MATH IS MURDER

MATH IS MURDER

ROBERT C. BRIGHAM
AND
JAMES B. REED

iUniverse, Inc.
Bloomington

MATH IS MURDER

iUniverse books may be ordered through booksellers or by contacting:

iUniverse
1663 Liberty Drive
Bloomington, IN 47403
www.iuniverse.com
1-800-Authors (1-800-288-4677)

ISBN: 978-1-4697-9728-1 (sc)
ISBN: 978-1-4697-9730-4 (hc)
ISBN: 978-1-4697-9729-8 (ebk)

Printed in the United States of America

iUniverse rev. date: 03/20/2012

For

Patricia and Deirdre

Robert C. Brigham

My Mother and Father

James B. Reed

ACKNOWLEDGEMENT

No book is created in isolation. The authors wish to acknowledge the support and encouragement given throughout the process by family and a host of friends.

Particular thanks are due Susan Myers-Feeney who designed the eye-catching cover. Eileen Daly suggested appropriate literary references, and Ben Goldfarb strained to keep our computer discussions on the right track. Any misrepresentation of their input is due to us alone. Karen Verity's careful reading of the manuscript saved us from many embarrassing errors.

While much of this story results from knowledge accumulated as a result of more than 40 years of university teaching on the part of one author and 35 years of experience in law enforcement and corporate security by the other, the people and places exist only in our minds. Any similarities to actual individuals and locales are purely coincidental.

CHAPTER 1

Late Sunday Afternoon and Evening

"Murder! Yes, MURDER!"

All stare with horror. One of the men screams, "My God! Look out." The standing Elmo Sherwin's massive right arm is aimed straight at the older woman who shouts, "No, please no!" The pleas have no impact. The offending limb, with increasing velocity, continues its downward arc while the miscreant's round cherubic face quivers and intelligent myopic eyes twinkle. The man who screamed and a young woman each grab their liqueur glass. The other man, Jim Albright, snatches both his and another's. Just in time! The gargantuan arm smacks the walnut table and only the hand-cut 24% lead crystal and expensive vessel in front of Elmo falls safely to the soft tablecloth.

All but Elmo sigh with relief. No damage has occurred, unless you count the expanding light orange stain on that cover. Theresa Bedlow, approaching 70, does seem to count it. She is not happy. Of course, it's her home, her glasses, her tablecloth. The others, again except for Elmo, know Theresa is capable of strict discipline to those who anger her. They await her reaction.

Theresa is Provost and Vice-President of Academic Affairs at Marcus Rome State University. Elmo is a mathematician at Sloane, a private university about 100 miles to the north. He's in a special class, absolutely brilliant! One of the best mathematicians in the world. It's strange, though, he's kind of a lost soul in most other areas of life. Like social situations.

The other three are faculty in the Mathematics Department. All are in their late thirties or early forties. They were hired within a couple of years of each other because their research interests matched an area the department wanted to build. Their collaboration has resulted in several papers in refereed mathematical journals. Of the three, Jim's relationship with Theresa is special. About twenty years ago, when he had no idea what he wanted to do with his life, he had enrolled in a criminal justice class she taught. She was the best teacher he had ever had.

There has been a conference at MRSU Wednesday through Saturday, attended by mathematicians from around the world, and Elmo gave the keynote talk. The research group prevailed on him to stay over to Sunday to discuss its work, which bears a relationship to some of his own activities. They had planned to invite him to dinner. Somehow Theresa learned about it and insisted everyone come to her home, said she had read about Elmo in the conference announcement and wanted to meet him. It's unusual for a provost to infringe on such an event. However, she always enjoys getting together with exceptional individuals and has maintained over the years a layman's interest in mathematics.

Theresa is questioning her interest in Elmo at the moment, but says nothing. Elmo breaks the silence. "Damn, oh, damn, damn, damn, damn! Why do these things keep happening to me? When I told my wife I was coming here, she reminded me not to get too excited," he whines like a child. He looks around, red-faced, and his eyes lock with Jim's, who nods toward Theresa. Thank God Elmo gets the signal. "Oh, right, right." A sheepish look engulfs his face as he glances at his host. Then, with eyes averted, "Terribly sorry. Tend to be a bit clumsy at times, you know." Now there's an understatement! He looks at her pleadingly.

So does the rest of the group. They know Theresa Bedlow does not suffer fools. Of course, Elmo's no fool. Just clumsy.

Jim has admired Theresa from the first day he walked into her class years ago. A dynamic instructor. Uses the Socratic method. Scared him to death, afraid he couldn't provide the deep analysis she demanded. And usually he didn't. But she found something in him, and has stayed in touch as he completed doctoral studies and wound up on the mathematics faculty. Before entering academe she'd been a lawyer, a chemist, and a homicide detective with the sheriff's department. Over the years she climbed the academic ladder at MRSU, serving as head of the Department of Forensic Science and Dean of the College of Science before assuming her present position. But to Jim and many of her other students she always will be a beloved and caring teacher.

Theresa eyes the penitent sternly, through steely gray eyes. She's not the slightest bit impressed with Elmo's mathematical pedigree. Intellectual dexterity is what she values. All hold their breath as she replies in a testy voice, "It's all right, Elmo. No real damage done. But perhaps it would be wise to curb your enthusiasm somewhat."

The mathematicians suppress sighs of relief. No storms for the moment. Jim looks at Elmo. My God, he seems to have no idea he's been gently rebuked, an impression he corroborates by jumping to his feet, sending his antique chair sprawling to the floor in the process. Oh boy, Jim thinks Theresa's really going to blow now. Her patience, never a strong point, seems to have diminished with advancing age.

Miraculously, there is no explosion. And, after another abject apology and terse acceptance, Elmo characteristically plunges ahead. "Well, of course I'm excited. Who wouldn't be after an evening like this? Fantastic food! Great discussion! God, what haven't we covered? Politics, religion, philosophy, literature, computers—even mathematics! The breadth of your knowledge amazes me, Theresa. And now murder! What on earth do you have in mind? Oh, this is so exciting!" As he resumes his seat, remembering to everyone's relief to set the chair upright first, he offers a beatific smile and with obvious glee rubs his hands.

Elmo looks at Theresa with interest. It's obvious he admires her razor sharp mind. But what is he seeing? No one would ever call him observant. An hour after he leaves her home he'll be incapable of recalling that she's tall—5'10"—and thin—barely 130 pounds. Nor that her face is long and angular, with a protruding jaw, slightly crooked teeth, and those gray eyes that miss nothing. Nor that her hair is fine, pure white, cut short, and straight. Nor that she's wearing an ivory pull-over blouse, navy blue slacks, dark comfortable low-heeled shoes, and no jewelry. Such details hold no importance for him.

Theresa Bedlow, on the other hand, misses nothing. Months from now she'll be able to describe every aspect of her guests' dress and demeanor. Take Elmo Sherwin, for example. Although Theresa probably wouldn't right now. Almost six and a half feet tall, easily 280 pounds, and a body having the firmness of a pillow. Brown eyes. Light brown hair. Mid 40s. And unbelievably brilliant. When Theresa phoned Jim to set up the dinner, he sang Elmo's praises. He told her about the 160 papers and 8 books Elmo's published, and that he was a consultant with the National Security Agency, the Department of Defense, and the National Science Foundation. Elmo's research has set the mathematical community on its ear. She listened, but she makes her own decisions about people. She'll base her opinion on personal observation, not on what Jim says. So far Elmo's receiving a failing grade.

Looking every bit the professor she is, Theresa stares directly at Elmo. "My secretary got me thinking last week. Tell me, Elmo, what do you think of *Dexter*?"

Elmo looks blank. "Er, I . . . I don't know a Dexter. Well, I guess there's Dexter Williams, a topologist at the University of Illinois. Is that who ya mean?"

She says, "No, Elmo, I don't know him. Why on earth would I? It's a TV show. I've not seen it, but my secretary never misses an episode."

Jim blurts, "It's a great series!"

This was a bad mistake. At his outburst, Theresa bequeaths her renowned stare reserved for those who don't measure up. Her eyes return to Elmo. "It's about a serial killer. His adoptive father, a policeman no less, recognized this tendency, realized it couldn't be controlled. So he steered it into productive activity."

"Productive?" Elmo's puzzled. "What can be productive about killing a bunch of people?"

"Ah, but you've hit on the heart of my question," she replies with a reluctant hint of approval. "He kills only those who deserve to be killed, those whom the rules of society can't touch. My challenge to you, Elmo, or to any of you, is to decide if there are people so evil that someone should take it upon himself to execute them?"

Jim recognizes her tactic so often displayed in the classroom. She's raising a controversial subject to make her guests think, state their views, and then justify them with coherent arguments. She expects them to challenge accepted beliefs. And, of course, she won't reveal how she herself feels. It's déjà vu for Jim. He had been terrorized in her class, afraid of being called on and even more afraid of not measuring up. God, he hopes this isn't going to be a repeat of those days. Why does he feel this way? He's a man now. At the moment it doesn't seem like it, though. Elmo has no such problems as he explodes, "No! It's never acceptable!"

"Would you care to explain your stand?"

"No," he mutters and slumps in his chair, his eyes filled with anger. She stares at him with disgust. Clearly her earlier tentative approval has vanished and she doesn't see the genius the others do.

"What about you, Jim?" And as feared he's no longer the man who calls her Theresa, at her insistence when he was hired. He's that skinny kid quivering under her gaze in a long ago classroom who wouldn't dare to address her by anything except Dr. Bedlow. You would never call her attractive, but her figure had dominated the room and commanded nothing less than total respect. It still does. Jim pushes back his chair, scratches his ear, and looks thoughtful. He's killing time while his mind races. She sees through the ruse. "Come on, Jim, get on with it."

Just like two decades earlier, he's scared he'll say something stupid which, of course, is enough to make him do just that. He doesn't think she expects much, though. He's pretty sure she considers him a philosophical lightweight. But he also knows she likes him. And she seems to be impressed with his math. She's been following his career, claiming not to understand the details of his research. And probably she doesn't. But, boy, can she ask penetrating questions! She's staring at him now, awaiting an answer. He wonders what she's seeing. Physically he's nothing special. Still kind of skinny, actually, but pretty strong from daily workouts at the gym. And almost six feet tall with light brown, almost blond, hair and hazel eyes. He knows one gorgeous woman says he's quite handsome and that's enough for him. Theresa's eyes are boring into him, and he's definitely at a loss for consequential words. All he can do is mumble, "Gee, I don't know. I just don't have much experience with violent death." She regards him with resignation.

Jim's colleagues enter the discussion half-heartedly, with routine observations about no pity should be shown to those monsters who torture their victims or repeatedly rape women, or that's what we have the courts for. Even Jim can see that these unimaginative responses are no better than his and won't cut it with Theresa. She gazes at them with dismay and disappointment, probably wondering about the intellectual depth of the math department under her sway. It makes him defensive and he thinks, *after all, we're mathematicians, not philosophers.* But he doesn't say it aloud.

Jim asks her for her opinion. She opens her mouth. Out of it comes nothing. Out of her slacks pocket arises a rousing rendition of *Pomp and Circumstance.* Theresa extricates her cell phone and strides to the kitchen.

The guests chat amiably about Elmo's presentation at the conference until Theresa returns. "I'm so sorry," she says, "but I have to ask you to leave. Something has come up I must deal with immediately." All rise in unison, but Jim's worried about the look on Theresa's face. Is it fear? Or worry? He's never seen her the slightest bit flustered, but she definitely is now.

"What's the matter? Is there anything I can do?" he asks.

"No, Jim. Everything's under control. Please, just leave."

Jim notices it's only 9:30. He's thinking about that gorgeous woman who believes he looks good. He's been thinking about her all evening. And fantasizing. Soon he'll be with her, earlier than expected. Any concerns for Theresa's problem pale in comparison with the visions now filling his head.

CHAPTER 2

Sunday—Late Evening

The cell phone rings as Detective Sergeant Tom Warren, tired but content after a weekend off, is watching basketball. He's looking forward to a good night's sleep before beginning his early seven o'clock shift. Instinctively he glances at his phone, his eyes focused on the caller's number. "Shit!" It's the University's Communication Center. He notes its 2121 hours.

"Yes?"

"Is this Sergeant Warren?"

"It is."

"Sergeant, the body of a male victim was found in Conroy Hall. Someone on the cleaning staff discovered him. Said there was a lot of blood."

Tom takes one of the unused stenographer's pads he keeps by the phone.

"What time was that?"

"The 911 call was received at 2108 hours."

"Where is he?"

"On the ninth floor, in one of the offices."

Tom knows the ninth floor houses the headquarters of the Mathematics Department. "Did the cleaning person go into the office?"

"No, sir. She took one look and ran away screaming."

"Who's at the scene?

"Two officers and two more are responding. Detective Chen is there. He was on campus when the call was dispatched."

"Is Doctor Bedlow still our contact person in Administration?"

"Yes. Should I give her a call?"

"Ok, go ahead. What's the case number?

He heads the first page of the pad with "2011-010445" followed by "S/7," a death investigation. On the next lines he puts successively

"Conroy Hall, 9th floor," "2108 hours 13 Mar 2011—911 call received," and "2121 hours—call from Communications Center." He terminates the conversation, saying he'll be there in about half an hour.

Tom pulls on a lightly starched white Oxford shirt, black slacks, black slip-on shoes, and one of his locally famous geometrically patterned ties. His Glock on the right hip and handcuffs and cell phone on the left complete the ensemble. Pad in hand, he's ready for work. Slipping into the department's unmarked Chevy sedan, he enters "2145 hours—left residence." His documentation of a new investigation has begun.

Over his police radio he says "Hotel-101, is 10-8/10-51".

"10-4" replies the dispatcher.

"A death investigation," he muses as he drives virtually on autopilot the familiar route to the campus. "It's been three years since the last homicide. Suicides, particularly among the students, and sudden health related deaths are more frequent. But this doesn't sound as straightforward, what with the blood and all."

Fifteen minutes on low traffic back roads bring him to Rome Drive, a four-lane thoroughfare leading to the main campus. After he passes the sign reading: "WELCOME TO MARCUS ROME STATE UNIVERSITY, 35,000 STUDENTS AND GROWING," he makes a quick stop: "2207 hours—arrived on campus."

Now it's a short distance along a circular drive to Conroy Hall. Invariably, contact with Conroy reminds him of his friend Jim Albright whom he still sees occasionally. They were both students here 20 years ago. At that time Conroy Hall was called the Science Center. When he heard about the renaming he had asked Jim if this Conroy fellow was a famous scientist. Jim had laughed. "Nah. Don't you understand how things work these days? Theodore Conroy was CEO of the Rivers Financial Conglomerate and filthy rich. He gave the university 10 million bucks, a pittance to him. The university in turn renamed the Science Center."

Tom parks in the faculty lot adjacent to the building. "2211 hours—arrived at Conroy Hall." The lot is empty except for a brown Honda Accord, a white Toyota Corolla, several police cars with flashing red and blue lights, and two Crime Scene vans.

As Tom opens the door, his cell phone rings. He shakes the notion that the door triggered the ring and instead looks at the screen. He sees a number he doesn't recognize and no caller name. "Hello."

"Tom, this is Theresa Bedlow."

Just what I need, he thinks. "Hello, Dr. Bedlow." He likes her. In fact she used to be one of his teachers, and a damn good one at that. It was due to her that he pursued a career in law enforcement. But he doesn't have time now to deal with her.

"What the hell is going on, Tom? I got a call saying someone was dead in the math department."

Knowing full well this former homicide detective was capable of interrogating him relentlessly, Tom was relieved he didn't yet have much information. "I'm just arriving on the scene now, Dr. Bedlow. I'm still outside Conroy."

"All right. Call me when you have information."

"It may be quite late."

"Any time, any time. Norman's going to want a full briefing in the morning and I'll have to deal with the media. You know they'll be all over the place. Remember, as soon as you have information."

Tom started to reply, but she had already terminated the call. Tom knew that "Norman" was Norman Mulholland, the University's fourth president.

The approved route from the car lot to the door of Conway Hall follows an L-shaped walkway for which Tom has no patience. He heads diagonally, zigzagging past bushes, trees, and a bench. He's met by Corporal Christopher, the first female to join the department, way back when Tom was a student.

"Good evening, Sergeant." She waves him in, and watches in admiration as he heads to the elevators. God, he's handsome, with a square-jawed face, friendly—unless you're a suspect—green eyes, wavy reddish-brown hair flopping haphazardly, and the most sensual deep voice she's ever heard. She remembers he had been a fullback on MRSU's fledgling football team. He looked good then and with his added maturity he looks great now. She had heard he competes in marathons and triathlons and she knows he works out regularly at the campus Wellness Center. She'd bet all those rumors about being a magnetic attraction to women are true. She sighs, and prepares for a long night at her post.

Tom brushes past the Corporal, all business, thankful the elevator is waiting. He hops in, punches the "9" and "door close" buttons and waits. And waits. Finally the doors creak, the device shakes and slowly ascends. Tom watches the numbers click on and off: 2, 3, 4, ... Just his luck to get the slowest elevator on campus. It must be as old as the university itself. The ride gives him time to ponder just what he'll encounter if the number 9 ever lights.

CHAPTER 3

Late Sunday

Tom plunges through the still opening doors when the elevator at last reaches its destination. Immediately his eyes focus on Officer Richards, a former partner in the Patrol Division, seated at a small table. The two friends greet, and Richards leans over the Access Control Log on the table and writes "2214 hours, Tom Warren, Detective Sergeant." No one will enter or leave this floor without being recorded in the log. Simultaneously Tom adds "2214 hours—arrived on 9th floor, crime scene" to his own record.

Tom surveys the area. His attention is drawn to a long hallway stretching the length of the building, about 75 feet he estimates. Its lights are dimmed in accordance with a recent university energy preservation initiative. Windows line the left side of the corridor. He notes the calm outside, giving no hint of the mayhem that has occurred within. Four doors can be seen on the right. All but one is closed.

In contrast to the subdued lighting in the hall, a brilliant blaze issues from the single open doorway about halfway down the corridor. Tom can see the yellow "Crime Scene" tape secured across the entrance. Three uniformed officers and Det. Stuart Chen are conversing in front of it. Tom realizes this is the office where the victim is located. He will learn more when Chen briefs him. At the end of the hallway Tom sees the members of the Crime Scene Unit. Three people, two men and a woman, stand patiently. The woman has a camera strapped around her neck in anticipation of videotaping the scene. Tom is familiar with her work. She's good. A large camera case and two equipment cases are nearby. Tom knows these are filled with the "tools of the trade." A stack of brown paper bags and boxes of latex gloves and shoe booties are next to them.

Tom strides toward Chen; his Oriental features are distinctive. He's a fourth generation American and little of his ancestral heritage remains. As always, his wiry 5'7" frame is clad to perfection, this time in a light gray suit, pale mauve shirt, black shoes, and a faultlessly dimpled maroon tie. The finishing touch is a brilliant white pocket-handkerchief. Tom has never seen him look other than elegant, even in the most trying of circumstances. He's never figured out how Chen does it. "Hi, Stu. How'd you get here so fast?"

"Hello, Tom. I was studying in my office. Have an exam on Wednesday." Chen is in his second year of a four-year evening program leading to a law degree. "I heard the call and headed over, arriving at 2115 hours."

"Well, I'm glad you're here. What have you got for me?"

"The Comm Center received the 911 call at 2108 hours. A member of the cleaning staff was making the rounds of the floor—emptying trash, dusting, and vacuuming." Chen looks at his notes and continues, "The cleaning lady is Gabriella Lopez."

"Where is she now?"

"She's in the staff lounge at the end of the hall with Officer Vasquez. Lopez's English is rocky at best so Vasquez is trying to get her statement."

Tom is pleased. Vasquez is an excellent officer and fluent in Spanish. "OK, go on."

"Lopez reached this complex of rooms—there's an outer office for clerical staff and then the department chair's office beyond—a little before 2100 hours. She can't be sure of the exact time. Apparently she was surprised at the open doors and peeked into the inner office to make certain it was empty. It was then she saw the body. Officer Galloway was the first to respond and he got what little he could from her and her supervisor. She kept saying, 'Sangre!' I learned from Vasquez that's Spanish for 'blood'."

"And she definitely didn't go in?"

"No way. According to Galloway, she took off screaming, ran to find her supervisor. He made the 911 call and stayed with her. They met Galloway as he stepped off the elevator."

Officer Galloway is standing next to Chen as he briefs Tom. He respectfully nods his head in agreement with Chen, but does not interrupt.

"All right, I'll speak with her later. Let's see if Vasquez can get her to write a statement. Galloway, you were first officer on the scene?"

"Yes, sir. I was dispatched at 2110 hours and was 10-97 at 2112."

"You were close to the building?"

"Yes, sir. I had just completed a foot patrol of the area."

"Did you see anything out of the ordinary?"

"No, sir."

"So, tell me what you did."

"I took the elevator to the 9th floor, where I encountered the two people from the cleaning staff. The woman kept saying, 'Sangre'; the supervisor said 'Blood'."

"Then what did you do?"

"They pointed toward the open office door. I walked slowly toward it, checking the floor for evidence as I did. I stood in the doorway to the outer office and took a quick look around. I then entered, walked up to the entrance to the adjoining, interior office and looked inside. I observed the body of a male victim, seated in a chair and slumped over a table. I could see blood on the back of his shirt."

"Did you enter the office?"

"Not the inner office, only the outer."

"You mentioned you could see blood on his back."

"Yes, sir. He's wearing a white shirt and his back from the shoulders to almost his waist is covered in blood."

"Then what did you do?"

"I called the Comm Center on my cell. I didn't want to put the information out over the radio."

Tom is pleased to hear that. The media and police buffs are glued to their scanners just waiting for something like this. "Then what did you do?"

"I requested additional officers to secure the scene. I asked if we had a Spanish speaking officer on-duty for translations. They advised me that Officer Vasquez was 10-51. I also requested they contact the on-call detective and the Crime Scene Unit. They advised me that Detective Chen was in route, but they would contact you."

"OK, then what?"

"Vasquez was the first officer to meet me up here. I asked her to speak with the cleaning people. About that time Detective Chen arrived and we secured the scene."

"Sounds like you did everything by the book."

"Thank you, sir."

"Stu, did you take a look at the body?"

"No, I wanted to wait for you."

"I guess you know me." Tom has a reputation for wanting to enter a crime scene by himself before opening it to others. He steels himself for the next step.

CHAPTER 4

Late Sunday

Tom strides to the Crime Scene Investigators. "Hey there. Looks like I'll be keeping you busy this evening."

Grinning, a CSI asks, "Can I interest you in some gloves and a nice pair of blue booties?"

"Sure. Nothing I like better than those god-awful booties."

The banter masks mutual respect between Tom and the investigators. He knows their work will be thorough and professional. They know he will demand nothing less, that every crime scene must be handled with as near perfection as possible.

Everyone appreciates that attractive is not the right word for the booties. But they and the gloves are effective. The booties protect investigators' shoes from being ruined by blood or any other material that might be on the floor. Even more important, they prevent contamination of the crime scene by external trace evidence brought into the area by the investigators themselves. The gloves will insulate their hands from contaminants as well as prevent inadvertent fingerprints being left behind.

"Dammit," Tom mutters. He's leaning against the wall, attempting to balance on one foot while pulling a bootie over the other. "One Size Fits All" sounds good, but ease of getting them on is nonexistent, especially if the foot is as large as Tom's. The CSI crew chuckles. Then, still smiling, the same CSI holds out a hairnet. Tom hesitates a moment, then takes it. Required by men and women investigators with long hair, few men bother. But Tom knows his is getting a little shaggy, and it sends a message to colleagues about taking proper precaution. Hairs dropped at a crime scene can muddy the water. And at least the hairnet and the gloves slip on easily.

Tom stands outside the door, examining the office inside. He'll check, but he's sure it's the room used by the clerical staff. Looking to the left he sees another open door. Experience tells him that's the important area, that this outer office has nothing to do with the crime. He's sure that's true, but he's not going to take it for granted. He's pleased the responding officers included this extended area in defining the crime scene. He'd pounded it into their heads often enough during training sessions. "You can always make a crime scene smaller. There's no way you can make it larger once it's been contaminated."

He lifts the "CRIME SCENE" tape and enters. The first task is to document the layout of this rectangular office. He flips pages of his pad to the first blank one. Initially he draws a rough diagram of the borders of the room, this time a simple rectangle. He pauses a moment, visualizing the orientation of the building, and then adds an arrow with an associated "N," meaning north, in the upper left hand corner. Next he estimates the size of the room using a trick he learned at one of the many classes he's attended. The ceiling is made up of square panels, 2' by 2'. He counts 15 panels along the side of the room that parallels the outside hall, and 8 panels in the other direction. The office is approximately 30' by 16'.

Now it's time to record the interior layout. Two cubicles, each containing a desk and an attached computer table, are noted. A third desk and computer table combination near the door to the inner office is in the open. The location of chairs, tables, file cabinets, faculty and staff mail boxes, copying machines, and other office equipment are added to the diagram. He's satisfied he has enough information about this room. He knows it's the next one where he'll be spending most of his time. He walks to the connecting door.

He does not immediately enter, but surveys the inner office from the doorway. It would be impossible to miss the victim about halfway down the right side, back to the door, slumped onto a round table with blood over that part of the body Tom can see. This is an important moment for Tom at the beginning of any investigation, his getting to "know" the victim. He wonders what he was like when alive, if he knew why he was dying. Tom wants to feel the pain of his last moments, mentally asking him to tell who committed this act. Unfortunately, Tom realizes this isn't going to happen, but taking this time and entertaining these thoughts always motivate him to do everything he can to bring justice.

Without entering the room. Tom begins another diagram on the next page of his pad. The rectangular border and "N" arrow are placed. He looks at the ceiling, 11 panels in one direction and 8 in the other: about 22' by 16'. There is only the one door, connecting to the outer office, situated on one of the shorter sides, and opening to the left as you enter the room. It's constructed from wood with a rectangular cutout at the top filled with window glass. The inside of the glass is covered with a small pull-down shade so, when the door is closed, no one can see inside. Obviously this guy didn't want anyone peeking at him. Now the door is fully open.

A large window, approximately 10 feet wide and 4 high, dominates the wall directly opposite. Tom notes it on the diagram. It faces northwest, and he envisions the view it affords of the campus green bordering Conroy Hall and the nondenominational chapel on the other side. A vertical blind, stretching from ceiling to just above the floor, is in the closed position, but the slats are rotated so one can see out. Tom wonders if the victim had been enjoying the view when struck down.

Tom turns his attention to filling in the diagram, beginning with the round table, 48 inches in diameter he estimates, with the slumping victim on it. He sketches the approximate position of the body and the fact that his left arm appears straight on the table while the right is bent. From where he's standing he can see an older model computer monitor, a keyboard, and a mouse. Colorful geometric patterns flow in and out on the monitor's face. To him it looks like something a mathematician would choose for a screen saver. He knows he'll be adding additional information once he gets closer, as well as producing a separate more detailed sketch.

Tom quickly notes three standard gray metal bookshelves lining the northeast wall from the far end of the room to about six feet from the wall containing the door. They're filled, with little space for growth, and with the book spines perfectly aligned. In that six-foot space are two black, four-drawer file cabinets. A whiteboard stretches approximately eight feet on the left wall. It contains mathematics foreign to him. He'll get someone else to take a look at it.

The remaining dominant feature is a large wooden desk, about 6' by 4', positioned at a 45 degree angle in the corner to the left of the window. It is highly polished and the shine reflects the overhead fluorescent lights. And there isn't a single item on it! This guy is some kind of neat freak. Behind the desk is a large high back brown leather chair, turned slightly to the left, and beyond it, on the left wall, are three framed certificates arranged in a pyramid design.

Finally he jots down the position of six unoccupied basic faux leather seated chairs, one opposite the victim at the round table, three in front of the desk, and two in front of the whiteboard. No one would want to sit in any of them for long. Tom notices the one the victim elected to use is of higher quality and comfort.

Tom considers his sketch and is satisfied. He knows the CSIs will create a precise diagram using computer graphics, but what he has will serve his purposes.

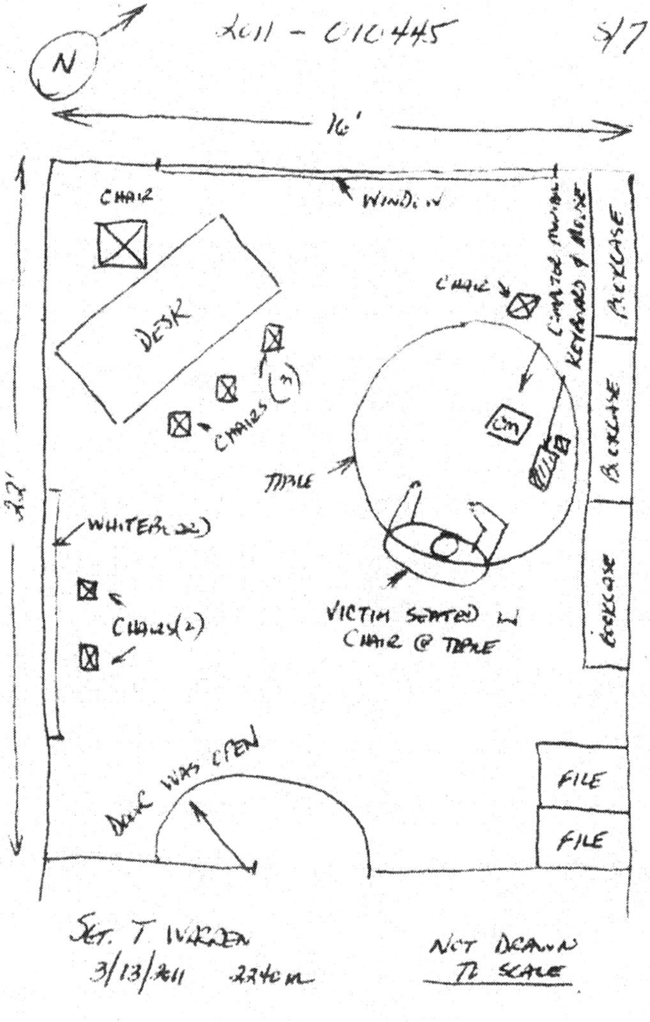

Sketch of victim's office

Tom enters the office, and walks toward the victim. He takes care not to disturb anything. The crime scene first must be documented using a video camera and then with digital images before he can make any form of contact. The body is off limits until an investigator from the Medical Examiner's office has had a chance to view the scene. But he can visually examine it.

As Tom suspected, the victim's head, turned to the right, lies on the table. The blood has soaked his back with some trickling down his left bicep. The medical examiner will say for sure, but there's a tear in the back of his white turtleneck shirt consistent with a knife wound. His pants are dark gray, and black socks and black wing-tipped shoes cover his feet. Tom inspects the carpeted floor near the victim, surprised there are no blood droplets. Usually removal of a knife would leave such residue.

During his initial inspection while standing at the door, Tom had noticed items on the table he could not identify. Now at closer range he sees several scattered sheets of paper on which there appear to be mathematical writings. It's as if the sheets had been knocked askew by the victim during some dying gesture. Another sheet is pinned to the table by his left arm. Blood that has begun to dry stains the lower left corner. A bright yellow "Ticonderoga" number 2 pencil remains clutched in the victim's right hand. A cell phone, face down, is located in the upper left quadrant of the table and is the only remaining item on it.

Tom's ready for a more detailed sketch of the table and turns to the next page of his pad.

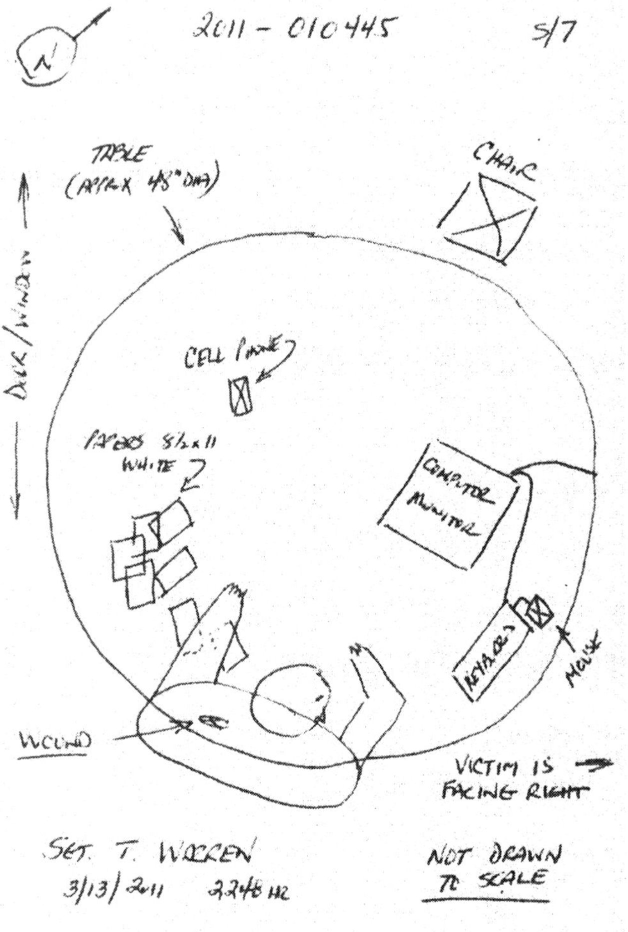

Sketch of table with victim

Tom turns his attention to the rest of the room, cautiously examining but not touching the file cabinets, all closed; the desk drawers, also closed; the bookcases; and the whiteboard which continues to mystify him with its incomprehensible mathematics. Everything looks normal except, of course, for the corpse. There seems to be nothing more he can do until the other experts complete their work.

He's ready to leave. When he reaches the door he turns, standing there for a couple of minutes. Looking, scanning, wondering—a strange and unconventional idea formulating in his mind.

CHAPTER 5

Late Sunday and Early Monday

Rejecting the unexpected and disturbing idea that had come to him, Tom retraces his steps to the hall and approaches the crime scene photographer. "Eva, we're ready for you. There are some papers on the desk and there appears to be a stab wound to the victim's back. Please get shots of all that."

"You got it."

"Oh, and make sure you get the victim's positioning, the writing on the whiteboard, the . . ." He stops, knowing she has photographed many crime scenes.

"Of course, Tom," she utters with a twinge of sarcasm. "Anything else?"

"No. Well, yes. Be sure to get a photo of the thermostat. I want the room's temperature recorded." He'd already noted it is 76 degrees, consistent with it being the weekend. The temperature is an important indicator when estimating the time of death.

Hairnetted, gloved, and bootied, Eva Wilcox enters the scene with her video camera. Tom keeps a respectful distance, but will observe all she does. He creates the newest entry in his log: "2244 hours—CSI Wilcox enters to obtain video and photographic evidence."

Wilcox makes a slow and meticulous circuit of the room, capturing every detail. Tom couldn't be more pleased. After exiting the scene, she returns with a digital camera and repeats the process. When she gets to the body, she places a small metric scale in her left hand and holds it next to the tear in the shirt while snapping a photo with the camera in her right hand. Tom can find no fault with her work.

Tom notices Lou Daly out of the corner of his eye. Daly is one of the investigators on the ME's staff. Tom gives a nod and advises him the photographer should be finished soon. The next three entries Tom places in his log are "2307 hours—ME investigator Daly arrives," "2320 hours—CSI Wilcox out," and "2322 hours—ME investigator Daly enters scene."

Daly is prepared, with a wheeled stretcher already in the hall. It's covered with an open body bag, white sheet, and a clear plastic sheet on top. Grabbing a digital camera, he enters the interior office and begins his initial examination. From the beginning he treats the victim with respect as he takes his own set of photos and examines the body, gently moving head and hands, looking for injuries other than the one to the back. He finds none. In 15 minutes he's done and Tom writes "2337 hours—ME investigator Daly completes initial examination."

"So, Lou, can you give me something about the time of death?"

"As I'm sure you've noticed, Tom, there's relatively little odor so not much decomposition has occurred. On the other hand, rigor mortis seems to be somewhat advanced. Taking into account that the temperature is a medium 76, I can only give you a rough estimate, say in the neighborhood of 1400 to 1900 hours. The doc doing the autopsy probably can give you a better estimate."

"Well, that's a start. You ready to take the body?"

Lou nods. "I'll need some help."

Tom addresses the officers. "One of you put on some booties and gloves and go in with Daly."

Daly adds, "And I'll have a lab coat for you." These coats afford protection if any blood or body fluids drip when moving the victim.

A white-haired officer says in a friendly manner, "Officer Rose, I do believe you're the newest one here."

Everyone laughs but Rose. He has a good nature, though, and, with a smile dons his booties and gloves and follows Daly who is wheeling the stretcher. Daly explains they must be careful so they won't disturb any possible evidence on the victim's clothing. CSI Wilcox enters to photograph both the movement of the body and afterwards any previously concealed areas.

Daly positions himself on the victim's left, directs Rose to the right side, and instructs him on how to lift the body. Together, on the count of three, they raise and with care move it to the stretcher.

Well, almost without incident Tom thinks. They did slightly jostle the table in the process. This in turn jiggled the mouse and suddenly the screen saver was replaced by an email message. Tom, prohibited from looking at the hidden version before, now legally can examine it since it's in plain sight. Ignoring the content, he zeros in on the line reading "March 13, 2011 5:07:47 PM EST." So now he knows the victim was alive at 5:07 in the afternoon.

When Tom returns to the corridor he asks CSI Wilcox to photograph the message on the computer screen. He turns to Daly who is checking the victim's clothing. From the right rear pants pocket Daly pulls a black leather wallet. The right front yields a simple one-inch round ring containing four keys. Tom notices one of them is labeled "Honda." That must be for the one in the lot. Judging by their size, shape, and markings, the remaining appear to be for a house, an office, and a desk. A white neatly folded handkerchief is pulled from the left front pocket. The victim is wearing a black leather belt, and attached to it on the left side is an empty cell phone case.

Daly opens the wallet to access a driver's license, American Express Card, University ID card, and two $20.00 bills. The license and cards all yield the name "Kenneth M. Salter," the same as what Tom had noticed on a nameplate next to the corridor door to the outer office. Underneath the name the nameplate had said, "Chair, Department of Mathematics." Tom notes the items found and the name in his pad.

The victim, presumably Salter but not officially until someone who knows him formally says so, is wrapped in the plastic sheet, followed by the white sheet. When the sheet is secured, the body bag is zipped shut. Officer Rose leaves with Daly and will remain with the body until it is secured in the ME's transport van. Tom enters, "2354 hours—body removed from scene."

Tom's exhausted, eager to get home. He sheds booties, gloves, and hairnet, tossing them into a brown paper bag marked "TRASH." He gives final instructions to Chen. "Stu, let's restrict the crime scene to the chairman's office, so seal its door when you leave. I'll be back around 0700 hours. By then have a list of all the evidence we've collected. Oh, and have the access log moved down the corridor so it's by the door to the outer office. We'll only need to log entrance and exit from this complex, so we might as well make the rest of the floor open for business."

Chen nods. "See you then, Tom."

Tom gives a small wave and notes it's now Monday morning. He logs out with Officer Richards, enters, "0024 hours 14 March 2011—10-98/10-7" into his pad, rides the sluggish elevator to the first floor, and wends his way to his car. Wearily he calls dispatch, "Hotel-101 is 10-98/10-7.

"10-4. Good night," is the quiet response.

Tom starts his car and is a couple of miles from MRSU. "Damn," he says aloud. He has forgotten to call Dr. Bedlow.

CHAPTER 6

Early Monday Morning

Tom, embraced by weariness, pulls to the side of the road. His watch shows 0032 hours, late but never for a second does he consider skipping the call. If Theresa Bedlow wants to be notified, she will expect it no matter the hour. And he isn't willing to risk her wrath. Bringing up the "Recent Call" list on his cell, he thumbs to her number and hits the "Call" button.

Answering on the first ring, Tom hears Dr. Bedlow's no nonsense and demanding voice, "Hello, Tom. What have you got?"

"Good morning Dr. Bedlow, I'm sorry it's so . . ."

"I know it's late, Tom. Don't worry about it. Get to the point."

"Well, Dr. Bedlow, . . ."

"Oh, Tom, it's been a long time since you were a student. Please call me Theresa."

"Er . . . oh, alright. I've just cleared the crime scene and am on my way home."

"I don't want to keep you, but I need to know what's going on."

Tom is angry. He doesn't have to talk to her at all and is doing a huge favor by contacting her. On the other hand, she is the Provost and a Vice-President with the ear of President Mulholland. Practicality assumes command. He stumbles over "Theresa." It's hard to push it out. "We have the body of a white male victim. Documents in his wallet ID him as Kenneth M. Salter." He hears a low gasp.

"My God, how awful. He's the Chair of the Math Department, Tom."

"Yes, that's what we understand from the nameplate on the department's main door, which also lists Susan Barber as Administrative Assistant."

"How did it happen?"

Tom is reluctant to supply too much information. But she *is* Theresa Bedlow and she will need something to tell Mulholland and the media. "It appears he was stabbed in the back.'

She peppers him with questions. "Was there a struggle? You could tell right away if there was; he was so unnaturally neat. Was he at his desk? Was he stabbed with a knife? Do you have the weapon?"

Tom is stunned at the intensity of the interrogation. He wonders if this is a top administration official speaking or is it the ex-homicide detective. "There's no sign of a struggle, and, no, we didn't find a weapon. He was seated at a round table. His computer was on and apparently he was engaged in some sort of mathematics when killed."

"Well, that's not surprising. He was a genius with a worldwide reputation. But why on earth would someone murder Ken?"

"At the moment I have no information about motive. Do you have any thoughts?"

"Not now, but I'll certainly give it some consideration. What did the ME's office give as the time of death?"

"Pretty much what they usually do, a broad range."

"Which was?"

"1400 to 1900 hours."

"What's going on at the crime scene now that you've gone?"

Tom can't help but smile. His teacher is back. She knows very well what's going on, or what *should* be going on. She's testing him. "The body has been removed. The Crime Scene Unit is still there. They've already taken the video and digital images. Now they're processing the scene for latent prints and collecting any other evidence they find. Then the scene will be sealed."

"That sounds right." Tom knows he has passed the test. "How about I call in some experts I know? Could you use them?"

Tom doesn't like this intrusion. "No, thank you. I have complete faith in our own people. They are extremely competent."

Sounding taken aback, she says, "All right. Let's meet in my office no later than 10.00 a.m."

Now this really is going too far. "That's impossible, Theresa." The name is coming easier now. "I have to be back at the scene at 0700 and the autopsy should be scheduled for 1000. You know I have to be present at it. With everything else to do, I'll be tied up at least until early evening,"

"Fine, we'll make it this evening at 7:00 at my home." Tom winces but doesn't object. Her voice turns to honey, "Now, Tom?"

He goes cold. Tom knows something is coming he won't like. "Yes."

"Do you know much about the mathematics department?"

"No, I don't know anything. And as far as math is concerned, I topped out at the Finite Mathematics required to graduate."

"So I guess you'll need to dig out some insights into the people?"

"Yeah, of course. I don't have a clue about any of them, the relationships, possible motives. Why do you ask?"

"Well, I'm sure you have to consider them as suspects?"

"You know that, Theresa. At this point I can't eliminate anyone. My God, on every case I've had I can hear you drumming that fact into me in your class. Hell, I can't completely eliminate anyone at the entire university at this point."

She gives a short laugh. "Well, you were paying attention after all. I thought all you concentrated on was those beautiful girls ogling you."

Tom figures he might as well press her for what she was thinking. "What were you getting at before, Theresa?"

"Well, do you remember Jim Albright? He was in the same class as you."

"Of course I do. We've lost close touch, but I see him around campus from time to time."

"He's in the math department, you know."

"Yes." Tom has an idea where this is going.

"I'd like you to bring him into the investigation. He has intimate knowledge of the department and I'm sure he could help with any mathematics you might run into."

"What!" Tom explodes. "You know I can't authorize a civilian to become involved. Besides, he has to be considered a suspect." But he's uncomfortable. He had briefly considered that same idea while standing in the door of Salter's office, before he rejected it.

"Well, I can personally vouch for him for a large part of the time frame of interest. He was at a dinner party at my place from about 4:30 in the afternoon until I got the call informing me of the murder. Take down these names of others who were there so you can verify it." She reels off three names that he records in his pad.

Tom believes from the email that the murder occurred after 5:07 and so Jim's alibi will hold. Still the idea is ridiculous. "I just can't, Theresa."

"Perhaps I'm not making myself clear. I can make this happen. I will make it happen if necessary."

Tom is stunned. She actually is interfering in an investigation. Tom hates university politics. How much pressure could she exert? What will he do? Does he have a choice? He's tired of this conversation. "Theresa, it's late, I have to be up early, and I need to wrap this up."

"I understand, Tom. Now here's Jim's number. Take it down." Tom is angry at her presumptuousness. But he scribbles the number in his pad. "I'm sure you'll do an outstanding job on this investigation."

"Thank you, Theresa. Good night."

Damn, he thinks, *I'm not her student any more. She's not even in my chain of command.* Deriving no comfort from such realities, he ponders, *what the hell am I going to do about Jim Albright?*

CHAPTER 7

Early Monday Morning

The cell rings at 0601. Tom, already up and mostly dressed, is ready to prepare his oatmeal and coffee before leaving for the university. His phone's display reads Communication Center. *What now?* he thinks, grabbing his pad.

"Yes."

He listens. "What . . . what's her name."

He's incredulous at what he next hears. "She actually said that? Well, you tell her *we'll* decide how we talk to her. I'll be in about 0640. Oh, and have somebody get me some whole wheat toast and coffee."

He considers a question from the Center, then responds, "No. It isn't necessary to call Dr. Bedlow about this." At least that will keep her off his back for a little while.

He ends the conversation, thinking hard. Theresa's demand had him tossing most of the night. What will he do about it in view of this new development? After a moment he picks up his cell. It feels like a five-pound weight. With deliberation he keys a number from his pad and presses "Call."

* * *

"Mmmmpff."

That's the second sound I'm hearing. The first is a periodic ringing. I rub my eyes, shake my head, strain to see the bedside clock. 6:15! What's going on? The unintelligible speech fragment had come from the woman next to me. Her name's Donna, Donna Albright, and I'm Jim, the guy lucky enough to be her husband. I was at a dinner party at Theresa Bedlow's last night. The conversation was good, but it didn't keep me from devoting erotic thoughts to Donna. For some reason she thinks I'm good looking.

I know she is, absolutely gorgeous in fact. I glance at her, noticing with satisfaction how her short nightie has ridden up her body.

That same body is showing movement. One arm approaches the bedside table. With a mathematician's deductive powers I realize she's reaching for the phone. Ah, that's what the ringing was! She grabs the cord to our landline and starts reeling in the offending instrument. With eyes firmly shut she positions the mouthpiece properly and utters, "Woosis." Who's this, she means. I think.

Not the most gracious greeting, but then poor Donna's not a morning person. Thinks it a sin to rise before 8:30, ever, and then only in the gravest of circumstances. After a pause, apparently while the caller is speaking and during which one eye flutters open, she says, "He's ite ere." She pushes the phone toward me saying, "Istm." I interpret that Tom's on the line and she's told him I'm here. But who the heck is Tom? Before I raise the phone to my lips I hear a gentle snore.

"Hello."

"Jim, It's Tom Warren."

"Tom! I couldn't figure out who it could be. My God, how long has it been? I don't think we've seen each other in a couple of years."

"Guess so. Now listen . . . ."

I interrupt, "It's great to hear from you, of course. But Tom, it's 6:15, a heck of a time to renew a friendship."

"Will you please shut up and let me talk?"

Stunned by the tone, I reply, "Well, sure, Tom, go ahead."

"Can you come to the campus immediately, the math office. I need you here by 0700."

Oh boy, I think. He's talking military.

"Er, I uh, I guess so. What's up?"

"I'll tell you when you get here. It's related to the incident last night. Now please hurry." He terminates the call.

The incident last night? What the hell is he talking about? I have memories, all right, of the previous evening. Very nice ones. They relate to the fantasies I'd entertained throughout that dinner party. Suffice it to say Donna and I were occupied until well past 11:00 when we finally fell into exhausted sleep. Whoops, maybe I'd better say 2300 if I'm going to talk to Tom!

What could have happened that made Tom contact me? I don't want to be at school this early. I have a class at 11:00 and I was planning on some last minute preparation at home. Well, I said I'd go so I guess I'd better.

It took me almost 30 minutes to bathe, shave, dress, eat, drive, and mount the stairs to the ninth floor of Conroy Hall. Yeah, I usually eschew the pokey elevator, and I think I can beat it anyway, When I open the door to the hall leading to the math department offices, I see Tom. "Reporting for duty, sir, at," glancing at my watch, "0650."

"Knock it off, Jim," Tom says offering his hand. "This is serious."

I realize my old acquaintance is a campus police officer and must have called me about some sort of criminal activity at school. I'd better stop screwing around. "I'm sorry, Tom. What is it?"

"As you know, Kenneth Salter was murdered here yesterday. This morning . . . ," Tom breaks off. He must see the astonishment on my face. "You didn't know? Don't you listen to the news?"

"Ken dead? How can that be? He was so, so *alive*! And no, I didn't hear any news. Er, Donna and I were busy last night"

"I heard you were at a dinner party, but I didn't know Donna was there."

"Oh, she wasn't. I'm talking about afterwards." Tom, who'd been around when Donna and I met had observed certain expressions of physical attraction between us. Do I detect a glimmer of a smile on that stern face? "But why am I here? You don't think I had anything to do with it?"

"No. I know you didn't, but I did have to consider it for a while. Now listen up. I'm really uncomfortable with this, going against my better judgment. Theresa Bedlow . . . ."

"Theresa? I had dinner with her just last night. Funny. She got a phone call that seemed to upset her. She then sent us home early. Oh, I guess it must've been about Ken?"

"Yes, that would have been our Comm Center informing her. Anyway, she suggested you could help us with the investigation, you being in the math department and all. It's completely against protocol, but even I had a brief moment where I entertained the same thought. And then, in view of what happened this morning, well . . . ."

Is he saying he wants me to be a detective? I suppose not in so many words. But he needs me to be involved in some way. And so does Theresa! God, I know it's awful about Ken, which makes my excitement about being asked all the more terrible, juvenile even. But I can't help it. I've always dreamed of being one of those super sleuths of fiction. You know, the kind who uses deductive reasoning to catch a culprit, sort of an amalgam of Sherlock Holmes, Hercule Poirot, Henry Merrivale, Ellery Queen, and, for a little dash, Kinsey Millhone. I do come fully equipped for the task, for don't I read at least one murder mystery a week? I enjoy them, but almost always feel cheated. It's because I like puzzles, and I think a mystery should plant clues to provide a path for the reader to take to name the killer. Believe me, if I ever write one, it wouldn't cheat.

Hey, maybe I will write one, about a real murder! This murder. I could start recording everything that happens in the next few days. Yes, that sounds good. And I'll write it like I'm talking to someone. I think I'd better not tell anybody yet, even Donna. I recognize it seems like childish and probably inappropriate behavior. Maybe I'll eventually turn it into a book. I wonder what I should call it.

Tom's getting impatient. "Of course I'll do all I can." Did that sound pompous? I didn't mean it to. Really. "Tell me about Ken's murder. How did it happen? What's this business about this morning?"

"Easy, Jim. I promise I'll tell you the whole story later. At the moment we have something more pressing to deal with."

Now I'm confused. "What?"

"Ms. Barber was signed into the office at 0558 hours. She . . . ."

"Susan here? At six o'clock! Impossible!"

"Impossible, why do you say that?"

"Every single day she arrives on the dot of eight. She's anal about it. Hell, when I had an early class a bunch of us would bet on the exact moment she'd appear. It was never more than a minute before or after."

"Well, she sure came in early today for some reason. As you can see, an officer is manning the access log just outside the complex door. She explained to him she needed to get some work done before everyone else arrived."

"I guess that makes sense. She probably knew about Ken and realized things will be crazy today."

"Maybe so. Anyway, after she logged in, she was warned to remain in the clerical part of the complex and to stay away from the chair's office. But when she saw the officer leave for a bathroom break she went to Salter's door and started to pull off the evidence tape. What she didn't know was that a relief officer was just around the corner. He caught her, stopped her from going in, and called the Comm Center which contacted me."

"Why on earth would she do that? Did she need something from his office?"

"I don't know, but I think it's more complicated than that. We'll find out more when we talk to her in a couple of minutes.'

I notice a man with a camera coming out of Susan's office complex. "Who's he?"

Tom looks up. "Oh, hi, Lamar. Please hang around. We're going to need you a little later." Tom turns to me and explains, "He's a CSI I called to photograph the torn evidence tape."

The man says, "Can I speak to you, Tom?"

Tom gets up and starts to walk off with him. I hear the CSI say, "I was processing the evidence that was collected most of the night and I found something I . . . ." By then they were out of earshot. But I saw this fellow Lamar hand Tom a small stack of papers and Tom give them a quick scan. He returns, papers in hand and his expression grim.

Wow, I feel a tenseness in the air and realize I'm in the middle of something serious here. This isn't a safe novel. It's real. A man I know was murdered. Suddenly I'm worried about my role. "So why did you call me?"

"She asked me to, says she won't tell us anything unless you're there. Jim, You're sitting in on the interview."

CHAPTER 8

Monday Morning

I stare at Tom, shocked. "No. Oh no, Tom. I can't do that." Maybe this detective thing isn't for me.

"Why not?"

"Well, who can tell what she'll say? And I do have to work with her, you know."

He's no happier than I. "You don't think this is *my* idea? Not exactly standard police procedure. But then, neither is having you involved at all. As I told you, Ms. Barber asked that I call you. Says she really likes you."

"Likes me! I didn't know she cared for anyone on the faculty. She's been the perfect doorkeeper for Ken. Protects him from everyone. Curt. Overbearing, despotic even. Not many want to be around her."

"How about you?"

I reflect a moment. "I guess I can't say I like Susan. But I do respect her. The office runs smoothly and she's the main one responsible. I try to get along with her."

Tom shrugs. "Well, it's you she wants here, Jim. And it might make her open up more. It's the only reason I'm allowing it."

Oh, great! He thinks I'll help trap her into revealing things she otherwise wouldn't. What does that say about me? How could I have been so excited at being involved in this murder investigation? I just want the interview to be over, and from now on I'll get my thrills from books. At least that's what I say now. I sigh. "All right."

"Okay, let's go." Tom's still carrying the sheaf of papers.

I nod to them. "What are those?"

"Later, Jim," is his curt response.

We're logged in by the officer outside the door and then enter the outer office. Susan's sitting at her desk. An officer stands nearby. Tom dismisses him and shuts the door to the corridor.

"Hi, Susan," I mumble.

"Thank you for coming, Dr. Albright."

I've tried over and over to get her to call me Jim, but all pleas have fallen on deaf ears. Ken encouraged the formality. It has always seemed so pretentious to me, but it's consistent with Ken's personality. I take a look at Susan. She's 37, a year younger than Ken. I'm pretty sure she has a great figure, but she does everything she can to hide it. Today's camouflage is a loose fitting light green blouse, off-white baggy slacks, and clunky brown low heels. The only bright spot is one of those striking Indian necklaces you find at flea markets. She was a red head when she first came to the department a year before Ken took over, but now her hair is a lustrous black. I couldn't tell you which, if either, is her natural color. I bet Donna could. Usually Susan's green eyes are piercing and unforgiving. Today they're puffy, red, and vulnerable. Has she been crying? Not surprising, I suppose. She's one of the few who got along with Ken.

Tom also is assessing her. He gets permission to record the interview and heads it with the date, time and names of those present. "Do you normally arrive so early?"

"No, but Dr. Salter told me he'd be coming in on Sunday. I thought he might have left me some work and I'd get an early start on it, while it was still quiet around here. Often he'll leave letters on his desk for me to type first thing in the morning."

"I see. So you didn't know he'd been murdered?"

"No. When I saw the officer I was shocked. Why should I have to be signed in to get to my own office? Then he told me about Dr. Salter. I couldn't believe it. Such a good man." She wipes her eyes with a lace handkerchief.

"Why did you break the seal on the door to Dr. Salter's office?"

"Well, you see . . . ."

"Didn't you notice it was clearly marked 'evidence,' as identifying a crime scene?"

"I guess I wasn't thinking. Somehow it seemed important to me to get and type any letters on his desk. Even if he was dead. It was just the right thing to do."

"Surely, Ms. Barber, you realize that makes no sense. You seem like an intelligent woman. Dr. Albright tells me you're unusually competent."

"I was upset, distraught at the news. I know I wasn't thinking clearly, but all I could feel was the need to get those letters done. He would have wanted it."

I have trouble correlating her current agitation with her cool, even frosty normal demeanor. I try to flash an encouraging smile, but I've never understood how one of those differs from any other kind. She ignores it.

Tom just looks at her a moment. I think he's trying to decide what tack to take. "Ms. Barber, you haven't been completely honest with us, have you?" With an ostentatious flair he waves the papers he's brought with him.

What can Tom mean? Is it one of those intuitive detective things? I feel I ought to jump to Susan's defense. Then I look at her face, now drained of color and staring at the papers.

"What do you mean?" she whispers.

Yes, what does he mean? I certainly have no idea. But something has Susan terrified and Tom's ready to pounce.

"Last night we found a diary in Dr. Salter's desk. He started it a little more than two months ago. Did you know about it?"

Although I wouldn't have dreamed it possible, she looks worse as she shakes her head.

She gulps twice. "No, I didn't know." Her hands twist the handkerchief. Her voice, a mere whisper, says, "Does it . . . does it mention me?"

"Do you think it does?"

"I . . . uh . . . I don't know."

"Would it make sense if it did?"

I'm beginning to understand. I bet those papers are a copy of the diary.

After a pause, Susan responds, "I think there's a chance." What on earth could it mean?

"There's more than a chance, Ms. Barber. You have a small but significant mention in it."

"Oh, my God." She folds completely, breaks into sobs, and places her head in her arms and her arms on her desk.

I glance at my watch. Soon the office will be a hive of activity. I don't want anyone to see her like this. She's always been so proud of her self-control. Fortunately, police at the door are turning away all comers.

She finally composes herself enough to mutter, "Ken . . . Dr. Salter and I were in a relationship." She looks at me and I suspect she's sorry she wanted me here.

I'm stunned. Susan and Ken in an affair? His exploits, I'm sorry to say, have been a source of office gossip for years. But with Susan?

Incomprehensible! Sure, she's good looking, but such a cold fish. At least that's what I thought. I'm going to have to adjust my thinking.

Susan, her voice still subdued, says, "What does the diary say about me? Does it say . . . he loves me?"

She appears so needy. I want to help, but don't know how.

"You're mentioned just once, near the beginning. He says he's busy now, doesn't have time to bother with you anymore. His words, not mine."

She looks like she's been slapped. "Does everyone have to know?"

Tom replies, "Only if it becomes relevant. But I can't guarantee anything."

"I'd never say anything, Susan," I interpose. I touch her hand. She glances at it, looks shocked, and pulls it back.

"I think, Ms. Barber, your best bet is to be completely straightforward with us. Tell us what you really wanted in his office. It wasn't this diary?"

She remains silent, thinking, and eventually deciding to cooperate. "No, not the diary. I really didn't know about it. But I'm so ashamed of the truth. I behaved like a teenager. I . . . I wrote him letters."

"Love letters?" She nods "And you wanted to get rid of them?"

"Yes. I heard about him on the early news this morning. I knew I had to get them. Before anyone else found them. It never occurred to me his office would be sealed. Please tell me, did you find them?"

Tom doesn't answer directly. "All I can assure you is that, if they turn out not to be relevant, they won't be made public."

I wonder if he has uncovered them. Poor Susan.

"Tell us how the affair began."

Bringing that so descriptive word into the open devastates her further. She looks at me, eyes imploring me to leave. But Tom's also eyeing me and the message is clear to stay. I stay.

Finally she begins, at first so softly we can barely hear, then in a progressively more normal tone. "It was about a year ago. But the story goes back much further."

She hesitates, her eyes mist. We wait. She opens her mouth to speak when my cell rings. I glance at the caller's ID and tell Tom I have to take it. He looks thunderous, irritated that the flow has been interrupted. Well that's just tough. I return to the corridor and answer. I listen for a moment, ask the caller to hold, and reenter the room. "Tom, could I talk to you a minute?"

CHAPTER 9

Monday Morning

Tom glares at me with disbelief, then strides from the room. "What the hell are you doing? Obviously it was a mistake to bring you in. You just screwed up an interrogation. Damn Theresa."

Now I'm a little ticked. "You're right, Tom, maybe I'm not the man for this job. I'm not a cop and don't do things the way you do. But give me some credit. I answered the phone because it was Donna on the line. I got you because I thought it was important."

"Well, I'm here now, and this better be good."

"Theresa rang Donna." I see this grabs him.

"Theresa again! What did she want?"

"She told Donna she had spoken to you about including me and was gratified to learn you had." Tom barely suppresses a groan.

"Okay, fine, let's get back in there. Or maybe I should leave you out here."

"There's more."

"Well, spill it out."

"Theresa also wants Donna to help. Says since she's already a consulting psychologist with several police agencies in the area, it shouldn't be a problem."

Tom stares at me, then seems to withdraw. Finally he nods and says, more to himself than me, "Yes, that might actually be a good idea. She does have a great deal of experience. Even assisted my department a number of times. Yes . . . I think it would be helpful and it makes a lot more sense than including you." Ouch! That seems unnecessary, don't you think? He continues, "All right, Jim, tell her, er, ask her to be here by 0900. I'm going to have a job for you both. Now let's get back to Susan Barber."

I remove Donna from "hold" and relay Tom's acceptance. She doesn't sound happy, but there's no time to explore, only to pass a small endearment.

Tom and I enter the outer office and once again sit with Susan. She looks at me questionably. I know to reveal nothing of what has transpired. How do I know? They never do in my books.

Tom starts it off. "Now Ms. Barber, you were about to tell us how your affair with Dr. Salter came about."

She's had time to compose herself, and she continues in a stronger voice than before. "As I started to say, it only makes sense if you go back further than the year Ken and I have been involved. My father drank—a lot. And when he did, which was almost every night, he got mean. He hit my mother, and my two brothers. I was the only girl. He never struck me." Her voice fills with bitterness. "He was saving me for something else."

I think I see where this is going and I don't want to hear it. I stir, make a half-hearted attempt to rise, but Tom's eyes rivet me to my chair. Susan doesn't notice.

"I was 13, almost 14. He came into my room. I was asleep. I felt someone shaking me. His breath. It's all I could sense as I woke up, his stinking alcoholic breath! He tore off my nightgown . . . touched me where he shouldn't . . . and then he . . . and then he . . . took me. Oh God, it hurt!"

Susan's composure has fled and she's crying openly. I feel so sorry for her and I don't know what to do. I wish Donna was here. But Tom doesn't want me doing anything. He's taking it all in. I suppose he's heard similar stories before. I mentally thank my parents for being normal.

Susan's voice reaches a feverish pitch. "From then on he had me whenever he wanted. Until I was 15. On my fifteenth birthday I ran away, lived on the streets, made money any way I could. What difference did it make what I did then? All I knew was men were filth and I'd hate them forever."

Oh, Susan. Who'd have thought your life was like this? I want to join her in tears and I sense one forming. I quickly wipe it away.

"One night, when I was 18, I was really tired, had no place to go. My last trick had stolen all my money—afterwards, of course. There was a church service. I went in and sat in the back pew. The preacher was a woman. A woman! Can you imagine? I fell asleep. When I woke, the church was empty. Except for the woman—sitting next to me—reading a book. I looked at her, horribly afraid. She just smiled, asked if I was hungry.

"She fed me, let me live with her. She helped me find a real job. And she made sure I got through secretarial school. I've been working ever since, dependent on no man. I've never dated. Men repulsed me. I'd have given anything to be gay. But even that solace was denied."

Tom breaks in, asking gently, "Ms. Barber, what does all this have to do with Kenneth Salter?"

"Don't you think it strange, Sergeant, that someone who so hated men would have an affair with him?" Tom settles back. "When I came here I was in my early 30's. That's a long time from 18. I began to wonder what I'd missed. Was it possible to have a normal relationship? Was every male a fiend? Before then I never questioned it. I knew the answer. But when I began looking at the men around here, I found many I could admire as people. For the first time in my life. I think you had the most influence on me, Jim."

I stare at her. For one thing she called me Jim. For another she's a hell of a lot more sensitive than I ever would have guessed. After all, she said I had an effect on her! But I am surprised. "Me?" I stammer.

For the first time there's a hint of a smile. "Yes. Observing how you treat your wife, the mutual respect you show, it made me realize that getting close to someone doesn't have to mean violence, threats, or fear. It was and is difficult for me to see how to build a healthy relationship, but I began to want something more than I had."

"How did you look on Kenneth Salter?"

She takes a minute to consider Tom's question. "I think I always admired him from the moment I met him. He is a genius, you know." A pause caused by realization of the situation. She corrects herself in a low voice, "Was a genius. And he was extremely courteous to me. Of course, I am a competent secretary. That's why I've become administrative assistant. I always did a good job on his work and he appreciated that. Said I saved him lots of time. He wasn't warm or friendly like Jim. But he respected me. One of the many men around here who appreciate me for my abilities."

"We all do," I say. Tom fires daggers at me. What the hell? He wants me to sit in on the interview and not say anything. Well, that's just too bad, old boy. Tom inclines his head in an invitation to Susan to continue.

"When Dr. Salter—Ken—became chairman, he called me into his office, told me he didn't want to be bothered with most of the details of running the department and was turning them over to me. He said he was impressed by my organizational skills and that he would support me in any conflict with faculty."

Well, that explains why she had so much authority over departmental affairs, and why faculty complaints to her were ignored.

"I was amazed. This world-class mathematician had faith in me! I swore to do the best job possible, even if it meant late nights and weekends. I devoted my life to what he wanted."

I'm so taken with her story I blurt, "And you're doing a wonderful job, Susan."

Again that half smile. "I know, Jim." Not a trace of arrogance. Just a simple statement of fact. She takes a deep breath. I think she's approaching the beginning of the affair. "One night, about a year ago, I stayed late, and Ken returned from home. When he passed my desk, he stopped, looked at me, and said, 'You're a damn fine looking woman, Susan.' No one had ever told me that. Not ever!"

It's hard to believe. 'Cause I've always found her attractive. On the other hand, as I've said, she hides her looks well.

"Except for my father who that last year called me his own pretty little girl."

I sense the hatred in her voice. Could she hate again—enough to kill?

"We started to talk. Ken could be a charming man."

True enough, I think, when he wanted something.

"Conversation was so easy. Except for Carole Witherton," seeing Tom's questioning glance she continues, "that woman preacher I mentioned, and now you, Ken was the only person I've ever told about my father. And he discussed things with me he said he'd never mentioned to anyone else."

"Like what?" asks Tom.

"Oh, how miserable his marriage was. How his wife Harriet—and she certainly is a mousy woman—showed no interest in him and how alone he felt."

Boy, wait 'til Donna hears about this. Ken really was a sorry specimen.

"I wanted to comfort him, something I'd never done for any man." She squirms in her chair. "Well, one thing led to another. For the first time ever I gave myself willingly. It wasn't electricity, but he was gentle."

"No one ever suspected, Susan."

She looks at me like I'm an imbecile. "You weren't supposed to, Jim." It seems as if Ken's demise has opened the door to first names on a permanent basis. "Ken told me early on that it had to be kept a strict secret. To protect *me,* he said! And I bought it. For a year I was in heaven. Then suddenly, without warning, it was over. He simply told me early one Monday morning he didn't want to be with me ever again. He'd like me to stay on as his administrative assistant. Said at least I was good at that." Tears form again. "Was I that bad a lover? He was so cold, so . . . so distant, like he didn't care whether I stayed or not."

I search my memory banks, suddenly remembering the unprecedented event of Susan leaving work because of illness. Could it have been that Monday?

Tom asks, "How did you respond?"

For the first time since she began her story, I sense hesitation, as if she's trying to word her answer carefully. I see Tom watching her closely. I'm sure he's getting the same vibes.

"Oh, I was devastated at first, in tears. The day he told me, well, I had to go home, pleading illness." Aha, so it was then! "But then I realized I'd had a wonderful year with a remarkable man, that I'd gotten more out of life than I'd ever expected. It was hard, but I'm a realist. I quickly came to accept the situation."

I stare at her incredulously. A proud woman, wretchedly treated by men in her early life and then unceremoniously dumped by another after her only meaningful relationship. And she came to accept it? Get real. But maybe. I will never understand people. "How could you continue to work here?" I ask.

"I love my job. And I'm good at it. And working for someone of Dr. Salter's reputation was exciting—typing papers that would startle his colleagues, assisting in the visits to our campus of distinguished mathematicians from around the world, and playing a major role in the building of this department. I wasn't going to lose all that because of some minor relationship problem."

Hardly "minor," I think. Tom asks, "You said you were devastated." She nods. "Were you angry?"

She takes a moment to respond. Again I have the feeling she's being careful with her words. "No. Of course not. As I said, I was hurt temporarily, upset. But that soon passed. Things have been fine since."

"So you wouldn't have wanted to kill Dr. Salter?"

"Heavens no! How could you think such a thing?"

"I have to ask you this. I hope you'll understand. Where were you from five o'clock on yesterday?"

Looking relieved she responds, "Every Sunday evening three other women and I get together for bridge." I didn't know anyone did that any more. "We gather at 5:30 and have a light supper first. Then we play until about nine. We all work so we have to quit early."

"What about between 5:00 and 5:30?"

She sighs, as with the release of a burden. "It's a 40 minute drive from my home to the university. Besides, my friend's house where we played is in the opposite direction. If that's the time period you're concerned about, there's no way I could have killed Ken."

"Please give me the names of the three women."

It's obvious Susan doesn't want to involve her friends, but she writes names, addresses, and phone numbers on a slip of paper that Tom pockets.

"Is there anything else you want to add, Ms. Barber?" She shakes a no. Tom says, "Interview ended at 0757" and turns off the recorder. Then he thanks Susan for her time and leaves the office.

I linger, uncomfortable with what's transpired. "Look, Susan. I know this hasn't been easy for you. I just wanted to reiterate that none of this goes beyond this room as far as I'm concerned."

She seems to draw herself up, looking once more the formidable commander of the departmental ship. "Thank you, Dr. Albright. Now I guess I'd better get to work making sure this place continues to function as it should."

It's a clear dismissal, and I see the mode of address has reverted to normal. I think I've been allowed a glimpse of a different Susan, a more caring one than is normally visible, but the public facade seems to be back in control. I leave and approach Tom in the outer office.

He gives me a sardonic glance and says, "She's lying."

CHAPTER 10

Monday Morning

I'm pretty sure Tom's right. Susan did lie. But I can't put my finger on any specific thing. "What about?" I ask.

"I don't know. But there's something. And we're going to find out!" I want to pursue this. Tom senses a question coming so hastens to add, "No time now to discuss it. I've got to return to my office to see how they're coming with the evidence."

Just as well, actually, as I'm eager to escape this scene. "So you want Donna and me here in about an hour?"

"Yes, at 0900—sharp."

Oh, my. Where is that fun-loving guy I went to school with? He at least talked normal. I decide to go to my office, one floor down, and get a little work done. I'm ready for my 11:00 class, but a review of the material wouldn't hurt.

I'm buried in an exciting math book—yes they are exciting—when a familiar scent pervades my space. I know that the love of my life has arrived. I look up and am struck for the umpteenth time by how hot she is. About 5' 3" with hazel eyes and soft golden hair falling to her shoulders. She's wearing a white blouse and gray slacks. Work clothes. She must have therapy sessions this afternoon. In addition to her consulting with law enforcement, she has a thriving private practice with clients who adore her. I reach for her but she evades my grasp with a move that is both artful and provocative.

"Easy boy, it's almost nine."

My watch provides verification. "You're right. Let's go."

"Wait a minute, Jim."

"What?"

"I know you. I know you're excited. I'm willing to bet you've had visions of playing detective."

Uh oh, I think. As always she reads me perfectly. "Well, maybe just a little," I mumble, head down.

She smiles, but her words are serious. "Just remember, Jim. This isn't a game. People will be hurt, most likely some we know."

Isn't she wonderful? So caring. She's in the right profession. I respond, "I know, darling. A little earlier I got a hint of that." Her eyes are questioning, but I say, "I'll have to tell you later. We've got to get to the math office."

When we arrive Tom's impatient stare verifies my watch's accusation that we're three minutes late. How terrible! "Hello, Donna. It's been a long time."

"Yes, Tom. It's nice to see you. I've heard good things about you."

"Thanks. And my colleagues tell me you've steered them in the right direction many times."

"Still single I hear. Still playing the field?"

"Not as much. There's no one special at the moment. I wish we could catch up more, but I have to attend Dr. Salter's autopsy at 1000, and there's something I want the two of you to do."

"How can we help?"

"Donna, I'd like you to take a look at Salter's office."

"Oh . . . kay. I can do that. But what good do you think it will do?"

"I wish I knew. I remember how intuitive you were when we were in school together. Maybe you'll see something I missed that would give me a better feel for the victim. Oh, and, of course, Jim, if you see anything I'll be glad to listen to you too."

Sure, throw the kid a piece of candy.

Then he continues, "There is something I definitely need *your* help with." Immediately I feel important again. "I'd like you to look at what's on Salter's whiteboard. It contains some math, and you might remember I barely got through Finite Math."

"Do you think it has anything to do with the murder?"

"I doubt it, but I want to make sure."

"Er, Tom."

"Yes?"

"Ken, I mean, uh, that is, Ken isn't . . ."

"No, Jim. The body was removed last evening."

"Well, then. Let's go," I say with more enthusiasm than is warranted. Donna shakes her head and her lips flirt with a smile.

Tom halts my steps with a sharp, "Not so fast. Lamar, we're going in now."

The CSI takes the lead, digital camera in hand. The officer handling the access log signs us in. Susan was able to remove only a single strip of the evidence tape. Lamar, I don't know his last name, meticulously photographs the destruction and then peels off the rest of it. Tom notes the CSI's entry into the crime scene on his pad, and simultaneously prevents me from following. I am able to observe Lamar take a broad-brush series of photos.

Tom explains, "Just to provide verification nothing has been disturbed since the crime scene was secured."

Lamar nods to Tom. "All yours. I'll be in the hall if you need me." Tom leads the way into Ken's office and records our entry.

Donna initiates a slow circle of the room, pausing to peruse the certificates mounted behind the desk and then continuing to the bookcases. She loves to learn what kind of books appeal to a person. But here they'll be math books, and that definitely is not her forte. So why does she appear so entranced?

I'm always amazed at how picked-up Ken's office is. It's usual for the desktop to be devoid of everything, but today so is the big round table that normally holds his outdated computer.

"Jim," Tom says, "Please take a look at the whiteboard and tell me what the hell it's all about."

What I see is

$$\sum_{i=3}^{\infty}\left(\frac{1}{i}-\frac{1}{i+1}\right)=\lim_{N\to\infty}\sum_{i=3}^{N}\left(\frac{1}{i}-\frac{1}{i+1}\right)$$

$$=\lim_{N\to\infty}\left[\left(\frac{1}{3}-\frac{1}{4}\right)+\left(\frac{1}{4}-\frac{1}{5}\right)+\cdots+\left(\frac{1}{N}-\frac{1}{N+1}\right)\right]$$

$$=\lim_{n\to\infty}\left(\frac{1}{3}-\frac{1}{n+1}\right)=\frac{1}{3}$$

"Hardly earth shaking, Tom. This is material from second semester calculus. My guess is Ken was helping some student with a topic called telescoping sums. You see these bold precise strokes? They exude confidence, don't they? That would be Ken's writing. Apparently he placed an illustrative problem on the board, probably asked the student to take it from there. Then he, or she, undoubtedly terrified, barely touched the board with the marker. I guess he, or she, got stuck at the end of the second line. And look at those bold square parentheses on that line. The poor kid left them out. And they're important. But my guess is Ken, thoroughly disgusted by now, inserted them with some sort of sneering comment. He had a pretty short fuse. It also looks as if he had to finish the problem. I'll bet that student will never ask for help again. No wonder so many wind up hating math."

Tom looks at me thoughtfully. I know his interest perked when I mentioned Ken's short fuse. By now he's heard several allusions from me as to the type of man Ken was, maybe from others too. I expect him to pursue it now, but all he says is, "I suppose this must have been written recently? Surely the boards would have been cleaned since Friday."

I can see why that's interesting to him since it might place a student in Ken's office yesterday. But I can offer no comfort. "I doubt it," I say. "In general, office whiteboards never get cleaned. Faculty rarely erase them, and it's possible an important piece of research may be on the board and nowhere else."

Tom in disbelief says, "You mean to tell me someone could make a significant discovery and not back it up anywhere?"

"Yeah, I know. But faculty can sometimes be a little weird." He looks directly at me and nods.

"Yes, I can believe it," he says. "So the janitorial staff wouldn't clean a board if it had something on it?"

"That's right. It's part of their training."

"But a student *could* have been here yesterday?"

"Of course. There's just no way to tell."

"Do you think a student might have killed him?"

I don't want to believe that. One of the reasons I took a university job is I like these kids and want to help them. But now it's different. After all, I'm a detective! Well, sort of. "I don't want to believe it, but I know young people commit horrible crimes. So, sure, it's possible. Ken definitely pissed off plenty of students."

"Any specific ones?"

I can think of some, actually a multitude over the years. But I'll be damned if I condemn them with no reason. Even for Tom. "No, no one especially."

"Tom," chirps my love from in front of the bookcases, "Can you come here a second?" Tom strides to her. "Jim will tell you I'm fascinated by the books people choose. Of course, here in a math office it'd be impossible to find many interesting ones." She gives me a wicked grin letting me know she's teasing me. "And most of the books do relate to mathematics. Over there is a section devoted to effective administration, which I suppose makes sense for a department chair. But what really interests me is this." Donna points to the second shelf from the bottom of the middle bookcase.

I see nothing special. "What about it?" I can see Tom's confused too.

Donna continues. "It seems a strange collection, especially for an office. It includes Machiavelli's *The Prince* and Stanley Milgram's *Obedience to Authority: an Experimental View* and a host of others that just seem inappropriate. Some of them actually are pretty horrible and some I've never heard of."

I say, "I've read *The Prince*, of course. But who's this Milgram guy?"

"I learned about him when I was in grad school." Did I mention she has a doctorate in psychology? "He was a professor at Yale University. He conducted experiments influenced by the Nazi *Holocaust* that explored the relationship between obedience and authority. They threatened electrical shocks for wrong answers. I can't remember whether volunteers actually were shocked or not."

"Yuck," I say.

"Well, he certainly was controversial."

Tom breaks in, "Do you really think this has anything to do with the murder?"

"I don't know, but I think it casts a little light on the kind of man Ken was." Donna appears to be disturbed by this discovery. "But that's not all, Tom."

"What do you mean?"

"Just look at these shelves. The books are perfectly aligned. You could use the spines to draw a straight line."

Tom says, "Yes, I had noticed that but didn't think much of it."

"Ken was a neatness freak," I mutter.

"Yes, Jim, I'd noticed that too." Is there a sarcastic note in his voice? "Do you see something more, Donna." He sure is more patient with *her*!

"Look at this." She points to a clear plastic report cover, the kind students use to enclose and secure a term paper. This one could be doing just that. It appears to contain about 30 pages. "See how it sticks out from the surrounding books. Impossible to miss. It's probably nothing, but it's just so out of place that I'd like to see it."

In response Tom walks to the corridor door. "Lamar, please come in and bring your camera." They return and Tom points to the report. "Photograph that and the surrounding books. Make sure you get close ups so we can read the titles. Then process the report and make a couple of copies of the contents. After we leave you can release the crime scene." Tom makes another note on his pad.

After the CSI returns to the hall, Tom asks, "Either of you have anything else?" We shake our heads. "All right then, I have to get to the autopsy."

That's fine with me. I'll still have about an hour and a half before my class, and I know Donna must get to her clients.

We are about to part when Tom says, "I almost forgot. Dr., sorry, I'm still not used to it, Theresa Bedlow wants all of us to come to her home at 1900. Can you make it?"

Ignoring the question, Donna says, "Theresa wanted both Jim and me to help you, Tom, and now she's requesting a meeting with all of us tonight?" Tom nods. "There's something strange about this, and a little unsettling."

"How so?"

"Think about the class we all took from her, when we met. Remember her technique?"

"Sure," replies Tom. "She'd divide us into teams of three. We formed one of them. Then she'd describe different types of crimes, coaching graduate students to play victims witnesses, perps. Then we had a week to solve them."

The memories flood my brain. We'd each contributed in our own way to the team. Tom brought unbelievable energy, spending hours pursuing facts in the library, interviewing "witnesses," and analyzing reams of data. And Donna? Oh, was she special! Still is for that matter. She supplied an intuitive understanding of events and individuals that allowed her to leap logical gaps and zero in on the correct interpretation of incomplete facts.

And she always looked for the hidden good in Theresa's actors, even the ones representing the most heinous of individuals. She was destined to choose counseling as a career.

I bet you're wondering what my contribution was. Well, when I could stop slobbering over Donna, I found I had a pretty good knack for logical reasoning. In fact, it was about then I decided to be a mathematician. Now don't even think it. Mathematicians can be pretty nice. Just ask Donna.

So all three of us made the team a great success. You think I'm being immodest, don't you? But no less an authority than Theresa herself indicated we were the most talented group she'd ever supervised.

"Well," continues Donna, "It seems to me Theresa is going back 20 years to resurrect what she felt was the best problem solving team ever. A bit of nostalgia maybe, for an aging academic?" She pauses. "Only this time, guys, the crime is more than an apocryphal puzzle."

CHAPTER 11

Monday Morning and Afternoon

Tom leaves for Ken's autopsy and whatever else police officers do in the afternoon. I decide to walk Donna to her car. Then I decide to hold her hand. And then I decide to stroke its palm with my index finger. She seems to find it as erotic as I. But enough of that. I am a detective and must move forward.

The trouble is I'm not sure where to go, so I follow up on Donna's comment. "I know, darling, it seems a little strange, what Theresa's doing, but what is there about it that bothers you?"

"I'm not sure. If I'm right and she's trying to revive the past, it just seems wrong." She pauses, trying to find a way to express her concern. "It's just, well, Jim, it's just that this isn't a game. And you know darn well that's what we thought we were doing in her class. Playing an interesting game. But this time a real human life was taken and there's someone truly nasty out there. I don't know, Jim. I just don't like it. We have no business being involved."

"Yeah, I know. I'm sure Tom thinks he's been forced into bringing us in. Me more than you." I wish I could lessen her worry. "Maybe you're wrong. Maybe she really thinks we have special talents that apply to this particular situation and we can get it solved quickly. You know how much she cares about our university. She's probably worried sick about potential damage to it."

"Maybe," replies Donna, but I can see she's far from convinced.

"She is pretty level-headed."

"Oh, I know. I'm probably overreacting." Then she smiles, lighting the world. "She's always been down-to-earth, hasn't she, not exactly a frivolous person?"

She squeezes my hand and I know she's left unsaid that I am—frivolous I mean—especially with this detective fantasy. In general she likes that part of me, understands it even. And more important, she accepts me for the way I am. And that's good, because, dammit, I *am* excited.

We reach her car. I, to my chagrin, receive only a chaste kiss for our parting, and then return to my office. Okay, how am I going to spend my day? Of course, I have my 11:00 o'clock graduate class, Then there's an hour break before I teach College Algebra from 1:00 to 1:50.

I love my graduate course. Mostly good students, and quite abstract. It's the type of course dear to mathematicians. And very few others ever come close to it.

College Algebra, on the other hand, is forced on huge numbers of undergraduates to satisfy their math requirement. Most who take it hate it, especially if they have a bad teacher. It's elementary of course. That is if you're a mathematician. But to many it embodies all of math's difficulties encountered since grade school. Unfortunately, I'm not a good enough instructor to overcome the fears. I know someone in the department who is, but he can't teach everyone. At least I treat the students with respect. They recognize and appreciate that, and I think they leave the course with no worse feeling about math than they had when they entered it.

If I grab lunch between my classes, I'll be free from 2:00 on. I figure detective duties will demand time the rest of the week. I have no idea what they might be, but I plan to be ready for the call. So I'd better prepare my classes for Wednesday and Friday. What, you say, that's all you teach? Just two courses, and you work only three days a week? Well, put like that it does sound cushy.

But it's not the whole story. Really. I have what's known as a half-time research assignment. I'd better find some original results and they'd better be good enough to publish. If I didn't do that before I got tenure I'd have been kicked out. Now there will never be a promotion if I don't produce. Well, it's an old argument and I don't want to defend my position any more.

What I do want is to work on my classes. So that's what I do, finishing by 5:00. That will leave me free Tuesday, Thursday, and before 11:00 and after 2:00 on Wednesday and Friday for detective duties. Probably no research this week. Or am I dreaming?

Traffic is wicked on the drive home and I don't arrive until 5:33. Well, yeah, mathematicians do love preciseness. Donna pulls into our driveway behind me.

"I brought us subs," she says. Now I love her even more.

We talk about our work, and how we have to call a technician to check the air conditioner before summer unfolds. But the murder is tacitly assumed to be taboo. At quarter to seven we leave for the short ride to Theresa's.

CHAPTER 12

Monday Evening

We arrive a couple of minutes before seven. Theresa answers the door, looking better than when I last saw her. Was it only 24 hours earlier? Of course, Tom's already there.

"Thank you for coming. I know it's an imposition, but I think you might be able to help. It's a devastating situation, public relations wise, for the university."

I think it's pretty devastating for Ken too, but I say nothing.

"Well, come into the living room. Sit down and we'll get started. What did you learn from the autopsy, Tom? Who did it by the way?"

"Doc Pritchard."

Theresa groans. Tom shrugs. What the heck is that about? Theresa sees Donna's and my confusion. "Doctor Reginald Pritchard is almost as old as I am and not nearly as bright. He's been in the medical examiner's office for decades—he was there when I was with the sheriff's department and you know how long ago that was. He's made no attempt to stay abreast of changing techniques. His one claim to fame, proudly and repeatedly stated, is his range for time of death has never been wrong."

"Isn't that good?" I ask.

Tom takes up the story. "It should be. The trouble is he always makes the window as large as possible. And he won't even guess a more realistic period."

"So what did his report say?"

"Several things, none of which is surprising. Salter was killed by sharp force trauma."

"What the hell does that mean?"

"It's a knife wound, Jim." Again I detect an unnecessary element of disgust. "The wound indicated the weapon was a double edged blade. It's horizontally oriented and is about one and one-half inches in length. It was located approximately 19" from the top of the head and 3" left of center. The cut was deep and nicked the aorta causing internal bleeding. Doc estimates Salter may have lived as long as two minutes before death occurred."

I feel sick. I wouldn't have wanted even Ken to suffer two minutes of agony knowing he was going to die.

"Then he reported," and Tom's voice betrays outrage, "that the death occurred between 1300 and 2100. Lou Daly, one of the ME investigators, gave a preliminary range of 1400 to 1900."

I ask, "Did Prichard explain the difference."

"He did not. I even called him on it. He said that Daly was a young whippersnapper who wasn't a doctor and didn't have the knowledge or the smarts to make such a decision. What a crock! Lou may not be a doctor, but he's almost never wrong." Tom shrugs. "Oh, well, nothing I can do about Pritchard, anyway."

Donna asks, "So who are you going to believe?"

"I'm going to believe Lou, but I have to act on Prichard's range. It's the official one and if I ignore it there could be trouble. Besides, I suppose there's an outside chance he's right." Tom pauses to look directly at me. "Jim, you've hinted that Salter was a difficult man. I've uncovered material I'll get to later that backs your opinion. But I'm curious, Theresa, what your thoughts are about him."

"Cold, ruthless, cruel, egotistical, driven. A thoroughly nasty bit of goods hell-bent on getting his way about everything and not caring who got squashed in the process," is the instantaneous reply.

Wow! Theresa's never been known to pull punches, but I'm left breathless by the force of her assessment. I'm sad to say, though, that I recognize its validity. However, it's not the entire story. Ken is more than that. I speak up. "All Theresa said is true, Tom. But you can't fully know Ken without recognizing him as a first-class mathematician. That's worth a lot in my book." I pause, recalling his accomplishments. "My God, he was such a young man, only 38 I think, yet already he'd published over 100 papers in respected journals."

"Is that really such a big deal?"

"Yeah, that's a big number, Tom, for someone that age. But it's not what's important. Every single one of his papers made a major contribution to our discipline. Some turned prior thinking upside down. So, yes, I'd say it's a very big deal."

"A genius, then?"

"Definitely!"

"But a bastard nevertheless?"

That knocks me down a peg. Unfortunately I have to agree, albeit reluctantly.

Tom turns to Donna and asks in a slightly mocking voice, "What's your opinion? I recall you usually can find good no one else can see."

She looks at him, forcing a small smile. "I do think it's dangerous to characterize people with a few adjectives." She looks at Theresa and is rewarded with a nod of understanding and apology. "And I didn't know Ken all that well, except through what Jim has told me, and most of that has been pretty negative. I saw him only at math department functions. Then he always was aloof, superior, difficult to engage in conversation. He showed no interest in me whatsoever. I'd hate to think he didn't have a 'good' side, but he kept it well hidden."

"So he was bound to have enemies?"

Theresa says, "I think, with few exceptions, anyone who came into more than superficial contact with him wound up hating him."

I chime in, "He was well respected as a mathematician, but I can't think of anyone in the department who liked his leadership."

"How the hell did he get to be chairman if no one could stand him?"

I look at Theresa. She knows the story better than I, although I have a damn good idea. She explains, "It began with MRSU's founding president, Maurice Chapman. He believed in dedicated teaching and promoted it at the expense of research. I think it was a mistake, but maybe it was expedient while getting the school off the ground."

"Why a mistake?"

"Well, most academics believe a university has two major functions: teaching, of course, and pushing the boundary of knowledge, what we call research. I, and I'm far from alone, also think good research fosters good teaching."

"So you're saying you can't be a good teacher unless you're doing research?"

"No, not at all. But I think at the college level you can't be a good teacher unless you're being intellectually challenged yourself in some way."

"So what does this have to do with Salter?"

"Our second president pretty much followed Chapman's philosophy. The third, Norman Mulholland's predecessor, started emphasizing research in his brief two-year tenure. He tried to hasten the shift by picking department chairs with international reputations and getting them to build their departments along the new lines. We went through a nationwide search for the mathematics chair, but it was a sham since, from its beginning, the president intended to pick Kenneth Salter. I was Dean then and fought against it, as did several others, but he overruled us all."

"He sure did," I say fervently. "Most of the faculty signed a petition protesting his selection, but it was ignored. He'd been here several years prior to the search, and we knew the sort of man he was."

"Has his selection had the intended effect, increasing your research output?"

"Definitely," I sigh. "The last four years we've hired only people with proven research records, and the message is pretty clear that tenure, promotions, and raises are available only to those with continuing and successful research effort along with the attraction of grant money. It's almost as if teaching counts for nothing anymore," I conclude a bit bitterly. I glance at Theresa, wondering if I'd opened my trap too much in front of an administrator.

"There's truth in what Jim says," adds Theresa. "I think we've swung the pendulum too far, although Norman has started practices to reward teaching too. We'll be all right in the long run."

"But Ken never responded to those new initiatives, Theresa," I object. "And at least one person's career has been ruined."

CHAPTER 13

Monday Evening

Tom pounces on my comment, guessing there's a suspect in the offing. "Who's career, Jim?"

"George Frazier."

"Ah, yes," agrees Theresa.

"Who's he?"

Theresa defers to me with a nod. "George is a really great guy. Joined us five years ago as an assistant professor—this is his sixth year—and it's time to consider him for tenure and promotion to associate professor. He came at the end of the old regime, when teaching was emphasized, and that's what attracted him to MRSU. He's a fantastic educator—innovative, caring, demanding, and fair. The kids love him."

"So what's the problem?"

"Ken wasn't going to support him, and without enthusiastic backing from a person's chair, advancement is almost impossible."

"Because of the research requirement?"

"Partially, although George has published some papers."

"Certainly as many as others Ken supported," interposes Theresa.

"Yes, with Ken there was more to it than just the research," I continue. "While most of us dealt with Ken's dictatorial leadership by maintaining as low a profile as possible, George fought him every step of the way. Ken didn't like being challenged, considered differences of opinion a form of insubordination."

"I suppose if he didn't get tenure his position here would be less secure?"

"It's worse than that, Tom. Denial of tenure means he'd get to stay only one additional year, and then he'd be forced to leave. And with the way the job market is these days, that's really a sentence to life outside academe."

"Sounds like a strong motive for murder to me." We ponder this statement. Then Tom continues, "So we have one suspect. And Susan Barber is another." Tom tells the unprivileged in the room, you know, the ones other than me, about our interview with her. "A jilted lover never can be ignored."

Tom lets the thought hang, then asks, "Can you think of any others I should be talking to?"

God, this is awful. He's asking us to produce people to be interrogated, people we know. I don't like it one bit.

Theresa has no such concerns, but then this used to be her line of work. She says, "Dick Brighthurst and Stephen Farnsworth come to mind." I understand her naming Dick, but mention of Farnsworth's name is a surprise.

"Who are they?"

"Dick has been the Assistant Chairman of the math department. Today I asked him to be Acting Chair until a permanent selection is made. It's a role he performed well previously, during the period prior to Ken Salter's selection."

"Why should he be a suspect?"

I know the answer and am sorry to have to reenter the conversation. "He thought he'd become permanent chair when Ken was selected. I have a feeling he believed the administration was behind him."

I look at Theresa. "And so it was—all but the president," she says.

"So was the faculty. Dick's a good man. Anyway," I continue, "thinking he was going to get the job, and the extra income associated with it, he made financial commitments that have been hurt by the current economy. He always blamed Ken, somewhat unfairly in my opinion, for his woes."

"But there's more to it than that, isn't there, Jim?" This from the love of my life.

"Yes. Ken knew the faculty liked Dick and hated him. He'd find that intolerable. I think he decided to retaliate by doing all in his power to make Dick's life hell."

"How so?"

"Oh, in little ways, nasty ways. For example, he'd load him down with menial tasks, ugly clerical jobs a student assistant could do. Then he'd exclude him from significant meetings, not let him in on major decisions, and get angry when he wound up not having all the facts. I never really thought about it before, but looking back I realize Ken treated him like dirt—over and over. And Dick never complained."

"Why do you suppose that is? And why didn't he leave if it was so bad?"

"Easier said than done, Tom. He'd have to face the same rotten job market George would, although he might have a better chance because his research record is stronger. Besides, it's probably scary to risk his assured income since his finances are already bad. And if he complained too much, there's no telling what Ken would have done."

"So you're saying Salter threatened Brighthurst's security and self-esteem?" He looks for the confirming glances Theresa and I give him. "Okay, we'll talk to him. What about . . ." Tom consults his notes, "Farnsworth?"

Theresa takes over here. "He's Dean of the College of Arts and Sciences. Came here 22 years ago as Chair of the Chemistry Department. Seven years later he was appointed Associate Dean of the college, basically a paper pushing position. He was promoted to Dean five years ago when I moved up."

"Why did you bring his name up?"

"I'm not really sure. But something strange has been going on. It's almost as if he was afraid of Ken. I have no idea why. He's kind of a weak fish, so maybe it's just that he was intimidated by Ken's forceful and domineering personality. But I can't help but feel there's more to it than that."

"Like he was being blackmailed?"

"Maybe. The thought has occurred to me."

"Not much to go on, though."

"No. It's just a sense I have. I don't know how much stock you can put on it."

"All right," Tom says, deep in thought. "We'll check him out. Anyone else?"

We remain silent. Theresa finally says, "You'll probably find many more as your investigation proceeds. You won't suffer from lack of suspects."

"How about the wife?"

"Harriet?" says Donna. "I guess you have to consider the spouse, don't you?"

"Absolutely. Usually people are killed by someone they know."

"Seems to me I read that somewhere, that it's a significant other most of the time."

"Well, that often is the case if the victim is a woman. Depending on the year, the husband or boyfriend is responsible for roughly 30% of the homicides."

Donna asks, "What if it's a man?"

"Only about four percent committed by wives or girlfriends."

Donna likes this last statistic. "So the odds are against our killer being Harriet?" Tom shrugs as Donna continues, "I saw her the other day, by the way, at a health food store. She looked better than she has in years. Lost 20 pounds, new hairstyle. Said she was taking their two children and leaving Ken. Told me he'd humiliated her privately and publicly for long enough. I've seen a little of that myself, at those math parties, and it made me uncomfortable. On top of it all, according to her, he's had a string of women. She knew about Susan Barber, by the way. She said she finally worked up the guts to do something about it. Couldn't believe how good it made her feel. I hate to think how he reacted when he heard about her leaving."

"He'd never accept it," I say. "He'd have done anything to prevent it."

Tom says, "Hmmm. Donna, what do you think she'd do if he tried to stop her?"

Donna takes a while to consider her reply. When it comes, it is not informative. "I really don't know."

Tom asks, "Anyone else?" When there's no answer he continues, "Well, we've made a good start. Unfortunately, we have more work this evening. I've brought some reading material for you."

CHAPTER 14

Monday Evening

Tom hands Donna a stapled pack of papers. "This is a copy of the report you found. I skimmed it, and frankly I don't know what to make of it. Please look it over later this evening and get back to me tomorrow." He explains to Theresa how Donna spotted this violation of Ken's geometrically precise bookcase.

Donna looks troubled. "Tom, I don't have much time tomorrow. I'm booked all day. What I'll do is take a quick look tonight. If it has nothing to do with Ken's murder I'll let you know immediately. But if it's important, I'll want to think about it and I won't be rushed. I do have some time both Wednesday and Thursday."

Tom doesn't like this. I think, though, he suspects what I know. Donna's spine is constructed from steel and no one bends it. Besides he knows of her good record with the department.

He says, "All right, whatever you can do." He reaches into his briefcase and extracts three sheets of paper, handing one to each of us.

"What's this," asks Theresa.

"This is a photo of what came up on Salter's computer screen after we accidentally jostled the table. It gives us a valuable piece of information."

This is what we're looking at.

From: Salter <salter@math.mrsu.edu>
Subject: **Collins Conjecture**
Date: March 13, 2011 5:07:47 PM EST
To: Analysis group

This is to announce that today I have answered the Collins Conjecture in the affirmative. I will publish the proof shortly, but interested parties can contact me directly any time.

Kenneth Salter
Marcus Rome State University

"Yes, I can see," Theresa says. "So the murder must have occurred after 5:07 in the afternoon."

I look at the email. Even I know that time on the third line is when it was sent. Of course, Theresa would understand immediately. Along with her other achievements, she's taught herself a lot about computers. I recall her discussion in class about introducing computational techniques to a reluctant Sheriff's Department. I've also heard that she's responsible for MRSU's prominent program in computer science, overcoming all odds to obtain the most up-to-date equipment. She even taught some of the startup courses in programming and system design before enough faculty had come on board.

My eyes move to the message content.

"HOLY SHIT!"

"Jim!" admonishes Theresa, "What brought that on?"

"I'm sorry, Theresa, but this is really special."

"What is? I see he sent the email to a group that might be interested in it. Obviously he copied it to himself and that's why it wound up on his screen. But what's got you so hepped up?"

And hepped up I am. I simply can't control my excitement. Filled with awe, I reread the message. "Isn't that something? To think Ken did it. He really did it!"

"Did what? What's the big deal?" Tom sounds pretty disgusted.

"He proved the Collins Conjecture, damn it. Can't you read?" Perhaps enthusiasm causes me to be the tiniest bit indiscrete.

"What the hell is the Collins Conjecture?"

"Yes, Jim," interposes Donna, "tell me, too."

Finally I remember I'm the only mathematician in the room, so I start to explain. "Andrew Collins is a mathematician, now retired I think. About 30 years ago he defined and investigated a new mathematical structure, examining over 100 special cases of it. In every one of those cases he found that two of the involved variables were related in a precise manner, and he conjectured in a paper that this was always the case. He was never able to prove the result in general."

Tom says, "I assume from Salter's email message no one else could either?"

"That's right. Lots of progress has been made, and it's been proven true for several large classes of situations. But no one has given a general proof. Until today, that is. But Ken did."

"Do you think he really was successful?"

"Oh, yes. Ken was an excellent mathematician. And fanatical about his reputation. He'd never make an announcement like this without being absolutely sure." I pause a moment and then add, "Of course, his work will have to be checked by an expert in the field, but I'm sure it'll stand up to scrutiny."

"Is it really such a big deal?"

"Maybe not to you. But to any mathematician it sure is. Oh, not as huge as proving the Four Color Theorem or Fermat's Last Theorem, but huge enough."

"Didn't I read a few years ago about that Fermat theorem?"

"You did indeed! That made the popular press in a big way. And it should have. That was an especially remarkable achievement."

"So do you think his work here could have anything to do with his murder?"

"How would I know, Tom? I kind of doubt it, but he did announce it on the same day he was killed, so maybe."

"Well, Jim, maybe that makes what I brought for you even more important." Tom digs into his briefcase and produces a stack of about 15 sheets of paper. "This is a copy of what was on Dr. Salter's desk. One sheet was separate from the rest so I left it on top. The paper is full of mathematics. What can you tell me about it?"

I take his offering and thumb through it. It turns into a reverential experience. I realize I'm holding a copy of the proof of the Collins Conjecture, and my arms start to shake. After all, I'm the first mathematician to do that. Except for Ken, of course.

"Jim, are you all right?"

"Yes, Donna. No, not really. Donna . . . all of you, this is history. It's Ken's proof!"

Tom, less moved, says, "It's also evidence in a homicide investigation."

I can't believe that and say so. Tom just looks at me. "What about that sheet I kept at the top?"

"Oh, that's just the last page of the proof," and I hold it up for all to see. This is what we're looking at.

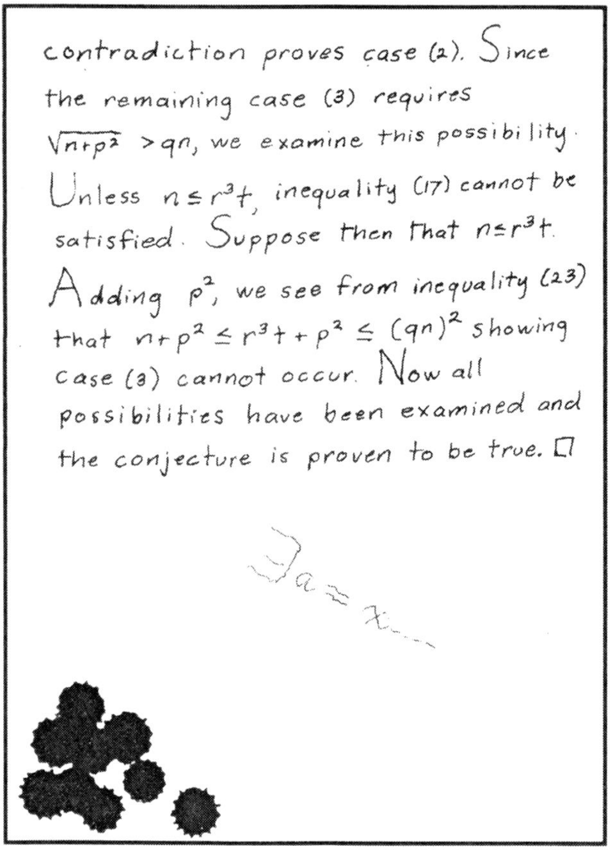

contradiction proves case (2). Since the remaining case (3) requires $\sqrt{n+p^2} > qn$, we examine this possibility. Unless $n \le r^3t$, inequality (17) cannot be satisfied. Suppose then that $n \le r^3t$. Adding p^2, we see from inequality (23) that $n+p^2 \le r^3t + p^2 \le (qn)^2$ showing case (3) cannot occur. Now all possibilities have been examined and the conjecture is proven to be true. □

I say, "I don't understand though, what are those black marks in the lower left corner?"

Tom replies, "It's not black on the original. There it's Salter's blood, some of which dripped from his shirt."

Now I'm sorry I asked.

After a respectful pause, cool as they come Donna speaks up. "What's that little square box?"

"It's a symbol marking the end of the proof."

"You mean like q.e.d.?"

"Right, that's kind of old-fashioned now and most people don't use it any more. I don't know why. Some people and journals use a solid box. By the way, it looks like he had just finished the proof shortly before he was killed."

"Why is that?"

"Well, the box and the wording indicate he was done. I can see him drawing the box Donna asked about, reflecting a moment on his achievement—as any mathematician would—and then sending out the email immediately."

"Okay, that makes sense. But why do you think the murder happened at that time?"

"Because, tidy fanatic that he was, he would shortly have stacked the papers with the last page properly placed."

What's that? Is Tom looking at me with newfound respect? If so, I think his response could be a little more dignified.

"Not bad for an amateur. So if you're right we can assume the murder occurred shortly after 1700."

I do a quick conversion to 5:00 p.m. and murmur, "Yes."

Tom says, "We'll take that as a working assumption, but let's keep in mind it could have happened anytime later." He pauses, thinking. "You said his work has to be checked by someone?"

"Sure. That's standard practice with research."

"I'd like to get that done as soon as possible, on the off chance it has something to do with the case. Know anyone for the job? Can you do it?"

"Don't I wish! But you need someone who's worked directly in the field related to the conjecture. It's pretty specialized." I mentally run through names of experts who might be appropriate and easily available. "Two people come to mind, Tom. The closest one is Harvey Delsanter." Tom's head jerks up. I wonder why. "He's at Reinhardt Tech." Reinhardt is a private institution located on the other side of town. It has a huge endowment and is making a name as a fine research establishment. "But I'm not sure I'd want to go to him."

"Why not?"

"He and Ken have been rivals for as long as I can remember, more a mutual and personal hatred than standard academic competition. Ken mocked him all the time, sometimes even to his face. Delsanter gave a colloquium here several years ago and Ken tried to make him look bad by asking tough questions."

"How did Delsanter respond?"

"I remember distinctly, after all this time. His face turned beet red, and he replied derisively, managing to cast aspersions on Ken's work in the process. I was extremely uncomfortable, and I wasn't alone."

"How will he take the news that Salter proved this Collins thing?"

"Conjecture, Tom. He'll be furious. I almost feel for him. After all, he's been working on it for over 10 years."

"How furious, Jim?"

"Plenty. He's an excitable and officious bastard. Probably yelling in frustration at everyone in earshot now." Then it hits me why Tom's asking. I gasp. "Oh, no, Tom. He wouldn't kill Ken just because Ken beat him to it."

"Are you sure?"

I suddenly realize that I have no idea. In spite of my outburst, I hardly know the guy. I shrug my shoulders in a discouraged way.

Tom says kindly, "We retrieved Dr. Salter's cell phone from his office. The last number he called was associated with the name Delsanter." I gape. "So you can be sure we'll look into him, Jim." I don't like the way he's contemplating me as he says it. I don't altogether trust Tom. "Now who's the other person?"

I'm remembering the fiascos of yesterday evening. I glance at Theresa and whisper, "Elmo Sherwin."

Theresa blanches. I can tell she had her fill of Elmo over dinner. Tom notices her reaction. Probably the reason he says, "Can you trust him?"

"Absolutely! First of all, he's brilliant. And, if it's a valid proof, he'll be thrilled and make sure Ken gets all the credit. He has no ego problem whatsoever."

Tom excuses himself, leaving the room as he pulls out his cell phone. I have an uneasy feeling about this, but I'm not sure why. I soon understand when Tom returns.

"Jim, I've just asked for two copies of what you say is the proof to be made and delivered here. They should be available shortly."

If I was uneasy before, I'm close to terrified now. "Why have you done that?"

"I'd like you to visit both Delsanter and Sherwin and ask them to check the validity of the proof. And I may want you to check out a few other things with Delsanter."

This does not sound good. What does he mean by "other things?" No one told me being a detective would be like this. The trouble with talking to Delsanter is that the little I've seen of him I don't like. Strikes me as a nasty sort, a worthy rival to Ken. "Don't you think that's a job for your people?" I ask with timidity.

"Normally it would be. And we'll certainly talk to him too. But you'll have a natural in, being fellow mathematicians and all. He'll probably respect you a lot more than us."

I doubt this. Some mathematicians, fortunately very few, take delight in tearing down others. Alas, Delsanter is in this group, and I dread thinking about how he'll receive me.

"So you will do it, won't you, Jim?"

"I guess so, but I don't like it," I mumble. Donna squeezes my hand. I'm sure it's a gesture of support, but I feel it's also a reminder there's a price for getting involved.

"When?" Tom presses.

"Well, it'll take most of the day to see Elmo," I realize tomorrow, Tuesday, would be the best time for that, but then the dread of Delsanter would last until at least Wednesday. "Suppose I see Delsanter tomorrow, and Elmo Wednesday?"

"Jim," interposes Donna, "don't you have classes Wednesday?"

"Yeah. But I'm giving an exam in my graduate course. Amy can administer it." Amy is my doctoral student and a joy to work with. "And she can cover my College Algebra class. I'll set it up."

Tom says, "That will work just fine." Well, thank you so much. Mission accomplished he dismisses me, saying, "I have further evidence that backs up all your suspicions about the various suspects." There is immediate interest, but he goes on to say, "It's getting late and I still have work to do so I suggest we adjourn. Donna, please remember about the report." I don't think she's likely to forget. "Jim, let's plan to meet at my office at 0900 and talk about plans for the day."

Plans for the day? I'm seeing Delsanter in the morning. That's all. I should have the rest of the day free. Why do I think I won't? The doorbell rings. Theresa rises to answer it and returns with two clipped sets of papers. Nodding at Tom, she says, "Jim, I believe these are for you."

We rise to leave. Seeing us out Theresa says, or perhaps orders, "I think it would be a good idea to meet every evening here at 7:00 until this crime is solved, so I'll see you all tomorrow. I'll have some sandwiches."

Outside the three of us look at each other and recall Donna's concern about our team.

CHAPTER 15

Tuesday Morning

Tom wants me with him at 0900. See, I can talk funny too. I've set my alarm for 8:00. I turn to give Donna a hug—yes just a hug—to start the day and find I'm embracing a pillow! Where is Donna? It's too early for her to be mobile. My shock dissipates when I remember her schedule is full from early morning to late afternoon. She will rise, with difficulty, if the needs of her clients call. When I reach the kitchen some twenty minutes later she gives me an alluring wave and leaves for work. I toast a bagel, douse it with peanut butter, pour a glass of tomato juice, and consume it all before I start for Tom's office.

"Hi, Tom."

He glances at his watch, so I look at mine. 9:04. Sigh. "Glad you could make it." Uncalled for, don't you think? He looks at me searchingly. "What's your schedule for the rest of the day?"

Ah, yes. What he hinted at yesterday is coming to pass. Seems to me I'm already committed enough by going to see Delsanter. "After I return from talking to the prick I plan to spend the day in my office, hopefully getting somewhere with my research."

"Good, so there's nothing important."

Well! You don't tell a research mathematician that his work is unimportant. No one else might think it is, but to the researcher it represents a major part of his life. "I'm not going to argue with you, Tom, but to me it's essential. If my efforts are unsuccessful I'll be stuck as an associate professor the rest of my life. Besides, it's fun."

"You're right, Jim. I apologize. It's just that I need your help."

Okay, now he's buttering me up. And it's working. "Tom, what is on your mind?"

"I want to talk to George Frazier. I thought you could pave the way."

"Aw, no, Tom. I really don't like this detective business."

"Bullshit. You're eating it up. You just don't like it when it hits too close to home."

I think Tom's got me pegged. It's disheartening to be so predictable. "Maybe you're right. But it would be even worse with George than Susan. After all, he's a colleague. It could make things pretty touchy in the future."

"Well, let's see how it goes. At least meet me for lunch and we'll discuss it more."

I resolve not to be roped into this, but even I don't know how strong I'll be about it. Then I get an idea. "How would you like to sit in on one of George's classes? It'd be a good show and you'd see for yourself the kind of teacher he is."

Tom isn't thrilled with the idea. Probably thinks it a waste of time. I'm surprised when he agrees. "Just a second," I say, "I'll check his schedule." I call the math office and speak briefly with one of Susan's underlings. "He has a calculus class at one o'clock. Will that be okay? I'll be glad to go with you to *that*." Emphasizing the class is okay for my presence is meant to imply the interview is not.

"Won't he mind someone just popping in?"

"Nah. People do it all the time. He has such a good reputation that graduate students and faculty often drop by just to see how a real pro acts. And he's a ham. I guess all good teachers are."

"All right, then. We'll have lunch, go to Frazier's class, and then visit with him."

Without enthusiasm I agree. Did you notice I've been conned, that I just agreed to be present when he interviews George? And if I'm honest with myself, I have to admit the sad fact that I'm torn between the distaste of seeing the police ask probing and probably personal questions of my friend and the ebullience of being involved in the chase. Somehow, I don't think Donna would be proud of my ambivalence.

Tom continues, "Got to run. I want to interview Brighthurst and Farnsworth this morning. See you at 1200."

Yes, sir! "Before you go, is there anything special you want me to bring up with Delsanter?"

Tom thinks for a moment. "Try to get a feel for how he's reacting to Salter solving that problem. Is he upset? Is he angry, furious even? Form an opinion about whether he's jealous enough to kill him."

Sure I'm going to be able to do that. What does Tom think I am, a fucking mind reader?

"And it'd be helpful if you can get an idea of his movements after five on Sunday." I nod forlornly, dreading the next couple of hours.

I return to my office, ostensibly to check one last time the exam I'm going to have Amy proctor tomorrow. The truth is it's a delaying tactic to spare me for just a little longer the displeasure of Delsanter's company. I think about my College Algebra class. It's one of my least favorite courses to teach, but I'd rather be taking on another section of it than going to see Harvey Delsanter.

I make a call. "Hi, Amy, it's Dr. Albright. I'm wondering if you can give an exam for me in my 11:00 class tomorrow and then take my College Algebra at 1:00."

"Sure, I'll be glad to. I guess you'll be busy helping the police about this murder?"

"Why would you think that?"

"Oh, come on, Dr. Albright. Everyone knows you've been in on it from the beginning."

My heart sinks. "Well, please don't spread it around even further."

She laughs. "I wouldn't have to. All the grad students are buzzing. Will we still be meeting tomorrow?"

"I think so, but I'll call you if there's a problem. I'll leave the exam and a note in your box saying what sections to cover in College Algebra."

"Great!" We ring off.

My delaying tactic can be carried only so far and I must be off to Reinhardt Tech. I've met Delsanter briefly only a couple of times. Once, about three years ago, at a conference. And before then, shortly after I joined the MRSU faculty, when he came to the math department and gave an incomprehensible lecture. Neither contact made much of an impression on me. But the stories I've heard have been enough to rattle my bones. He's successfully argued against tenure for every mathematics candidate at Reinhardt for the last four years. He's lambasted speakers at conferences, driving one graduate student presenter to tears and causing her to run from the room. He's scathingly responded to journal articles by debunking the importance, as opposed to the accuracy, of the content. I'm not looking forward to this meeting.

I haven't called ahead. I'm secretly praying he's not in. Then I can tell Tom I tried, leaving the contact up to him. So I'm hopeful as I pull into a visitor's space on the 600-acre urban campus. I've been here many times and know exactly where the math department is. But I don't know Delsanter's room number so I go to the main office. A secretary looks up, recognizes me, and says, "Hi, Dr. Albright. What brings you here?"

I smile at the attractive 20-some woman. "I was hoping to see Dr. Delsanter." Now there's a lie! "Is he in?"

Her face clouds over. "Yes, he's here. But he's in a foul mood. Worse than normal. I don't know if he'd like visitors or not. Do you have an appointment?" I shake my head. "Oh, well, it's up to you."

Great! Just what I need, to see a nasty man who's having a bad day. Of course I know why. I ask for and receive directions to his office. The secretary looks at me with pitying eyes. Slowly I trudge to Delsanter's domain, Ken's proof clenched in my left hand. His door's closed and I cling to the hope he's left.

Tentatively I knock, and with immense disappointment I hear a roar, "Come in!" I open the door, Delsanter, standing behind his desk and facing the entrance, stares at me and says, "Who the hell are you?"

He's a good 15 years older than Ken. And like Ken he's a wonderful mathematician and an awful man. I don't think he's in Ken's league though. Ken made tremendous advances in several areas of mathematics. This guy has concentrated only on that part of math involving the Collins Conjecture. But he has made significant contributions to the problem. I remember 10 years or so ago someone told me that, if the conjecture was ever solved, it would be Delsanter who did it. Now there's a prediction that went awry!

Delsanter has a Slavic look—big square face, bushy eyebrows, prominent nose, full and wavy gray hair, massive shoulders, and stocky body. He hasn't shaved, his light blue shirt's top two buttons are open showing a portion of his undershirt, and his navy blue slacks have been stretched to their limit. Even from where I'm standing I can smell his foul breath. Definitely been drinking! Before 10:00! How the hell am I going to get through this? "I'm Jim Albright, from Marcus Rome. I've met you briefly a couple of times."

He looks at me through hazy eyes. "You're the one with that worthless paper on manifolds that came out recently," he growls. "I forget the journal. Not a major one was it? Still don't know how it survived the refereeing process. Why on earth would I want to talk to you?"

Nice beginning, don't you think? I feel the anger boiling in me. After all, the paper he mentioned is the best work I've ever done. And I'm not alone in thinking that, dammit. The three referees were uniform in their praise, asking for only minor modifications before publication. Nevertheless, for just a moment, this cretin makes me doubt my abilities.

I guess you'd agree that everything I've heard about him seems to be true. I'm regaining my confidence, suddenly glad of his comments. Because I realize he's just a rotter and that I'm no longer afraid of him. But, mature as I am, I want to make him as uncomfortable as possible. So, like they do in all those mystery books I read, I say, "I'm not here to talk about that, but about Ken Salter's solution to the Collins Conjecture." I know that'll get to him. I hope what I say next will be even worse. "The police sent me."

His eyes flash angrily. I was right, I observe with malicious glee. It's all I can do to keep from grinning. I really am a child, aren't I?

He says, "Shit. Why should the police care about me? Just 'cause Salter proved a silly conjecture, *if* he did prove it."

"Oh, as to that," I say sweetly, "I've a copy of his handwritten proof here for you. I can't testify to its accuracy, but I'm taking it to Elmo Sherwin tomorrow. He'll be able to give me a reading on it."

"Sherwin!" Delsanter snorted. "Another flaming idiot."

At least I'm in good company. No one doubts Elmo's abilities. Except for Delsanter, I guess.

"He'll probably try to take the credit for it himself."

Now that *is* going too far. "Elmo Sherwin is the most ethical man I know," I storm. Then, because I know it'll annoy him, I add, "And in order to protect Ken's proof, we had it notarized." This had been my idea, expressed to Tom last night after he pushed Delsanter on me. While I trust Elmo implicitly, I don't have any feel for this man's integrity.

I'm pleased to see he's sputtering. I know, I know. I'm a slimy individual. "Very well, I'll look at it," he stammers, "let you know if it's right. I assume that's what you've been sent to find out."

Oh, this is wonderful. "Actually not," I say. "We'll be satisfied with Dr. Sherwin's evaluation. This copy is just a courtesy for your personal edification." He looks murderous and I'm glad there's a desk between us. Makes me think he could kill if sufficiently angry. Was he that mad at Ken? "I was wondering if you could tell me if you've had any communication with Dr. Salter lately about the conjecture." Pretty cagey, huh? See how I'm cleverly getting him to talk about the relationship he had with Ken?

"Communicate with that son-of-a-bitch?" he roars. "Not a chance! The bastard did call me though."

Now here's what sounds to be a verification of what we already know. I search for the perfect question. Ah, I have it! "When," I ask.

"Yesterday, sometime in the afternoon."

Better yet. "What did he want?"

"Just crowing, the shit. Left a message on my machine saying he'd solved the Collins Conjecture. We'll see if he did."

Ken was scum. I have no love for Delsanter, but I know what it's like to work on something and then find out it's already been done. "Bet that made you mad?" I say, surprised at the sympathy in my voice, a wasted emotion it turns out.

"What are you, some two-bit amateur psychiatrist? Of course it didn't upset me. What do I care if someone else solved the problem before me?"

Oh, come on. You haven't worked on anything else for over 10 years. You were devastated and we both know it. God, look at you. And smell you.

He continues with, "But I am going to look at that proof damned carefully. If I find, as I suspect I will, that Salter stole my ideas, there's going to be hell to pay."

What a crock! Ken was so arrogant about his abilities, with good reason I have to add, he'd scorn taking anything from this blowhard. Undoubtedly Ken's work was built on previous results of Delsanter's and many others, as well as his own. That's standard. But, and this is the only way he resembled Elmo, he'd never steal another's work. I think it's time I sneakily find out about his alibi. So I say, "Where were you yesterday after five o'clock?"

"Why the hell should I tell you?"

I shrug. "You can tell me or you can tell the police."

"Which you say you're working for."

"Unofficially. Call Sergeant Warren if you want to check it out. He's at the MRSU police department."

His voice oozes scorn. "MRSU. Your math department is the weakest I've ever seen." Don't you love this guy? "But I guess there's no harm in telling you. I was at home. My wife and I were having a barbecue with one of our daughters and her kids."

I hate to think what kind of a father he was. But his next words surprise me, and his voice takes on a dreamy quality.

"A lovely girl. Married a nice fellow and presented me with two wonderful grandchildren. They came about five and we all spent the rest of the evening on our patio until we were driven inside by mosquitoes." The moment passes. "Does that answer your question, Mr. Detective? So go tell your hot-shot police buddies I've got a perfect alibi."

I make a mental note to have Tom see if he really was in sight of his family all that time. But I have a sick feeling it's true. "I will, Dr. Delsanter. I will." I can't resist a parting shot. "What will you work on now, since the Collins Conjecture is solved?"

"There's plenty, Albright. And deeper stuff than anything you'll ever do. Good day."

I nod goodbye and leave, not exactly slamming his door but not closing it gently either. I'm still ticked about his remarks concerning my paper and Elmo. I don't feel like much of a detective. They always know what to ask in books or TV, even people like me who aren't supposed to be experts. Take Jessica Fletcher, for instance. I feel like I found out nothing about Delsanter. And I'm a little discouraged that the lout seems to be completely innocent. I guess I was wishing for an incriminating statement elicited by brilliant questioning on the part of Detective Albright. Well, it's a good thing I make my money from mathematics, 'cause I'd be a dud as a detective.

CHAPTER 16

Tuesday Noon

Oh, how glorious it is to have left Delsanter's office! What an asshole! There aren't many like him in mathematics, but the few there are make us all look bad. I'm feeling a little guilty about how I treated him. Just a little. In fact, just maybe the tiniest of bits. But I didn't *have* to needle him. It just felt soooo good at the time! I'm surprised my watch says it's only quarter to eleven. I probably was with him less than 10 minutes, but it seemed like an eternity. I'll be on my own campus well before it's time to meet Tom for lunch.

It's 11:20 when I do get back. After I remove my mail from my box in the math department, I pass George Frazier in the hall. We exchange greetings. George starts to move on, but I arrest him—oops, that's probably not the right word—"George, would you mind if I sit in on your calculus class today?"

"Of course not, but why?"

Now comes the tricky part. "I have an old acquaintance from college and I told him about what a great teacher you are. I'd like to bring him."

"Well, sure. Be glad to have you."

I know Tom won't approve, but I've got to say more. I just can't find a good way, so with usual lack of aplomb I plunge forward, "He's a detective with the campus police, working on Ken's murder." That rattles him, and I hate to see it.

"Why would he want to come to my class?"

I shrug, at a loss for words. This is when George's kindness appears.

"It's okay, Jim. I know this isn't your doing." I'd feel a lot better if I didn't realize that it was, at least partially. "See you at 1:00." He leaves me standing there, his look detached and his gait slow.

I wander to one of the school cafeterias, near to Tom's office but on the other side of the campus from Conroy Hall. I reach the entrance and find no Tom. Did I beat him for once? The associated smugness is magnified by the inconceivable fact Tom's late, it now being 12:06.

Ah, here he comes, striding across the bright green lawn separating the police building from the cafeteria. I remember him as a gregarious friend, so it's been somewhat of a shock to see the working no-nonsense police officer he has become.

Wasting no time, he asks, "How did it go with Delsanter?"

"Let's get our food and sit down," I say. He looks at me impatiently, but I guess he decides it's not an unreasonable request. We go through one of the two parallel food lines. I create a masterpiece from the salad bar at 20 cents per ounce, get a bowl of soup, and dispense a diet Coke. Tom orders what cafeteria personnel claim is lasagna, along with mashed potatoes, green beans, and coffee. We're surrounded by students and I despair of finding a table. It's my lucky day, though, if any day with Delsanter in it can be lucky. Four students crowded around a table for two are leaving. I dash for it, deftly and courageously shunting aside what must be, judging from his size, one of our linebackers. His lack of ability to stop my run certainly would have embarrassed the guy's coach. The table also has the advantage of being in an out-of-the-way corner so conversation will be fairly private. Not that anything could be overheard, anyway, with the noise created by a couple of hundred boisterous students.

I plunk my cafeteria tray on the table and wave to Tom who has fallen behind. My linebacker looks a bit less threatening when he sees Tom's size. Tom has not forgotten his mission. As soon as we've transferred plates from trays to table and taken our seats, he repeats, "So how did it go?"

"He's a real horse's ass, Tom. Accused Ken of stealing his results and even hinted Elmo was incompetent and unethical."

I don't think Tom cares as much as I about Elmo's reputation. He ignores my comment and asks, "How's he taking the fact that Salter solved his pet problem?"

"Not well." I outline the secretary's interpretation of his mood and then repeat as closely as possible the conversation the two of us had, attempting to imitate the tone as well as the words. Tom seems amused at my theatrical shenanigans and childish digs.

Tom's interest seems to focus on two points: Delsanter's denial that this is a major blow to his work and his alibi.

He says, "I suppose his family would stick up for him, but it sounds like he's in the clear. We'll definitely have a chat with him though."

Now it's my turn. "Did you get to talk with Dick Brighthurst and Dean Farnsworth?"

"I saw Brighthurst, and I have an appointment with Farnsworth for late in the afternoon. After you left this morning, I went to the math office early and hung around 'til 0945, hoping Brighthurst would show. Ms. Barber didn't know when he would arrive, but told me most days it wasn't until ten." I nod agreement. "I was about to call him at home when he phoned Barber to tell her he'd been in a meeting with your dean and would be over momentarily. So I waited for him."

"Find out anything?"

"He wasn't happy to see me. Tried to postpone our talk. Said he'd been appointed Acting Chairman yesterday and there was too much work that had to be done."

"He does tend to be pompous at times. But underneath it all he's a good guy."

"Maybe so. I never completely shook his attitude, but I did shake him."

I look interested, and concerned. After all, this man is now my boss. "What happened?"

"Why don't you read the transcript? As soon as I was finished with him I took the recording of our conversation . . ."

"Dick agreed to your recording him?"

"Oh, yes. No problem there. As I started to say, I took it to headquarters and got it entered into the computer and then printed. Just barely in time to get back here. It's why I was a little late."

He hands me several sheets of paper. I skim over the identification of who's present and Dick's agreement to the recording, as well as Dick's reiterated concern that he's extremely busy and hoped this wouldn't take long. I bet Tom really worried about that! Then I get to the interesting part.

Warren: Congratulations on your selection as Acting Chairman.

Brighthurst: Thank you. It's an enormous responsibility, especially coming at a trying time like this.

Warren: But you've done it before, haven't you?

Brighthurst: Er, yes I have. How did you know?

Warren: When was that?

Brighthurst: Oh, four or five years ago.

Warren: What was the reason?
Brighthurst: Uh, our previous chairman took a deanship at another university and we were conducting a nationwide search for a replacement. I was privileged to lead the department in the interim, until Dr. Salter was selected for the permanent position.
Warren: Did many apply?
Brighthurst: Oh my, yes. Over 80 I believe.
Warren: Any others from MRSU?
Brighthurst: Er, no. (pause) I can't recall any.
Warren: None at all?
Brighthurst: I believe I answered that question. Can we please move on? You don't have any idea how much I have to do.
Warren: Dr. Brighthurst, you haven't been honest with me.
Brighthurst: What! How dare you? I . . .
Warren: Sir, we know you also were a candidate for the position that eventually went to Salter.

I glance up. "Why would he lie about something that's so easy to check?"

Tom shrugs. "Who knows? But it's fairly common. In Brighthurst's case there's embarrassment at least. And, of course, maybe something more sinister. Read on."

Brighthurst: (pause) Oh, that. Yes. I thought you were referring to others.
Warren: We also have it on good authority that you were confident you were going to receive the appointment.
Brighthurst: With so many candidates, one can never count on anything like that. While I was hopeful, of course, I wasn't surprised when Dr. Salter was picked. He was a wonderful choice.
Warren: That's not what the faculty tell me. And we also know you were bitterly disappointed to lose out on the job. In fact, I understand your financial situation became precarious as a result.
Brighthurst: Where . . . where did you hear that?
Warren: It doesn't matter. Is it true?

"Was he rubbing his right ear at this point?" I indicate to Tom where I am in the manuscript.

Tom looks amused. "He was indeed. What made you ask?"

"He always does when he's worried, or deep in thought. We kid him about it all the time." I return to my reading.

Brighthurst: (pause) Yes . . . it is. I was foolish, and it's painful to admit. I did think I'd get the job. Theresa Bedlow virtually assured me it was mine. Poor Theresa. I think she was more upset than I was when it didn't come through. I gather the president overrode her recommendation.

Warren: How did this affect you financially?

Brighthurst: My wife and I always have wanted some land in the mountains where we could build a small vacation home. We found a beautiful spot. Out of our price range, but it was just what we were looking for. We remortgaged our home so we could buy it, creating monthly payments that the mortgage company considered right at the limit of what I could afford. And they were right. But what they didn't know is the situation was even worse.

Warren: How so?

Brighthurst: (pause) I don't know why I let myself get into this mess, but Angie, my wife, wanted the land so badly. So I, er, I didn't tell the mortgage company about another loan I was paying on, for my daughter's education.

Warren: Didn't the mortgage company run a credit report on you?

Brighthurst: Of course, but the loan was from my brother, off the official books. He covered all her education costs, and I was paying him back. Between the two loans I was forced to dip into our savings every month. I wasn't too worried at first, 'cause I thought we'd be okay once I got the chair position.

Warren: Would it really have made that much difference in your income?

Brighthurst: Definitely, for two reasons. My basic salary would have increased. And in addition I'd have been guaranteed summer employment. Faculty have no such assurance and the university's fiscal problems almost always preclude significant summer income. I figure the difference would have been about $35,000 a year.

Warren: So how have you been surviving?

Brighthurst: As I said, using savings. But they're almost gone. Angie and I have some stocks, but their value has plummeted in the last few years.

Warren: But now things should get better for you.

I don't like reading this transcript. There's so much it doesn't tell you. Like how do the people look? I can imagine Dick, a short wiry man, in his gray pinstripe suit, one of several he owns so he never has to worry about what to wear. And then there's his perennial maroon bow tie. And what's the tone of voice being used? And how about body movement? Rereading Tom's last comment, I can hear his purring voice, a cat stalking its prey, and I sense the wariness with which I'm sure Dick responds. For he's no fool.

Brighthurst: Perhaps I'll be better off. At least as long as I'm temporary chair. But I know what you're thinking. And I didn't kill Ken to solve my own problems.

Warren: How did you feel when he originally got the job?

Brighthurst: Obviously I was disappointed. But these things happen.

Warren: Were you ever angry at the way things worked out?

Brighthurst: Of course not.

Warren: Really, Dr. Brighthurst. How can you expect me to believe that? There you were, in terrible financial shape with your only hope of getting out of the mess suddenly dashed. Then, on top of it all, I hear Salter treated you like dirt in your role as Assistant Chairman. And you tell me you weren't mad?

I notice Tom has almost finished his lunch and I've barely touched mine. I don't like the way he's eyeing my salad. I pull it slightly closer. "Aren't you being kind of rough on him?"

Tom replies, "That's nothing like what I'll be if he keeps trying to hide things from me. And he's such a sanctimonious ass!"

"Like I said, he does come across that way sometimes. But he's okay, Tom. And he did a great job when he was acting chairman. I hope he gets the permanent position this time." I return to my reading.

Brighthurst: Much as you might not want to believe it, Sergeant, I don't lose my cool every time something goes wrong.

Warren: We're not talking in general. I'm interested in this particular situation between you and Salter. It isn't hard to believe you'd be furious at him, blaming him for your loss of financial security and hating him for the way you were being treated. Wouldn't it have occurred to you that if only Salter was dead you'd have a good chance to get this job? And if you did, your problems would disappear. Sounds like a good motive for murder, Dr. Brighthurst, doesn't it?

Brighthurst: That's enough! What right have you to talk to me like this. Everyone doesn't think about committing murder to solve problems, you know. What a distorted mind you must have! Please just get out!

Warren: Ah. So you can get mad. And here it was over just a few words. I have to wonder how you'd react to years of stress.

Brighthurst: Are you done, Sergeant?

Warren: Not quite. Please tell me where you were Sunday after five o'clock.

Brighthurst: Home. So if that's the time Ken was killed, I have a perfect alibi.

Warren: Was anyone with you?

Brighthurst: Off and on. I was watching a golf tournament on TV. My wife was outside weeding our garden. Then at seven o'clock I turned on "60 Minutes" followed by a mystery. Want me to tell you the story?

Warren: That would be easy enough to have found out. Was your wife with you?

Brighthurst: From seven on, as was my oldest son, Michael. He had a friend over and the four of us played backgammon during "60 Minutes."

Warren: How about before seven?

Brighthurst: I was alone in the living room.

Warren: So you could have slipped out, come to the university, and killed Dr. Salter.

Brighthurst: That's preposterous! I live 20 minutes from here. The chances of being away from home, unnoticed, on a Sunday afternoon for almost an hour are negligible. My wife could pop in at any moment, and in fact she did once or twice.

Warren: When?

Brighthurst: I have no idea. If I'd known it was going to be important I'd have kept a record.

Warren: Did you receive any phone calls?

Brighthurst: As a matter of fact, I did. Around 5:30 one of our professors called to say he had the flu and wouldn't be in yesterday.

Warren: Why did he ring you?

Brighthurst: To arrange for someone to take over his classes. That's one of my jobs. Or it was.

Warren: Can you do that? Isn't it hard to find someone with the necessary experience?

Brighthurst: It depends on the class. If it's in the professor's area of specialization, as one of his two is, I normally just cancel it, which is what I did. However, his other one is the third semester of calculus and any of our faculty could teach that with a little preparation. We try to help each other out in situations like this. I phoned Maureen Baker, one of our professors. She wasn't in, so I explained the problem to her husband. About 6:15 she returned my call and indicated she'd be glad to take the class.

Warren: Any other contacts after five?

Brighthurst: None. Still think I'm guilty?

Warren: Please, just give me Dr. Baker's number, as well as those of the sick professor and your son's friend.

Brighthurst: Do you have to involve them?

Warren: Yes.

That's all there is, except for a closing statement by Tom and a place for Dick's signature. "He hasn't signed it."

"No. I'll get him to later today or tomorrow."

"His alibi seems pretty good to me."

Tom nods. "I'm afraid so. With the timing of his various contacts, I don't see how he could possibly have killed Salter."

I glance at my watch. "It's almost one. We're going to have to move if we're to catch George's class."

CHAPTER 17

Tuesday Afternoon

We rush across campus to the appropriate room on the first floor of Conroy Hall, arriving on the dot of one. Two back row empty chairs beckon. The room is close to square. Whiteboard replacements have not yet relegated the blackboards lining the front and two sides to historical obscurity. It can handle a class of about 40.

George is just beginning to speak. I've known him for over five years and his appearance barely registers. But I wonder what staid Tom is thinking. Today George is clothed in typical math teacher garb—short-sleeved orange shirt, tan slacks, and brown sandals. His long and unruly brown hair coupled with his lush moustache and beard touched with gray could satisfy anyone's vision of how a mathematician should appear. The course is Calculus III, not surprisingly the third in a sequence. Tom wasn't enthusiastic when I told him that. You see, he'd selected engineering as a major, his parents' choice. Luckily, Theresa talked him into law enforcement. Lucky because he barely made it through Finite Math and he would have had a terrible time completing the math requirements. I know his dad was mad for a while. I hope now he's proud of his son's career.

I've heard George give formal presentations, but never have attended one of his classes. This should be fun. Glancing at Tom's face, I see I may be the only one to enjoy it.

"Good afternoon. Anyone have any questions?" begins George.

"Yes, Dr. Frazier. Could you do problem 17 of the homework?" This from a young woman wearing a tight yellow blouse and blue shorts, very short blue shorts, in the third row. Just a casual observation.

George whips out his book, takes a look at the offending problem, and responds, "Tell me what you've tried." This turns out to be the first step in a cleverly contrived sequence of questions and suggestions that enables the student to wind up solving the problem herself. "That's wonderful," says George as she gets the final answer. "Well done!" I'm a fair teacher. It's clear, though, I've a lot to learn. That student was thoroughly lost when she asked her question, but now she understands the necessary math and has a good feeling about what she accomplished. George truly is unusual. I glance at Tom. He seems impressed too. "Any more?" George asks.

"Yes, sir," a boy two rows in front of us says.

"Yes, Mr. Simmons, what is it?"

Tom jerks his head to look at the student. He seems strangely interested. "Do you know him?" he hisses.

"Yes," I whisper back. "I had him in Calc II last semester. Why?"

"I'll tell you later. Now shush. I want to hear this."

I look at David's back, that's his first name, wondering what's behind Tom's interest. The youngster is hesitant, obviously uncomfortable with speaking out.

He begins weakly, "I know this is a silly question, but I just don't see why the example on page 826 works."

A boy in front of us nudges his neighbor and whispers loud enough for Tom and me to overhear, "What an asshole! It's obvious."

I want to club the guy. Hell, David never opened his mouth in my class. George must be doing something right. His answer shows me he is. "Thank you for asking that, David. It's certainly far from a silly question and I think I know what's bothering you. There's a subtle point hidden in that problem and I bet most of us have missed it."

George continues with a thorough and clear explanation of the example, emphasizing the obscure step he felt, quite correctly I'm sure, the majority of the students had glossed over. I bet the creep in front of me had.

The class continues and I'm intrigued by the informality that prevails. Kids interrupt George frequently, often cracking jokes. There's a lot of laughing. Tom looks disgusted. I sense he thinks time is being wasted. I make a mental note to tell him just how much material is being covered. Frankly, I'm amazed by it. Turns out I won't have to do that.

The girl sitting immediately to Tom's left grins at him and whispers, "I've never taken so many notes in a class in my life."

Ah, now I see Tom's looking a little more thoughtful. Perhaps he's getting a hint of what's really going on here.

Uh, oh. The kids are becoming restless, and still 15 minutes left. That happens in my classes all the time. Somehow, I feel vindicated that George has the same problem. At such times I usually just forge ahead.

I'm wondering how he'll deal with it when suddenly he screams, "Look at that!"

What he's indicating is a flake of chalk that has released its hold on the blackboard and is creeping slowly towards the tray lining the board's bottom. "Isn't that great?" The students look at each other and start to smile. "We're not so lucky today. Sometimes two of the specks occur at the same time and we can place bets on which one reaches the tray first." He grins at the class and continues, "You know, I often fantasize about being interviewed on my 100th birthday—no, believe it or not I'm not there yet—and being asked what was the most meaningful part of my teaching career. Oh, I know what I'm supposed to reply. You do, too, I bet. Probably seen such interviews on TV."

What a ham, I think admiringly. He shifts into an old man's voice.

"Well, sonny. If I have helped just one person develop a love of mathematics, my whole life will have had purpose." He pauses, smiles broadly, and shouts, "ONE PERSON INDEED! Spent my whole life teaching and then be satisfied with having an effect on only one person. No sirree. I'm going to talk about the pieces of chalk drifting down the board as my most exciting moments."

Most of the class is laughing outright, joined unashamedly by me. Even Tom is grinning. Now George continues with the class. What's he wasted here? Only two minutes, and it broke the fidgeting I'd seen earlier; the students are back to full concentration. I really am observing a master teacher in operation. It's hard not to be envious. But I'm trying. I truly am.

As the class closes, George reminds his students of an exam for this coming Thursday, a statement greeted with good-natured groans. He hands out several review sheets. I take and scan a copy. God, where does he find the time? This is a beautifully written summary of what I assume is the material since the last exam, clear and concise. I'm impressed and wonder if his students know how lucky they are. The class files out, but Tom motions me to stay behind. I'm being suckered, aren't I?

Three students have remained to ask questions. George goes to the blackboard to explain a point. A couple of them want to accompany

George back to his office for additional help, but my colleague sees Tom approaching and apologizes to the students for not being available today.

"Sergeant Warren, isn't it? Jim said you were going to attend my class. Was it worth the effort?"

"You're an intriguing instructor, Dr. Frazier. It's hard for me to evaluate the subject matter, but you seem to have wonderful rapport with the kids."

"Damn right, George," I interpose. "You sure do live up to your reputation."

"Thanks, both of you. But that's not why you're here, is it?"

CHAPTER 18

Tuesday Afternoon

Tom says, "You're right, Dr. Frazier. Is there some place private we can talk?"

"Sure. Come back to my office."

I'm getting queasy again. "George, if you have any hesitation about my being here, please say so."

I'm hoping he'll ask me to leave. Alas, he says, "No, Jim. I want you to stay."

We take the elevator from the first floor to the tenth. After we settle in his office, George says, "I suppose this has to do with Ken's murder."

Tom replies, "Yes it does. What was your opinion of Dr. Salter?"

"A first class bastard," George responds in such a calm and controlled voice it's hard to believe the hatred it projects. "It couldn't have happened to a better guy." Watch yourself, George. This is serious business, as I'm learning myself.

"Why all the anger, Dr. Frazier?"

"Oh, there are so many things. Where can I start?" I mentally implore George to be careful. His mouth gets him into too much trouble.

"You could start with your tenure application."

"So you've heard about that?"

He looks at me. I squirm, but his eyes show understanding rather than anger. I know I've said it before, but he really is a super guy.

"That's certainly part of it," he continues. "But it's more complicated than that. Have you ever wanted something so much and worked for it all your life?" Tom remains impassive. I wonder what George is getting at. "Ever since I was a kid, even as far back as elementary school, I wanted to be a teacher. I was bright, able to pick things up quickly. Others weren't so lucky, and I enjoyed helping them. It was an incredible high when I saw they understood. And, while I didn't analyze it closely, I sensed that not only was I able to get the academic points across, but also I could do it in a way that encouraged the other kids and made them feel good about themselves."

George pauses, probably recalling those early days. "What's amazing," he continues, "is this desire to teach was more than just a passing fancy. It burned in me. As I passed through high school and college, I continued to tutor successfully."

"Yet you majored in math, rather than education?"

"Yes, Sergeant. Doesn't seem to make sense, does it? But I loved math too, and somewhere in my immature 20-year-old mind I thought I could do both. I spoke to several people on the faculty where I did my undergraduate work, the ones I thought were good teachers."

I'm becoming interested. "What did they say," I ask.

George grins at me. "'Teach math at a university!' So I said, 'Sounds good to me. Where do I start?' Then they threw me the curve. 'You'll need a Ph.D.' Hell, Jim. I didn't even know what a doctorate was at the time." I nod in understanding. "And I sure had no idea how hard it would be to get."

"But you did," I say.

"Yes," he responds softly. "And for the first time, as a teaching assistant, I stood in front of a real class."

He pauses. "And?" Tom prods.

"And it would be impossible to tell you the thrill it was. Finally I was in the right place! Even then, without any experience, I knew I was doing a good job. I'd never been happier in my life. I eventually got my doctorate, the passport to a university career. My parents were so proud. So was I. All I had to do was find a job."

"Did you have any trouble?"

"Hell, yes! The job market's been terrible for years. There were some Post Docs around, but . . ."

"Post Docs?"

"Visiting appointments for some fixed period, usually between one and three years, for new doctoral graduates. But all of them were solely research positions. No teaching at all. Now I like research, but my real love has always been the classroom. So I kept looking. But I couldn't even find a post at a community college. Finally I was offered a visiting instructor spot at a New Hampshire liberal arts school. I snatched it and loved the work. But I could barely live on the pay so I continued hunting. Then I heard about MRSU through an ad in the *Notices*."

Seeing Tom's questioning glance, I explain, "A journal for mathematicians—contains articles of general interest, announcements of meetings, advertisements, and miscellaneous other stuff."

Tom indicates George should continue. "I was attracted because it was one of the few places that claimed an emphasis on teaching over research."

How sad. George was pulled in by a lie. That view certainly was our previous chair's preference, but he stood more or less alone. The university had long before decided to emphasize research. Oh, the administrators state for the record that teaching is still important. But certainly as far as tenure and promotion are concerned, it's a distant second. Or even third behind research and university service, you know, committees and such.

"Anyway, I applied. And fortunately got the job."

I'm thinking back to how close a decision that was. I hope George never finds out. Our faculty was divided into two camps, with one not wanting to employ any but the most outstanding researcher. The rest of us prevailed, with the chair's help in George's case, but it was the last time. Under Ken's leadership our hires have all been brilliant mathematicians. A few are acceptable teachers, but some are awful.

George continues, "At last I had achieved my goal. I couldn't imagine anything better. I was prepared for a lifetime career here."

"What happened when Dr. Salter became chairman?"

"The entire atmosphere changed. He instigated rules for evaluating performance that concentrated heavily on publication of papers, writing research monographs, and obtaining grant money. Excellence in teaching was stated to be a minimum expected requirement for the job. What he meant was it didn't matter what kind of teacher you were as long as the research was strong."

"What was your reaction?"

"I think Jim will tell you I fought it with vigor." I nod. "I was outspoken at faculty meetings. I'm not against research. I just don't think it should be the only criterion for success. And early on, when I thought Ken was someone I could reason with, I went to see him."

"What was his response?"

"He told me he was tired of my opposition and if I couldn't accept his decisions I should get out. And then he said he didn't want to see me in his office again—about *anything!* Can you believe the guy?"

"Were you angry?"

"What do you think? You're damn right I was. Who wouldn't be? But sometimes I'm my own worst enemy."

You've got that right, my friend. George is a principled man who finds it as hard to compromise his ideals as it would have been for Ken to agree with someone else's views.

"I stupidly continued to fight his changes in faculty meetings and through informal discussions."

"Any success?"

"None. And, with each addition to the faculty, those supporting my vision for this place became less powerful. I paid for it too."

"How's that?"

"Ken gave me the smallest raises he could get away with, the minimum mandated by the legislature. He refused to discuss the possibility of any merit funds. Money isn't all that important to me. God, you'd never go into education to get rich. But being recognized for what I do means a lot. And there's been none of that since Ken became chairman."

I can't let that go unchallenged. "Aw, George. You got the 'University Outstanding Teacher' award last year. And people always turn to you for help on teaching techniques. I sure understand why, after seeing you in action."

"You're right, of course, Jim. I didn't mean to imply that *nobody* appreciated my contributions. Only the official channel, my boss. Unfortunately that's the one dealing with tangible measures."

"You mean money?"

"Partially, I suppose. But what if I don't get tenure? Jim would tell you finding another university position would be close to impossible. Everything I've worked so many years for would be gone. No other job would give me anywhere near the same satisfaction. And all because of a fucking bastard like Salter!"

I'm stirring uneasily. The venom in George's last words settles thickly over us, and his passion for his job is almost embarrassing to behold. It sounds like a good motive for murder to me. I bet it does to Tom, too.

As if he can read my mind, Tom asks, "How has your situation changed as a result of Dr. Salter's death?"

I can tell George has been waiting for this. Probably since earlier today when I told him we were coming to his class. So why has he said all he has? He's smart enough to realize it could only hurt him. Remember, though, about his suffering from foot-in-mouth disease, that stand-by-your-principle business even at great personal cost. Admirable, I suppose. But not very many of us are that altruistic.

George smiles sadly at me, shrugs, and looks Tom squarely in the eye. When he speaks, it's with a tired and resigned voice. "Greatly improved, Sergeant. My dream now lives. Dick Brighthurst will support my tenure application. I think there are enough faculty in the department who will give me a positive vote." I nod my head with vigor. "And I don't anticipate trouble further up the line."

"So Salter's death has saved you from what must have seemed like intellectual suicide?"

"Interesting way of putting it, but yes, it has. I even briefly thought of suicide in the literal sense, although it was for only a fleeting moment." He pauses, and then continues forcefully, "I didn't kill Kenneth Salter, Sergeant. Much as I might think he deserved to die, and much as my situation has improved, I just couldn't take another life."

God, I want to believe him. Everything I know about him verifies what he said. One day, for example, I was walking with him across campus when he spied a roach on the sidewalk, right where he was about to step. Now who would like to give a discourse on the worthiness of roaches? I don't know if George would, but he did deliberately extend his stride so the roach was saved. I remember looking at him quizzically. He smiled self-consciously and muttered, "I'd squash him without hesitation in my home. But how could I out here when he was only doing his thing on his own turf?" That's the kind of guy he is. I've never seen him purposely hurt anyone. Even his arguments with Ken were civil—on his side at least. How could he kill a fellow human? I don't think he could. But I realize there's a world of difference between a roach and someone who's ruining your life. Damn, this detective business has its down sides.

Tom is unmoved by George's protestation of innocence. "You realize, I'm sure, we have to check all possibilities. Would you please tell me where you were after five o'clock on Sunday."

George looks relieved. He's got an alibi, I think. Thank God. "Right here, in this office." Tom looks interested. Probably thinking he's finally found someone with the necessary opportunity, just one floor up from the victim. His hopes crash with George's next words. "Two graduate students and I are developing a software system I dreamed up to animate mathematical principles in some advanced undergraduate courses."

I interpose, "George is a computer genius. Knows more about those machines than almost anyone I know."

"Hardly, Jim. Anyway, we worked together from about half past four until nine."

Tom looks disappointed. "And then?"

"We went to O'Reillys and I bought the kids a beer." That's an excellent local Irish pub. I speak from experience. "Stayed about an hour. Then I headed home."

I sense Tom suppressing a sigh. He keeps hoping for someone without an alibi, and George's sounds pretty good to me. "Please let me have the names and phone numbers of your two students."

Tom thanks George and we prepare to leave. I flash my colleague a thumbs up and he grins. When we're alone, Tom says, "It's almost time for my appointment with Farnsworth. I'll see you tonight at Theresa's."

Thank goodness, no assignments for me the rest of the day. Except, of course, for the scholarly pursuit of research, class preparation, and reflection on murder.

CHAPTER 19

Tuesday Evening

Donna and I arrive at Theresa's at the appointed hour of 7:00, a remarkable feat, as you shall see. I worked to rather late in the afternoon and didn't arrive home until 5:55. My playful wife offered an invitation to attend an interval of marital machinations. Being the caring and unselfish individual I am, I agree. It is unnecessary, indeed crass, to give details. Suffice it to say it was an enormously delightful time that occupied only a very few minutes even though the hands of the clock on the dresser somehow sped forward a full 40 minutes. Einstein probably could explain it, but not I.

I see Tom's car so we'll be the last arrivals—again! We ring and it's Tom who admits us. He motions us to the sofa. Theresa's sitting in a matching chair and Tom sinks into a love seat. The three pieces of furniture form a rough "U" around an oak coffee table, with Theresa and Tom on opposite sides of the "U." A plate of sandwiches and coastered glasses of water sit on the table. Tom's somber countenance implies there'll be no idle chitchat this evening. I know he's ambivalent about these meetings, and especially with dealing with the three of us.

He starts the instant our rears contact the sofa. "One of the drawers of Dr. Salter's desk contained a small book with lined pages."

"A journal?" asks my love.

"I guess so although I've been calling it a diary. One of our Crime Scene Investigators found it and contacted me before I spoke with Susan Barber. Jim saw me with a copy of it."

Uh, oh. Donna has that reproachful look she's mastered. "I forgot, darling. I wasn't keeping it from you."

"Can it, you two." Yes, his patience is thin. "I've been so busy I didn't get a chance to read it until last night."

Good Lord, I think, he works day and night. How can he look so fresh? I'm feeling beat myself and my schedule has been relatively normal.

But then, in justification of my exhausted state, I realize I've been engaged recently in strenuous activity that would sap any male's strength.

Tom continues, "Most of it was mathematical garbage." I wince. "But some of it is pretty interesting. I've picked out portions I'd like you to read." He's prepared copies, clipped into sections, which he gives to each of us. "The first set of pages is the initial entry in Salter's book, dated a little more than two months ago. Read it. Then we'll talk."

I start. What I see is reproduced faithfully here. Obviously Tom has had it typed so we don't have to look at Ken's prissy scrawl.

> I am positive I have found an approach that will answer once and for all the Collins Conjecture. I still am not sure whether I will prove it true or find a counterexample. But either result will be a remarkable achievement. The unique beauty of my approach is its ability to decide the answer, no matter which of the two possibilities. It represents a brilliant shift in the way one thinks about the problem. I have done marvelous work in the past, but this surpasses everything I've already achieved and will finally place me where I belong, in the ranks of the top mathematicians of the world. I expect to be awarded the Fields medal.
>
> I suspect many will want to know more about my life story once news of my breakthrough appears, much like the attention Andrew Wiles drew after proving Fermat's theorem. Perhaps an article in *The New York Times,* maybe even my picture on the cover of *Newsweek.* Undoubtedly there will be interest in how the work on the problem progresses as I move toward its solution. I have decided to create this journal to remind me of information the media may request. As background, today I enter some of the important milestones of my life.
>
> It was obvious at an early age that I was special. I read third grade books when I was two, and started solving elementary mathematics problems at three. My mediocre parents didn't know what to do. They had me tested. I, of course, was in the super genius category. They consulted education specialists. I hate to think what kind of jerks they were. They got me mathematics tutors, but I quickly surpassed their capabilities. I was ready for high school when I was 10, but my conventional,

unimaginative parents wouldn't let me go until I reached 12. Then they wanted me to attend the local public school. I could not contemplate wasting time there. I insisted on studying at a private academy that had a good mathematics reputation. Even when told about that, my miserable parents tried to talk me out of it. They were such hopeless failures themselves that they couldn't even afford it. Why, my father had to find a second job to pay for it, and my mother started to baby sit! She didn't have any useful skills so her financial contributions were negligible.

At the school I quickly became the academic leader. Straight A's, of course, and I was reading mathematics at a level beyond anything my teachers had ever seen. We entered a team every year in the state high school mathematics competition, and it was natural I was selected as captain. My final two years we were the winners, although my personal satisfaction was diminished the last year due to a clerical mistake on some incompetent's part. I undoubtedly had the best individual score in the state, but the official tallies listed me second. They claimed some girl in a small town 250 miles distant had beaten me. As if any girl could outdo Kenneth Salter! I'd like to know who made that error.

I entered MIT when I was 15, graduating at 18, the age most of those cretins were just beginning college. Again I led our team, this time to the Putnam competition, placing second one year and winning my last year. I stayed on and received a Ph.D. in just 23 additional months. No one could believe the problem I solved for my dissertation. My inept advisor had been working on it for years. He gave me a special case, thinking if I successfully dealt with that it'd make an adequate thesis. The fool! Within a couple of months I'd solved the general situation. Really made him mad. God, that was a good feeling!

Then there were my two years at the Institute for Advanced Study. How many people get asked to spend time there? Only the very best.

This should be sufficient. My career since Princeton is portrayed adequately by my well-documented accomplishments. A quick look at my vita will confirm an illustrious career. And I'm still a young man with many productive years ahead.

Not so many years, I think. I raise my eyes and see Theresa waiting for us to finish while Donna contemplates the last page. Ken was a nasty bit of goods, wasn't he?

When my wife turns toward Theresa, our mentor's acerbic tongue lashes. "I think that describes Kenneth Salter rather well."

Even Donna seems unable to find a compensating factor. I suspect she didn't react well to the comment about a "girl" besting Ken.

She says quietly, "His poor parents. How they must have sacrificed for him. And look at the contempt they received in return. Are they still living?"

Tom has this information. "Yes. In their late 60s. I contacted them Monday. They've retired to Florida, said they hadn't been in touch with Salter for over 10 years. His choice, not theirs. They tried, but he told them to stay away from him, that he'd call them if he ever felt the need."

"What a bastard!" I exclaim.

"It was sad talking to them. They appear to be decent people who tried their best to give him what he needed. Apparently they have two daughters who live nearby and present no problems. They seem bewildered by their son, unable to understand what they did wrong. And now they feel guilty, almost as if they're blaming themselves for his death."

"A natural reaction," my lovely psychologist says. "I hope they'll get help. Ken has hurt them long enough."

Theresa points out, "You read this and realize how many people recognized Ken's genius and worked hard to give him every opportunity. And how does he repay it, by heaping scorn on them. It's sickening."

Her comments express my views. "It's so typical of him to think someone made an error on his test scores. He never could deal with his own inadequacies." I reflect a moment. "Of course, he didn't have much opportunity; he rarely was wrong."

"Except in relationships," remarks Donna.

"Yes," I respond sadly. "Except for relationships."

Tom asks, "What is the Putnam exam? And the Fields medal?"

This is my bailiwick. "The Putnam is a difficult mathematics examination given every year to interested undergraduates, usually math majors. Scores are individual, and they are used additionally to evaluate teams entered from a school."

"Is winning it a big deal?"

"Oh, yes, Tom. Usually the winners come from the name schools—like MIT, Harvard, Princeton, or Cal Tech, and placing high is a big plus when applying to grad school. I try to do the problems every year. They're always published after the exam. I have trouble with most of them, even when I take all the time I need. These whiz kids answer all of the questions in a restricted time frame."

"Did you ever attempt it for real?"

"I was afraid you'd ask. Yes, once. But I got only one right answer. Even at that I was in the upper 20%."

"Is it any surprise Salter did so well?"

"Not at all! As I've told you, there are very few mathematicians in his league."

"And the Fields medal?"

"Ah, that's something else. It's sort of the Nobel prize for mathematicians. Everyone calls it the Fields medal because it was established through the effort of a mathematician named John Charles Fields. Its official name though is the International Medal for Outstanding Discoveries in Mathematics, a more descriptive designation. It's awarded every four years for mathematicians no older than 40, and only the best receive it."

"Would it have been awarded to Salter for solving this Collins problem?"

"Who knows? He'd be pushing the age limit. And would the selection committee have considered the entire body of his work, not only the proof of the Collins Conjecture, a sufficient contribution? I think there definitely would have been a chance. But it seems to me what's really significant is *Ken* had no doubts he'd receive it. That's the sort of man he was. Probably couldn't conceive of any other outcome."

We're silent for a while. Then Tom asks, "Did anyone like this guy?"

No one has a name to offer.

CHAPTER 20

Tuesday Evening

We think about that a moment. Then Tom continues, "Well, apparently their feelings were reciprocated. I couldn't find a single civil reference to anyone in his diary."

"So others were mentioned?" asks Theresa.

"Oh, yes. Sprinkled throughout, as you'll see. Mostly people who'd had a run-in with him during the past two months, or he felt impeded his work in some way. And each had a motive to kill him. Look at your next sheet to get an idea of what I mean."

We all turn to the second set of clipped papers. I suppose Tom wants us to take them one at a time, but I can't help thumbing through them all. They seem to be a series of short paragraphs about different individuals. The first refers to Susan Barber.

> Susan has become a sniveling neurotic bitch, demanding more and more of my precious time. What nerve! She actually thinks I'd divorce Harriet for her, that I'd replace one dullard with another. She's been a useful interlude, but it's time to put an end to it. Now my research demands every bit of my energy. I'll get rid of her today. Hope she'll stay on as administrative assistant, but there are plenty of others who'd be glad for the job if she goes.

Theresa reacts first, her voice laced with cynicism. "A truly caring individual." No one adds to that, but I sense uniform agreement with the implied message.

Tom asks, "Do you know her, Theresa?"

"Not well. Only an occasional greeting when I see her around campus. I think my secretary is a friend."

"What's your secretary's name?"

"Elsie Martin. Why?"

"You remember Ms. Barber played bridge with three other women Sunday evening. It turns out Ms. Martin's name is on the list Ms. Barber gave me, and I'd like to speak with her. Would she be a reliable witness?"

"The best! If Elsie says she was with Susan all evening, she was. She would never lie, even to protect a friend. If you talk to her though, call her *Miss* Martin. She's an older woman and disgusted by the new form. Becomes quite agitated on the subject."

"I'll probably see her tomorrow." Tom grins. "And I'll call her *Miss* Martin."

Donna says, recalling the interview Tom and I had with Susan, "That poor woman! I've been thinking about what you told us yesterday. Inexperienced, she was ripe for Ken's exploitation. And most probably equally unready to handle the rejection."

Theresa agrees. "Such a cruel man. I hope Ms. Barber survives it. From what you've told us it sounds as if she'll be all right in the long run. Well," she sighs, "I suppose we should move on. Who's next?"

"Professor Delsanter, from Reinhardt Tech. Jim spoke to him this morning. Run through your chat again, Jim, exactly the way you did for me earlier."

I don't think it's necessary for Tom to be grinning. Nevertheless, I take this to be a ringing endorsement of my interviewing and theatrical reporting techniques. Maybe detective blood is coursing throughout this body after all. Uh, oh. My ruminations have delayed my response and Tom stares at me impatiently. I see a hint of amusement in Donna's eyes, and have a sick feeling she's divined my thoughts. Quickly I start to speak, describing almost word and tone perfect the conversation I had with Delsanter.

When I'm done, my loving, non-judgmental wife says with disdain, "Mathematicians!" I look pained. "What a perfect pair those two are!"

I object with a pout. "Sure they are. But you know full well most of us aren't anything like them."

She rubs my leg and whispers, "Especially you, lover boy."

Pink rises from neck to brow. You doubt that? Clearly you can't see Theresa looking at us with exasperation etched on every line of her face, obviously feeling this is too serious a business for adolescent chatter. I, on the other hand, believe no business is that important. I squeeze Donna's hand and await Theresa's simple words. "Did Ken mention Delsanter in the diary?"

"Just once, in the second day's entry when he discusses his research for the first time. It's on the next sheet of paper you have."

We start to read. Actually there's only a small paragraph outlining the general approach Ken was taking to solve the conjecture, not nearly enough to understand it. Certainly not by me. Or most mathematicians! I know that sounds like rationalization for my ignorance, but what more can I say? Here's the part that relates to Delsanter.

> Everyone thought Delsanter would be the one to solve the Collins Conjecture. But it's going to be I. I find it hard to contain my glee when I think how pissed Harvey's going to be.

"Once again Ken has shown us his unique ability to interact with others," says Theresa.

I reply, "Delsanter is hardly one to feel sorry for, Theresa." She gives an eloquent shrug of dismissal and again I feel I've goofed in her class. Why do I put myself through this?

Theresa asks Tom, "Have you checked his alibi?"

"Not yet, but I expect it to hold."

"Very likely. It sounds almost impossible that he could have sneaked off unnoticed for a long enough time. By the way, I saw Dick Brighthurst today at a committee meeting. He asked to speak with me when it was over and informed me you had interviewed him."

"Yes, immediately after he returned from seeing Dean Farnsworth. In fact, Brighthurst's interview is the next item on the agenda. Dr. Salter didn't mention him much in the diary, just a few passing comments. They're given on the next page, excerpted from various spots."

I flip to the following sheet that reads in part as follows.

> Chairs meeting this afternoon. No time for such shit. I'll send that ass Brighthurst.
>
> . . .
>
> Brighthurst has been begging for a meeting about Frazier's tenure. Told him I didn't want to discuss it and not to bring it up again.

. . .

> Needed someone today to count the number of student credit hours over the last five years. Susan could do it, but gave it to Brighthurst. Seems sufficiently menial for him.

. . .

> Faculty backed a resolution Brighthurst offered in our meeting today. I'd told him I was against it. They'll all pay, and Brighthurst's life is about to get more miserable. I'm tired of all this crap distracting me from my work.

. . .

There are a couple of other entries, but you get the picture. We've all seen it, of course. The way Ken treated Dick, I mean. I know Tom was put off by Dick's mannerisms, but, as I've said before, he's okay. Tom now is passing around copies of the transcript of Dick's interview, the one I've already seen. I try not to show superiority for being privy to its content. Donna's bemused glance informs me with striking clarity that I'm failing. Oh, well, I never could fool her. Or have I said that? I sit back and, with Tom, watch the two women read.

When both heads lift Tom says, "Once again we have a suspect with a seemingly perfect alibi. I've yet to check it, but I'm sure it too will stand." Tom pauses a moment, collecting his thoughts. Then he moves on to George Frazier, accurately describing our joint chat with him. When he's done, he asks us to look at the next sheet.

> That bastard Frazier keeps pestering me, thinks he can persuade me to support him. What a moron, after all the trouble he's caused me. I told him straight out he'd be gone at the end of next year, sooner if I could think of a way of accomplishing it. I don't need his distractions now.

Theresa remarks, "Frazier's an interesting fellow, don't you think? Stands up for what's right even when he knows how it'll be received. I'm glad he's at MRSU. And especially glad he has such a good alibi, for his motive seems strong."

"Theresa, I know you and Jim felt Frazier's chances for tenure were virtually nonexistent with Salter being opposed to him. Yet everyone, including you, speaks so highly of him. It seems crazy to me that one man could block it. Aren't there safeguards?"

"Oh, Tom, you've been around long enough to learn how bureaucratic politics work. I know there was a former lieutenant who blocked many in your own department from advancing."

"Touché. But how does it happen in the academic side of things?"

"You wouldn't believe the steps supposedly designed to make this process academically pure."

You can taste the sarcasm oozing from this person who distrusts committees as much as I do. How can she stand her present position? She must spend over half her time in meetings.

"First a department committee reviews the file and makes a recommendation. It probably would have supported George. Then the chair, Ken, adds comments, devastating in this case. And that's the rub. You see, the rest of the university community would place great stock in what the chair says."

"So there's no further review?"

"Oh, but there is. The file is then examined in succession by a committee made up of faculty from the College of Arts and Sciences, the dean of the college, a university wide faculty committee, and lastly by myself. Of course, the final decision is made by President Mulholland, but it would be rare for him not to follow my recommendation."

"And you think all these decisions, including yours, would be negative?"

"I think so. And I'm not proud of my role in this. You have to understand that faculty are an elitist bunch, many of them highly competitive. They tend to search for reasons not to grant tenure rather than otherwise. So I think it's a sure thing the two upper-level committees would seize on the chair's evaluation and be opposed. And I don't believe Dean Farnsworth would dare counteract Ken's position for that unclear reason I mentioned yesterday. Of course, even without extra pressure he'd probably fold. He's a weak man and Ken was a steamroller."

"It turns out you're right about Salter having a hold on Farnsworth. We'll get to it soon. First though I'd like to hear the reasoning for your stand. It doesn't sound like you."

"Things are not as easy or straightforward as you might think. I'm not always happy with my actions or free to do what I want, especially when politics are involved. But in my position you can't ignore them. There's a limit to how effective I could remain if I reversed faculty decisions capriciously. I have to pick my battles with care, and I don't think I would consider this to be a sufficiently important matter to risk alienating the faculty."

"Even if it ruins a man's life?"

I can sense Tom's dismay. Our teacher has always been a person of principle. She looks at him sadly. I realize it would be a decision that would weigh on her, and that the admission to us of her views was painful for her.

She responds to Tom's accusation softly, "Even then. You have no idea how constrained I am." She sees my look of disbelief. "Not what you thought, is it, Jim? You believe we in the administration sit around all day creating silly memos of no import other than to get you to take on inconsequential work in addition to your normal loads?"

I shuffle uneasily. It's bad enough that Donna understands me so clearly. But now Theresa has read my mind.

She continues kindly, "I understand, Jim. I used to think the same way myself. There's a lot about this job I hate. Sometimes I feel sick about the lack of action I'm able to take."

None of us has seen her as vulnerable as she now appears. I've watched her face obstacles before, and effectively eliminate problems through unorthodox approaches and force of will. Now she seems so frustrated. We want to help. But I can find no appropriate words, and I suspect the others are in the same boat. Eventually Donna moves to Theresa's side and hugs her. Is that a tear forming in Theresa's eye? No, it couldn't be.

Tom brings us up short. "And then there's the matter of Dean Stephen Farnsworth."

CHAPTER 21

Tuesday Evening

Ah, that's right. Tom saw Farnsworth this afternoon. I never liked the guy, although he's pleasant enough in a face-to-face encounter. As Theresa said earlier, he's been at the university forever.

He's constructed from spheres—a small one for the head and a much larger one for his torso—and ellipsoids for appendages, four of which make up the dean's legs and another elongated four form his arms. An ellipsoid? Oh, that's math talk for being egg-shaped. Very prissy, about his looks and everything else. When Tom saw him, each of his few remaining strands of white hair was plastered into place across his almost bald pate. I guess he thinks it hides that increasingly bare spot. I've wanted to tell him it's not working, but I haven't dared. His spit-polished black shoes were the most striking contrast to his dark gray suit and starched white shirt. I hear you. You're saying I wasn't even there so what am I doing telling how he was dressed? Well, he's always bedecked the same way. No genius is required to guess this afternoon's garb.

His office, by the way, is decorated in a similarly colorful manner. Ecru walls provide the splash of cheerful diversion, beautifully offsetting a black carpet and steel gray furniture. Whenever I'm there, which is as little as possible, I think I've returned to a movie set predating the advent of color.

I wish I could tell you his sparkling personality compensates for the drabness of his environs. Alas, I cannot. It's merely an extension. A nitpicker who's main excitement seems to be issuing memos. I've learned to ignore most of those sent to faculty. Rarely does he follow up on requested information, so there's no point in supplying it. Pretty clever, huh? I think he read a book at some point about micromanagement. He's wonderful about pointing out misplaced commas, but seems incapable of thanking you for all the work involved in the offending document.

He's a company man. I hate that about a person, don't you? In the early days research meant little to him. But what do you suppose happened when a new president changed the university's emphasis? You're right, of course! Farnsworth suddenly developed an intense interest in building our capability in original work. Before my time, but I've heard about the memos he issued exhorting adherence to the new policy! What gets me is, as far as I know, he hasn't done any research himself in years. Certainly I've never heard him utter an original thought. After all, he's been in administration for at least a quarter of a century. I wonder what Tom learned from him.

Tom surprises me. "Of the motives we've seen so far, Farnsworth has one of the strongest." What can he mean by that? "Take a look at your next sheet." My eyes return to the page dealing with George Frazier. I thought it was the last in the second packet, but now I see there's another. I flip and start to read.

> Just back from the Ontario conference. Not much there mathematically. Did show me how far ahead of everyone else I am. And something came up I think I can use. A 65 year-old geezer saw I was from MRSU and inquired if I knew Farnsworth. I admitted I did and asked what his association with the ass was. Used those words, so the guy knew what I think of our illustrious dean. He told me the following story. Should give me plenty of pull in the college. Seems he was a professor when Farnsworth was in grad school. Farnsworth was having trouble getting started on his dissertation. No surprise there. He has the brains of an acorn. Suddenly he made tremendous advances in his research and developed an interesting new polymer that everyone thought was a significant contribution. Farnsworth published it to wide acclaim. I think it's the last paper he ever got accepted.

I look up. "So what's the big deal?"

Tom, confused, comes over to see my sheets. "You're missing the last page," he says.

Donna states, "I think we all are, Tom."

He looks in his briefcase. "Uh oh. I forgot to collate it in." Pulling out three sheets, he distributes one to each of us. I start to read again. Then I feel sick, unable to believe what my eyes transfer to my brain. See for yourself.

> I thought the old codger was rambling. I was about to brush him off when he said there was something funny about it all. He didn't want to reveal any more, but I pressed him. There was an associate professor—his name was James Willett—productive but paranoid. Didn't trust anyone. Hid his research notes. Not cleverly and most people knew his favorite hiding places. He was killed in a motorcycle accident. It was shortly after that that Farnsworth's investigations started to advance. My source said most people didn't connect the two events, but he had always wondered. So do I.

"So that's why Farnsworth has been dancing to Ken's tune lately," exclaims Theresa.

"Wait a minute," I object. "Sure the Dean has backed Ken, but maybe it had nothing to do with this. After all, this guy only suspected something. And obviously Farnsworth's committee didn't see anything unethical."

Tom knows more. "Here's another diary entry I've been saving for this moment." He hands it around and once again we set to reading.

> Hit Farnsworth with my suspicions today. Wasn't sure it was true, but decided to bluff it out. He tried bluffing too, but doesn't have the stomach for it. I knew he was a weak-livered worm, but even I was surprised at how easily he folded. I realized I had him where I wanted when he asked what I was going to do. Told him nothing if he supported me in getting rid of Frazier, increased money for the department, and backed me whenever I asked him to. He accused me of blackmail, like I didn't know what I was doing. When I shrugged and said it was his choice, but I'd get word of what he'd done to Bedlow, he capitulated immediately. It was such a pitiful battle. It would have been more fun if he'd had some guts.

Tom asks, "Did Farnsworth blow this out of proportion? After all, the incident happened over 30 years ago, and presumably he's been doing his job since then."

It seems like a naive question to me. But perhaps I'm being unfair. Tom, of course, isn't familiar with the academic side of university life.

It's Theresa who deals with this. "No, Tom. He understands it would spell the end of his career if it became known. I don't know what disgusts me more, Ken's cruel exploitation or Steve's unethical behavior."

She looks so sad lately. She's seen enough of the down side of life, you'd think she'd be immune, but these transgressions so close to home have hurt her.

She continues, "Everyone knows, of course, that occasionally someone steals another's work. I'm sure you've seen articles in the newspaper. But it's rare."

"So what will happen to Farnsworth?"

"There'll be an investigation. For faculty we have a standing committee to search out the truth and suggest penalties to the administration. They could range from a declaration of innocence to a period of probation to outright dismissal. In the last case, assuming the President agrees with the findings, we may permit the offender to resign, but he will go."

"But a dean would be handled differently?"

"Not in the final outcome. I'll have to talk with Norman Mulholland, but I'm sure we wouldn't want faculty investigating someone in the higher administration."

Of course not, I muse. They only want it the other way around.

"I'll probably chair an ad hoc committee of administrators to deal with this. But if he did steal the work, we'll have no choice."

"I can see what Farnsworth did is contemptible. But you know it happens all the time in business. I know the city police have an economic crimes unit. Why wouldn't you just reprimand him, perhaps demote him?"

"Think what we're trying to do here, Tom. We're an *educational* institution, trying to mold young minds. We not only give them intellectual *knowledge,* we also serve as an example on what intellectual *honesty* is. Maybe if we'd done a better job the city wouldn't need the special unit."

"So Farnsworth's motive is as strong as I thought?"

"Definitely," responds Theresa.

I don't know what's wrong with me. I feel like bawling, and I don't even like Farnsworth. And it's clear to me Theresa's also trying to stem tears. I take Donna's hand. She's no longer joshing me. She knows when support is needed, and the way she responds to my pressure tells me she understands.

Tom says, "I think it's time you heard about my conversation with Dr. Farnsworth."

CHAPTER 22

Tuesday Evening

I know this will be bad, whatever it is Tom's going to tell us. It's awful to see the lives of people I actually know bared. I guess I'm having one of those moments when all I want is to be rid of this investigation. You don't believe that? You think I'm so superficial that the excitement of being in on the chase will soon envelop me again. I wish I could dispute you, but I'm afraid you may be right.

Tom says, "I've decided to play the recording of the session so you can judge his voice." Tom pulls the digital device from his pocket. "I'll start after the preliminaries."

In order to present a complete record of all proceedings to which I'm privy, I've reproduced the conversation here. "W" stands for Tom, well, okay, Warren, while "F" for Farnsworth.

W. "Has Dr. Salter's death created problems for you?"

F. "Indeed it has. In addition to dealing with the personal loss, I have to be concerned with the future of the mathematics department. Who should replace him? Should it be an internal appointment or should we initiate a national search? What about the morale of faculty and students after such a traumatic event? And that's just the beginning. I think you can see I have much to do so please make this as quick as possible."

W. "So his loss is a major blow to the university?"

F. "Oh my, yes. Dr. Salter was a brilliant leader and mathematician. He'll be sorely missed."

W. "I gather he was well liked then?"

F. "Well . . . perhaps respected is a better word. No one questioned his abilities. Without a doubt he was among the best in the world."

W. "Would I be right in surmising, then, that there were some who didn't get along with him?"

F. "I think that would be a fair statement, yes."

W. "Enough to kill him?"

F. "Oh, heavens no, I wouldn't think so. We have academic disputes all the time. We take them seriously, but there's never malicious intent."

W. "So, for example, Dr. Salter was never malicious?"

Tom halts the playback and says, "He's another smooth one, like Brighthurst. But he was beginning to get nervous as my questioning continued. With what I knew from the diary, I was certain he wanted to avoid the subject of people hating Salter. As I continued from this point he started fidgeting in his chair and his finger tapped his desk continuously." I nodded, having seen this nervous twitch often. "Let's continue."

F. "Well, I guess some of the disagreements with him have been intense, but I'm certain no one associated with the university could be responsible."

W. "That's hard to believe, Dr. Farnsworth, since he was killed on campus. Who's had problems with him?"

F. "I'm sure it's nothing, and I hate to bring it up. But I know Dr. Salter was engaged in a continuing argument with Dr. Frazier, one of his faculty."

W. "About what?"

F. "About department policy, mainly, I think."

W. "Just policy then? Not Frazier's tenure application?"

F. "Oh, so you've heard about that?"

W. "Of course. It seems to be common knowledge. Why on earth didn't you tell me? Let me remind you, Dr. Farnsworth, that we're in the middle of a murder investigation, not one of your ivory tower discussions. I expect you to hold nothing back. Is that clear?"

Again Tom stops the recording. "He didn't like being spoken to that way."

"I'll bet he didn't," I say. "He's a guy very impressed with his own status. Always wants to be called 'Dean.' Gets annoyed if faculty use his first name. Of course, that makes me want to all the more."

"We all know your maturity, Jim," Donna says with debatable sweetness. I fire figurative daggers in her direction.

Theresa's annoyance with our asides reasserts itself and she demands of Tom, "What did he say next?"

The interview continues.

F. "Quite clear, Sergeant. As to others, I suppose I'd have to include Dr. Brighthurst. There's been bad blood there ever since Dr. Salter was appointed to the chair position. But I certainly can't think of anyone else."

W. "Come now, Dr. Farnsworth. Surely at least one other person comes to mind."

F. "What are you suggesting? I've answered you honestly, and now, as I've said once already, I have a great deal of work requiring my attention. I'd appreciate it if you'd let me get at it."

Again Tom hits pause. "I'm about to confront Farnsworth with Salter's accusation. I was worried, because I didn't know positively whether there was anything to it or not, thought it could just have been something Salter made up. I couldn't tell whether Farnsworth was trying to get me out of his office because he feared what was coming, or whether he really was swamped with things to do."

"Well, Tom," interjects Theresa, "I could have told you that if Ken said it was true, it was. He didn't deal in fantasies."

"You're right, of course. Farnsworth began to fold as soon as I brought it up. You'll hear it in his voice, which drops its initial bluster and becomes almost a whine. That's why I wanted you to listen to the recording rather than reading a transcript. At this point Farnsworth paled, started fidgeting in his chair, and kept wiping his face with a gigantic handkerchief."

Ah, yes, the handkerchief. Usually its purpose is to buy Farnsworth time when he's trying to out-think a smarter subordinate. On such occasions our eminent dean will pull it out and carefully and slowly wipe his big round glasses. My personal feeling is that no self-respecting speck of dirt would want to get as near to that man as his glasses. Tom's finger returns to the pause button.

W. "I believe, sir, that *you* have an excellent motive."

F. "Me! You think *I* have a motive! That's preposterous! How dare you? Why I . . . , er, I think I'm going to have a talk with your superiors."

W. "So there's nothing to the rumor you stole research that formed the basis of your dissertation?"

F. "Why . . . um . . . um, what do you mean? Where did you get an idea . . . I mean why would you . . . . I'm sorry but you simply have to leave."

W. "Not just yet, sir. We know about James Willett. We know how he would hide his research; that he died suddenly in a traffic accident; and shortly after his death your own work, which had been stagnant, took off. We haven't even begun to investigate that lead yet, but I can assure you we will. We'll find colleagues of Willett's who will be able to give us an idea of what he was working on. We'll locate others who were graduate students the same time you were and see what they think. And we know of one person who has held onto suspicions for decades. I'm sure he could help us obtain damning evidence. We can do all that, and we will if necessary, but it will be to your advantage to tell me the entire story now."

Tom's finger now is nowhere near the pause button, yet we hear little sound. I can picture Farnsworth debating whether Tom can come up with proof or not. Frankly, so do I. It seems to me that, if anyone were able to recognize the theft, they would have done so at the time. Even this guy Salter had spoken to didn't seem to have hard proof, at least according to the diary. But then, I know Farnsworth's a bully, benevolent, but still a bully. And he's more than met his match with Tom. I bet he folds as bullies will. I can't believe how I'm feeling, but I'm actually beginning to be sorry for the guy. Suddenly the recorder's speaker comes to life, although we have to strain to hear the next words.

F. "Does anyone have to know?"

W. "We keep all our findings confidential, unless it's necessary for a conviction. However, I must inform you that Dr. Theresa Bedlow has been asked to consult on this case, and all information will be available to her."

F. "Oh, God! I'm doomed. They'll never let me stay here now. What will I do? Who will hire a 59-year-old man? I don't have any practical skills at all. Sergeant, what can I do?"

W. "That's hardly for me to say, sir. But as far as my investigation is concerned, you are certainly best off telling me everything. After all, we are talking about murder and at the moment your motive seems awfully strong. I want to hear the entire story, so please start at the beginning."

F. "I suppose you're right, but it's terribly embarrassing."

W. "So is being dragged down to campus security, or staying overnight in a cell. It's time for you to come clean, Dr. Farnsworth."

I inch forward in my chair. Everyone else is equally attentive. Again we wait for a pause to pass. Occasionally a slight sigh can be heard. Then Farnsworth begins in a soft and resigned voice.

F. "I was always clever. I breezed through school. As an undergraduate I had a straight A average. It seemed natural to seek a Ph.D. Graduate courses were almost as easy for me as the earlier ones. And I passed my qualifying exams with flying colors. Everyone, including me, thought finishing my degree would be a snap."

W. "But problems arose?"

F. "Yes, Sergeant. What a nice way of putting something that was about to ruin all I'd been aiming at. Problems did arise. Research requires a vastly different set of skills from successfully completing a course—and no one had prepared me for it. I found an area of study I thought would interest me, and an advisor willing to take me on. I still remember his first words. 'Outline an experiment which will tell us something new about your subject.' I must have shown some of the panic I felt because he assured me it didn't have to lead to a major result, or even be directly related to the problem I eventually wanted to solve."

W. "What was the difficulty you were having?"

F. "I simply couldn't do it. I didn't have any idea how to define a new question. Oh, sure, I could think up things I might investigate, but then I didn't have a clue on how to begin the research. The things I thought I could do involved only trivial ideas, ones almost identical to those I'd seen in classes. I floundered for almost a year. I felt my advisor losing interest. Then Willett was killed when his motorcycle skidded on wet leaves and he slammed into a wall."

W. "You were familiar with his research?"

F. "No. It was in a somewhat different field from mine, or at least from what I intended to do. But it was close enough so I could keep the same advisor. That made it easier."

W. "How did you know where to look for Willett's notes?"

F. "It's so far-fetched, unless you knew Willett. He was paranoid about someone stealing his research. Don't look at me that way, Sergeant. I see the irony only too clearly. He always hid his notes. Paradoxically, he made no great attempt to obscure the concealment. One time I was passing his office. His door was open and I saw him placing papers in his boots. I said hello. He looked up angrily, nodded to me, and slammed the door. I didn't think much of it. Willett was a strange man. Because of that it never occurred to me to question why he had boots in his office then—in the middle of June."

"Wow," I hoot. Tom hits pause so my interruption doesn't make us lose any of the interview. "Hiding his research in a pair of boots. That guy must have been a real flake."

Tom, annoyed at this diversion, frowns at me and restarts the recording.

T. "So you heard about his death. Then what? Did you go immediately for the research?"

F. "No. I never even thought about it. But then, the day after he died, I passed his office. The door was open, just like when I'd seen him before. He must have left it that way when he went for his ride."

"What?" I explode. "This paranoid jerk didn't even lock his door. How can such things happen?"

"Perhaps he had other things on his mind," my wife says sweetly.

"Really, Donna, how could he neglect to do something like lock his door?"

"Well, you know scientists, Jim. Absent-minded—a lot of them anyway. I imagine chemists are as bad as mathematicians."

God, she looks so innocent, but there's a familiar mischievous glint in her eyes. I know something's coming, but I don't have the slightest idea what. Foolishly, and I should know better by now, I accept the challenge. "Come on, Donna. I admit some of us are a little strange, but I think most of us act pretty rationally." Then I make my big mistake. "I know I do."

She gives me a smile of pure love and asks Tom, sitting just across from me, "Tom, I'm too close to Jim to see. Could you please tell me what color socks he has on?"

Now Tom has a healthy respect for Donna, but he's confused by the request. I'm sure he thinks it's out of place in the present discussion.

Nevertheless he complies and peers at my feet. Then he grins widely. What on earth is the matter with these two? "On which foot, Donna?" he says.

I look down. Okay. Is it really such a big deal that one sock is blue and the other brown? After all, I have both colors in my drawer. Someone must have placed them there mismatched. Honesty forces me to tell you something, but there's no need to repeat it. I do the laundry in our house so it's going to be hard to find a way to place the blame on Donna. What should I do to extricate myself from this embarrassing situation? I take the time-honored approach and grin foolishly.

Suddenly Theresa spits, "Stop this, all of you. It's getting late and I want to finish our discussion. It's just like when the three of you were in my class. Always kidding around. Can't you understand this is serious business? Get on with the recording, Tom."

We look at each other, shocked at her outburst. She's always had such a good sense of humor. And we *are* taking the situation seriously. But Donna and I, especially me, aren't used to violent death, and we need diversions. I guess it's part of the aging process, and she's bound to be upset about what's happening around the university. She's devoted such a large portion of her life to the institution. Tom shrugs and restarts the recorder, and Farnsworth echoes my original outburst.

> ". . . Unbelievable, isn't it? Here he is so worried about keeping his precious research private, and he leaves his door open to the world. I felt myself drawn into the room, as if by a magnetic force. The boots were there, apparently unmoved from the last time I'd seen them. I told myself I should leave. I actually took a couple of steps toward the door. But then something came over me. I quickly closed the door and dove into the boot. His papers were still there. I couldn't believe it. I took them, stuffed them under my shirt, opened the door, saw the corridor was clear, and raced for my room."

W. "And the notes did refer to his research?"

F. "Yes. It was brilliant work. There was still a lot of experimental effort required, but a complete plan was laid out for carrying it forward. Any fool could have finished it."

W. "And you did."

F. "Er . . . yes."

Theresa snaps, repeating her earlier comments, "He had the integrity of a con man then, and he does now. It makes me sick. That man is finished. The only thing worse is Salter's using Farnsworth's weakness for his own gain. God, what a mess things are here."

Donna gently reminds her, "He's served MRSU for many years, Theresa. Isn't that worth something?"

"Normally, yes. But we've already gone over the importance of academic integrity. Does Farnsworth have an alibi, Tom?"

Tom sighs. "Yes, he does. It's on the rest of the recording but I can summarize it easily. He, his wife, and another couple went to an early-bird dinner at a Chinese restaurant, took in a movie, and then stopped for ice cream."

"Sounds like a teenage double date," I put forth helpfully.

Tom looks at me and shakes his head before continuing. "Farnsworth drove and dropped off the other couple at 10:30. I still have to talk to them, but he wouldn't lie with a story that's so easily checked."

Theresa says, "So everyone you've spoken with so far has a pretty good alibi. You've got your work cut out for you, Tom."

"You sure do," I mutter through a yawn. "I think Donna and I should get home. Remember, I'm planning to drive up to see Elmo Sherwin early tomorrow morning."

Donna seems amenable to our impending departure, although I think she has some pre-sleep activity in mind. I believe I'll be able to find the required energy for that.

As we start to rise, Tom says, "Just a minute, you two. We still have to discuss what you're going to do tomorrow, Jim."

CHAPTER 23

Tuesday Evening

I'm getting wary. "What do you mean?" I say. "You know I'm going to see Elmo. I've even arranged to miss my classes in order to do it."

"Yes. And I appreciate that. I really do. Er . . . you should be back fairly early in the afternoon, right?"

"Yeeees," I say, drawing the word out, not sure where this is headed. "Well, I'm not positive actually. It'll take me a couple of hours to drive there and another two back. Say two more with Elmo."

"So if you started at 0700 you should be back by 1300?"

Why do I have to keep translating times when I'm with Tom? "If I'm lucky, I guess."

"Good." Tom seizes the best case option. "Here's what I'd like you to do. You should be the one to talk with David Simmons. Figured you could get more out of him than I would. I remember you said he was in one of your classes last semester."

"Who's David Simmons?" asks Donna. A glance at Theresa tells me she knows already. That surprises me.

"He's a former student, a computer science major. Very shy. We saw him in George Frazier's class today, and I was pleased to see that George has gotten him to open up a bit. It's something I was never able to do. Tom seemed interested in him, but I don't know why." I look inquiringly at him.

"Let me answer that by giving you one last page from the diary." Again your faithful scribe reproduces its content accurately.

> David Simmons made a scene today. Actually had the temerity to threaten me. I'll make short work of him.

"Wow," I say with typical originality. "I wonder what that's about."

"I think I know," says Theresa. We turn to her. "He came to my attention after the boy's father attempted unsuccessfully to make an appointment with Ken. Ken simply refused to see him, a really stupid move. Mr. Simmons wasn't about to be put off, so he turned to Steve Farnsworth."

"What happened?" I ask. As a teacher, I'm always worried about problems with parents. So different from when I was in college. We'd never have considered getting a mother or father to fight our battles for us. Hell, we wouldn't even have dared have an argument with our teachers. Was it better then? I don't know. Just different, I guess. It's another age now.

"Not much, from what I can gather," Theresa responds. "The father, along with David, came to see me, I presume as a last resort. He said Steve listened politely, muttered some inconsequential platitudes, and ushered him out of the office."

"Sounds like him," I mumble.

Theresa responds, "I think it's more than that, especially in view of what we've learned tonight. He wasn't about to take any action opposed to Ken."

I can't imagine what this is about, so of course I blurt, "What the hell was going on with David Simmons?" I can see Tom has the same question.

Theresa answers, "Something which illustrates all too well what a cruel man Ken was." I think of that poor introverted kid and wonder what I'm about to hear. "For years there has been a steady stream of complaints about Ken ridiculing students if they had difficulty following his lectures. I've even heard he made sure to ask questions of youngsters he was certain didn't know the answers."

"Yeah," I interject. "That's the scuttlebutt around the department."

"Well," Theresa continues, "David Simmons seems to have been a favorite target. You're right, Jim, about that young man. He's painfully shy. He hung behind his dad, barely whispering a greeting. I've looked up his record, and he's done well here, A's and B's, especially in computer courses where I understand he's quite a whiz. His only poor grades were in speech and English composition."

"He did well in my calculus class. Sorry, Theresa, I didn't mean to interrupt."

"I asked David to step outside so I could talk to Mr. Simmons alone. He told me David had been sick as a child and never strong physically. This had made him the butt of jokes from classmates and he had withdrawn socially. He panics when he has to talk in front of a class, which I guess is the major reason he did so poorly in speech. The first time Ken called on him, his mind went blank. That's all Ken would have needed to select him over and over. Made him look silly, and I guess several in the class were amused. Makes you wonder about our future leaders, doesn't it?"

Tom's more interested in whether Simmons could be a murderer. "What's this about a threat to Salter?"

"His father was up front about that. Of course, whether he would have been if he'd known Ken was going to be killed I have no way of telling. I guess Ken picked on David once too often. The boy was practically crying. He fled the room, but before he left he turned and said, 'I'll get you, Salter. You'll never hurt anyone again.' I've looked into the incident, talked with a couple of others in the class, and that's pretty much the way it was."

Of course it's my wonderful and empathetic Donna who senses the boy's pain the most. "The poor kid. He's probably felt inadequate most of his life. Then, for an instant, a more fiery personality broke free. That must have terrified him. I hope he'll get some therapy."

"I think he is," responds our former teacher. "I suggested it to his father and told him about our campus counseling center. Mr. Simmons said he'd take him there. I assume he did. I was afraid David might drop out of school, so I'm pleased to hear he's in George Frazier's class. There isn't anyone who would be better for the boy at this point."

"He's doing a terrific job," I reiterate.

"So you will speak with David, right, Jim?"

"Aw, Tom, after I get back from Elmo's I'm supposed to meet separately with two graduate students. Besides, I'm not particularly close to David. There's no reason to think he'd open up to me. And there's a good chance I won't be able to find him."

"Oh, I think you will."

Damn him. He's right. I can check David's class schedule for starters. I recall George's four-hour calculus class meets Monday through Thursday so I probably can catch him after it. Tom grins at me. How could he and I ever have been friends? I sigh. "All right, Tom, I'll give it a shot. I guess I can put off my students until late afternoon." I look to Donna for her reaction to my discomfort. The damn woman also is smiling. I try to look sullen, but the cycle is on the upswing; once again I'm thrilled to be entrusted with an important task, two if you count the visit to Elmo. And I do. But I need a passing shot, so as I get up to leave I say, "Can we go now?" Pretty devastating, huh?

"Wait just a minute. I want to get Donna's reaction to that manuscript she found."

Theresa immediately jumps in. "I think that can wait, Tom. We're all tired and it can't be that important. Let's discuss it tomorrow evening."

Donna nods agreement. "Actually, I would like another day to reread it and think some more. But, Theresa, I disagree with you. I think it's terribly important and might provide a significant clue to the murderer."

CHAPTER 24

Wednesday Morning

I'm lying on my back, attempting to formulate a scheme to get me going for the day without expending any energy. Remember my telling you I thought Donna had plans for us last night? Turns out I'm as perceptive as she is. At least in this one rather restricted area. Sorry. Again, no details. Alas, I find my body depleted, even after the extraordinarily deep sleep of the righteously exhausted, with no enthusiasm for the jobs that lie ahead.

It's 7:10, just 10 minutes later than when I told Donna I'd definitely be leaving. Not bad. There's no point in waking her. Instead I roll over and stroke her arms. She emits a delightfully provocative sigh and her lips form a half smile. It's almost enough to make me dump my appointed tasks and stick around to see what develops. Almost, but not quite. This having a sense of responsibility is a real drag at times. But it will be fun to see Elmo again. It's been less than 60 hours since we last met, but it seems like an eternity, what with all that's happened since.

Heaving a silent sigh of resentment and self-righteousness, I force myself erect, bathe, shave, and gulp a banana and bowl of cereal. By half past seven I'm on the road north to Sloane University. If I don't speed it'll take me slightly under two hours for the 100-mile trip along mostly interstate highway. Only a short urban portion at the end.

That's plenty of time to think. I attempt to ponder my research, but my mind always returns to the murder. What are my feelings? I keep telling you about the excitement. It makes me sound so crass. What excites me is the possibility of contributing to the solution. I love puzzles, and this is one. Sometimes I tend to forget the horror that is the puzzle's source. But I want you to know that frequently I do think about it. And then revulsion is what I feel, revulsion for the fact that anyone could consider life to be so cheap, even the life of a shit like Ken. So please excuse my zest for deductive reasoning. I'm not as insensitive as I sometimes seem. Really!

I reach the campus at 9:10. Okay, maybe I exceeded the lawful limit by just the tiniest of bits. I've been to Sloane before, but never to see Elmo. We've collaborated on a couple of papers, but all our communication has been via email or his occasional visits to MRSU. It's been a thrill for me to work with him. You should see his mind whirl. At the beginning of a project he'll work through dozens, maybe even hundreds, of examples to glean some understanding of the properties common to them all. Then he'll draw on his vast reservoir of mathematical knowledge to formulate and prove general truths, things we call theorems. It's beautiful to watch him produce mathematics. What's that? You've never associated the words "mathematics" and "beautiful" in the same book, let alone the same sentence? Oh, if only I could share with you the ecstasy of discovery that mathematicians experience. I know you feel you had quite enough of that kind of ecstasy when you were in school, and sharing with a mathematician is not high on your priority list. I can only feel for you.

I'm in the math building now, a towering 14-story modern edifice of stucco over block. Are you ready for this? Climbing the sides, just up to the second floor so far in this relatively new building, is ivy! So in a few years this really will be a hallowed hall of ivy. I'm sorry. I'm sorry. Time to go in.

I've been here many times, but, as I said, never to Elmo's haven. I knock once. And I wait. Then I knock again.

"Come in," roars forth.

I enter a paper factory. It's stacked everywhere. On file cabinets. On bookshelves. On every chair. And all over the floor. Piles three feet tall line the front of a desk, obscuring any person, hopefully Elmo, sitting behind. I see two large hands emerge and remove the top half of the middle pile, creating a "U" effect with Elmo's head appearing in the interior.

"Oh! Jim, is that you?"

He's looking right at me. I figure he knows it's me. But then he's Elmo. "Yes," I answer, "it truly is."

"Well, good to see you, of course. What are you doing here?"

"Elmo, I called you yesterday. Remember? Asked if I could drive up to meet with you today."

"Is that so? What did I say?"

"You said sure, come ahead."

"Well, there you are. And here I am. What can I do for you?"

I purposely hadn't told him I wanted to consult him about Ken's proof to the Collins Conjecture. I knew the first mention of that would have him demanding I drop whatever I was doing and bring it to him at once. I don't know if he's even heard that Ken claimed to have solved it. "It's about Ken Salter's murder, Elmo."

"Oh. Why would you want to talk to me about that? Thought about it quite a bit since I heard the news yesterday. Terrible thing! The guy was a real son-of-a-bitch, of course. I was forced to entertain him once when he was up here for a presentation. Had to be nice all day. About killed me. But what a mathematician! And what a wonderful talk he gave! Very few like him in the world. He'll be missed."

It's nice to hear someone speak positively of my former boss. Then I recognize that I've gotten to labeling comments positive if they aren't 100 per cent negative. "He claims to have solved the Collins Conjecture!"

"Yes, I know! Got an email message from him announcing it." So Elmo is on the list of recipients. I should have realized that. "Isn't that something? After all these years and so many bright people attacking it, it finally falls. Worked on it myself some. Made some minor contributions, but never came close to a full argument."

Notice the difference between Elmo and Harvey Delsanter? Not a jealous cell in Elmo's body.

"Salter's name will be a household word in math circles. Shame he won't be around to enjoy it. Can't wait to see his proof. Hope he wrote it up before he died."

"Well, actually, Elmo, that's why I'm here. Tom Warren . . ."

"Who?"

"The campus police detective directing the investigation."

"Oh."

"What I was going to say is Tom took me over to the murder scene with him." I'm trying. You've got to believe me. I really am trying to keep the triumph of being included in the investigation out of my voice. Alas, I believe I'm failing. Fortunately, Elmo is not overly perceptive, but I can see his eyes light up. I have a sick feeling he'd like to be involved too. I hope I'm wrong.

"He actually took you with him? Sounds rather unusual, I'd say."

Again I strive for modesty. Again I fail. "Well, I guess he felt I might be able to shed a little light on the case, my being familiar with the department and all, you know."

"Yes, yes. I'm sure you've been a big help." There's a slight suggestion of a pout. Is he envious? "But why come to me. And what does this have to do with the Collins Conjecture?"

I describe the pertinent facts to Elmo. "Apparently he was stabbed shortly after he finished writing his proof."

I'm guessing Elmo's sensing why I'm here. He lets me know I'm right. "You want me to look at it?"

I nod. "Tom sent me to see you. He doesn't think the proof is connected with the murder, but he's not leaving anything to chance, wants to know if it's right. He asked me who could check it out. I told him that the only two nearby were you and Harvey Delsanter, and I recommended you."

"Hmmph. Harvey would have been fine." Those were Elmo's words, but I can see he's pleased. "So where is it?" I take it out of my brief case and give it to him. He comes around his desk. Suddenly he notices I'm standing. I never sat, there being no place available. "Sit down, Jim, sit down. Why on earth haven't you made yourself comfortable?"

"Er, where?"

He blinks, not comprehending the problem. "On a chair, of course." He gives me a puzzled look and returns to the other side of his desk, replacing the previously moved stack of papers in the front. He's disappeared.

I sigh. I select the chair with the fewest papers, gingerly lift them and set them atop another pile on the floor, crosswise so I can return the room to normal—normal for Elmo that is—before I leave. It's an armless wooden chair, not at all comfortable looking. I sit. And I wait. And wait. Why didn't I bring something to read? After about 20 minutes I hear Elmo whistle. Then I wait more. After what seems an eternity I notice an hour has elapsed. Do you have any idea how long an hour is when all you're doing is sitting and waiting? Think about attending a math lecture, on a hard wooden seat, for that length of time. Does that help explain the misery I'm feeling? Ten more minutes and Elmo says, "Damn! Wonderful!"

Then more silence. I've been here almost two hours. I'm going to have to get up and walk around. I should have left when I first gave the proof to Elmo. But once I started sitting I didn't want to move, afraid I'd disturb Elmo's concentration. But I can't take it anymore.

Just as I'm about to rise, Elmo screams, "Magnificent! The man's a genius!" He stands and I can see his head. "It's brilliant, Jim." In his excitement he waves his left arm and knocks two piles of papers from his desk, distributing them on the floor.

I'm appalled, thinking mathematics research has been set back years. It's hard to believe Elmo could have found anything in the mess I originally saw, but now it'll be impossible. He doesn't seem the slightest perturbed. How on earth has he succeeded so well all these years without me to worry about him?

"Jim, Ken Salter has found a damn clever way to attack the problem. So simple, but no one ever before even considered the approach. I hope they catch the bastard who ended this man's life so prematurely. He could have made many more fundamental contributions."

"So you think the proof is correct?"

"Oh, yes. Of course, I'll have to go over the details carefully. It'll take me a couple of days to do that. But I'm sure they'll stand up. Salter didn't make mistakes, and his approach is certainly the right one."

"Do you see how the proof could be involved in his murder?"

"Impossible, I'd think. After all, who cares anything about it, except a few of us."

"Delsanter, I suppose."

"Well, yes. But to kill? Harvey's another bastard, but I don't think he'd go that far. He's more comfortable trying to terrorize people intellectually."

"Well, if you do think of anything, will you let me know?"

"Sure. By the way, what's this stuff on the last page, after the proof is finished?"

"I've wondered myself, but haven't figured it out. I do know the marks in the lower left hand corner correspond to a bloodstain on the original. But for the rest, I have no idea. I suppose Ken was just doodling after completing his work."

"Well, maybe so." He seems doubtful. "Hey, I just remembered. I've printed out Salter's message announcing his result. I've got a little program that lists all my messages in order. Saves me having to mess around with my computer. Always hit the wrong key, then have to call someone to straighten things out. Going to frame it and put it in the graduate student lounge. Want to see it?"

Now why would I want to look at a piece of paper that's simply a repeat of the message I'd already viewed on Ken's monitor? But of course

I say that would be fine because I'm such a nice fellow. Elmo rummages around his desk top, finally producing a sheet of paper.

"I bet you'd like a copy for yourself, wouldn't you?" he says.

"Uh, of course, Elmo," continuing my role as Mr. Politeness. All I need is another piece of paper to deal with. But then I think maybe Tom would like to see it, although I have no idea why. Elmo prints a copy that I accept with grace. For your edification, I've reproduced it here.

From: Jordan <Jordan@sci.mit.edu>
Subject: **Colloquium**
Date: March 12, 2011 11:53:14 AM EST
To: Elmo@mat.sloane.edu

Elmo, can you speak at our mathematics seminar April 15 on a subject of your choosing? Please let me know by Friday.

Nancy

From: Salter <salter@math.mrsu.edu>
Subject: **Collins Conjecture**
Date: March 13, 2011 5:07:47 PM EST
To: Analysis group

This is to announce that today I have answered the Collins Conjecture in the affirmative. I will publish the proof shortly, but interested parties can contact me directly any time.

Kenneth Salter
Marcus Rome State University

From: Singh <singh@mat.sloane.edu>
Subject: **Dinner**
Date: March 13, 2011 1:35:14 PM EST
To: Elmo

Elmo, just a reminder you and Michelle are coming to dinner Thursday night—6:30. S.

From: Albright <albright@math.mrsu.edu>
Subject: **Conference on Differential Equations**
Date: March 13, 2011 2:15:20 PM EST
To: DE

A conference on differential equations will be held at Marcus Rome State University next year in October on dates to be announced in the near future. Please direct all inquiries to James Albright, Conference Chairman.

I hadn't realized the message I'd sent from home would be on the same sheet. Certainly adds value to the document, don't you think? Well worth Elmo framing now. I might even keep a copy myself. After all, it's as near as I'm ever going to get to a great mathematical discovery like the solution to the Collins Conjecture.

I thank Elmo for his time and am about to leave when he says in a beseeching tone, "Er, Jim."

Uh oh. "Yeah?"

"You know, I've got a pretty good knack for solving problems."

I see it coming, but all I say is, "You sure do. One of the best *mathematicians* in the world." I emphasize the word 'mathematicians,' but I'm afraid his thoughts are on another field.

I'm not wrong. "Well, I believe I might be able to be a bit useful in this little problem you and that policeman fellow are having. I thought perhaps I could return with you for a few days and devote some time to it."

My heart sinks at the confirmation of my fears. Theresa considered Elmo a bumbling fool last Sunday. I know having Elmo "help" is the last thing in the world she'd want. Or Tom either. Then I think of two outs. "We'd love to have you, Elmo," I lie. "But what about your classes." I'm sure he never gave a thought to them before his gracious offer.

Any hopes this would dissuade him quickly dissolve. "No problem at all, Jim. I'll get one of my grad students to take the undergraduate class, and I'll just cancel my other. It meets only once more this week." That's too close to what I'm doing today, making any potential rebuttal hypocritical. "This sort of thing occurs all the time," he continues, "with the traveling I'm forced to do." It's true. Someone of his stature is constantly in demand.

Okay, time to pull out all the stops. "I did happen to notice, Elmo, that one of your emails referred to a dinner invitation tomorrow for you and Michelle." There, that should end the threat.

"Mighty nice of you to be concerned, Jim, but don't think anything of it. Singh's been trying to get us together for some time and I'm sure he wouldn't mind waiting until next week."

Well, I've tried. Now I'm grasping at straws. "Well, if you come it would be for just a day or two, right?"

"Certainly no more than the end of the weekend. Have to be here Monday. So what do you say?"

I calculate that's four days, not counting this evening. A long time if a dentist is boring into you. Would Elmo be as bad? Probably not. And his childish importuning visage is hard to resist. "All right," I say, mentally kicking myself, "if it turns out you can make it."

"Great! I'll drive down this afternoon and find a nearby motel."

"I'm sure it would be all right to stay with us," I blurt. What the hell is wrong with me? I'd better call Donna the minute I get on the road and see if I'm in hot water. "Will Michelle be coming?"

"Mighty kind of you, Jim. Afraid Michelle won't be able to make it. She's got a heavy week booked. Kind of think she'll be happy not to have me under foot."

I have no trouble believing that. We part and I spend my drive contemplating the similarities between me and Pandora. I must remember to call Donna. I'm sure she'll take it in stride. But what about Tom? And especially what about Theresa?

CHAPTER 25

Wednesday Afternoon

I get back to campus a little after 1:30, again due to a slightly unconventional interpretation of the speed laws. I hadn't intended to spend so much time with Elmo, and now I've got to find one of my grad students and delay seeing him until I'm finished with David Simmons. I don't look forward to speaking with David. I didn't get close to him at all last semester and I can think of no reason why he'd want to talk to me.

I locate Hamil JaWan, my master's student, in the graduate teaching assistant office. I'm supposed to see him at 3:00 to discuss his research report, but he's happy to delay our meeting until 5:00. With that change I'll be able to speak with David and easily make my four o'clock appointment with Amy.

I get to George Frazier's classroom moments before his students leave. I hang around the door and when David appears say, "Hi, David. How are you doing?"

"Oh, er, hi, Dr. Albright."

He ducks his head and begins to slink off. "David, do you mind if we talk a few minutes?"

"Talk? What about? I've gotta get moving."

"This won't take long, and it's really important. Come on, I can walk with you."

"Well, okay, I guess. What do you want?"

We're outside now. "You've heard, of course, about Dr. Salter's murder." He appears nervous. But that's his normal behavior so I don't know how to interpret it. I sure could use some of Tom's experience. I continue, "Sergeant Warren, the detective in charge of the case, asked me to speak with you. He thought it'd be easier for you to talk to me than with him."

He looks ready to bolt, but fortunately he doesn't. I don't know what I'd have done if he had.

"Why . . . why do the police want to talk to me? I don't know anything about who killed him."

The poor kid is shaking now, looks ready to cry. Am I in over my head? I spy an empty bench partially hidden by trees and suggest we sit there. He agrees. After we're settled I say, "I don't know too much, myself, about why the police want to talk to people." I'm being pretty modest, don't you think? "But it is a murder investigation, you know, and for that they pull out all the stops. I think what the sergeant is worried about is the problem you had with Dr. Salter a couple of months ago."

"What do you mean, problem? I don't know what you're talking about."

"David, don't make this hard on yourself. No one wants to create difficulties for you if you had nothing to do with the murder. But Sergeant Warren knows about your threat to Dr. Salter."

His eyes are darting everywhere, landing on everything except me. I hope his legs don't follow suit. He gulps several times. He knows what I'm talking about, but he attempts another bluff. "Threat? You've lost me."

I sigh. How can I convince him to come clean? "Let me assure you, David, that Sergeant Warren is an excellent detective. I know him well. He's an old friend. He's not going to charge an innocent person with a crime." I sure hope that's true. Tom wouldn't do it on purpose. But mistakes happen. I don't want this boy hurt.

"He does, however, have an obligation to check into any situation he hears about, if for no reason other than to eliminate innocent people as suspects. What occurred between you and Dr. Salter is common knowledge, and he wants to learn your side of the story."

I hope to get him started by telling him a little of what I've heard. "We know Dr. Salter embarrassed you in class to the point you felt you had to leave. Now that wasn't right, David. He had no business doing that. And I'm sorry it happened. But it did. And so did what you said to Dr. Salter. The sergeant simply can't let something like that go without checking it out. Unfortunately, if you don't talk to me, he'll come see you, so please give me your version of what happened."

He remains silent a long time. Should I try to prod him, maybe even a mild threat. All my mysteries have the detective in such situations just sitting back and waiting for the suspect to break the stillness. That's what I do, mainly because I don't have any idea what else might work.

And what do you know, David starts to talk, all the time straining to hold back tears. "That wasn't the only time the bastard shit on me in class. The first was when he called on me near the beginning of the semester. I think he picked on me because I always sat in the back row. It's where I like to be, dammit."

"It's not where you sit in Dr. Frazier's class," I say softly.

"No. But Frazier's a really good guy. Treats me nice. Not like most teachers I've had." I feel like slime. Was I one of the bad ones? I don't know if he senses some reaction in me, but he goes on to say, "Oh, I don't mean you, Dr. Albright. You're okay. But Dr. Frazier's special."

"Yes he is. I'm delighted you have him. So you think Dr. Salter asked you questions because you sat in the back row?"

His voice becomes bitter, and angry. "Yes! Probably thought if we picked such a spot we wouldn't be able to answer correctly. And he was right. At least about me. I clammed up, couldn't get anything out."

"Did you know the answer?"

"Sure, it wasn't hard."

"So why, David?"

"Because he scared the hell out of me, that's why. He didn't just stand in the front of the room and ask politely. He came to the back and towered over me. When I didn't answer right away he loudly demanded if I'd studied, and why was I in college anyway if I wasn't going to take my work more seriously. And I had studied, Dr. Albright. I swear it. Then he said maybe I was a little too slow for his class and started asking me questions about earlier subjects. My mind went blank. I just sat there, wishing I could crawl out of the room. And some of the guys started laughing."

"And this happened more than once?"

"You're damn right it did." I'm startled by his vehemence, not at all like the David I know. "At least every two weeks, sometimes more often."

"And one day you decided you'd had enough?"

"I didn't decide anything. I was exploding inside. And I was so mad. I didn't even remember yelling at him until later. Then I was scared shitless, afraid he'd do something awful to me. So I phoned my father."

"Do you remember what you said to Dr. Salter?"

"Not exactly. Something like he'd never treat anyone that way again."

"What did you mean by that?"

"I don't know. I didn't have any idea what I was saying. I know what it sounds like, now. Maybe that's what I wanted it to sound like. But I didn't mean anything by it. Honest."

"David, did you kill Dr. Salter?"

He looks at me in horror. "No! I swear it, Dr. Albright. I couldn't kill anybody. Even when I was so mad at him that day. You do believe me, don't you?"

I want to believe him. And I think I do. But, when I saw his anger, I sensed a power usually foreign to him. How was he so different from a battered child? People can take only so much. I know Tom will expect me to see if David has an alibi.

"David, I hope you won't be offended, but I've got to ask you what you were doing Sunday evening, say from 5:00 on."

"Is . . . is that when he was killed?"

"They believe sometime in that time frame." I think I'm supposed to say we can't reveal information like that. But I'm no cop, just a teacher dealing with a student who needs my help. "So were you with anyone?"

"Nah. I really don't have friends. I guess I don't have an alibi." He looks scared and again close to tears. "I was in my room studying."

"Alone?"

"Yeah."

"Do you live in the dorms, have a roommate?"

"No. I live at home. I'm a commuter."

"At home! With your parents?"

"Sure."

"Well, David, were they there?"

"Of course."

"Did you see them? Can they give you an alibi?"

"Gee. I guess they can. I saw them several times when I'd go to the kitchen for a snack."

"Where do you live?"

"About 25 miles south of the campus."

"It seems to me, David, that you don't have much to worry about." Once more I've said something I hope is true. I believe it *should* be because I find myself believing David. But I bet Tom will put limited stock on his family confirming the story. Or maybe not. "I'll tell Sergeant Warren about our conversation. If I were you, I'd just forget about this and get on with your life. Thanks for speaking with me."

I rise, ready to leave our hideaway bench, when David stops me. "Dr. Albright?"

"Yes."

"Er . . . thanks for being so nice."

"I'm just sorry that we had to have this discussion at all. I know it hasn't been easy for you."

"I'm getting counseling, you know. I thought I was going to be screwed up my whole life. But now I'm beginning to think I can be somebody."

"You can. You've a lot of ability. And I'm glad you're seeing a therapist. My wife is one, and I know how a good counselor can make all the difference in the world. Good luck, David. And drop in my office once in a while to let me know how things are going."

"Thanks, Dr. Albright. Maybe I will."

We part, and I watch him shuffle off, head bowed, I'm afraid I don't see much change in him. Except his belief that things can improve. Seems like a good start at that, doesn't it? He certainly deserves better than what he's had.

Unless he's a murderer.

CHAPTER 26

Wednesday Afternoon

After leaving David, I stroll to my office. I have well over an hour before my meeting with Amy. Damn. I needn't have changed Hamil's appointment after all. Maybe I can catch him now. Heading toward the grad student office a three-tone chime erupts from my shirt pocket, right behind my pen and pencil. Text message. Damn, it's from Tom. I read, "Something's come up. Can't see Elsie Martin. Please talk to her today." Shit! What am I, his slave or something? I'm annoyed. So why am I trudging over to Theresa's suite of offices?

The main administration building differs from all others on campus. Like them, it's coated with brick, but there all resemblance ends. For one thing it's only two stories high. And far from a box-like design. Indeed, the front forms a semicircle with a canopied walkway leading to the main door. Small columns support the canopy and guide you to the entrance. Upon achieving admittance you immediately sense an unusual lightness of foot. Careful inspection indicates this is due to the thick carpet that bears no kinship with the threadbare remnants lining the offices and corridors of the math department. It's quiet, too. Unbearably quiet in my opinion. Of course, those pesky and noisy students rarely cross the threshold to this land of the academic mighty.

All right. All right. Perhaps I'm being just a wee bit nasty. And I know you're thinking I'm jealous. Nothing could be further from the truth, though. About my jealousy, that is. But I do think the nasty part may be on target. I get so steamed when I see the opulence of this building and compare it with the math department's tight budget that makes even copying a class handout a major expense.

But enough of this. It's time to get down to business, which means I've got to make my way to Theresa's office and find her secretary. I'm not a frequent visitor to the building and it takes me a few minutes to locate my destination.

When I do it is to be reminded that vice-presidents don't have offices like yours or mine. Certainly not like mine, anyway, an 11 by 12 windowless box in which are crammed a desk, two visitor chairs, two file cabinets, three bookcases, and a computer table. In Theresa's outer office is a phalanx of four secretarial cubicles with unseen entrances off a corridor on the opposite side. A visitor sees only a blank wall and a small counter manned—actually today *womanned*—by a student assistant ready and willing to do her job. "Can I help you?" she says.

"Yes, thank you. I'm here to see Elsie Martin."

"Do you have an appointment?"

I'm shocked that an appointment is required. "No, I don't. But I think she'll talk with me. Please tell her I'm here."

The student is dubious. "And you are?"

"Dr. James Albright."

"Well, let me ask Miss Martin." She punches a four-digit code and I silently thank her for reminding me not to say "Ms." The young woman cradles the phone and, glancing at me with surprise, says, "You can go right in." She points to a door at the far left. "Have a seat and Miss Martin will be with you in a moment."

I thank her, and pass through the indicated door to a room containing a sofa and three large easy chairs. Another door, now closed, is on the opposite wall and an empty, glassed cubicle is off to the right. I assume the door leads to Theresa's office while the cubicle is *Miss* Martin's domain. Clearly I'm to wait, and I elect to sit at one end of the sofa.

In less than two minutes a gray-haired woman of about 60, carrying a steno notebook, exits Theresa's office, glances in my direction, and says, "Dr. Albright, I assume. Sorry to keep you waiting. If you could just give me one more minute." She goes into her cubicle without waiting for my assenting nod. After all, her words were more statement than request. True to her promise, she beckons me in almost immediately. "I was in Dr. Bedlow's office and picked up the receptionist's call there. I don't have much time, but Dr. Bedlow says I should talk to you. Something about poor Dr. Salter's murder, I understand. I'm not clear why it's necessary to discuss it with you. A . . . er, let's see," and she glances at her appointment calendar, "ah, yes, here it is. A Sergeant Warren was supposed to see me, but he cancelled." Her tone indicates this is an egregious *faux pas.*

She gazes at me with intelligent light-blue eyes. She's wearing a navy-blue suit coat and matching skirt, and a cream-colored blouse with one of those ruffled collars. Her shoes are navy also, with no-nonsense one-inch heels. I return her look, figuring it would make me seem more honest. "Tom Warren had planned to see you, and then I got a message saying he'd been called elsewhere and asking me to stop by." Again I strive for a diffident demeanor. "I'm assisting him on the case."

"Indeed!" she replies, and I sense she knows I'm a highly educated flunky. "Well, then, I guess I should help in any way I can. What is it you wish to know?"

"Thank you for your cooperation. I'm sure the Sergeant will appreciate it." She impatiently waves me on. "I understand you and Susan Barber are friends."

"Yes, we are. For over 10 years. I'm the one who found her a job here."

"I'm glad you did. She's a wonderfully competent woman."

"She certainly is. As I'm sure you're fully aware, she's been the one running the math department's day-to-day operations for years. In addition to her normal duties as administrative assistant, she, among other things, prepares the budgets, schedules classes, and completes the annual reports. And those reports are better than all the others we receive. She's an excellent writer."

I think back to all the memos reaching my desk, under Ken's name but, as is common knowledge, authored by Susan, and I have to agree.

"And such a lovely woman, heart of gold. Are you aware she volunteers every Saturday at the Battered Women's Shelter? I know the director, and she told me Susan connects easily with the residents, giving them moral support and the courage to strike out on their own."

This is a different Susan from the one presented to our faculty, one much closer to the person Tom and I got a brief glimpse of Monday. Interesting that she's working with abused women. I wonder if Miss Martin is familiar with Susan's past. Then I recall Susan told us that only the woman preacher and Ken were previously privy to that information. "Susan mentioned she was playing bridge with you Sunday evening."

"Yes, although why that should be of interest to you . . . oh, is that when Dr. Salter was killed?"

"We think so."

"And you feel Susan needs an alibi?" I'm not sure how much she knows and don't want to break any confidences. My fears are laid to rest with her next words. "I suppose it's because of her affair with Dr. Salter. So ill advised. I tried to tell her several times. But I guess the attraction was just too strong. The poor dear hadn't had much experience, you know."

"Those situations are always hard, and so difficult when they go bad."

"Yes," she responds slowly. "Susan's having a great deal of trouble putting it behind her."

Ah, maybe we're getting to Susan's lies. It sounds as if she's still carrying a grudge. Not over it like she said. "It must have been terrible continuing to work for the man," I offer.

"It certainly was! Every bridge night she'd complain about him. I'm not sure why she stayed on. It would have been easy for someone with her ability to change positions."

"Any hunches why she remained?"

"I'm only guessing, but I think she thought someday she might get even for being dumped, and wanted to be around to seize any opportunity."

"Like killing him?"

She's shocked. "Of course not!"

"Well, in what way would she get even?"

She appears flustered. "Oh, I don't know. I'm not even sure I'm right. And what difference does it make anyway? If Dr. Salter was killed Sunday night, Susan was with us all evening. Two others beside myself can verify that. And I wouldn't lie to save her skin."

I smile. "I know. Dr. Bedlow made that clear. And I'm glad Susan has such a good alibi. Thank you for your time. I'll be going now." Just as I'm about to pass through her cubicle door I think of another question. I turn back to Theresa's secretary. "Was Susan still complaining about her situation this past Sunday?"

She looks startled, remembering the evening. Then she says softly, "Why, no, I don't believe she was."

CHAPTER 27

Wednesday Afternoon

I have a little time to clear up some paperwork before meeting Amy, but not enough to see Hamil. On the dot of four my doctoral student appears. She's a wonderful person, extraordinarily bright, and it's been a pleasure working with her. She started her dissertation about a year ago and has made significant progress. I expect her to finish the research in another few months, and then she can start writing it up. Some of it already is in near final form and has appeared in published papers. Many women who study mathematics are physically attractive. But Amy isn't, and she has no sense of how to make the most of what was granted her. She's not overweight, but large bones and short build give the impression she's constructed from Lincoln logs. Her face is indistinctive. Unless you look for the intelligence in her dark, almost black, eyes. Today her drab, brown hair hangs in strings to her shoulders, she wears no makeup, and she's in a muumuu and sandals with a strap missing on the left foot.

I've gotten to know her fairly well, and she's told me some of what she's had to put up with. Her looks and lack of any fashion sense whatsoever made for a difficult adolescence. And coupled with the fact that she was brilliant in the sciences—which in her high school was okay for a guy but weird for a girl—she initially was the recipient of nasty taunts and had few friends. I don't think I could've dealt with that. But Amy's made of sterner stuff. She worked on her personality, forcing herself to be outgoing. She joined school organizations and a church. Eventually people discovered the kindness and caring that lurked under the unattractive exterior, and by the time she graduated from high school she was popular, in the platonic sense, with a large group that included class leaders. Her friendliness is more apparent now, and all our graduate students love her. And so do the undergrads she teaches. Last year she won our annual award for best grad student instructor.

I also can report that lately there's been a glow on her face I've never seen before. She hasn't said anything. But I've observed her in the company of another of our Ph.D. students. A lot. He's a guy all the females drool over. It's hard not to be jealous of him. But he's also a serious person who maybe is looking for more than looks in a woman. I just hope he's good to Amy.

We don't get much done in our session. She opens with, "Hi, Dr. Albright. What can you tell me about the murder investigation?"

It was clear from what she said yesterday that word has gotten out I'm involved in the case. No, I haven't been broadcasting it. Well, not much, anyway. Everyone wants me to spill all. I don't, of course. I really don't! And, no, the reason isn't there's just not that much to spill. I'm ashamed to say, though, that Amy, whose virtues I've been so forcefully extolling, is demonstrating membership in the expanding student group displaying ghoulish interest. What's that, you say? I'm a fine one to talk? Well, I'm not condemning Amy. In fact, I must admit to enjoying talking with her about it, although I don't reveal which people have been interrogated or what anyone has said.

"Not much, Amy. Tell me what the grad students thought of Dr. Salter."

One thing I like about her is her no nonsense approach to life. She can be brutally honest and now she gives me an earful. "Oh, they respect his mathematical ability, but I can't think of a person who didn't hate him."

"What're the main complaints?"

"Where should I start?" Her tone is angry. "He was brusque in class, rude in conversation, condescending, and often cruel."

"Had any thought of asking him to be an advisor?"

She looks at me like I'm crazy. "You're kidding, right?"

I guess it was a dumb question. We've had a masters program for years and a doctorate for the last eight. Ken has not directed a single student.

"Do you think any of the students felt strongly enough to kill him?" She gives me another of those incredulous looks and simply shakes her head.

I see Hamil waiting for me in the hall, so Amy and I agree to meet in a week, with the standard stipulation, of course, that she contact me immediately if any problems arise in her research. Hamil's a serious young man who has no interest in murder. He wants to finish his project, get his degree, and return to his homeland. We have a productive hour, and agree it's time for him to start writing his final report. This often is an exhausting process for both the student and me, and I hate it. You see, most students have terrible writing skills. I don't anticipate the normal problems with Hamil, though. His English is superb and I've seen samples of his writing. He's good.

Finally I'm on the way home. I'm tired and wish I could just crash for the evening. Unfortunately we have that meeting at Theresa's, changed to 7:30 this evening, and I've got a lecture to prepare for Friday's class. I've given up hope of finding time for research until the murder is settled. I see Donna's car in our driveway, so I honk as I pull behind it. She meets me at the door, and she's looking great. She's wearing a tight short-sleeved blouse, more like a sweater, and painted-on jeans. My eyes never get down far enough to see what's on her feet. I start salivating. She grins and indicates there's no time for what I've got in mind. So I have to settle for a long, passionate kiss that leaves both of us weak. I really am one lucky fellow.

Donna cooks up spaghetti with a vegetarian sauce she'd made in quantity on Saturday, and I whip a salad together. It's a simple meal we both enjoy. We finish eating around 6:30 which leaves me a little over half an hour to work on my lecture before we have to depart. Just as I'm settling down, the doorbell rings. Donna answers it and I hear Elmo's voice. Lead fills my stomach. I'd forgotten all about him. I never did call Donna so she knows nothing. Oh, boy, am I in trouble. I don't feel any better as he says, "Damn good to see you again, Donna. Where d'ya want me to put my stuff?"

By then I'm working up the courage to face the situation—until I hear Donna shout, "Oh, Jim. Can I speak with you for a minute?"

I haven't been very fair with her about this, have I? I enter the living room and see Elmo ensconced in one of our more substantial chairs. "Hi, Elmo," I say weakly. "Have a good trip?"

"Wonderful. Love my car. Got it just last week. A Lexus. Let me tell you how I bargained with that salesman. Boy, did I show him. See, he . . ."

I interrupt. "Sounds great, Elmo. But give me just a minute."

He airily waves me off and I follow Donna's previous exit into the kitchen. She's standing there leaning against the table, arms folded, with an exasperated look on her face. "Is there something you haven't told me, Jim?"

"I'm so sorry, baby. He talked his way into joining us down here for a few days. Seemed to think he could help solve this murder." She doesn't seem impressed. "I tried to discourage him. I really did, but he was insistent."

She glares. "And did you by any chance suggest he stay with us?"

I look sheepishly at my feet. "I, well I . . . I think maybe something like that might've slipped out."

"All right. I'll go make up the guest bed, but you're going to pay for this."

"Er, what do you mean?"

Suddenly any trace of anger disappears and she grins mischievously. "You're going to have to perform when we get back tonight, and I won't take any excuses."

All right! I'm wondering what other transgressions I can commit to receive similar adjudications. Then I remember my lecture, which I've accomplished nothing on. Fortunately I can put its preparation off until tomorrow. I have a hunch that once I've served my sentence with Donna, I'm not going to feel like working this evening.

It's time to leave for Theresa's, and I've got to figure out some way to explain Elmo to both her and Tom. I don't think I can count on much help from Donna. I begin to rationalize that Elmo's one of the best mathematicians around, so he's bound to be adept at the deductive reasoning required for interpreting a set of clues. Think they'll buy that? I don't either.

Suddenly I'm overwhelmed by an absolute certainty. I do buy it! Elmo will be instrumental in finding the killer!

CHAPTER 28

Wednesday Evening

We arrive at Theresa's on the dot of 7:30. Once again Tom has preceded us. He opens the door in response to our ring, greets us, sees Elmo, and blurts, rather impolitely I think, "Who the hell is this?"

Theresa, standing behind him and remembering, I'm sure, the events of Sunday's dinner, chimes in. "Elmo, just what *are* you doing here?"

Tom says, "Elmo? Are you Elmo Sherwin?"

"Yes, I am, young fella. And I bet you're that nice detective Jim told me about. Tom Warner, isn't it?"

"Warren, sir. I'm terribly sorry, but I'm afraid you're going to have to leave."

I glance at Elmo's disappointed face. I swear it resembles a basset hound's. With my newfound enthusiasm for his presence, it's time to leap to his rescue. A spirited, vehement and, if I do say so myself, brilliant case for his inclusion elicits, "I'm afraid it's impossible, Jim," from Tom. "I'm out on a limb enough discussing it with you."

Theresa nods agreement. "That's right, Jim. Elmo simply has no place in these discussions." Then she, a dog lover, looks at Elmo and softens. "I'm sorry, Elmo. You're welcome to wait in my den if you wish. Please understand this has nothing to do with you."

But I think it does. Theresa did not appreciate his Sunday antics, and I've got to admit his clumsiness created some awkward situations. But that's the way he is, and it has nothing to do with his thought processes. I realize even more how much I want him to join us. So I go for broke. "Tom, you asked for my help. I've tried to give it to the best of my ability. And I'm still trying when I say Elmo should be here. I believe he'll be able to make significant contributions. Frankly, I think you've got to trust me on this. I feel so strongly about it that I don't want to be involved any longer if he isn't." I know you think I've flipped. To give up this puzzle I've been vicariously enjoying, all for Elmo? But surprisingly, I'm comfortable with my stand.

Tom stares at me, eyes blazing with anger. I think he's about to tell me my leaving is just fine with him when suddenly Theresa becomes an unexpected ally. "Tom, maybe it would be all right, especially since Jim feels it's so important."

I'm shocked. Why is she taking my side? Tom appears equally dismayed, but then states with singular lack of grace, "All right then, but I don't like it."

I respond, "It'll be okay, Tom. You'll see." God, I hope I'm right. The sad truth is, I'm never sure what Elmo's going to do next.

As Donna and I walk to our accustomed places on the sofa she whispers, "I'm proud of you for sticking up for Elmo, although I'm afraid Tom may be right to exclude him. Anyway, I've decided to commute your sentence for tonight."

I'm horrified. I fully intend to do what is right. "No way," I say. "I've committed a grave sin and I've got to pay for it."

Donna squeezes my hand and runs her middle finger lightly along its palm. I'm ready to leave now. Unfortunately, Tom wants to get down to business.

"Why don't we start with Jim telling about his activities today, visiting Elmo and then speaking with David Simmons."

"Before I do that, Tom, suppose I fill Elmo in on what we've learned so far?"

"You mean you haven't done that already," Tom replies, rather nastily, I think.

"Of course not," I respond with dignity. "I wouldn't have done that until we'd agreed Elmo would be working with us."

"All right, go ahead. But make it snappy."

Tom's growling now and I fear this case may strain our relationship. I hope not. It takes me about 10 minutes to present Elmo with the essentials gleaned so far. Elmo listens intently to every word, barely moving, hardly ever blinking his eyes. I know his mind is recording each detail and even now is starting to process the information. Tom, never long on patience, asks if I could please get started with my report. Tossing all caution to the wind, I suggest Elmo himself cover the conversation we had. Tom throws up his hands in a helpless gesture and slumps in his chair.

I think Elmo stuns them all. He speaks passionately of Ken's proof, how brilliant it is. He indicates he still must examine the details to make sure they're correct, and he'll do that while he's visiting us. Then he extols Ken's mathematical abilities, fervently stating his views on cutting off the life of such a genius. He's concise, coherent, and believable. He's impressed them and I heave an internal relieved sigh.

I suppose it was too much to ask. Elmo just doesn't know when to shut up. He concludes with "Happens all too often. History's full of great mathematicians who've suffered a premature death, often being forced into war by power hungry leaders. It's why I'm so glad you asked me to help. Think I'll be able to come up with some ideas."

Oh, Elmo. They were accepting you. Now you've reminded them you're here on shaky grounds, and they don't like that. I doubt very much your comment about being asked to help set well either. That's not how they remember what's happened. Hell, it's not the way *I* remember it as I recall how I tried to find excuses to offset your importuning.

Elmo's remaining comments are brief. After all, there isn't much to tell. The two of us hadn't talked a great deal. Mainly he had hidden behind his desk examining Ken's proof and I had sat interminably on that increasingly solid chair. Also he doesn't require time to describe the impressive disarray of his office, or the papers flying through the air after an enthusiastic arm sweep. These are unimportant to him and to the investigation. But there's something else he doesn't mention, probably equally unimportant. Nevertheless, I think it should be shared.

So I tell them about the sheet of email communications Elmo gave me. Remember, the one with the four messages on it that included Ken's announcement? You've already seen it. When I got back to school I made copies for everyone here. Then I promptly forgot to look at them. I haven't had any time, anyway, and I can't imagine what role they could play. Nevertheless, I pass the copies out. My colleagues' singular lack of interest tends to verify my own evaluation of the sheet's worth. Only Theresa is marginally encouraging, reminding us it's important no input be summarily dismissed.

Now it's time for David Simmons. As I've modestly said previously, I've good recall and am able to reconstruct the discussion almost verbatim, trying simultaneously to convey my impression of David's tone, mood, and nervousness. I conclude by saying, "He's a nice kid. I'd hate to think he had anything to do with this. And his alibi sounds pretty tight to me."

“But you did have some second thoughts about him when you saw how angry he was?” asks Theresa.

“Yes,” I say slowly and sadly. “I don’t think you can dismiss him if his alibi can be broken.”

Tom sighs. “I’ll talk with the parents, of course, but I’ve a hunch Jim’s right and Simmons was home Sunday evening.”

Elmo blurts, “Wouldn’t parents lie?”

“It’s a real possibility, but usually I can detect it.”

Theresa adds, “I met his father, you know. He seems like a straight shooter.”

“Besides,” I say, “David didn’t even consider they could provide him with an alibi. You’d think he’d have a more prepared story if he really needed one.”

“Unless he’s a lot cleverer than you’re giving him credit for,” cautions my trusting and caring wife.

CHAPTER 29

Wednesday Evening

I find Donna's comment valid, and it makes me sad. I like David Simmons, more than I expected, and I don't want to admit he might have me fooled. It's easy to do, though. Fool me, that is. And I saw enough anger in him to make me think there's at least a possibility he could kill. I'm glad these thoughts get pushed away by Tom saying, "Let me tell you about my talk with Harriet Salter."

Harriet's always been a cipher to me. We've encountered each other briefly only a few times, mainly at department social functions. At them she was what I call a "peripheralite," huddling in the background. Theresa confirms my evaluation. "A rather drab woman, don't you think? Always dressed in grays or browns, with her dull, straight hair parted in the middle and brushed unbecomingly to the two sides."

"Have you talked with her much?" asks Donna. I'm interested in Theresa's response because I know Donna thinks there's more to Harriet than most people see. Certainly more than I do.

"Rarely. I'm afraid I haven't gone out of my way to encourage contact. I found her conversational fluency virtually nonexistent. And she just seems so mousy, much too timid a woman for my tastes."

The words sound judgmental, but Theresa's sympathetic expression belies such an interpretation. I'm sure she's truly sorry for Harriet whom she probably thinks is wasting her life.

"Was Ken with her while you were speaking?" pursues my lovely wife.

"Always. Why?"

"Because I've seen her that way too. And every time Ken was by her side. But I've also spoken with her alone. At those times she became a completely different woman—intelligent, articulate, incisive—a pleasure to be with. I've even had lunch with her a couple of times." I didn't know that. I wonder why she never told me.

Tom, who's been listening to the conversation with interest, asks Donna, "So you think Salter's presence suppressed her normal personality?"

"Without a doubt. I don't want to speculate too much, but I believe he must have been demanding, controlling, and impatient. I got the impression he constantly berated her, told her she was useless, couldn't do anything right."

I burst in. "You're right. Something happened at work several months ago. I'll never forget it. One day Harriet came to the math office looking for Ken. Said she'd locked her keys in the car and needed to borrow his. Had walked more than a mile to get there. The secretaries kidded her about it. One of them said Harriet gave a half-hearted grin but seemed nervous, not seeing the humor of the situation. I came into the office just as Harriet was entering Ken's."

"What happened?"

"It was pretty ugly. All we could hear was Ken yelling—a lot. Things like, 'Can't you do anything right? You're the stupidest bitch I've ever known. Here. Take my keys, but make sure you get them back immediately.' All of us in the outer office looked at each other, but no one said a word."

"Then what?"

"There was a moment of silence. At least we didn't hear anything, but Harriet must have been speaking because soon Ken's voice again came roaring through. 'Well, your inane little charity will just have to wait, won't it? Maybe next time you'll be more careful where you leave your keys. Do you think you're smart enough for that? God, sometimes I wonder. Get out of here. And I mean it about getting my keys back soon.' By now each of us in the office had found something to engross our individual interest. We didn't want Harriet to emerge and catch us staring."

"Was that the end of it? Sounds awful."

"It was. Awful and nearly at the end. Almost, but not quite. There was another silent moment. Again with Harriet speaking, I guess, because soon we heard Ken say, 'Oh, for Christ's sake, did you ever think of taking a cab. Just leave. I've important work to do.' Harriet did appear then, only to find an office of people diligently attacking various tasks. Even Susan Barber, who normally has a word or two for a departing visitor, had her head glued to her precious computer, typing furiously. I wonder what she was thinking, given what we now know. I stole a glance at Harriet as she passed. Her face was flushed and I saw tears. I was torn. Should I say anything? I just remained still and felt terrible."

Donna takes my hand. "That's one of the situations she mentioned to me."

Ah, now I understand. I'm sure Harriet has been seeing Donna professionally, which is why I've been kept in the dark, and why she's unwilling to go into much detail with Tom.

"Always knew he was a son-of-a-bitch," growled Elmo.

He'd been uncharacteristically quiet and I'd almost forgotten he was here. I wasn't even sure he'd been listening. Most of his time was spent pouring over that sheet of email messages I'd gotten from him in the first place.

Tom scowls at Elmo, then says, "Tell me a little more about your impressions of Mrs. Salter, Donna."

I sense her hesitation as she ponders what's appropriate to reveal. Actually, her rules are pretty simple. If it's said in a therapy session, it's off limits to anyone else. Even her adoring husband. So whatever she has revealed or will reveal must come from contacts outside the professional ones. My guess is they did occasionally do lunch.

"She's an educated woman. And obviously intelligent. Has a degree in accounting."

"English, too," interposes Tom. "She told me she took a double major. And loves writing."

"I didn't know that, but I'm not surprised. She said she had derived a lot of strength over the last few years from Emily Dickinson's poetry. Did you know she used to have a job in a large firm with excellent prospects for advancement?" Tom nods. "She gave it up when she married Ken. He said no wife of his was going to work. And then their two kids came along and she devoted her life to raising them. She doesn't begrudge sacrificing her career, although she was bitter about receiving no recognition or help from Ken. I feel that underneath her public persona lies a vivacious, charming, and intelligent woman."

"I agree," says Tom. "I met her this morning about 1000 when I went to her home."

I picture the single-story, white frame house with black shutters I visited the one time Ken held a department party there, shortly after his appointment as chair. It's the last social event he ever planned for us. The house is situated on a pleasant suburban oak lined street of upper middle-class homes.

Theresa says, "You didn't see her the night of the murder?"

"No. I sent Detective Chen to break the news. He said she took it—what was the word he used—oh, yes, stoically. Not a single tear. But I didn't attach much meaning to that. After all, people react to tragedy in so many ways."

"But you feel differently now?"

"I don't know. Maybe. Let me get to that in a minute. First, though, guess who answered my ring."

"Oh, come on, Tom. This is no time for games." Theresa sure does seem to be edgy. I hope she's feeling okay.

"Sorry, Theresa. It was Mrs. Farnsworth, the dean's wife."

"Probably felt it her duty to comfort the grieving widow," Theresa says cynically.

"Now that's the interesting part—about the grieving. Mrs. Farnsworth, by the way, was not pleased to see me. Probably knew something about my talk with her husband, although I doubt he had confided the whole story to her. Anyway, she attempted to keep me from seeing Mrs. Salter, said she was too upset for visitors."

"Bet that stopped you," says Theresa with a grin. It's good to see a bit of her sense of humor remains.

Tom smiles. "Hardly. Mrs. Farnsworth finally conducted me into a den where Mrs. Salter was seated in a large leather chair."

I put in, "I've seen that room. Really dark. Walnut paneling, bookcases, and furniture. Deep brown carpet and the same paneling on the ceiling as is on the walls. Don't see how Ken stood working in it, but he told us he got his best ideas while sitting at the desk there. What a depressing place for Harriet to pick."

"Maybe," says Tom. "But 'depressed' or 'upset' are not the words I'd use to describe her, nor does your account, Theresa, accurately portray the woman I met. Colorful, not drab, is what came to my mind when I saw her outfit. A deep yellow blouse with matching shoes, flowered skirt, pearl necklace and earrings, and a green emerald pin. And her hair was lustrous, cut short, and curly. Pretty chic, I thought."

"Not exactly funereal, then," says Donna. She's smiling and I sense she's proud of Harriet.

"Not even close. I offered condolences on her loss. Asked her if she minded a recording of our conversation. She immediately acquiesced. Then she smiled at me and started to speak. Her response is not what you might expect and I want you to hear it directly." He gives Donna a look I don't know how to interpret. "I'll be interested in your reaction."

Tom pulls out his recorder, already set where the playback is to begin. He presses a button and Harriet Salter's voice blasts throughout the room. Tom hastily adjusts the volume.

"I appreciate your expression of sympathy, Sergeant. But you're not here out of kindness. You want to know if I murdered my husband. I certainly had motive enough. He treated me horribly. Wait. That's not entirely fair. He did treat me badly, but I took it. For years."

I sense Donna's hand in helping Harriet see her own responsibility. It's not the first time I've been impressed with my wife's work.

"*Our* life meant *his* life. Everything was arranged around *his* schedule, *his* work. I was a tool to facilitate *his* wants. For years he told me I was worthless, so often I came to believe it. Lately, I've rediscovered myself. I've been seeing Donna Albright. Do you know her?"

Donna looks startled. So Tom has been aware of this all along! Hence that look.

"Good. Then you may realize what a marvelous therapist she is. Ken would have had a fit if he'd known. But I've begun retrieving my identity. I don't think I'd have stayed much longer with Ken if he'd lived. But now I feel so free. I can't even mourn. I want to celebrate."

Tom looks at Donna. "You never mentioned Mrs. Salter was a client," he says accusingly.

I shift uncomfortably. Donna's not going to stand for that. "That's right, Tom. Nor should I have. The fact that she's seeing me is just as privileged as the content of our sessions. If she wants to reveal anything, that's up to her. But *I* can't, and you know it."

And Tom does know it. He doesn't like it, but I think he understands and respects the privileged communication between client and therapist.

Tom says, "A little later I indicated that it sounded like she had a good motive for killing Salter. She just smiled at me. Listen to her response."

He finds the correct spot using the recorder's counter. It's clear he's put some thought into how to present the interview. He's ready now and presses the play button. "It may seem that way, Sergeant. But in actual fact it wasn't enough to make me kill Ken. Not now anyway. Perhaps some time ago. When I first learned of his flings. Oh, yes. I knew about his other women, including Susan Barber, and I knew when he dumped them, as he always did. Susan should have known better! We women let ourselves get fooled so easily, don't we? I did, so I guess I can't blame Susan.

"It's funny. I can't tell you how often in our marriage I wished Ken was dead. He'd go on trips and I'd fantasize about the plane crashing. Then I'd feel guilty because of the others on board. I did occasionally think about murder, although I can't imagine ever killing someone. The trouble is, I'd been humiliated for so long that in the past I'd have been too scared to try. Lately, though, I've rediscovered just how strong a woman I am, something that was true once, but wrung out of me by Ken's treatment. If I could convince myself murder was necessary, I'd now have the courage. The nice thing is I don't have to. Because that same courage would have allowed me to leave Ken. Murder simply wasn't required."

Tom's looking at Donna now. "What do you think? Do you think she could have killed Kenneth Salter?"

Donna returns his look squarely. "I'm not even going to begin to discuss Harriet with you, Tom. I wish I could comment based just on the statements she's made to you. But it would be impossible to separate that from what I know from our sessions. What's your view on what she said?"

Clever, huh? Turning it back on him?

"She sounds genuine. If she's lying, she's good at it. And she might be; she's so damn self-confident now." He gives Donna a rueful smile. "You *must* be good."

Theresa says musingly, "She sounds completely different from the woman I knew. I think I like the new Harriet Salter. Does she have an alibi?"

"Of course," says Tom with disgust. "When Salter said he'd be at work the rest of the day, Mrs. Salter knew he wouldn't be home until late. Apparently that's been the pattern. So she invited some neighbors over for drinks and sandwiches. They began arriving at half past four and the last couple, especially close friends, didn't leave until shortly before ten. It seems pretty solid." He pauses, then adds wistfully, "She's got a humdinger of a motive though, and I don't mean the way Salter treated her."

I sense a bombshell coming. "What is it?" I say brilliantly.

"The old reliable. Money! Salter carried a $500,000 life insurance policy. Bought it when they were first married and kept up the premiums. She's the sole beneficiary."

"Did she know about it?"

"She certainly did. Brought it up herself. She was smiling when she told me it'd make her transition to widowhood even easier."

"That's a lot of money," I say. Boy, what I couldn't do with that. But I guess I don't want me or anyone else to die for it. I don't think. But it *is* a lot of money. "Wonder what she's going to do."

"She told me she plans to return to an accounting career. Says she'll take some courses at the university to brush up her skills."

Theresa says, "I'm going to call that woman tomorrow and offer her the courses free. She deserves something for the years she endured Ken."

"She can afford the tuition," I put in wryly.

Theresa trains her steely eyes on me and replies, "James Albright," and I know I'm in trouble. "You have no idea what hell she's been through. No man could. Even I can't, never having been in a situation like hers. But I do know this. There isn't enough money to make up for all those years. She'll get the courses free."

I huddle down in my seat. Donna grins at me. I feel as humiliated as Harriet was. Of course, I realize that's a stupid thought. The situations aren't even close. But I sure feel like dirt.

Donna asks, "Did you see her children, Tom?"

"No. She'd sent them to friends' houses to stay."

Donna says, "I bet they're taking it hard. How awful it must be to have your father murdered."

"Mrs. Salter indicated as much. Her boy is 14 and the daughter is 11. I gather Salter was a fairly good father, although he didn't devote much time to them. According to her, she was the one who attended PTA meetings, school plays, soccer games, and band parent affairs. She said the kids are upset, but thinks they'll work their way through this. She indicated she'll get them counseling if necessary."

"Good for her," says Donna. "Anything else to report, Tom?"

"Not much. We checked on everyone's alibi, except David Simmons', of course. I'll get to that tomorrow. Most of the afternoon was spent on paperwork on other cases."

Theresa asks, "What about fingerprints and other forensic evidence?"

"Nothing. Salter's and Barber's fingerprints are all over the office. And Mrs. Salter's. But so are dozens of others. When you think about all the people who've been in that room—janitorial staff, students, faculty, secretaries—we'll never identify them all. I don't think physical evidence from the scene is going to help us much." He momentarily appears discouraged, but the mood quickly passes.

After a moment Tom says, "Tell us about Elsie Martin, Jim."

Did you notice? Not "Did you get a chance to see Elsie Martin, Jim?" He just assumed I followed his orders. Well, you say, why shouldn't he? After all, that's exactly what I did. Sigh. I just wish he'd left open the possibility I'm my own man.

Swallowing my pride, I relate my conversation with Theresa's secretary. When I'm through Tom expresses the thought I had had earlier. "I wonder if that's what she was lying about."

"I think so, Tom."

Elmo asks, "What are you talking about?"

"Oh, that's right," puts in Donna, "you weren't here last night. Susan Barber, Ken's secretary, . . ."

"Administrative Assistant," I correct automatically.

Donna flashes me an impatient look. "Whatever. Anyway, she said she had long ago put her affair with Ken behind her. Miss Martin's testimony disputes that."

Elmo replies, "Probably thought it made her look better if she wasn't harboring a grudge."

"I suppose," says Tom. "I wonder what was different this past Sunday, why she wasn't complaining anymore."

Donna, ever the optimist, offers, "Perhaps at last she had made peace with the situation."

"Or," says Tom, "she knew she'd had her revenge."

CHAPTER 30

Wednesday Evening

We think about Tom's statement. "But she has a perfect alibi," I say.

Tom replies, "I know, dammit, I know."

After a moment Theresa smiles at my lovely wife and says, "I think it's time we heard your thoughts on the document you discovered."

I'm interested, too. Donna's kept it to herself, so I haven't had a chance to review it.

Everyone looks at Donna expectantly. Except for me. I look at her adoringly. Even at a time like this I can't help noticing how beautiful she is. But she appears troubled. I hate that.

"I wish, Theresa, you could have seen where this report was found. Ken, of course, had rows and rows of books, mostly math stuff." I wince at the "stuff." "But one shelf was different. The books varied in subject matter, but a common theme ran through them. When I was in Ken's office with Tom and Jim I noted that *The Prince* and *Obedience to Authority: an Experimental View* were among them. Tom later provided me with a photograph showing all the books on the same shelf. There's Nietszche's *Thus Spoke Zarathustra* that among other issues expresses loathing for victims; Greene's *48 Laws of Power*, which is along the lines of *The Prince*; Taylor's *Brainwashing: The Science of Thought Control*; and Carnegie's *How to Win Friends and Influence People*, to name just a few."

I'm impressed by my wife's knowledge. "How did you know about all these?"

"I already was familiar with the ones I mentioned, except for the *48 Laws*. I had not heard of many of the others. However, *Google* and the internet gave me a quick superficial education."

She pauses, marshaling her thoughts. "I've investigated all of them. Every one, in some way or other, relates to manipulating people and getting one's own way. There are a couple on hypnotism and one discusses effective blackmail techniques. There must be 20 or more titles. Many are classics and no one alone raises significant questions. But taken as a whole, that shelf represents a pretty ugly scene. Not what you'd expect in a typical office."

Elmo halts his continuing perusal of the email sheet long enough to say, "Bet there were books on administration in that mess." The disgust in his voice shows he and I share the same view of that organizational activity.

"No. They were in the office, all right. But on a different shelf nowhere near these. And there's no comparison, Elmo. Given the type of man Ken was, these represent a nasty insight into him."

I can't help wondering what tricks Ken has pulled on us to get his way. In particular, I'm concerned about what tricks he's pulled on me. I knew he was a rotter, but I didn't realize how much.

"The report was near these books?"

"Right in the middle, Theresa. It was sticking out, so much it would have been hard to miss." Donna holds up her copy. "The original, which I guess Tom's keeping with the rest of the evidence, had a clear plastic cover."

Ever the detective, Theresa asks if the document contained any fingerprints or other evidence.

Tom adds, "No information yet. The CSIs are still processing it, the diary, and all the other evidence. As you know, that can take up to five days. By the way, the cover to the report had MRSU's logo on it."

I say, "That's how many of our students submit reports, even masters theses."

"Well, that's where the similarity ends. Unlike most research papers, there's no acknowledgement, abstract, table of contents, summary, or list of references."

Theresa asks, "Is the author mentioned?"

"Yes, but just the single word 'Avila.' Mean anything to anybody? There's no indication whether it's a first or last name."

We all shake our heads. I search my memory banks for a student with that name, but come up empty.

Elmo seems intrigued by this. "Avila, Avila. Sounds familiar." He softly repeats this litany several more times, then reverts to his study of the email messages.

Tom surely must be wondering why I pressured him into accepting Elmo. I'm beginning to question it myself. I notice the mathematical whiz is still mouthing the name silently.

Tom gets us back on track. "Do you still think this report has anything to do with the murder, Donna?"

"Instead of answering you directly, let me read you some excerpts."

She pulls her glasses from her purse. Donna is not in the least concerned what others think of her, except for me, of course. And except for one other thing, the fact she needs glasses for reading. To me it's no big deal. Besides, I think she looks especially sexy with them on. But she just doesn't like the idea they're required and other people knowing it. It's a quirky thing for someone so well adjusted. She's getting better about it, though. There's a slip of paper in the report and she opens to the page it marks, finds her place, and starts to read.

"'A professional man places family second to his work, demanding that his wife arrange all aspects of their joint life to ease his own individual one. He is disrespectful to his wife, downgrading her in public, humiliating her in private. He allows her no creative room, and seems to take pleasure in the misery he inflicts on her.'

"Here's another one. 'A man in a leadership position has an affair with his secretary. The woman, in her thirties, is sexually starved and hungry for affection. She is putty in his hands, yielding willingly and planning a life together. He promises her it will happen, although he shows no inclination to divorce his wife of many years. One day, without warning, he tells her the affair is over. He says he no longer has time for her.' Do these vignettes remind you of anyone?"

My mouth has been open for some time as I marvel at what Donna has found. I get it moving up and down sufficiently to say, "Harriet Salter and Susan Barber."

"I thought so, too."

"What's the context in which these were found?" asks Elmo. Good point, I think.

"Maybe some feeling for the layout of the entire report would be useful. It's composed of three short chapters. I've made a copy for each of you. Except for Elmo whom I didn't know about until a few minutes before our departure from home."

Uh, oh. I sense a dig here. A small reminder of my transgression. Of course, my harsh sentence then flashes through my mind and I vow to bear the latest barb stoically.

Now it's Donna's turn to delve into a briefcase to retrieve copies of the report, which she distributes. "I suggest you read this before we meet again. It won't take long, as the chapters are short. The first of the three, lengthier than the others, begins by describing a person in power who achieves his goals by repeated application of fear, mental coercion, and economic threats. It then proceeds to castigate such a leader, describing in detail the suffering of the individuals working for him, and how the organization under his control will eventually break down as a result of his approach. It paints this kind of leader as an evil man who must be removed from power. It ends with what appears to be an attack on the premises of the books on Ken's shelf that had surrounded this document."

"Wow!" I exclaim. Did you notice I'm rather innovative in the ways I find to express myself? "Do you think someone slipped the report onto Ken's shelf just to annoy him? Not a bad idea," I muse.

"It seems to me there's more to it than that, Jim," says Theresa. "What do you think, Donna?"

"I agree. There's an implied threat in this first chapter, but as you'll see, there's a much more explicit one appearing later on."

"So what's in the second chapter?" I ask.

"That's where I found the quotes. The title is 'Victims'—the first chapter, by the way, is headed 'Perpetrator'—and it contains a series of five short sketches of situations in which one person behaves abominably toward another. I've read portions of two of them. For each of them, as well as the other three, there's an analysis of how the treatment can have lifelong implications, and possibly lead in some cases to suicide. It's a somewhat scholarly work, but while references allude to the literature, no citations are identified, nor, as I said, is there a bibliography."

Tom breaks in to ask, "Can the other three be matched with suspects as Mrs. Salter and Ms. Barber were?"

Donna looks at him with troubled eyes. "Let me read the related portions of them. Here's the first. 'Two men compete for an administrative position. One, well-liked by the workers, loses out to the more brilliant competitor who resents the other's popularity. The winner retaliates by reducing the workload of the loser to meaningless trivia and clerical nightmares. The loser's financial position is precarious, and the winner does all in his power to limit efforts of the loser to add to his income.'"

Tom whispers, "Richard Brighthurst."

Donna replies, "Sounds like it to me. Here's the next one. 'A person in authority has power over a much younger, not yet educated, man. He can greatly control how much of a future that man has. He decides on purely a whimsical basis to drain the youngster's already low self-esteem and attempt to ruin his career. His intelligence and experience, coupled with the other's self-doubts, make the job easy.'"

I feel sick. "Obviously David Simmons," I observe.

Donna nods. "Here's the last. 'A man responsible for determining the advancement prospects of another bases his judgment on personal biases rather than a thorough and fair analysis of the other's contributions. Failure to receive a promotion means loss of position, income, and status.'"

"Clearly about George Frazier," says Theresa, the disgust in her voice aimed at my former boss. "I don't see how we can consider this to be anything other than an intended indictment of Kenneth Salter."

There's a moment of silence as we think about her words. Then Tom asks, "And those are the only ones? Nothing we can associate with Delsanter or Dean Farnsworth?"

"No," replies Donna. "Nothing."

"I wonder why," says Theresa musingly.

"Can think of a couple of reasons," Elmo pipes up.

Theresa looks at him coolly. "And what would they be, Elmo?"

"Writer might not'a known about 'em all."

"I can see that about Farnsworth. None of us was aware of his indiscretion. What about Delsanter, though, Jim?"

I take a moment to consider our suspects. "Well, Dick Brighthurst knows of him. He was at Delsanter's talk at our colloquium. And Farnsworth would have had to approve our honorarium payment to him, but that is more or less automatic and the name might not have registered. I wouldn't know about Harriet. Probably Ken mentioned him to her at some time, but who knows? David Simmons would have no reason to be familiar with him. Both Susan and George joined our department many months after that talk, but Delsanter's a big name so they may have heard of him anyway. Hey, now that I think about it, George and Dick were present at a colloquium Ken gave where he spent at least five minutes vilifying Delsanter's work. Not a comfortable time for us in the audience—one of the longest five minutes of my life. It certainly gave us a clear view of how Delsanter rated in Ken's eyes." I examine the frustrated look on my colleagues' faces. "I'm afraid this doesn't help much, does it?" I pause a moment, then look at Elmo. "Is what you're saying that we can eliminate Delsanter and Farnsworth as suspects because they're not in the report?"

"Mebbe. Or maybe the writer deliberately left his own name off."

Tom sighs. "In which case the murderer is one of those two."

"Not the only possibilities, though, are they?"

"What do you mean?"

"Think about it logically." With that, Elmo sinks back into his chair, refusing to add to his cryptic remark. I try to understand, but I'm not sure what he's getting at either.

Theresa reminds us there's more to come. "What about the third chapter?"

"That's the scariest to me, and makes me sure the murderer wrote this. Its title is 'Resolution.' It asks the reader to suppose that a single man was responsible for all of the situations outlined in the previous chapter."

"Kenneth Salter," I blurt.

"Obviously! The report reminds us that this individual hasn't broken any laws, but what he's done has been unacceptable in any reasonable system of human behavior, with consequences easily as devastating as those caused by unlawful acts. It states in so many words that this man is as morally reprehensible as the worst criminal. The conclusion? The man deserves to die. Basically, the chapter's a justification for murder! The reader is asked to consider the possibility that it is right to eliminate such a man, and it specifically mentions killing him, although the word used is 'execution.' I suppose that's a part of the rationalization process."

"The author must be insane," mutters Elmo.

Donna responds thoughtfully, "Without a doubt. But you might never know it if you were to meet him."

I'm puzzled. "What do you mean?"

"Remember, I'm extrapolating from the very small amount of information in this report. But the writer is obviously intelligent . . ."

"Like everyone in this damn case," Tom mutters.

". . . and able to provide a seemingly rational defense of irrational concepts. The insanity may be manifested in this one area only, fostered by a false sense of justice. If you stay away from the subject of one person's cruelty towards another, the author may seem as sane as any of us."

She looks at Elmo and I wonder if she's thinking he should be excluded from the general group of sane ones.

Then she adds, "Even in that area the person is probably intelligent enough to hide his true feelings, unless you're looking for indications."

"His? Donna, do you think the murderer is a man?"

"I didn't mean to imply that, Theresa. No. This could have been done by anyone, although I don't know about the strength required to plunge a knife in Ken's back."

But Tom does. "It wouldn't take great strength, assuming Dr. Salter wasn't expecting trouble."

"So you think it was someone he knew?" asks Theresa.

"Well, there's no sign of a struggle, and the person had to be behind him."

I can almost see him, perhaps anxious to finish his proof. If so, he might well ignore his visitor and go on working. Possibly told the killer to wait. Hell, I do the same thing myself if I'm in the middle of an idea I'm trying to get on paper. But I'd say "please" when I asked them to wait. I bet Ken didn't. I explain this to the group and they seem to understand that could happen. After all, even non-mathematicians get busy.

Theresa says, "I definitely agree with Donna that the author is our murderer."

Tom also seems convinced. Nevertheless, he'll explore every possibility to make sure he misses nothing. "How can you be so sure the writer and killer are one and the same?"

"Of course, I could be wrong, Tom. But you saw Ken's office. You know how neat it was. The only papers lying about were those he was working on. And his books, all arranged so the backs were exactly aligned. It would drive me crazy to live like that."

It would, too. I've tried to indicate the many lovely characteristics of my delightful wife. But I'm sorry to report that housekeeping isn't one of them. Or mine, either, if truth be told. We always seem to have so much else we'd rather be doing. But Ken was a nut on the subject. Drove our secretaries crazy.

Donna continues, "Now remember how I noticed the report in the first place. It was *sticking out* from the other books a good two or three inches. Can you imagine Ken not noticing such a flagrant violation of the order he loved? I can't."

"So you think the murderer left it at the time of the killing?"

"I'm virtually positive of it."

"Me too."

We look at Elmo. I'm never sure when he's going to enter the conversation. Seems to come at such odd times. I gulp, wondering how his latest comment will be received. But I manage the courage to ask, rather intelligently, "Why?"

"Just a feeling I've got. This thing's well planned. Obviously the report took a lot of effort. Something funny about these email messages too." Here he waves the paper in the air, striking a floor lamp in the process. I jump up just in time to prevent it from contacting its namesake in a shattering explosion. The action momentarily diverts him. Then he says, "Can't figure out what, though."

I look at my copy of the sheet. "Elmo, these are just normal messages. What's the big deal?"

"Don't know. Probably nothing there, after all. The hell with it." He shoves the copy of the messages in his pocket and relaxes with a petulant pout.

There seems nothing more to discuss. Theresa says, "I'd like to keep our future meetings at 7:30 if that's all right with everyone. It gives me a little extra time at the university."

We nod in agreement. Actually that's better for me too. We start to rise when Elmo, now recovered from his doldrums, asks, "Who do you suppose this Avila is?" He's probably been thinking of this since he adopted the name as a mantra.

Tom shrugs and looks at Theresa. "Is there an easy way to check university files for any association?"

"Sure. I'll see that it's done tomorrow. If anyone with that name, first or last, has been a student, faculty member, or on the staff, we'll find it. Anything else?" She scans her guests who remain silent. "Very well. Let's call it quits. I have a big day tomorrow."

Tom replies, "Tomorrow will be busy for me, too. I want to check on Simmons' alibi and make some inroads on my stack of paperwork.

Theresa says, "You might want to look at Ken's student evaluations. I'm sure they'll give you additional insight into the man."

"I remember having to fill them out. I don't know, though. Do you really think it would be worth my time to examine them?"

I pipe up in support of my former teacher. "Theresa's right, Tom, you may learn quite a bit about the kind of person Ken was. You should look at George Frazier's too."

"Why?"

"Oh, I don't know. I just think you'll see a huge difference between the two sets. I thought it might be interesting for you."

"Do they still have questions you give a numerical value to as well as space for written comments?"

"Sure do. There are 15 questions you rate the instructor on from 1 to 5 with 5 being the best. Administrators love it, giving them a number with which to evaluate faculty." Then I remember Theresa's in the room. I steal a glance in her direction, catch her smiling, and give a silent relieved sigh. "They're still filled out by hand, but they'll be done online beginning next semester."

Tom says, "Well, I'll think about it." He adjourns the meeting and Donna, Elmo, and I rise. I'm looking forward to beginning the penance Donna has imposed. I'm also grateful that tomorrow will be a day free from investigative duties. I sure can use the time, because I have the exam to grade that Amy administered today as well as my preparations for Friday's classes. I learn complacency is a false friend as I hear Tom's final words.

"What are you doing tomorrow, Jim?"

CHAPTER 31

Thursday Morning

As soon as Tom asked about my schedule I knew he'd decided to look at the evaluations and wants me to be with him. I'm surprised he's heeding Theresa's suggestion, given his initial lack of interest. Tom will learn something about Ken, but I can't imagine what they can tell him about who killed him.

Again I'm torn. I'd like to help, but I have my own work to do. And I'm still not ready for my classes. One of them, the College Algebra, I've taught before, so all I have to do is review my old notes. But the graduate course is one I'm handling for the first time, trying to stay a day or two ahead of the students. It takes me several hours to prepare for one lecture. Fortunately, tomorrow morning I'm continuing a subject I began on Monday, so I've made some preliminary plans already.

Ah, I can almost hear you. You want to know why I didn't get my preparation done last night after we returned from Theresa's. Wink, wink. What evil minds you have! It turns out we spoke to Elmo for a while, then bid him good night. My sentence? You want to know the details? Well, I really don't think it's necessary to tell all. Suffice it to say that I carried out all terms as prescribed by the adjudicating officer, and I received special compensation for bad behavior.

It's early now, barely seven o'clock, and I'm bleary eyed with less than six hours sleep. Stop computing how long I must have stayed up carrying out my sentence. Tom wants me to meet him at Dean Farnsworth's office at 10:00; that's where evaluations for chairs in the college are kept. So I've got some time. I'd better take advantage of it because, with Tom making all his demands, I'm not sure I'll have another opportunity.

I kiss the comatose Donna, shuffle to the kitchen, and make coffee, leaving a couple of cups warming for her. Hope she gets to it before Elmo does. I wolf down an egg salad sandwich I forgot to eat for yesterday's lunch and settle into my work. By 8:15 I have a good outline of what I want to cover. I'll try to steal time to fill in the details, but at least I can wing it now if I have to. I return to our bedroom to find Donna stirring, with one foot tentatively exploring the world beyond the sheets. I dress, and by the time I'm finished she's alert enough to give me a most satisfying goodbye kiss. What a woman!

When I arrive at school, I extract the exams from my box where Amy placed them and head for my office. Fortunately the class is relatively small and I get about half the grading done before I have to hoof it over to Dean Farnsworth's suite, arriving just a couple of minutes after 10:00. Tom, of course, is pacing the hall outside the entrance.

"You're late!"

"Come on, Tom. Not by much. Do you want to go in now?"

"Wait a sec. First tell me again what I might expect to learn from the evaluations."

"Well, as we said last night, the kind of person Ken was. The numerical scores will give a quick feeling for how the students feel about him as an instructor. A summary sheet gives the average for each question over the entire class. The comments will provide additional insight."

"Does the instructor get to see the responses?"

"Yes, but not until the semester's over and grades are out. The students answer the questions anonymously, but the delay is to ensure an instructor doesn't somehow find out his evaluations and penalize those who give poor ones."

"Do you think I'll be able to learn anything useful to my investigation from them?"

"To be honest, Tom, I doubt it."

Tom walks a little further, pondering what I've said. Finally he says, "Okay, I'm ready. Let's go."

We enter the dean's suite and Tom approaches Vivian Melrose, Farnsworth's secretary, who views him with loathing. Reacting to his earlier visit, I suspect. Probably she sensed Farnsworth's subsequent distress, and her resentment shows. She's a good secretary and very protective of her boss. Tom, of course, is not concerned in the least about her lack of enthusiasm.

"I understand Dr. Salter's student evaluations are stored in this office. We'd like to see them please."

"I'm afraid we view those documents as private. They couldn't be turned over to you without a warrant."

I know that's bunk. Almost all public records are open in this state. There are some exceptions, but student evaluations aren't among them. I point this out, so Vivian, eyeing me with contempt, adopts another tactic.

"Really, Dr. Albright. I didn't realize that." Her voice is super-cooled ice. And what she says is bunk again. "I'll have to check it out with Dr. Farnsworth. Call me this afternoon and I'll have an answer for you."

Tom's voice is soft, but its steady and studied calm speaks volumes about his anger and determination. "Get approval now."

She's shocked. Probably used to the power she wields over much of the academic community. Doesn't like it when someone fails to succumb. "I . . . er . . . I can't. Dr. Farnsworth's not in his office."

"That doesn't matter. You can give them to us without receiving official approval. You do realize this is a murder investigation?"

This is a side of Tom I haven't seen much of. Most impressive. It would certainly keep me on the straight and narrow. And Vivian recognizes defeat. Her manner remains haughty, but she pulls six folders from a file drawer, each containing anywhere from 10 to 50 sheets, and plunks the pile on her desk in front of Tom.

"We keep them for only three years, and require one course be evaluated per semester. I'd like a receipt for them, please."

Tom's amused. Like he's going to steal them! He hurriedly prepares the requested document and says, "We'll need a private spot to go over these."

She sighs, a drama queen in the making, and announces the Dean's Conference Room will be available for two hours. She leads us to it and unlocks the door. I've cleverly remembered to scoop up the folders and bring them along.

Once we're settled, Tom takes a moment to familiarize himself with the forms, learning about what I have become all too familiar with over the years. On one side is the set of 15 questions getting the numeric responses. The opposite has three open-ended queries: "What did you like most about the course?" "What did you like least about the course?" And "How would you change the course?" There's also a computer printout presenting the average of all responses to each of the 15 questions.

Tom thumbs through the numerical portion of a few of the evaluations, but soon turns his attention to the course summaries. "Salter got some excellent evaluations on the statement 'Is the instructor knowledgeable about the course material?' but others are awful. Look at this, the average score for 'Does the instructor set aside adequate time for student consultations?' is 1.34 and for 'Does the instructor show concern for the student?' is a miserable 1.02."

"It's really hard to get that low a score, Tom. What it means is virtually every student in the class gave him a 1. I guess I'm not surprised, though."

"Maybe he just worked them hard and they didn't like it."

I don't think so. "It's true most students don't like to work. We didn't either when we were undergrads, if you recall. And some will give the professor low evaluations if he demands a lot. But not most. They appreciate an instructor who works hard himself to prepare a good course and who expects a lot from them. I'd say that, to get scores like Ken did, you'd have to be universally hated."

"Does George Frazier expect a lot?"

"He sure does. And I think you'll see later that doesn't stand in the way of him getting high evaluations."

Tom's beginning to scan the reverse sides of the sheets, where the written comments are. He shoves three of the folders at me and tells me to look through them. "What am I looking for?" I ask.

"I don't have the foggiest idea. But I've a hunch you'll know if you find it. Just tell me if something strikes you as out of the ordinary."

I begin my task. It doesn't take long to read each one. Many are blank. Those that aren't really blast Ken. They don't like the hard work, but mainly they hate the way he is with them, his superiority, his lack of patience. I bet Ken relished reading these. He'd have taken it as a badge of honor to have the students detest him. There were few comments in the section dealing with likes, and most of them were similar to the terse entry "nothing" appearing on several.

Tom's taking longer than I. Once he exclaims, "Look at these. Don't these kids know how to write. Hell, they don't make sentences, they can't spell, and they don't know the difference between 'there' and 'their.' What are you guys teaching them?"

I smile. After all, I deduct points for incorrect spelling or poor English. Most math profs don't, but I do. The students don't like it. But, you know, a funny thing happens. Their writing gets better as the semester advances. I shrug and say, "Some of them come from atrocious backgrounds."

I've finished two of the three packets Tom gave me and think further examination would be a waste of time. Tom's about half way through his second. "What do you say we skip the rest?" I say. "There doesn't seem to be anything here."

Tom's incensed, and I remember the stickler he was for following all leads in that course we took. "Absolutely not. I want every one of the sheets examined. You never know."

I sigh silently and continue my perusal. Tom interrupts my labor with a chuckle. "Listen to this." He picks up a sheet and reads,

> "'Doctor Salter was here to teach,
> But all he ever did was preach
> That we're too dumb, we'll never pass,
> He really is a horse's ass.'

I hope to hell he's not a creative writing major." Tom continues to smile.

I'm chuckling too. "Sometimes you get strange things on your evaluations, but I've never seen a poem before. But the message is the same as all the others, isn't it?"

"It sure is. The kids just don't like him."

"Some students always try to find something nice to say, but it looks like even they were stymied when it came to Ken. It's sad, really."

"What's sad, Jim."

"Oh, I guess I was thinking of what we try to do here. After all, what could be more important than our teaching? And Ken didn't give a damn about it."

"I thought you were a big research guy."

I shrug. "I like research. It's fun for me. But I still think my teaching is the significant part of my job."

Tom appears unimpressed by my sanctimonious statement. "Let's finish these," he says.

So I return unenthusiastically to my task. I'm about a third of the way through my final folder when one of the forms arrests my rapid scan. I stare at it a minute. "Tom, look at this."

I pull the sheet out and hand it to him. It doesn't take long for him to read the comments. They're short and simple. Under what was liked most is written "This is the last class Salter will ever teach," and under what was liked least, "Salter will never know what hit him." A pretty clear threat, don't you think? Finally, the suggested improvement is "Rid this earth of Salter."

Tom's excited. I think he feels he's got himself a major clue. "What course was this from?"

"Let me see it."

Before Tom gives it to me, he places it in a plastic cover he had in his briefcase. It's just like in my books, trying to preserve fingerprints and all. I'm impressed. I bet he doesn't like how much I'd handled it already. I guess if I was a real detective I'd have been more careful when I first discovered its significance. I turn the cover and enclosed sheet so I can see the numerical side, noticing that the student had filled in the 1 box on every question. At the top is the course being evaluated, along with the semester. I'm shocked.

"Tom, there's something funny going on here. The course and semester shown don't refer to the one they're supposed to."

"What do you mean?"

"Look here. This folder is for a course Ken taught last spring. But the semester given on the form is from this past fall."

"Is it the class David Simmons took from Salter, the one where he had the trouble?"

I'm jolted by the possibility and look at the course number more closely. Then I feel sick. "Yes. It is," I say softly. I pause a moment. "But that doesn't mean he's the one who filled this out."

"No. But it is suggestive, don't you think?"

I have to agree, but I don't like it. "How do you suppose it got with the others?"

"I don't know." Tom looks exceedingly grim. "But I sure as hell am going to find out." We continue our perusal but nothing more of significance emerges. "Okay," says Tom, "let's tackle that secretary again."

Tom takes the offending evaluation with its protection and indicates I should gather up the six folders and follow him. He strides over to the dean's office and I lumber after him. He takes the files from me, hands them to Vivian Melrose, and requests a receipt of their return. He can play the paper game as well as Vivian. Then he informs her he's taking one of the forms and will, of course, give her a receipt for it.

She's shocked. "You can't do that. I simply won't permit it."

Tom isn't having any of her nonsense. Even I can't see why she's making such a big deal. "Ms. Melrose, I'll get a warrant if necessary. It's a lot of work and the outcome will be the same. I assume you want to help us catch the murderer and don't wish it known you've impeded our investigation. Now, what's your decision? I don't have a lot of time."

Again she's forced to face the reality that with Tom she has no bureaucratic power. "Very well. It seems I have no choice. But Dr. Farnsworth will hear about this, and he won't like it."

Now that threat might mean something to academics at MRSU, but it shakes Tom nary a whit. "Thank you for your cooperation," he says, and I detect none of the sarcasm I know he's implying. "Now we're going to need some further help."

"Indeed. In what way?"

"Tell me how the evaluations for Dr. Salter have been handled, once they were collected."

She appears relieved it's such a simple question. "Well, that's no secret. The student who administers the evaluations . . ."

Tom interrupts. "Salter wouldn't have done that himself?"

She looks shocked. "Of course not. That would invalidate the integrity of the results. Now, as I was saying, the student brings them here. We send them over to computing where they run the summary sheets. After that they're returned to this office, the dean looks them over, and then they're held until the following semester when they're forwarded to the chair—Dr. Salter in this case—for his examination. We allow them to stay a maximum of two months, and by the end of that time the forms are to be returned here for storage."

"You have just the department chairs' forms here?"

"Yes. Those for ordinary faculty are kept in the appropriate department offices, but the procedure is much the same."

I don't like the word "ordinary" being applied to me. I never liked Vivian, and today hasn't done anything to improve her status.

"Is there any way someone could add an extra form to a set?"

"Absolutely not," she snaps.

But I know that's not true. "Really, Vivian. You know that, when they're returned, your student assistant often places them on that counter by her desk where they could stay an hour or more until they're filed. Anyone could come by the office while they're easily available."

"They shouldn't be left out like that."

"But they are. I've seen them several times."

"Well, I'll make sure it doesn't occur again."

Tom reenters the conversation, "But apparently it could have happened with Dr. Salter's latest evaluation?"

She's forced into the admission. "I guess so, but only if it was last Friday. That's when he returned his from the previous semester."

"Who would have access to the office while the evaluations were on the counter?"

I see Vivian's defenses building again and decide to answer myself. "It could be anyone, Tom. Faculty, students, staff, even parents, are in and out of this office all day long."

"Students, huh?"

I know he's thinking of David. I'm beginning to worry about that boy.

CHAPTER 32

Thursday Morning and Afternoon

"What's next, Tom?" I ask.

"Let's go to Conroy Hall and look at Frazier's student evaluations. You said it'd be a good idea."

As we begin the jaunt to the math department I reply, "All I meant was so you could see how they compare with Ken's. I certainly don't believe you'll learn anything useful about the murder. You're not thinking you will, are you?"

"No. It's mainly because you've aroused my curiosity. You and Theresa have heaped such high praise on him that I want to see if his students feel the same. By the way, what's Sherwin doing today?"

I'm startled. I'd completely forgotten about Elmo, ever since I worried about him finding Donna's coffee. He must have been still asleep when I left this morning. I have a feeling if he'd been awake he would have been painfully obvious. That means Donna had to deal with him on her own. I don't imagine that will improve my standing. Then I perk up. Maybe I can be disciplined again. "I don't know, Tom. But he said yesterday he wanted to spend the day going over Ken's proof."

We were almost at the entrance to Conroy when who should emerge? You guessed it. Elmo. He positively beams when he catches sight of us.

"Tom, Jim! Great day, huh? Off for some lunch. Want to join me?" It's only shortly after 11:00, so we demur. "Damn. Like to have your company. Gotta go now, though. Kinda hungry. Donna gave me a wonderful breakfast, bran and other terribly healthy stuff. Loved it, but stomach's growling." I don't know how he did it, but to prove his point his stomach did a fair imitation of Niagara Falls.

I ask him, "How's the proof holding up?"

"Hardly started to look at the details. Got myself situated in your office. Hope you don't mind. Secretary didn't want to let me in, but I said you'd okayed it. Well, got to run."

He's gone before I have a chance to be polite. In reality, though, I don't feel polite. I don't like the idea of him being in my office, mainly because I've got to find some uninterrupted time to finish grading those damn exams.

Tom seems suddenly cheerful. "Still glad you asked Elmo to join us?"

What can I do? Pride makes me hiss, "Of course."

We're now on the ninth floor of Conroy Hall, about to enter the math office when I spy George Frazier coming towards us. "I'm going to tell him we're planning to look at his evaluations."

I thought that might upset Tom, but I just don't like doing things behind a colleague's back. Tom surprises me by saying, "Sure. Why not?"

"Hi Jim, Sergeant. Still searching the hallowed halls for a murderer, I see."

Appears much too cheerful for a homicide suspect, seems to me. Especially one who gained so significantly from the victim's death.

"It's a serious business, Dr. Frazier."

"Of course it is, and I wish you success. Now, if you'll excuse me, I want to get back to my lab and work on that program I told you about."

"One thing, George. Tom wants to look at your student evaluations from the last few years. Any objections?"

George's puzzled. "Certainly not. But why on earth would that be of interest to you?"

Tom speaks up. "I must confess to a certain curiosity. I've heard so many wonderful comments about your teaching, and, of course, I saw you in action Tuesday. I'd just like to see how students respond to your style."

He shrugs. "Well, feel free. See you later, Jim." As he starts to leave, George turns back and says, "Say, why don't you stop by my class again at 1:00. I'm doing something I always enjoy and I'd love for you to see it."

Tom seems hesitant, and I say, "I thought you were giving an exam today."

"I am, but I usually like to take the first five minutes to try to relax the students. That's all of your time it would require, and then you could leave when I distribute the tests."

I want to see George in his element again and say so. Tom, without much grace, agrees to accompany me.

I look at Tom's grim visage. "Cheer up," I say. "He'll give you a good show, and before then we'll just have time to look at his evaluations and grab a bite to eat." Secretly I'm hoping this will speed up our examination of those forms. Tom likes to eat.

He agrees to the plan. We can't find Susan Barber in the math office and we need her to get the evaluations. One of the secretaries says, "She's helping Dr. Zhang. Something about his computer not working."

"Thanks, Ellen, we'll go to his office."

Tom looks at me. "She fixes faculty computers?"

"You bet! She probably knows more about the way they work than anyone in the department, even George. She's taken all kinds of special courses, even a couple for technicians at the vocational school. When something goes wrong, with either software or hardware, we all turn to her."

"Pretty handy."

"She's been a godsend many times. Here's Zhang's office." I poke my head in. "Hi, Xin, having computer problems?"

"Hello, Jim. Yes, but I think Susan's about got it licked."

Our administrative assistant says, "Just a bad setting. I think it should work fine now, Dr. Zhang, but let me know if you have any more problems."

"Thank you, Susan."

I say, "Susan, we need your help."

For the first time she notices Tom and her eyes fill with alarm. She comes into the hallway and warily asks, "Yes?"

"A simple request. We want to look at George Frazier's student evaluations for the last three years. He says it's okay." She seems perplexed, but says nothing.

In silence we return to the main office where she retrieves George's six folders and hands them to me. We settle in an unused conference room to peruse them. The process goes fast. Tom really is doing this out of curiosity, not hoping for anything enlightening to show up as far as the case is concerned. Occasionally he mutters some of his findings, which reflect exactly what I expected we'd see. "They sure give him high marks for being prepared, making himself available, and caring about the students . . . here's a person that thanks him for taking the time just to talk to her when she was having problems with her family . . . gosh, he even came in on Saturdays to hold extra help sessions. I guess you're right, Jim, about being demanding not meaning low evaluations. This one says he's never worked so hard in a course in his life, or taken so many notes, like that girl in his class told me. Then he continues that he's never learned as much either and concludes with a simple 'Thanks, Doc.'"

"Had enough?" I ask.

"Yeah. And I think it was worthwhile. Now I can more easily believe that Salter's evaluations were an indication of the man rather than the fact he was a tough teacher."

"Well, I could have told you that! In fact I did!" Am I sounding a bit petulant? "Ready to eat? There's a fast-food spot not far away and we can be back in plenty of time for George's class."

Tom agrees and we carry out the plan. Now we're settling in the same classroom we visited Tuesday. George already is at the front and on the dot of one he starts. He smiles at the students and says, "All excited about your wonderful opportunity today?"

Of course, he's referring to the upcoming exam and not surprisingly a good-natured moan sweeps the room. A lad in the third row attired in a tee shirt promoting a rock group's tour and pants whose legs meet in an anatomically incorrect position speaks up, "I heard the exam was canceled."

George laughs outright, along with several others. "Good try, Randy. Now, you know how I like to spend the first couple of minutes on exam days talking about subjects I find interesting. Today's little discussion is on language, the language of mathematics. Remember how I've told you a bit about that?"

Do you recall that girl I inadvertently noticed with the short, short, short shorts in George's class? Alas, today she's ensconced in traditional jeans. She's the one who replies. "You mean, like, parentheses are different from braces and you've got to use the right type or the reader may not understand what's being said?"

"Exactly! Today I want to mention something that's related and which I think is really neat: symbolic equivalences for entire word expressions. Let me show you."

And George writes the following on the blackboard:

$$\forall \varepsilon > 0 \ \exists \delta > 0 \ni |x - x_0| < \delta \Rightarrow |f(x) - f(x_0)| < \varepsilon$$

"You may or may not recognize this from the first semester of calculus. It's the formal definition of continuity, and we didn't dwell on it in Calc

I. The thing that turns me on about this is it so compactly says so much. Now, don't take notes. Just listen and have fun. Let me read its meaning. 'For all epsilon greater than zero, there exists a delta greater than zero such that the absolute value of x minus x sub 0 less than delta implies the absolute value of f of x minus f of x sub 0 is less than epsilon.' Notice how long that sentence is, and how efficient the equivalent notation is. Are you familiar with the symbols? Of course, you know those vertical bars refer to the absolute value of the enclosed quantity, and the Greek letters epsilon, the character that looks like a small e, and delta that looks a bit like a d. Then there are other symbols that help to make the expression so compact. Take that one at the beginning that seems to be an upside down A. It means 'for all' or 'for each.' Then there's the backward capital E which can be interpreted as 'there exists' or 'there is' or some similar expression. Finally the backward small e means 'such that' while the arrow stands for 'implies.' Now you've got to admit that's neat."

One of our fellow back seaters pipes up with, "And you say this is what turns you on, Dr. Frazier?"

"Sure does."

"Get a life, man!"

George joins the laughter. I notice the pre-exam tension apparent at the beginning of the class has evaporated and again I admire George's art. He's done all he can to prevent the students from freezing from math anxiety and doing poorly on the test. He begins distributing the examination and Tom and I leave.

Tom heads towards the exit and I tag along. He looks at me, shaking his head. "What was that all about? If I were taking an exam I wouldn't want a bunch of crap interrupting my thoughts at the beginning."

I smile at him. "Remember, Tom, when you took math classes? What do you remember the tests being like?"

He'd told me once and he repeats it now. "You know I'm terrible at math. I'd be shaking so hard it'd be 15 minutes before I'd calm down enough to remember anything."

"And just maybe you're not as bad in math as you think, but you did poorly on exams because all you could think of was that *is* how you'd perform. I think George was just trying to relieve the anxiety a bit."

It's clear Tom hasn't considered that possibility. "Do you think it works?"

"I don't know," I admit. "I'm strictly a 'hit 'em with it the moment they come to an exam' guy. The mathematically oriented people aren't going to be bothered one way or another, yet people like you might be helped."

"Maybe." He's unconvinced. Of course, his job and his past mathematics experience make him a doubting fellow. "Frazier doesn't do much by the book, does he?"

"More so than you might think, but there's nothing that says following the book produces effective teaching." I notice I've followed Tom outside. "This is where I leave you," and I start to turn back.

"Hold on. I'd like you to meet an old friend."

CHAPTER 33

Thursday Afternoon

"Tom, I have a job I get paid for, you know. And I've got to start doing it."

"Come on. You'll like him. Barry Schwartz. Know him?"

"I think I've served on a committee with him. What's he got to do with this?"

"Just bear with me." I follow Tom's lead to the building housing the English department. We climb the stairs to the main office on the second floor and Tom approaches the secretary nearest the door. Another beautiful young woman. I swear the pretty females on a college campus are innumerable.

"What ken I do for youse?"

As so often happens, I'm suddenly reminded that not only is Donna gorgeous, but she's also smart and knows how to talk.

Tom replies, "I'd like to see Professor Schwartz, please."

"Sure. His room's 237. Let me call him foist ta see ifin he's in. Kin I tell him who y'are?"

"Tom Warren, an old friend from college."

She looks at him wide-eyed. "Hey, aren't youse the one here 'bout that murder. Gor. You don't think Dr. Schwartz done it?"

Tom laughs. "No. Nothing like that. I was passing by and thought I'd drop in."

Just passing by? I think not. She's clearly excited as she dials. Her voice is breathy.

"Dr. Schwartz? There's a Mr. Tom Warren and some other guy here to see youse. Says he's an old friend . . . Sure, I'll send 'em right down."

She points the way and we thank her. In the corridor a big—tall and wide—man is coming towards us, waving with enthusiasm. He's not the one I'd served on a committee with. I'd have remembered this guy.

"Tom, you son-of-a-bitch. God, it's good to see you. How long's it been now? Two years? Three?"

"Too long, Barry, that's for sure." The two friends shake hands and Tom introduces me. "Barry was on the football team when I was. A guard. Made it possible for me to hog all the glory."

"Yup. The unsung hero is what I was." Barry has a charming grin. Like another big man—Elmo—he turns out to be a gentle and engaging guy.

"You have a wonderful secretary for the English department."

"Ah, Effie. Yeah, she has a bit of a problem with the language, doesn't she? But a heart of gold. And can she type! I've heard about the murder, of course, Tom, and that you're directing the investigation. How's it going?"

"Frustrating at the moment. I wish this was just a pleasure call, Barry, but I need your help."

I glance at Tom sharply. How can an ex-buddy ex-football player English professor help solve a mathematician's murder? Suddenly I don't seem to mind the lost time one bit.

Barry rolls his eyes. "Might have known. Do I have to run interference for you again?"

"Nothing so strenuous, I hope. Something more intellectually challenging. After all, you were the team genius, Academic All American as I recall."

Barry looks at me, "Be careful where you step, Jim. He really must want something. Okay, let's have it."

"You told me about your dissertation once. As I recall, you analyzed Elizabethan poetry of unknown authorship and attempted to determine characteristics of the writer. The goal was to identify whose work it was. Am I right?"

"Yes and no. That was what was intended. Mostly what I was able to accomplish was to take works by known poets and try to determine their personality characteristics just by interpreting what they wrote, checking my findings against what was generally understood about their lives. Then I tried to apply the techniques to works by other poets that were submitted to me by my advisor, but without telling me who wrote them. Finally, I'd go back and again check against known facts."

"How did it work out?"

"Mixed results. My final conclusion was that more work might refine the technique, but I didn't believe it to be a reliable method for determining who wrote a specific piece."

"Still, it might be possible to tell something about the author?"

Barry's hesitant and answers only after some heavy thinking. "Maybe," he says doubtfully. "But what does this have to do with your murder?"

I think I know, and Tom soon confirms it. He tells Barry about the report and, to my surprise, the extra student evaluation, giving him a copy of each.

"Once you read these, I think you'll understand my interest. I'd like to learn two things. First, anything you can tell me about the authors. And, second, are the two authors the same?"

"Aw, I don't know, Tom. Like I always say, the main benefit of my dissertation work was to get me my degree." I like this guy. Unpretentious, honest. So many of us in academe become bloated with our importance. "I'd really be hesitant to apply it to an important situation."

"Look, Barry. I'm sure as hell not going to arrest somebody just because of what you tell me. This is a tough case and, quite frankly, I'm stuck. I need all the help I can get and anything you can provide would be appreciated. I'll take it in the spirit in which you offer it."

Barry continues to look unhappy, but he says, "Well, all right, under those conditions. What's your time frame? Next week be okay?"

Uh, oh. I know Barry's problem. He already has a full schedule, like me, and he'll have to fit this extra work in, like me. But Tom doesn't worry about such picayune matters. "Sorry. I need your answer by tomorrow."

"Tomorrow! Impossible. I've got a grant proposal I have to finish by Monday."

"Oh, then you should have plenty of time." Tom does not understand the difficulties of preparing a winning proposal. "Please, Barry. It's important."

Barry is not thrilled, but I can sense his mind calculating and rescheduling his immediate future. "Okay. But I have limited time I can devote to it, so all you'll get will be an off the cuff opinion."

"Anything you can do will be helpful. I really appreciate it. Can I take you for some coffee?"

"Are you kidding? I didn't have any time before you came. What do you think it's like now? Just get out and let me start working." I wave goodbye while the two friends clasp hands. Barry may have sounded annoyed but he's not. "Don't make it so long next time."

Tom smiles. "How does tomorrow sound?"

Barry punches him in the shoulder in that way athletes do to each other, and we take our leave. Tom finally sets me free and I return to my office, ready to spend an hour grading. I've forgotten about Elmo. At least until I find my door wide open and hear mutterings. Entering, I find Elmo firmly installed behind my desk, my papers pushed aside. He doesn't even notice my presence. I decide he's involved in Ken's proof, so, not wanting to disturb him, I extract my briefcase in the utmost silence and find a table in the lounge. A couple of graduate students are drinking coffee and working out a problem on one of the whiteboards, but they won't bother me.

I open the briefcase, intending to remove my ungraded exams. But on top is the copy of the email messages Elmo had received. I figure it won't hurt if I spend a few minutes with it. After all, Elmo had thought it worth a great deal of his time last night, although he confessed to me later he didn't see anything significant in it and had abandoned it as a clue. I figure that, if Elmo couldn't, surely I won't be able to either. But it can't hurt to look, can it? So I place the sheet on the table in front of me and give myself 10 minutes to examine it. Twenty minutes later I see it. I can't believe my eyes.

It's going to blow the way we've been thinking about the case sky high.

CHAPTER 34

Thursday Evening

I can't wait for our regular evening meeting to begin, bursting as I am with my mind-boggling discovery.

I know you're worried about my exam. Yes, I finished grading it. I never did find enough time for additional preparation for tomorrow's classes, but any experienced teacher can fake his way through at least one period without the students sensing too much wrong.

When I'm grading, my mind is riveted on the task. Worries, pains, and dreams; which might have seemed so important earlier, fade into oblivion. Thus I gave no thought to my great discovery. Until exactly one second after the last exam was added to the completed pile. From then on I could think of nothing else. On the drive home I kept envisioning myself as the conquering hero whose startling deductive reasoning has pulled the investigative team from its morass of confusing facts. Okay, okay, so chasing windmills is fun for me. Don't knock it. You'd be surprised at the vicarious thrills you can get that way, and without encountering the dangers of real life.

Then I recall. This *is* real life. The thought sobers me. For about 10 seconds. Then, as I pull into the driveway, I once again am consumed with the wonder of my discovery. I fear I'm building it up too much and when you hear it you'll be disappointed. Nah. Not this.

I've poured the last of my after-dinner decaf down my throat and shout to Donna, who's gone upstairs to change, "Isn't it time we get going?"

We're due at Theresa's at 7:30. It's a 10-minute drive from our home. It's 7:05 now. You work it out. Donna certainly did as she entered the room, looking particularly luscious I might add in tight jeans, a gorgeous green blouse, tight jeans, sandals, and tight jeans. She grins at my lascivious look. "I think we have plenty of time to get to Theresa's," she says with amusement. "You're onto something, aren't you?"

"Maybe." I don't want to reveal anything ahead of time, even to my soul mate. I really do crave center stage. I try not to think that way, but what can I do? I'm a ham.

Donna knows me. "Don't worry, lover. I'm not going to spoil your evening, so you don't have to spill your guts."

I'm relieved. Because if she demanded edification I'd have been putty in her hands. Which she would have made use of to obtain her goals.

"Do you think what you've discovered will pinpoint the murderer?"

I'm brought up short and have to face the limitations of my brilliance. "Er, no, I don't think so. But it should get us thinking in another direction." Momentarily depressed by the thought of being unable to say, "And this means that you, (fill in the proper name—do you have a guess yet?), killed Kenneth Salter on Sunday last." No I can't do that. But I do reconvince myself that my input will be valuable. It really will. You'll see.

Donna gives me a hug. Then she gets serious. "I hope it does help. I don't like murder, and I want whoever killed Ken caught."

"Me too, baby."

Then Donna finally says the beautiful words I've been hungering for. "It's time to leave."

Suddenly I remember our guest. I seem to be forgetting him a lot lately, and, given the way he is, that's fairly remarkable. "Where's Elmo?"

"He called just before you got home. Said he suddenly realized the time; he'd been completely wrapped up in Ken's proof. He's picking up his own dinner and will meet us at Theresa's."

"Does he know how to get there?"

"I assume so. He was there last night, after all. Now let's go."

So we do, again arriving at the appointed hour and, again, later than Tom. We enter and find Elmo not yet present. The phone rings and Theresa excuses herself. When she returns she says icily, "That was Elmo, from his cellular phone. He's lost. I've given him explicit directions so I hope he can negotiate the remaining distance."

"Where is he?"

"The next block over. Honestly, that man! He'd better prove himself useful, Jim."

The remark from my former teacher sort of takes the edge off my excitement. Again I wonder how wise it was to include Elmo. We make small talk until a loud crunch interrupts. Tom and I rush to the door to see Elmo, who has parked in the drive, emerge from his car and inspect a city issued recycling container now ready for its own reincarnation. I notice "Bedlow" painted on its mangled side. I sense this is not going to improve the already strained relations between Elmo and our host.

Theresa's at the door now, taking in the damage. Elmo sees her, then hangs his head. "Terribly sorry, Theresa. I'll arrange to get you another one, of course. Just came at me out of nowhere."

Now that's a bit hard to swallow, so I'm shocked when Theresa responds, "It's all right, Elmo. The garbage men often place emptied containers onto my driveway, and I didn't get around to putting them back in place today." I start to breathe easier.

Finally all of us are settled and Theresa turns to Tom. "What have you accomplished today?" Seems to me she could have turned to me. After all, I'm the one with the exciting news. Of course, only Donna knows that. And she might not be so sure how important it is.

But no, I've got to listen to all the stuff I'm already familiar with. Okay, so the other people aren't, but then they're not bursting with information. Tom describes our examination of Ken's and George's student evaluations, emphasizing the threatening one. He's made a copy of both sides of it for everyone and indicates he's convinced it was added to the original set of evaluations while the folder containing them was sitting on a counter in the Dean's office.

"Should be easy to check," says Elmo.

Tom shows interest. "How so?"

"Well, can't tell for sure when it was incorporated, but should be able to determine if it wasn't handed in with the rest."

"It does have a different date on it from the others. But how could we find out for sure?"

"Don't know if the date's important. Probably is, but we have a clever murderer who might have planned ahead. Whatever. Up at Sloane we get a summary sheet with our evaluations."

"Same here," I offer.

"For us that sheet includes the total number of respondents, so all you'd have to do is count the evaluations and compare 'em to the value given on the sheet. If you've got one extra, you'd *know* something funny was going on."

My God, I think Tom's looking at Elmo almost with respect. Great strides are being made tonight. It's an obvious check and I wish I'd thought of it.

Tom says, "Sounds like a good idea. I'll look into it tomorrow. Of course, I suppose the person adding the new evaluation could have removed another."

"Sure. Anything's possible, but I bet he didn't."

Tom shrugs and reiterates his determination to make the requisite count. Now he's describing our visit with Barry Schwartz and the assignment he's given the English professor. "He promised me his opinion tomorrow." He does not describe Barry's reluctance to respond so quickly or even to take on the project.

Tom looks at my beautiful wife. How can he do that without salivating? I barely can. Of course, if he did we'd probably have to have words. "You've had another day to think about that report by Avila, Donna. You've told us what was in it. But now I'm asking the same question I posed to Barry. Can you deduce anything about the author?"

"I've been giving some thought to that, but all I can come up with are general observations."

"Anything, Donna. Anything at all."

"There's a troubling dichotomy throughout. On one side is moral outrage at the evil actions of the manipulator, supposedly Ken, and on the other is the completely amoral justification of murder. Then there's the sensitive understanding of the feelings of those hurt, and the cruel lack of sentiment for Ken. Finally there's almost an appeal for the reader to approve of the advocated actions, and simultaneously a haughty disdain for disagreement about them. I think our murderer has both a strong feminine side and a strong masculine one."

"Which, of course, makes me ask if you have a feeling for whether the killer is a man or woman?"

"I don't see any way of telling. Both a man and a woman can demonstrate characteristics normally attributable to both. Jim, for example, has an extremely lovable feminine side."

Great, I think. Just what a guy wants said to a group of his friends. Especially in front of a former fullback. On the other hand, there are benefits directly attributable to Donna thinking that way about me, and those benefits without a doubt relate to my male side. I see Tom's ready to move on. It's going to be my turn now. In my fondest dreams, it turns out. Well, not my fondest ones. He then indicates he took the offending evaluation to a handwriting expert this afternoon, and again expected a report tomorrow. Where was I, I wondered. I'm unwilling to accept the fact I'd been bugging Tom all afternoon to turn me loose. Well, he did and apparently carried on just fine without me. Unbelievable, isn't it?

Anyway, now surely it's my time. Aghast, I listen to Tom. "Late this afternoon I made a list of our main suspects, along with their motives and alibis. I've got a copy for each of you." He distributes them and I glance at mine. Maybe waiting for my exposé was a good idea, for this seems the perfect segue. I repeat Tom's list here, although I know you'd prefer to hear my revelation.

Suspect	Motive	Alibi
Harriet Salter Wife	Mental abuse Other women Need to assert self	Neighbors over for drinks, sandwiches 1630 to 2200
Stephen Farnsworth Dean	Blackmail about research Fear for position	Early bird dinner, movie with another couple, parted after 2230
Richard Brighthurst Assistant Chairman	Jealousy, wanted chair Financial difficulties Shabbily treated	Call from ill professor 1730; Call to Professor Baker—spoke to her husband, she called back at 1815; family and son's friends in and out, 1700 to 2100
George Frazier Assistant Professor	Fear of promotion/tenure denial	Working in office with two graduate students 1630 to 2200, then out for beer
Susan Barber Secretary to Salter	Rejected lover	Bridge party 1730 to 2100
David Simmons Student	Mocked in class Possibly unstable	At home. Seen frequently by parents
Harvey Delsanter Rival	Long-term feud Jealous of Salter solving Collins Conjecture	Family barbecue 1730

After we've all had time to examine the list, Tom complains, "Every damn one of them has a perfect alibi!"

This is my moment. "Maybe not," I say much louder than is absolutely necessary.

CHAPTER 35

Thursday Evening

Donna smiles, knowing how I've been looking forward to this moment. Tom is startled and Elmo appears interested. Theresa, who seems to get annoyed so easily these days, says, "You've been fidgeting all evening, Jim. If you've got something to contribute, spit it out."

I wonder what's bugging her, but her words do serve to remind me of the seriousness of our work and I settle down. "It has to do with the email messages Elmo received. Do you have that sheet I gave you last night?"

Everyone but Elmo has remembered to bring all pertinent materials, and Donna says Elmo may look on with her. Donna and I squeeze together on the couch—a sacrifice I am only too willing to make—so Elmo can sit on her other side. He says, "Spent a lot of time pondering that sheet myself. You might have noticed. Couldn't see anything, though. Say you did, huh, Jim?"

"I think so. Examine the communications and see if anything strikes you as odd." I know Elmo's failed to find significance in the messages, but I don't believe the others have given any thought to them at all.

I've goofed. I'm still in game mode while the others aren't playing. "Just tell us, Jim," snaps Theresa.

"Okay. Look at the times."

```
From: Jordan <Jordan@sci.mit.edu>
Subject: Colloquium
Date: March 12, 2011 11:53:14 AM EST
To: Elmo@mat.sloane.edu

Elmo, can you speak at our mathematics seminar April
15 on a subject of your choosing? Please let me know
by Friday.
                              Nancy
```

```
From: Salter <salter@math.mrsu.edu>
Subject: Collins Conjecture
Date: March 13, 2011 5:07:47 PM EST
To: Analysis group

This is to announce that today I have answered the
Collins Conjecture in the affirmative. I will publish
the proof shortly, but interested parties can contact
me directly any time.

             Kenneth Salter
             Marcus Rome State University
```

```
From: Singh <singh@mat.sloane.edu>
Subject: Dinner
Date: March 13, 2011 1:35:14 PM EST
To: Elmo

Elmo, just a reminder you and Michelle are coming to
dinner Thursday night—6:30.   S.
```

```
From: Albright <albright@math.mrsu.edu>
Subject: Conference on Differential Equations
Date: March 13, 2011 2:15:20 PM EST
To: DE

A conference on differential equations will be held at
Marcus Rome State University next year in October on
dates to be announced in the near future. Please direct
all inquiries to James Albright, Conference Chairman.
```

Tom's annoyed. "We've been through that. Salter's message was sent at 5:07 Sunday afternoon. That's why we know he died after then."

Wow, I didn't know Tom could talk regular time. "Yes. But look at my message too." Light dawns in Elmo's eyes, but the others stare blankly. Not wanting to risk further reproof, I move on. "I also transmitted a message about a conference I'm chairing. I was at home at the time, remotely logged onto the MRSU network. Thus two messages initiating at MRSU and terminating with Elmo were sent Sunday afternoon."

Donna's learned enough about computers to handle word processing, but she studiously has avoided assimilating one more byte of information than absolutely necessary. So I'm not surprised when she says, "I don't even see why those two messages came to Elmo. At least his name appears in the 'To' field of the others."

I'm dismissive. "What both Ken and I did was create mailing lists, his called 'Analysis group' and mine 'DE.' When you send a message to such a name, it's automatically transmitted to everyone on the list. The key here is the times of the messages."

Elmo's nodding enthusiastically, beaming at me. He never minds when others accomplish things he fails at, massive results like Ken's or minor ones like this of mine. Tom and Donna, however, remain perplexed, but I think I see understanding dawning in Theresa's eyes. She says, "Your message was sent about quarter after two in the afternoon."

"Exactly! And I know that's right."

"So what?" from an exasperated Tom.

"Well, I'm no expert, but here's what I understand. MRSU has something called mail servers that handle all the email routed to the university. The source for them might be local or remote. The servers then deliver these emails to the proper destinations."

"Like I said, so what?"

"Here's the key point. The servers transmit the messages to their recipients in the order they're received."

"Yeah?"

"So if my message was created at 2:15 and Ken's at 5:07, *why did Elmo receive Ken's first?*"

Utter silence, as we all ponder the implications. Tom appears impressed. "What do you think it means, Jim?"

"I know it doesn't make sense, but Ken's message had to have been sent before mine, before 2:15."

Donna asks the obvious question. "Then how did the wrong time get on Ken's message?"

"I wish I knew, darling. But it had to have happened."

Theresa offers a path to an answer. "I think Oscar Shepinfield could help you explain it."

"Who's he?"

"He's the Manager of Networks and Systems."

That's the outfit that supplies central computing facilities to the university. Most of the people there work in the background, so it's not surprising I've never heard of this guy.

Tom's looking at me. "Jim?"

Oh no. He's going to use me again. "Yeah?"

"How about talking to Shepinfield tomorrow; see if you can dig up an explanation for this."

Actually, I don't mind. I have my classes but I'll find the time. As I've said before, research will have to wait. "Okay."

"And, Jim," says Theresa, "let me know if he gives you any problem." She seems amused I'll be speaking with him.

"There's no reason he should, is there?"

"You'll see. He's an interesting individual. Of course, you all realize what this means."

It's Tom who speaks for all of us. "All those perfect alibis don't count worth a damn."

CHAPTER 36

Friday Morning

I pull myself from bed at an ungodly hour. I want to see Oscar Shepinfield before my 11:00 class. It has been a restless sleep, thoughts of the case drifting in and out of consciousness. And I'm worried about my brilliance of the previous evening. Could my conclusion be wrong? I don't see how. If Elmo got Ken's message before mine, then Ken must have sent his first. It's that simple. I'm looking forward to talking with Shepinfield.

I glance adoringly at Donna, but realize it's a minimum hour and a half before she'll be communicative. I get up, shave, and dress. As I make my way to the kitchen I hear the guest shower running and a barely recognizable version of *Old MacDonald had a Farm*. The words are unfamiliar, obviously the product of an eccentric mathematician. ". . . and on his farm he had a skunk, eeyi eeyi o, with a phew, phew here and a phew, phew there, here a phew, there a phew, everywhere a phew, phew. Old MacDonald had a farm, eeyi eeyi o." Other singularly uninspiring verses follow. I listen with awe before shaking my head and advancing to the kitchen.

I scramble enough eggs for three—one share for me and two for Elmo—pour some orange juice, and start coffee. Elmo lumbers in as I finish setting the table. "Mornin', Jim. Looks like a beautiful day."

"Sure does. Here, have some eggs."

"Thankee, thankee. Quite a good cook, aren't ya? Tried cooking myself once. But now Michelle's banned me from the kitchen. She didn't like it when the fire department had to come. Suppose I shouldn't have left the cookbook on the burner. And I guess it wasn't a good idea to throw the damn book, burning like it was, across the room towards the sink. Was it my fault I missed and hit the curtains instead? Could have happened to anyone, don't you think? Can't understand why Michelle was so upset, especially since she got to redo the kitchen. Insurance company was real nice."

For a moment I stare at this genius, wondering how on earth he could be such a klutz. And questioning how safe it was to have him in my home. But then he erases all doubt from my mind.

"Mighty nice piece of work, Jim, on those messages. Completely missed it myself."

"Thanks. Had some doubts for a while this morning. But I don't see how the conclusion can be wrong."

"It isn't. Have faith in yourself, young feller."

Now Elmo's maybe five years older than I am—at most. But I guess being thought of as a young "feller" isn't so bad. "You know, Elmo, I was so caught up last night in those emails of yours I forgot all about Ken's proof. How's it coming?"

"Real well. The bastard was a genius. His prissy scrawl drives me crazy, but what it says is magic."

"No mistakes, then?"

"None yet. Just beauty and elegance."

"Have you gone through all of it?"

"Not in the detail I need to. I should be finished today. By the way, is it all right if I use your office again. Got a nice atmosphere to it, easy to concentrate."

No. But I say, "Sure. Want to ride in with me?"

"That'd be great if it's no trouble. When will you be returning?"

"Late afternoon. How's that for you?"

"Perfect. What are you gonna do today?"

"I'll try to see Oscar Shepinfield first thing. I've got classes at 11:00 and 1:00 with a meeting at 12:00."

"Sounds like a busy three hours there. This Oscar feller is the network guru?"

"Yeah. I've never met him, but I swear I've heard his name somewhere. Wonder what Theresa thinks is in store for me. She seemed pretty amused about my speaking with him. Probably some weird hacker."

"Well, I'll be glad to hear what you learn. Wish I could make more of a contribution."

"There's still time, Elmo."

"True. By the way, feel free to use your office today. Won't bother me a bit."

A weak smile is my response to this magnanimous gesture concerning *my* office. We leave shortly thereafter, but first I return to the bedroom to nuzzle Donna's awakening face. After arriving at school, I install Elmo in my office and then head to Oscar Shepinfield's locale.

I've formed a mental picture of the man. He's in his mid-twenties, large boned, long hair, granny glasses, never sleeps, pocket protector doing its job against several pens and pencils, leather sandals, and spaced out. The reality couldn't differ more. I find a small man in his late forties with a crew cut, shirt and tie, dark-blue suit pants, and spit polished shoes. I was right about the glasses and pocket protector, though. His eyes flash over me and continually dart around the room.

He has no idea who I am and appears uncertain why anyone would want to speak with him. "You were looking for me?"

It's tough to know what form of address to use around a university. This guy doesn't inspire the use of his first name, and I doubt he has a doctorate. But I might be wrong. Do I insult him by not calling him "Doctor" when he has the degree or do I humiliate him by using the title when he doesn't? Ah, life is hard. I settle on the following. "Mr. Shepinfield, I'm Jim Albright from the math department. You've heard about the problem we've had over there?"

"Something wrong with your computers? Oh, my. Haven't heard a thing. You've certainly contacted the wrong person, though. Definitely. I'm not the one to come to. People never do, you know. You should be calling the Help Desk."

"No, no. It's not our computers. I was referring to the murder last Sunday of our chairman."

I thought his eyes moved rapidly before. Now they're in hyper mode, a mouse searching for escape. I'm sure he's uncomfortable outside his normal work habitat. He says, "Oh, yes. Terrible, Yes, terrible. What's that got to do with me?"

"Well, in the investigation," and I swell with self-importance, "we've come across something puzzling about the way email works, and I understand you're an expert."

"What is it? Email's pretty simple to use. If you're having trouble understanding it, we've put out a manual. The receptionist can get you one. Or you can download it. Hope that helps. Now, if you'll excuse me I've got to get back to work."

"Actually, Mr. Shepinfield, it's not basic user info we want. We need to understand how you actually process the messages."

"Oh, I couldn't discuss that. No. No. It would take too much time and I simply don't have it. There are books describing it in detail. You can find them in the library. Sorry. Wish I could help more. Got to run."

"I'm afraid I'm going to have to insist. It's vital to the investigation. You do want us to catch the murderer, don't you?" Do I sound like a detective or not?

"Certainly, certainly. Wish I could help. But I simply can't give you what you want. Besides, although the algorithms and protocols are well known, revealing specific configuration details could compromise security. I'm right, am I not, you're just faculty? Faculty have no authorization. So couldn't help you. No sir. Sorry."

What is it with this guy? And I certainly don't appreciate the status he's assigning faculty. Besides, every computer nut I've known hasn't given a damn about rules. Until now. "Would it help if Vice-President Bedlow okayed it?"

He looks relieved. "Oh, well, yes. Of course. No problem there. Tell you what. I'll write a memo requesting authorization. Try to get to it today. Monday at the latest. Or maybe by the middle of next week for sure. Should have an answer shortly thereafter. Why don't you call me in about a week?"

I can see Tom calmly listening to my explanation of why we're waiting a week for the answer. And I can see him responding to Shepinfield's bureaucratic mumblings. I think I'd better get tough. "Mr. Shepinfield, I don't mean to upset you," (there, didn't that sound threatening?) "but we're in the middle of a murder investigation and the detective in charge isn't going to wait a week for this information. Whether you like it or not, and whether I'm faculty or not, you're going to have to explain what I need to know. Now I suggest you call Dr. Bedlow's office immediately and receive the authorization."

"You mean right now? Talk to her in person? Oh, no. I couldn't do that."

"Here, I'll get you started." Notice how kind and understanding I'm being?

I look up Theresa's extension and dial. I identify myself to Elsie Martin (that's *Miss* Martin, you know) and she puts me through immediately. I sense my mentor's amusement. "With Oscar, are you, Jim?"

"Yeah. How did you know?"

"I figured you'd need me to get him to cooperate. The guy's a computer wizard, but such a finicky milquetoast. Put him on."

I hand the phone to Shepinfield. "Dr. Bedlow wants to speak with you."

I'm afraid he'll pass out. He's shaking as he takes the phone. I wish I could hear both sides of the conversation. "Hel . . . er, hello? . . . yes, came by a few minutes ago, wants me . . . no, certainly not. I wasn't trying to obstruct the investigation, but . . . yes. I see. Regulations be damned, you say?" He's staring at the phone, not believing what he hears. "Yes, sir, er, ma'am. Whatever you say . . . er, . . ." The poor guy's sweating. ". . . could you tell Vice President Johnson? Oh, thank you, ma'am . . . oh, yes, you have a nice day, too." Johnson is the VP of Information Systems and this guy's boss, and I gather Theresa has agreed to cover his ass. He replaces the phone on its cradle, still shaking his head. He looks at me resentfully. "Says I should tell you anything I can."

"Good. Now take a look at this sheet of email messages sent to someone at Sloane State."

He looks, and gasps. "These are to Professor Elmo Sherwin!"

I look at him quizzically. "Yes. Is that important?"

"No. Not at all. I used to work at Sloane before coming here. One time I got a call to go to his office. He was having some problems."

Interested, I couldn't help pursuing it. "What was wrong?"

"He couldn't get his computer to work, was terrified he'd lost all his files. Really panicked. I asked if he had backups. Of course, he didn't. So silly. How can people be as smart as they say he is and not make backups?"

He's indignant, so I vow not to tell him I have the same problem. Of course, I'm a saint compared to Donna's delinquency in observing this basic computer ethic. "Were you able to help him?"

He smiles smugly. "Most certainly. I plugged it in. One of the cleaning personnel apparently had knocked the cord with a vacuum."

He shakes his head in disbelief. He has a point. Even I would think to check the plug. On the other hand, I couldn't understand the proof to the Collins Conjecture. And neither could Shepinfield. But Elmo can.

Oscar seems to recall the purpose of my visit and his annoyed frown returns. "All right, let me look at that sheet again." It takes him less than a minute to find the problem. I should have brought it to him at the very beginning. "I see. Yes, yes. Very strange. The two messages from here seem to be out of order, judging by the times."

I'm impressed. Oscar may be a prissy dude, but he seems to know his stuff. I voice the only misgiving I've had. "Of course, I suppose it's possible the order got shuffled up at Sloane . . ."

He's incensed. "Absolutely not! I know their mail servers inside and out and I configured those systems myself. The emails will appear in the order in which they are received. The one from . . . let's see," he examines the sheet, ". . . from Kenneth Salter definitely arrived before yours."

"Then how do you account for the timing discrepancy?"

"I, er, um, I don't know. The only thing I can think of is . . . er, well, it's impossible."

He appears deeply troubled. "Impossible?" I say.

"Yes. You see, if Dr. Salter's message really was transmitted before yours, but the time says otherwise, then it means someone altered the clock in Salter's PC."

"Could Dr. Salter have done it for some reason."

"Oh, no." He's shocked. "Only someone with proper authorization and access codes could do that, assuming the computer was on our university network."

"It was."

"Well, then, that settles it. It couldn't have happened because no one on the access list would do such a thing."

This guy is going to drive me crazy. "Just pretend for a minute that someone was unscrupulous enough to do it. What would be required?"

He looks like he's dealing with an idiot. "Of course, he'd have to be able to edit the 'group policy.'"

"What's that?"

"It's administration software that controls system behavior throughout the network. Off limits to the typical user."

"Is time setting one of these functions?"

"Yes, there actually are several time stamps that are associated with any email. When the writer presses 'send' his local computer creates the initial one. Then additional time stamps are added as the email traverses through various servers including the one, in this case on the Sloane campus, that finally transmits the email to the recipient."

"I never see any of those on emails I receive."

He shakes his head in disgust. "Of course not. Mail clients usually are configured to hide all but the original one when the email is sent. That's the only time most are interested in."

"So are you saying that if that time was changed, as it appears to be here, the other times, presumably correct, would still be attached to the message in some way?"

"That's right."

"Could those times be obtained?"

"Of course. Mail clients usually provide a way to display them."

"And they would be able to show the message traversed the system in roughly the two o'clock period?"

"If that is what happened."

"Isn't that what must have happened?"

He shrugs.

I continue, "Now tell me how it could have been engineered."

"I told you it couldn't happen. None of our authorized people would do such a thing."

"But it did happen, didn't it?"

He barely whispers, "It seems so." Then, with more force, "But I don't believe it."

I'm becoming impatient and the need to get to my class is increasing. "Just tell me!"

"Well, there are a couple of necessary steps. The first of course, is having a login name and password for a domain administrator. Then the person would have to change the group policy to allow time on the computer to be altered."

"Is that easy?"

"It is, but it isn't fast because the change has to propagate through the network,"

"How long does it take?"

"It varies, but maybe as long as five minutes."

"Then what?"

"The person would change the time on the local computer, send the email, and then reverse the process so future time stamps would appear normal."

"Who's on this access list?"

"I can't reveal that. Sorry."

"Shall we call Dr. Bedlow again?"

This shakes him and he continues with little grace, "Oh, all right. I am, of course, and my boss. And a few key administrators, but only as a courtesy. For all practical purposes, all actions at that level are taken by me."

"I guess there's also another possibility."

"What do you mean?"

"Someone who isn't authorized. Couldn't a clever hacker break through your security system?"

"Absolutely not!" He's offended.

"At what level of security are grades and salary information kept?"

"The highest. Why?"

"Didn't you have someone bypass your security provisions not too long ago and change a grade, and at the same time set some salaries to zero. In fact, I've been trying to recall where I've heard your name before. Wasn't your salary one of them?"

He has the grace to look embarrassed. "Where did you hear that? It wasn't supposed to be revealed to outsiders."

"But it did happen?"

He scuffles the floor and examines his moving shoe. "Yes," he mutters so softly I can barely hear. "But that's completely different from the email system."

"Is it easier or more difficult to crack than the email?"

Again he's forced into an admission, "Harder."

"So why couldn't a computer geek somehow outwit your scheme and change the clock?"

He reacts to "geek" like I do to "math stuff." "What occurred before was a fluke. I've already upgraded the security on all systems and networks so it couldn't happen again."

"You mean, don't you, so someone couldn't break through in the same way as before?"

"Well, er, yes. That's what I had in mind when I did the reconfiguration."

"Can you positively eliminate the possibility some hacker could outwit your system."

He is decidedly unhappy. "No. I can't."

CHAPTER 37

Friday Afternoon

I couldn't wait to get away from Oscar Shepinfield. It's like I felt when I left Harvey Delsanter. Different people, different levels of decency, but same relief. I return to my office, again to find Elmo immersed in Ken's proof. I pull a chair up to my computer desk, shove the keyboard aside, and attempt to confine my papers to the cramped quarters.

My cell rings. My stomach sinks. It's Tom. "Hello, Tom."

"When are you free today?"

"My last class is over at ten to two. But I have lots of work."

"No time to talk now. Meet me at Barry's office at 1400."

"But, ..." He's disconnected. Damn. I consider calling him back. But you guessed it. Curiosity is my enemy and I decide to do as bid.

I look at Elmo. He has evidenced no movement. I doubt he's even noticed my presence, let alone my speech. Fascinated, I watch as I make a concerted effort to create an annoying noise by scraping my chair across the floor. Nothing. Maybe that's what separates him from us mere mortals. Intense powers of concentration. And, of course, a super intellect. A glance at my watch tells me to get to my graduate class.

The first job is to return the exams. Most will be happy. They're a talented group of students, except for a couple. On the two worst papers I've penned a note asking them to see me. Maybe I'll be able to get them on the right track, although I'm not too hopeful in at least one case. I still have 45 minutes to fill. It's my lucky day. I'm hit early on with a question about one of the assigned homework problems, and, even luckier, I know how to work it. Not always the case, I'm sorry to say. Newly motivated by my observation of George Frazier, I guide the class through a self-discovery of the solution, and it works well. Better yet, it takes up 15 minutes of the remaining time. I stumble through the last half hour finishing the subject begun Monday. I'm not great, but I'm not that bad either.

Gathering my notes I rush to my meeting, the bane of all faculty. Well, not all I guess. For reasons I will never understand, some of my colleagues love wasting an hour pontificating. But I hate to. Fortunately for me, university meetings usually are limited to an hour because of scheduling conflicts among the members. And on rare occasions even I think a meeting is important. Today's is one of those. It's the Graduate Committee and we have to plan the next doctoral qualifying exam. The session goes well, a minor miracle, with several subcommittees being formed to construct the various portions of the exam.

I flee from the meeting to my College Algebra class. Here I wing it rather successfully and the students don't realize how little I've prepared for them.

It's almost two and I'm starved. But I have to be at Barry Schwartz's office in exactly 37 seconds. Well, if I'm going to be late, I'm going to be very late. I stop at a kiosk, pick up a bagel, and with malicious delight take the time to have it toasted.

Munching, I head for the English department. Tom intercepts me before I enter the building and directs me to a nearby bench. A marvel! He doesn't berate me for tardiness. Instead he asks about my session with Shepinfield, so I present the details. He gets a kick from my efforts to force the expert to talk. I fail to mention the wimpiness of my "get tough" approach. Tom sees right through me. I can tell by the way he grins.

Now it's time to see Barry and we walk to his office. Tom enters without knocking and I follow discreetly. "What do you have for me?"

Barry looks up from the paper he's writing and grins. "And a good day to you, too."

"Okay, I'm a little rushed. Were you able to uncover anything for me?"

"Not much, I'm afraid. You recall I told you I had serious reservations about what I might be able to find. Also, all my experience has been with poetry. Except in especially gifted individuals, the mind sets of poets and prose writers are vastly different."

"Yeah, yeah. Don't give me this shit. All you experts dish out the same disclaimers. You want an out if things don't go the way you predict."

Barry doesn't appreciate this. "Enough, Tom. If you don't want my opinion, don't ask for it. But if you listen to what I say, you've got to know what it's worth. Which isn't much in this case."

"I know, Barry. Sorry. This investigation is frustrating. I shouldn't take it out on you. I do need all the help I can get, and I value anything you can give me."

"Okay. Fair enough. Let's talk about the evaluation first. Not much there. Three short sentences. But in some sense they tell a story. Salter's teaching his last class, he doesn't know it, and the earth will be better off without him. What can I say? I think the writer is an intelligent person able to express key points in pithy style. Knows what he's doing."

Tom sighs. "Everyone related to this damn case is intelligent. After all, it's a fucking university we're dealing with. You said 'he.' So did Donna Albright the other night when discussing that report by Avila. She's a super psychologist dumb enough to have married Jim." Barry smiles at me. "When I questioned her about it, she said she was not implying anything. Is it the same with you?"

"Oh, yes. I have no way of determining whether the writer is male or female. I certainly didn't get any hint from the evaluation, but when reading the report my thinking would vary depending on the passage. Some parts seemed definitely male while others were distinctly feminine."

"Yeah, Donna said something along the same line, but with more psychological jargon. Anything else you can tell me about the report?"

"Not much. At least I don't think you're going to consider it much. But I do have some vague feelings."

"Well, spit them out."

"Take it easy, Tom. I believe the author is particularly sensitive to the pain being endured by the victims of the piece. I assume you're casting Ken Salter in the role of villain?" Tom nods. "Well, the author obviously understands the consequences of Salter's cruelty. I can't help but wonder if he, too, wasn't treated unfairly at some point in his life."

Tom doesn't seem impressed. He waits for Barry to say more. When the silence extends, Tom says, "That's it? Nothing more?"

Barry elegantly shrugs his huge shoulders. "Sorry. I told you how limited this process is. I wish I could do more."

Now it's Tom's turn to shrug. "I knew it was a long shot at best. And I do appreciate your help. As one last favor, could you write a short report outlining what you've told us?"

"Already have. Here." He offers a single sheet. After all, how many words does it take to describe his findings?

We part, and as soon as we're clear of Barry's office I say, "What do you think about his comment that the killer has been treated badly?"

"Not much. You don't have to have suffered to understand suffering."

I wonder. In Tom's defense I realize I have known many caring people who truly can empathize with the less fortunate even though their own lives have been blessed. For example, have I mentioned Donna lately? So I guess Tom's conclusion might well be correct. But would it be possible for a murderer?

"Have you checked alibis for before five?" I ask.

"Stu Chen is coordinating that. I hope to have a report for our meeting this evening. One last task for you. I want you to come with me to see Madelaine."

"Who's Madelaine?"

"Madelaine Thompson. She's the document examiner I met with yesterday about the evaluation form, and she is especially proficient in handwriting analysis. Her office is just a couple of miles away."

This sounds like fun. Handwriting experts are people you read about, but never see. We travel in Tom's car. It takes less than eight minutes to reach our destination. Tom parks in a lot appended to a two-story office building and we climb the stairs to Suite 2B. I can't believe there's enough business to support handwriting analysis, but Tom tells me I'd be surprised. He doesn't elucidate, but I am surprised.

Tom knocks and a loud feminine voice bids us enter. We obey and step into a single-room office, so maybe business isn't that good. What the room lacks in size is more than made up for in high tech equipment. There's barely space to walk. A counter along the wall to the left as we enter holds a complex appearing computer and multi-function printer along with twin opaque projectors. I wonder if they're used to make comparisons between handwriting samples. Then on a continuing counter on the back wall are a large dual eyepiece microscope and a camera mounted on a stand with spotlights attached to flexible arms. Completing the picture to our right is a small desk with phone and answering machine. On the wall above hangs a screen for the projectors.

Rising from the desk is a tiny woman, no more than 4' 10" tall. My first reaction is I'm seeing an Olympic gymnast. She's extraordinarily thin and her brown hair is held in a ponytail by a green elastic band. Unfortunately, she's not in a leotard, just jeans and a green blouse that matches her hair band. She has brown eyes and eyebrows that almost meet. Her red lipstick is delicately applied. She's perhaps 15 years too old for the gymnastics team, which probably makes her even more enjoyable to admire. Now don't you worry. Donna knows I like looking at other women. But Donna also knows she's the only one I want. So let me luxuriate in my observation. After all, I'm almost a detective, aren't I? But it is hard to believe this small creature could have issued that authoritative command answering Tom's knock.

I receive immediate confirmation that it was indeed she, for, although the volume is down, her voice is strong. "Hey, Tom, good to see you again, even if you are a bastard."

"How ya doing, Madelaine? What do you mean, bastard?"

"Hell, calling on me yesterday and demanding an answer today. And me with a hot date last night that kept me from my beauty sleep until the wee hours. Had to get up at six just to finish your damn job."

I feel her beauty has not been at all diminished by her traumatic time, and wish to assure her all is well. However, I simply respond politely to the introduction Tom performs. Tom doesn't seem too upset about her problems and I know he's eager to learn what she's discovered. My curiosity, though, has to be satisfied first, so, before Tom has a chance to ask anything, I say, "Tom tells me local police use your services frequently. But surely that's not enough to keep you busy."

Tom smiles, knowing he'd whet my appetite. She also beams. "Most of my work is for law enforcement agencies. But a lot of them. I receive requests from police departments around the state and even beyond. It's getting so much, I think I'm going to have to hire someone else and move to larger quarters."

"No one else can do what you do, Madelaine," interjects Tom.

No false modesty about her. "Yeah, and that's something I worry about. I'd have to check a new person carefully, but I've some good prospects." She smiles at me. "Then I also perform at parties, for a hefty fee I might add, and I've even written a program used by those instant analysis computers at state fairs. I'm doing okay."

"She sure is, Jim. Don't worry about her. Now let's see what you have for me. As you know, Jim, I asked Madelaine to take a look at the student evaluation."

"You sure didn't give me much to work with. Just three sentences."

Tom sighs. "Don't you start feeding me excuses. I've just come from another expert telling me how hard his job is. Besides, I know what you can do. Hell, I've seen you derive enough from a single word written on a torn sheet of toilet paper to catch a killer. This should be a piece of cake."

Madelaine smiles. "Well, I might have a point or two that could help." She picks a piece of paper from her desk and places it on one of the opaque projectors. She switches it on and the display shows the written portion of the evaluation. Madelaine turns a rotary switch near the door and the lights dim so the projected image is readily discernible. "Look at these strokes." A laser pointer has materialized in her hand and she sweeps it over the three sentences. "Notice how bold they are, and firm. Furthermore, the writing is large, taking two lines for each short sentence."

"What do you conclude from that?"

"I think the writer is self-assured almost to a fault, absolutely positive about his or her views. Are you working on the assumption that the writer is Dr. Salter's killer?"

"We are."

"Was this written before or after the murder?"

"We're not certain, but we think two or three days before. Why?"

"I'm not surprised. It's what's alluded to here, of course, a future elimination. But it's also in keeping with the type of person I think the killer is. Bold. Willing to take risks in future actions and to say so, as in this form. Maybe even creative. And proud. Furthermore, this person won't exhibit any remorse about Salter's death. It may be difficult to catch him. Or her."

Tom's silent a while, mulling the information. So am I. It's impossible for me to believe someone could form so many conclusions from such a small amount of information, and I wonder about their validity.

Finally Tom speaks. "That's very helpful, Madelaine. As usual, you've given me something to chew on. You've been careful not to designate the writer as either male or female. Do you have any thoughts?"

"A few years ago I might have guessed that the writer was male, based on the belief only males pen bold strokes. It was probably malarkey then and it certainly is now. These days I believe writing is much more indicative of character traits than gender. The bottom line is I don't have a clue about the writer's sex."

Tom replies, "Well, what you've given us is terrific. Thanks. You know where to send the bill?"

She smiles. "Of course. First thing I check into. By the way, here's a copy of my findings." She hands him two pages stapled together. "Any other questions?"

Tom shakes his head and looks at me inquiringly. "I was just wondering why you haven't taken a look at the report," I say.

She gives Tom a perplexed look, obviously having no idea what I'm talking about. He explains about the document prepared by the mysterious Avila. Then he looks at me. "That report was typed, Jim. Madelaine deals with handwriting."

Boy, do I feel dumb. But in detective stories they always check mechanically prepared documents to determine the machine that created them. In embarrassment I steal my last look at the diminutive and delightful Madelaine and bid her adieu.

I feel better when Tom and I are alone and he says, "It was a good question about the report, Jim. Just asked the wrong person. I've an expert in the department working on it. He's sure it was created on a laser printer and he's spending the day at the university trying to discover which one."

"Tom, the number of printers there must be in the hundreds, maybe thousands? And how do you know it was even printed out there?"

He looks weary. "We don't. And I'm fully aware of the unlikelihood of finding the machine. But we've got to try. And Felix is really good at his job. If anyone can discover it, he can."

I assume Felix is Tom's expert. I want to voice my concerns about Madelaine. "Tom, do you really think it's possible to determine so much about a person from his writing. It's hard to believe."

Tom answers thoughtfully, "I felt the same way when I first employed Madelaine on a case, very wary. I'm still cautious, but less so. I've been astounded by what she's been able to do, both for the campus police and for my colleagues in law enforcement. There are many creeps doing time because of her."

I hear him, and believe him. But I think it would be a mistake to place too much emphasis on Madelaine's findings.

CHAPTER 38

Friday Evening

Tom drops me at Conroy Hall. Walking down the corridor towards my office, I hear an excited voice. Elmo's, of course. It's coming from the lounge, and as I approach the words become clear. "And so that's the idea of his proof. Ingenious, isn't it? You notice, of course, how he brazenly ignored all the approaches taken in the past, and how simple his basic concept is." He pauses, then continues in a voice filled with awe, "Simply amazing!"

I slip into the room to find several of my colleagues in rapt attention as Elmo strides back and forth in front of a whiteboard he's filled with mathematics. He continues, "As I've said, what I've discussed is the overall outline of the proof. The details, of course, go on for pages. But I've been through it carefully, and it's all there. Your chairman was a genius." His tone is reverential, an expert paying homage to a brilliant practitioner of his art. It seems he's definitively determined the correctness of Ken's proof. He's being peppered with questions and doing a masterful job of answering with clarity. The bumbling klutz disappears the minute the mathematician emerges.

I slip out, go to my office, and work until Elmo enters. "I see you're finished with the proof," I say.

"Sure am. Saw you in the room there. Marvelous work. Simply marvelous. Damn shame his life was cut short." His voice is fervent. "Jim, we've got to catch the bastard who did this."

I nod. But I worry. Even with Elmo's brilliance available to us I'm not sure we're ever going to discover this killer. I suggest we leave for home and Elmo agrees, asking if he can take us to dinner.

"Sure," I reply. "I'll call Donna and tell her. We'll have to go early enough so we can get to Theresa's on time." In truth, I don't feel like attending our daily meeting. Do you suppose it's because today I don't have any startling revelations to share?

Donna is delighted to accept Elmo's invitation and we reach a medium-priced restaurant about ten after six. Elmo's captivated with the mechanics of operation. Servers carrying food emerge from the kitchen through one door and return empty plates through another in an endless rotation. It's sort of a merry-go-round effect with waiters suddenly appearing, doing their thing, and then disappearing, only to reappear later. Elmo puts a mathematical twist on it, pointing to the doors and saying "source" and "sink."

Donna looks confused until I explain that in certain flow problems, such as mathematical models of oil distribution networks, there are sources (like where tankers unload) from which all flow originates and sinks (like storage tanks) where flow ceases.

Donna looks fondly at Elmo. "Only you, Elmo, would see the restaurant operation in such terms."

He's surprised. To him it's just a natural way to view what he's observed. The system, whether mathematically described or not, works fine and we have an enjoyable dinner, following which we drive directly to Theresa's. Even though we're a couple of minutes early, guess what. You're right. Tom's already there.

He immediately initiates the discussion. "Theresa, did you have any luck tracing Avila?"

"I don't think so. We have computer data going back 25 years and I had someone from Records do a search of three files: students, faculty, and staff."

"Do they include administrators?"

"Yes. Academic officials are filed under faculty as they all have departmental appointments also. Others are included in the staff list. Everyone will be in one of the files."

"Okay. But you didn't find any matches?"

"We did actually, but I don't think they'll be helpful. There were no hits for first or middle names, but we found four having Avila as a last name. It turns out to be a fairly common one." Seeing my look of surprise, Theresa says, "Look in the phone book, Jim. I did."

"Tell us about them."

"Two, Eduardo and Michael were students. Eduardo graduated seven years ago and Michael three. Orlando was in our custodial department until his retirement last year. Victoria spent two semesters as a Visiting Professor of Languages four years ago."

"So what's the problem with these four?"

"I had my secretary attempt to determine where they all are now, through our records here. Of course, we haven't actually checked to see that the records are up-to-date. But it doesn't sound like any of them will be a likely suspect."

Tom sighs. I bet he's thinking that, if Theresa doesn't think there's a chance, there isn't. "Let's hear it," he says with resignation.

"According to the Alumni Office, Eduardo attended medical school after leaving MRSU and is now in his final year of residency in San Francisco. Michael graduated in Computer Science and works for a young software company in Silicon Valley. Orlando's retirement checks are being sent to Florida. And Victoria went from here to a tenure track position at the University of Massachusetts. Here's a list of their last known addresses and phone numbers. I did call a friend in the language department at the University of Massachusetts and he assured me he knew Victoria and she's been there all semester, even attending a department party Sunday."

"Sounds like you're right about them not being involved, but I'll check them out. You're sure there's no one else?"

"There's always the possibility of a data entry error, although I had my people vary the spelling a bit in case there was. Nothing turned up. The only other thing we could do would be to hand search our older records."

"The ones more than 25 years old?"

"Right."

"I don't think that's worthwhile. I'm sure the answer lies in the present rather than the past. But thanks for the effort. Now, let's get you all up to date on what Jim and I have accomplished."

He indicates I should describe my interview with Oscar Shepinfield, which I do with aplomb.

Theresa says, "A bit of an ass, isn't he. His protest about it being impossible to break through our security codes is bunk. Hackers try those things all the time and often they succeed. Just read the papers."

"He did say he couldn't guarantee it wouldn't happen," I say, surprised to be rising to his defense.

"Bet it killed him to admit it," mumbled Theresa.

Tom says, "There's further evidence someone hacked in."

"Oh," says Theresa, "what's that?"

"I took another look at the sketches of Salter's office I made Sunday. As you remember, he was seated at a round table which contained his computer, keyboard, and mouse."

"So what?"

"Well, we think he just typed that email announcing his result, right?"

"Yes."

"So then his keyboard should be directly in front of the chair he was in. But it wasn't."

Donna asks, "But couldn't he have pushed it out of the way."

"Sure, but then he probably would have shoved it straight back. In actual fact, it was turned about 90 degrees, as if someone else had been using it."

"The murderer!" I exclaim.

Tom says, "Yes. I think so." Donna appears unconvinced. "And there's even more damning evidence," Tom continues. "When Jim told me how various times are applied to email messages as they advance through the process, I called Detective Chen. He tracked down Oscar Shepinfield and got him to recover the information, at least as far as the times appended locally."

"And?"

"All but the time the message was sent showed up in the 1403 range."

Pretty convincing. Even "Doubting Donna" seems on board now.

Tom asks, "Are any of our suspects computer savvy enough to do it?"

A good question, and I hate to mention the two that spring to mind. "George Frazier certainly is. His software work is complicated and he'd have had to learn a lot about the system. And we know David Simmons spends hours with machines."

"What about Susan Barber?"

"Definitely," says Theresa. "She has single-handedly established the mini-network connecting the math department computers and has taken advantage of every course we've offered. My secretary tells me Susan got so interested in computers, before she got interested in Kenneth Salter, that she bought two for her home use and has actually learned to program at the machine language level. If she wanted to break in, I think she has the ability to find the way." This agrees with the assessment I gave Tom earlier. "The same could be true of Dick Brighthurst. Doesn't he use the computer a lot in his research, Jim?"

I nod. "But I don't know how deep he gets into them," I respond loyally. "They're simply tools as far as he's concerned."

"You're right," agrees Theresa. "He probably doesn't program at the system level, but he's got the mind to figure out how to do it if he wants to." Again I'm forced to concur. "And," she continues, "I called another friend at Reinhardt. Harvey Delsanter received a masters in computer science before becoming a math major. Of course, that was several years ago and things have changed a lot."

"I bet he's kept up, though," is my brilliant contribution.

"Maybe," Theresa responds doubtfully.

Tom asks, "Can we at least eliminate Stephen Farnsworth and Harriet Salter?"

Theresa shakes her head. "I don't think so, although I believe they're less likely. Probably Steve doesn't have enough moxie to do it himself, but in view of what we've learned, I wouldn't put it past him to pressure some student, maybe threatening him with expulsion if he failed to do what he wanted. Even Harriet might know someone to help her."

Tom says, "One of the neighbors she had over Sunday night, Sharon Williamson, is on the computer science faculty." He pauses a moment, then says without conviction, "I suppose she would have the requisite expertise, but why in the world would she help?" After another pause, he attempts to sum up. "I guess what we're saying is that any of the suspects could have caused the time change, but some are more likely than others?" Upon seeing our agreement he adds, "Well, that's progress."

Tom then describes our visits with Barry Schwartz and Madelaine Thompson. "When we were with Madelaine, Jim asked about the machine used to print Avila's report. I told him Felix Cox, our expert, was checking printers on campus."

"Not much hope of success there," says Theresa.

"The odds were small, certainly. But it turns out he did find it. He called me just before I left for here. He checked the machines in the math office, an obvious place, but they all failed. On the second floor of that building, though, is a computer lab."

"More a classroom," I say. "Some of us use it to illustrate how to employ computers in math and research."

Tom's annoyed at the interruption. "Whatever. Anyway there are several long tables, each with four computers. They all feed a single printer. And that's the one that's our baby."

"How could he tell?" I ask.

"It turns out there's a deal between the U.S. government and printer manufacturers. Most laser color printers nowadays insert tiny virtually invisible yellow dots on every single sheet printed. They encode among other things the printer serial number. Felix took the report into a dark room and shone a blue LED light on the paper. That's what you do to make the dots visible. He lucked out. They were there, meaning the report was printed on a color laser printer."

"What's so special about that type of printer?"

"They're the kind that are best suited to counterfeiting money and that's what got the government involved. Anyway, once he had the dot array it was straightforward to decode the serial number of the printer used for the report. Then, hoping it was located on campus, he checked the university database of printer serial numbers and found a match to the one in that lab."

"Wow!" I say. I'm getting better at producing non-inane exclamations, aren't I? "I don't suppose those dots can tell you when the report was printed?"

"As a matter of fact, they do. It was done the Thursday night before Dr. Salter's death, actually early Friday morning at 0213."

Theresa interposes, "Probably wanted a time when it was unlikely there'd be a student present."

"I suppose so," replies Tom.

I have a brilliant thought. "I bet we could find a copy of the report on one of the lab computer's hard drives. Might tell us something."

"Surprisingly, Jim, Felix thought of that, too." Don't you think sarcasm here is uncalled for? "None was apparent. He even ran programs on each of them, first a simple search, then a more sophisticated one to recover a deleted file. No luck. He says either the user did something special to make recovery impossible, or, more likely, simply had the document on a flash drive and printed directly from it."

Donna says, "I guess anyone smart enough to alter the time on the email messages would know how to hide a file from us."

Tom nods glumly, although he's not entirely without hope. "Can the fact the report was printed there help us eliminate someone?"

Theresa is equally grim. "I'm afraid not. That lab's open 24 hours a day, and anyone can walk in when there's no class there. I suspect the room is empty much of the time, especially in the middle of the night."

"Even Harvey Delsanter," I chirp helpfully.

"Thank you, Jim." There's that sarcasm again. Really! "I have just a couple of other items to report. First, I followed up on Elmo's idea of how to determine if that student evaluation was added to the others at a later time."

Elmo, who's been uncharacteristically silent, perks up at the mention of his name. "What's the result?"

"The summary sheet showed there had been 37 respondents when the evaluation was carried out. Counting the one of interest to us, there are 38!"

Donna asks, "So it definitely was added later?"

Elmo says, "Just realized how you could check it out for sure."

Tom responds, "I believe I know what you're thinking, Elmo, because it occurred to me, too." Elmo smiles with pleasure, as he might when a student has volunteered an especially clever point. "I took the 37 supposedly legitimate sheets—and what a fight to get them out of the hands of that secretary in the dean's office—to the man in charge of scanning evaluations."

Theresa smiles. "You mean Derek Connelly?" Tom nods. "You two have had a day. First Jim with Oscar Shepinfield, and now you with Derek. Have any problems?"

"That was the most rule bound creature I've ever seen. Even worse than Shepinfield sounds. I bet he's never done a daring thing in his life. He spouted nonsense about confidentiality and you simply couldn't use state resources indiscriminately and the administration would never allow it and a long list of other reasons not to take one minute to run a bunch of anonymous forms through what essentially is a counting program."

"But you didn't deem it necessary to have him call me as Jim did with Oscar."

She's smiling, but the words bite to the quick. So I'm not as tough as Tom. So what? I also don't have the persuasive powers of a police badge.

"No," responds Tom, looking at me wickedly, "I was able to convince him he should willingly assist a murder investigation."

"And the result?"

"When he reran those 37 forms, he reproduced the original summary sheet exactly."

To reestablish my credibility I voice what's in all our minds, "So the extra evaluation didn't replace one of the original ones? It had to have been included at a later time."

Tom nods and adds, "And probably last Friday when the folder containing the original 37 was lying on that counter in the dean's office."

Donna asks, "What does that tell us, Tom?"

"Not much," he admits. "We'd figured that all along."

"Anything else for this evening?"

Once again Theresa's eager for the session to end. She looks tired. She's probably under pressure from the president about the murder. Maybe it's too much for her at this point in her life. It's sad to think of her aging. She's always been so vital, and played such an important part in Donna's and my younger lives.

"Just one thing. In view of Jim's discovery about the email times, I increased the possible window for the killing to the maximum stated by Doc Pritchard, from one o'clock to nine. I hate to think the old geezer could be right, but it seems to me the murder had to occur before two, since the clock was reset before Jim's message was sent."

Donna says. "I'm not as quick with the technical stuff as you, so let me clarify something. What all this means is Ken typed the announcement of the greatest achievement of his life, but was killed before he had a chance to send it. Is that right?"

"I don't see how it could be any other way," responds Tom.

"So the killer did all that manipulation with the clock right from Ken's office. God, how cold blooded can you be?"

"And quick witted," I add.

"What do you mean?"

"Well, the killer couldn't have known about Ken's message ahead of time. When he saw it, he must have realized he could create a perfect alibi by sending it then, but with a later time appended when he knew people could verify his whereabouts."

My statement meets with more thoughtful consideration than most of my utterances.

Tom breaks the silence. "Naturally, we had to go back and check everyone for an alibi for the period between 1300 and 1400. Stu Chen had officers doing that today, going up to 1700, and I've summarized their findings on this sheet."

He hands us each a single page containing the following:

Suspect	Alibi (1300 to 1700)	Alibi (1700 to 2200)
Harriet Salter	Shopping alone until 1600	Verified
Stephen Farnsworth	At work, alone	Verified
Richard Brighthurst	Taking nap, wife and children on a picnic	Verified
George Frazier	Bicycling to 1530 alone, then into work	Verified
Susan Barber	At home gardening, lives alone	Verified
David Simmons	Taking a walk, alone	Verified
Harvey Delsanter	At Reinhardt doing research, alone	Verified

We all take a moment to digest the implications of the sheet, but it's Theresa who voices our common conclusion. "So none of the suspects has an alibi for the time we now think the murder occurred?"

"Not a damn one." Tom's disgust pervades and emphasizes every word.

My doubts about our finding the killer grow. My gloom seems to be a reflection of everyone's feelings.

Only Elmo offers a further comment before we leave. "There's something funny about the last page of Salter's proof."

CHAPTER 39

Saturday

It's 8:00 Saturday morning. Normally I'd be home all day, accomplishing various chores and working on my classes or doing research. Today, though, I have a meeting at school. You can imagine how I feel about that. This is a rarity, but we simply couldn't find a compatible time during the week. Donna usually goes to her office on Saturdays, seeing clients until 2:00, accommodating those who can't get to her during normal working hours.

I'm still in bed, wicked thoughts coursing through my mind. When we got home last night Donna complained of fatigue and headache. Oh yes, I know what you're thinking. Oldest excuse in the book, right? Well, I want you to realize you're wrong. Because she also told me she had no client today before ten and wondered if I could delay my departure this morning. Then she donned this sheer nightie that removed all element of choice from my response. Accordingly, I'm glued to the bed. Dammit, woman. Wake up!

Fifteen minutes more of torture and I can stand it no longer. I reach over to my beloved and drag her toward me, initiating a full-body press. Her eyes open. I've never understood books giving emotions to eyes—happy, sad, worried. Eyes are eyes, round orbs moving over a background of white—or sometimes red. But I swear her eyes are smiling—and inviting! Oh my, her mouth is open, and her tongue is darting over her lips. She languidly moves her arms above her head and I remove the virtually nonexistent covering.

Twenty minutes later we lie exhausted, but oh so happy. Disappointed? Did you really think I was going to go into all the details, even though it's only to my personal journal? Don't be ridiculous. You never know who'll wind up reading it. Suffice it to say I can't recall a better moment in my life. Although I hope to have one, several actually, in the future.

Suddenly Donna is "Miss Efficiency", after discovering she has only an hour to get to her office. I could stay in bed all day, except of course for my meeting at 11:00. While I'm slowly extricating myself from the tangled sheets, Donna does those unseemly early morning bathroom things, showers, and power dresses. Actually, she dresses rather simply in a yellow blouse and full ankle-length multicolored skirt. But it seems powerful to me.

She smiles at me, pecks me on the mouth, and a quick lash of her tongue gets me thinking again. Then she says, "If you'll get a move on, I'll have some cereal ready for you." How's that for a mood breaker? But I do as she suggests and arrive in the kitchen in time to share a few minutes before she leaves.

Shortly after Donna's departure, I also head for work. I spend the time before my meeting preparing for Monday's College Algebra class, redoing my notes from the last time I taught the material. I'd scratched an indication that an example I'd given had stupefied every one of the students. Looking at it from my perspective a year later, I couldn't make anything of it either. Those poor kids. Well, I've come up with a better one now. At least I hope it is. I'll find out next week.

The meeting was a horror. We hassled for over an hour attempting to create a document outlining merit criteria for evaluating faculty. Each department has to come up with such a list, and it's damn hard. Surprisingly, the good instructors want teaching effectiveness emphasized while researchers demand that published paper output be the determining factor. What the administration wants is an inventive teacher simultaneously publishing several articles in leading journals while volunteering in the community and serving on committees at the department, college, and university levels. I don't know how anyone fits the mold, but some do. I bet they don't have experiences like I did this morning, though. They have no time for that. After all, it's not what the administration wants. Cynical, you say? Right, I say!

Surprise, surprise. We attendees at the meeting can't resolve the differences so, alas, we must gather once again. But at least it's over for today, leaving me more preparation time before Donna gets home. I'm brown bagging it, having brought a sandwich, apple, and banana. While munching, I sit back in my chair and don't think about my class. Instead, I concentrate on the murder. I think. And I think some more. I wish I could have my choice as to who the murderer is.

I'd certainly go for Harvey Delsanter, as unpleasant a man as I ever want to encounter. But then I think of his family and decide maybe he wouldn't be such a great selection after all. Please don't let it be David, though. So young, with a lot of promise and finally getting his life in order. Or George Frazier, one of the world's good guys. If it's Harriet Salter, the killing would seem justifiable to me, although I could never condone it. She surely endured enough suffering to have pushed anyone to the limit. Of course, I don't think the law would take such an open view of assisted death, and her children have already lost one parent. So let's not let it be her.

What about Stephen Farnsworth and Dick Brighthurst? Farnsworth's an ass, but could he kill? The hold Ken had on him would have been a powerful motivating force. I can't imagine Dick murdering anyone. He's like Harriet in a sense, abused by Ken for years. How might he react? Again, I could understand Dick taking action, but I sure don't want it to be him. It's a selfish wish. I want Dick to be my boss. Finally, there's Susan Barber. Not an endearing woman, except for that glimpse Tom and I were privileged to see. And she is competent. I don't like her, but I admire her. I bet she'd have the nerve, but it's hard to imagine her in the murderer's role.

Naming our seven suspects clouds more than illuminates the issue. I've started thinking of them as people. Human beings I know—and human beings I know don't kill other human beings I know. I'm getting nowhere. Obviously, I should quit thinking about the murder. That works with my research. Get away from the problem and sometimes ideas pop into place.

Good advice, but I don't take it. So I stare at a blank wall, trying to open my mind to new thoughts. I glance at my watch. One-thirty. I put in another half hour on preparation, this time for my graduate course. In the back of my mind, though, the Salter murder percolates. Suddenly I slam my pencil on the desk. The germ of an idea hits me, right in the middle of a particularly clarifying sentence I'm writing.

I've got to think more about this. Certainly nothing conclusive, but a new slant. It's worth a call to Tom. As if on cue, my cell clamors for attention. What a coincidence! It's Tom.

"I've an idea," he says. "Not a convincing argument, but maybe a pointer in the right direction. Think we can all get together at 6:30 and discuss it before we go to Theresa's?"

"Sure. How about meeting at our house? We're closest to hers."

"Sounds good. I'm going to bring Stuart Chen. Will you ask Elmo?"

"Will do. Sounds like you're beginning to have some faith in him."

"Don't push me, Jim." Then, after a pause, "He has had some good thoughts, though. Well, I'll see you later."

"Oh, Tom, I've also had a couple of ideas I'd like to discuss."

"Good. Maybe things are starting to fall into place. Be seeing you."

And just like that, Tom's gone, leaving me wondering what Tom's figured out, and whether it will mesh with my own vague machinations. Guess I'll know soon enough. The next step is to inform Donna and Elmo about the extra meeting, and that's best accomplished by returning home. And there's also the small matter of apprising Donna I've set it up for our house. Normally she doesn't appreciate such short notice, as we saw with Elmo's arrival, but I think she'll understand in this case.

And she does. She indicates, though, that I can straighten the magazines littering the living room and pick up papers I've left scattered on the floor and coffee table. Was it only last weekend I'd been doing research while seated on the sofa? It seems like ages ago, a more peaceful time when murder was only a literary concept.

After returning from my appointed task, Donna takes my hands in hers, her expression troubled. She says, "I'm glad we're getting together early. I've had some ideas too. They're mainly feelings, discomforting ones, and I don't know if they mean anything. But I guess I've got to voice them."

She seems to be bothered in the same way I am. I pull her to me, attempting to comfort her but realizing I need comfort, too. Finally I say, "Maybe we should push our meeting back to six, since we seem to have more to discuss than Tom thought."

"Good idea. If you'll prepare coffee, I'll make some sandwiches."

"Okay. And I'll call Tom. By the way, where's Elmo?"

"He went out for a walk shortly after I got home. Said it helps him think. He was really strange. Subdued. Not at all his normal self. Didn't want to talk, and went around the house muttering. I was glad to see him leave."

That doesn't sound like Elmo at all. I wonder what's up. Shrugging it off, I call Tom and learn the earlier time is fine for both him and Detective Chen.

I don't hear Elmo return. That in itself is unusual, considering his proclivity for disruption. But as I turn from the phone, there he is, standing immobile near the front door, forgetting even to shut it. Is he all right? It's clear what I should say. "Elmo, are you all right?" I discreetly pass him and close the door.

He looks at me blankly, with no hint of the familiar joviality we've all come to love, well, to accept. After several seconds he suddenly seems to notice my presence. "I know who killed him, Jim."

I stare. After all, Tom, Donna, and I have thoughts, but were far from positive. Every one of us. And here's Elmo saying he's sure. "Are you absolutely certain?"

"Oh, yes. There's no doubt."

I'm struck dumb. Finally I find enough presence of mind to ask, "How can you be?"

"Because Salter was a clever bastard." Elmo shakes his head in admiration before he continues. "He named his killer."

> What do you think? I know for a fact that Elmo has no more information available to him than I've dutifully recorded. So can you see what he sees? Or what any of us does, for that matter? I know I'm having trouble, except for my own contribution, of course.

CHAPTER 40

Early Saturday Evening

Donna enters the room just as Elmo makes his announcement. She shoots me a questioning glance, as if I stood a chance of understanding what he means. I shrug the shrug of the ignorant. "Come on, Jim," she says. "Let's get started on supper."

We adjourn to the kitchen and attack our appointed chores. I place the proper ingredients in our Mr. Coffee and switch it on. Exhausting work. Meanwhile Donna slices bread, coats it with mayonnaise, scoops chicken salad onto half the slices, tops them with the other half, and neatly severs the resulting sandwiches in two. Obviously an equal division of labor.

We remain silent as we work. There's tacit agreement not to discuss the murder. Since it's the only subject on our minds, nothing is said. Donna arranges the sandwiches on a tray and carries it to the coffee table. I follow with five plates and napkins. It's ten to six. We know Tom and Stuart Chen will appear on the dot, but there are times when 10 minute waits seem infinite. That's math talk. We, including Elmo, endure it by sitting quietly in the living room. I suspect Donna's using her time similar to the way I am mine, which is going over my argument searching for flaws. Elmo doesn't appear to have any doubts. But he doesn't look happy.

Time, as is its wont, does advance, and promptly at six Tom and Chen arrive. Donna passes the tray of sandwiches and I return to the kitchen to pour coffee and deliver the cups. Tom wolfs his sandwich, interested only in the purpose of this preliminary meeting.

"It was my intention to go over my ideas with Stu after I called you, Jim. But then I decided to wait and let him be a sounding board for both of us. I've told him he's to be a devil's advocate. For you too, Donna. I understand you have a contribution." She nods gravely.

"Turns out Elmo has an idea too," I say.

The big man has remained uncharacteristically silent, barely acknowledging Tom or his introduction to Chen. He did find the energy to down two sandwiches, in a discreet manner, of course. But my words have stirred him. "Not an idea," he says. "I know who the killer is. Salter told me."

Tom and Chen stare at the massive man. It sounds like Elmo's received a message from beyond. I know that's not what he means, but perhaps it's not the best phrasing to inspire confidence.

To divert doubts I insert, "He's figured out something, Tom. He hasn't explained it to me, but I'll wager you can count on it."

Tom looks skeptical. "All right, Elmo, let's hear it."

Now Elmo *never* relinquishes center stage when it's offered, so you can imagine how stunned I am to hear him say, "Not yet. I'd like to learn what you're thinking first."

Tom's annoyed, probably guessing Elmo's just seeking attention. But I know differently. Elmo's a ham, but not when the subject is important. Suddenly I get an idea. Not a mature one, I admit. But unable to resist, I pursue it. "Tom, Donna, does what you've discovered lead to a particular person?" They both indicate yes. I'm thankful, because now I can implement my plan. "Do you remember what we did in Theresa's class?"

Donna looks puzzled, but Tom says, "You mean when we neared the end of one of her hypothetical cases?" I nod. "Let's see. Didn't we each write the name of whom we thought was guilty on a separate piece of paper?"

"Right! And virtually every time we all picked the same person."

Donna gives me a pained look, and even Elmo, who never passes up an amusing opportunity, looks disgusted. My lovely says, "Come on, Jim. This isn't a game."

"I know it," I say more sharply than perhaps my case warrants. "But do you recall why we did it?"

Got her there, and I'm pleased to see a bit of guilt flash across those lovely features. She smiles self-consciously. "I do. I think I said something about it ensuring that none of us would be influenced by another. But, Jim, I was a lot younger then, and surely we aren't going to change our opinion just because someone has a different view."

"Well," I respond with virtue, "I admired your argument then, and I think it's equally valid now."

Tom's angry with this diversion. "Jim, you admired *anything* Donna said back then. But if it'll get things moving, let's do it so we can proceed with our business." Then he adds, in somewhat a rueful tone I think, "It actually might be interesting, if for no other reason than to see how far apart we are."

So I'm not the only one captivated by the idea! And I detect Elmo's showing a little more enthusiasm. Even Donna's bestowing a sad but benevolent smile on her adolescent husband. So I tear a sheet of paper into fourths and give all but Stuart Chen a piece. Everyone pulls out a pen, even Elmo! Everyone but me. I hastily excuse myself, returning in a few seconds with the requisite instrument.

It takes only a moment for each to write a single name, fold the papers, and hand them to Tom. He opens and examines them, shakes his head in wonder, and says, "They're identical."

It's a sobering statement. Each of us in our own way has detected clues pointing to the same individual. But there's not the joy we felt in that class 20 years earlier. In real life, accusing someone of murder is too serious a business.

As if reading my mind, Tom says, "Okay, let's carefully go over our reasoning. We don't want to be wrong. And I sure as hell don't want to goof in front of Theresa."

"Amen," I say, and I know I speak for Donna too. After all this time, we still have vivid memories of sharp cross-examinations of our deductive processes, and woe be to anyone arguing capriciously. I'm surprised that Tom, even with all his experience and successes in detection, shares our apprehension. Only Elmo seems unconcerned.

Tom says, "I'll begin."

He outlines two points, one admittedly vague and one possibly more damning, but so esoteric you can't help but wonder if he's not stretching unacceptably. I admire his thought processes, though. He's a clever guy.

Chen doesn't seem impressed. In fact, his reaction matches mine. Being diplomatic—and of course holding down a subordinate position—he doesn't come right out and call Tom a fool, but he doesn't blindly accept the argument either.

Tom doesn't mind. He likes his people to challenge him. He says, "You're next, Jim, if you've come up with anything in addition."

He's like all of us, I guess. We study a subject for a long time and finally see something, so we expect everyone else to see the same thing. Interestingly, Tom's deductions don't overlap mine at all. But listening and critiquing his makes me think my argument is equally weak. But I forge ahead anyway.

When I'm done, Tom asks Chen what he thinks now. "It's still awfully iffy, Tom."

"We're not talking about making an arrest, damn it! But you've got to admit the level of suspicion is increasing."

Chen shrugs, not deeming it worthwhile to argue. Tom nods to Donna and she makes her pitch. Amazing. Nothing she says duplicates either Tom's or my contributions, and when she's finished I'm feeling there can't be many more nails needed for this particular coffin. Actually, I think her arguments are more cogent than either Tom's or mine, although all points take on added importance as the evidence grows.

I can see Donna has begun to make a believer out of Chen, for his reaction this time is more positive. "The case is getting stronger, Tom. None of your arguments singly are convincing, but taken together they begin to paint a pretty damning picture. But, and I'm sorry as hell to say it, there's not even one piece of evidence pointing conclusively to your suspect."

Elmo breaks his silence by emitting an immense sigh. "Yes, there is," he says.

"Okay, Elmo. It's time to tell us," I insert.

He nods, and then begins a clear and devastating description of the single fact that convinced him, and now is removing the last vestige of doubt from us, of the identity of the killer.

When he's through Tom bestows on him an admiring glance. "I think you've done it, Elmo. You really meant it, didn't you, when you said Salter had named his murderer?"

Elmo nods and Chen says, "Even I think the case is solid now. A good prosecutor should be able to make the charge stick."

Elmo can't resist repeating, "That Salter was a damn clever fellow. Cool enough, too, to leave us a clue as he died. The person who did this mustn't get away with it."

Tom, impressed by the intensity of Elmo's words, replies, "This killer won't. I promise you. Now let's talk about the next step, which I guess is going over all of this with Theresa." He glances at his watch, "In less than 45 minutes." He looks at me. "That gives us what, another 30 minutes here?"

"Thirty-five, maybe. I guess we could be a bit late." Tom and Donna look at me incredulously. No one's late for an appointment with Theresa. "Sorry," I mumble, "wasn't thinking."

We use the time to examine all the other suspects in detail and convince ourselves there's sufficient reason not to consider them further. Then we review yet again the evidence against the person we now are convinced is the killer. Putting it all together in a single cohesive argument serves to increase its persuasiveness, and at the end none of us harbors a doubt.

It's hard for me to believe that someone I've spoken with can be a killer. I don't like the situation, and it rests heavily on me as we drive in Tom's car over to Theresa's.

> I'm stunned. We all recognized different clues. But, like I said before, every one of them was there for all to see. Now that I know about them, they're pretty obvious. It's similar to a math problem you work on for days, getting nowhere. Then someone shows you how to do it and you realize the solution's been staring you in the face. I bet you have some ideas too. Maybe it's something we've all missed. Let us know. We need all the help we can get, even though Elmo's contribution is pretty damn convincing.

CHAPTER 41

Saturday Evening

Theresa greets us warmly. Even Elmo, I'm pleased to say. She's looking better this evening. Rested, more her normal, vital self. She's prepared decaf and presents each of us with a cup. Once we're positioned on sofa and chairs, she takes her seat in an adored rocker, next to a small, round walnut table on which she places her cup and saucer. Once settled she looks at Tom. "Well, have you made any progress today?"

"Indeed we have, Theresa. We know who the killer is."

She's surprised. "And you have proof?"

"Definitely."

"Well, then, let's hear it."

As agreed earlier, Tom acts as leader. "You know we've been concentrating on seven individuals, all of whom had reason to hate Kenneth Salter." Theresa nods. "So let's look at the cases against each of them. We think five definitely are weak and even a sixth can be eliminated."

"Well, that should do it! Who's first?"

"Several should be removed from consideration immediately. Dr. Brighthurst is one of them."

"But what about his motive? It's a strong one."

Already it feels like the old days, with her incisive demands that we not make invalid assumptions. And it's probably a damn good thing she's that way. Tom holds up well under scrutiny.

"Of course he has his reasons. Jealousy, shabby treatment for years, financial insecurity. Strong motives. Remember, though, we've learned a lot about our murderer."

"Yes," responds Theresa. "He probably has an academic background or at least is familiar with the way our reports are created, he's probably a caring person as indicated in that report by 'Avila', and he should know something about computers. Seems to me Dick meets all these criteria."

"Perhaps, but it's not so clear about his computer knowledge. Remember, we're not looking for a person who 'knows something about computers.' We want an expert. From what Jim told us, we know Brighthurst uses computers in his research, but not at the level necessary to break through the protection required to alter the clock. And there's no evidence at all he has that knowledge."

On cue, I hop in. "And he does know Harvey Delsanter. Remember he was at that talk Delsanter gave to our department. Yet no allusion to anyone who might be Delsanter appears in the Avila report."

"Maybe he felt Delsanter wasn't wronged to the same degree the others were."

Now it's Donna's turn. "I don't think so, Theresa. We've agreed the writer—whom we're sure is the killer—is attempting to justify the murder. Surely he or she would search for any reason, no matter how minor, to include another name. And we know Ken did attack Dr. Delsanter at every opportunity, so it seems reasonable that Dick, if he is our man, would have created a small vignette about him."

Theresa bestows a bemused look upon us. "It appears you've gotten together earlier to coordinate your arguments."

Tom grins sheepishly. "Surely you didn't think we'd present a case to you without preparation?"

A flicker of a smile flashes across her face, but then her eyes harden and bore into Tom. "It's not very convincing. About Dick's innocence, that is."

Tom snaps a response. "Nor is the evidence awfully damning. As you know full well, judgments have to be made, and, as you'll see, we have evidence that's so strong against one individual that cases against the others pale by comparison."

I'm proud of Tom. He's standing firm against our former teacher in spite of her sharp questioning.

"Very well. I suppose you're going to give me a similar argument about Harriet Salter?"

"Certainly a spouse has to be considered carefully. You taught me that. And her motivation is great."

"But not her current attitude," pipes Donna. "As I told you, she's self-possessed now, wouldn't have felt it necessary to kill to save her life."

"Right," continues Tom, although I suspect Theresa's thinking Donna's just protecting a client. "And she probably knows of Delsanter. We can't imagine living with Salter and not being exposed to some contact with the man. Yet, again, no reference to someone who could be Delsanter appears in the report."

I pick up the argument. "We talked about the possibility of her convincing her friend to break into the computer system. Remember, though, using Ken's computer to alter the time stamp was a spur-of-the-moment decision by an unusually knowledgeable killer. It's impossible to imagine anyone taking the time to get help, even in the unlikely event someone was willing. Especially with Ken's body in the room. No. Our murderer and the computer hacker have to be the same person, which means Harriet Salter can't be the killer."

"I suppose she could have picked up the requisite computer knowledge somewhere," Theresa says doubtfully.

"Be reasonable, Theresa. Her candidacy just doesn't wash," says the light of my life.

Our mentor sighs. "I think you're probably right." Donna always was the teacher's pet. "Who's next?"

Tom resumes control. "Stephen Farnsworth is not a viable candidate."

"And why not?"

"For many reasons. For one, we've agreed the author of the Avila report is a caring individual. From what I've seen and what you've told me, Farnsworth is a self-centered egoist not overly concerned with others. He doesn't meet our criteria."

"Besides," says Donna, "he was aware of Dr. Delsanter since he approved an honorarium for him."

"That's not significant, Donna. He might very well not have known anything about the man."

My turn. "True. But, if for no other reason, we have to eliminate him using the same argument we employed on Harriet Salter. He simply doesn't have the necessary computer expertise. God, he's one of the most incompetent men I know."

"You're right, of course," Theresa surprises me by saying. "I agree we can eliminate Stephen, although his motive is compelling. How about that poor boy, David Simmons?"

I'm gratified she's concerned about David because, as I've said, I've taken a liking to the lad. "David's out of it," I state forcefully.

"I thought he was a computer whiz."

Tom steps in. "He is, and it's possible he could have hacked into the system."

"Surely that's a major factor. After all, how many people have that kind of expertise?"

"More than you might think. Don't get me wrong, though. We're not dismissing it lightly."

"So what else do you have on him?"

Tom says, "That's the problem. Nothing! We don't believe he could have created as sophisticated a document as the Avila report. That boy is no writer. You told us yourself about his poor grades in composition. Sure, he's probably familiar with the form of a university report, but his record shows he lacks the skills and maturity to prepare a document of the type we've seen. Furthermore, would he be familiar enough with the people indicated in the report to write so cogently about their relationship with Salter? It stretches the imagination."

"Yes, it does," agrees Theresa. "So we're left with George Frazier, Harvey Delsanter, and Susan Barber."

"Correct. Let's start with Delsanter. It seemed as if Salter was leaving us a clue pointing to him."

Theresa shows interest. "You mean having the cell phone's last active screen being the 'Recent Call' list, showing the last call placed was to him? I wondered about that."

"Right. It appeared to be such a logical way for Salter to finger his killer."

"You sound hesitant."

"I am. There are several problems. Including getting that screen up while dying and realizing Delsanter's name was on top. Also it's improbable he would know everyone outlined in the report. Especially Simmons. Hard to believe he would have come into contact with that young man anywhere. The others maybe, although Frazier and Barber definitely are iffy. Even more telling is the fact that no one has ever thought of him as a caring person. Besides all this, there is no evidence of the necessary modern computer expertise. I'm afraid we have to eliminate him."

"But how do you explain the phone?"

"Remember Salter called him earlier in the day, leaving that taunting message on his answering machine."

"Ah, I see. So it was open at that spot for no more reason than he was the last person Ken called. Okay, so Delsanter's out, I guess."

I say, "Let's discuss George Frazier next."

"With this man," Tom says, "we have a real possibility. He satisfies virtually all of our criteria, and has a strong motive. He's well versed in computers, quite possibly possessing the knowledge required to break through the security. He has academic experience and Jim told us he writes well. He could have prepared the 'Avila' report. He's a compassionate guy just like we think the author is. And he's familiar with all the victims of the report."

"Are you saying he's our culprit?" Theresa asks softly.

"No. For two reasons."

"Oh?"

Tom looks nervous. I don't blame him, because I know what he's going to say next. I'm not looking forward to it myself. "Er, the first one is Jim doesn't think he's capable of murder."

"What! Since when has Jim been an expert on murderers?" Obviously she doesn't know how many mysteries I've read. "That's the craziest thing I've ever heard. I'm ashamed of you, Tom, for listening to him!"

Now Donna's annoyed. "Theresa, I have a great deal of faith in Jim's opinion of people. He has a good feel for that sort of thing." Isn't she a lovely girl? "And I also think it makes sense from a psychological point of view. All I've heard about the man leads me to believe he couldn't be a murderer."

"What's with you people? That's a pile of shit, Donna. If you had any knowledge of homicide, you'd know the gentlest people can be the vilest killers."

Tom's reply is sharp. "Theresa, Donna has extensive experience as a consultant to law enforcement agencies, so I listen to her views. Of course we're all aware of the validity of what you said. But there's also the fact Frazier knows how Ken hated Delsanter. If he's the murderer, why isn't a reference to Delsanter in the report?"

"Weak, Tom, weak. The case against George is strong."

"Agreed. But not as strong as against another."

We're nearing the end and I sense everyone, including yours truly, tensing for the conclusion. Theresa can count. "The only one we haven't discussed is Susan Barber."

"Yes," sighs Tom. "Let's talk about Susan Barber."

So how did you do? Were you able to eliminate everyone but Susan? Tom tells me he often zeros in on the guilty party because all other suspects have been shown to be innocent. Didn't Sherlock Holmes say something like that once? Were you surprised the only suspect left is Susan? I bet you're not, for I'm sure you've discerned the evidence yourself. It forms a strong case, doesn't it? Especially with what Elmo discovered on the last page of Ken's proof.

CHAPTER 42

Saturday Evening

Theresa is subdued. "I must admit I'm surprised. Tell me what you have against her."

Tom says, "It's a strong case."

"So why do you look so glum? Do you have doubts?"

"Oh, there's nothing wrong with our reasoning. You'll see. It's just she's such a remarkable woman. I quite like her. I'm sorry she wound up in the mess she did because of a selfish, egotistical man."

Theresa undoubtedly sympathizes, but is eager to move on. "She's not the first to be taken advantage of by a man—or to let him," she snaps. I wonder if she's remembering experiences she's had to endure. "Tell me why you think she's the one."

Donna takes over. "She fits our profile better than any of the others. She writes well. Remember what Elsie Martin and Jim told us about the memos and departmental year-end summaries she's prepared. I've seen a couple myself, and I agree. And certainly she's familiar with the format for reports."

"Damned right she is," I chime in. "I bet she's informed hundreds of our graduate students of the guidelines."

"Furthermore," Donna continues, "she's aware of all the people we believe were discussed in the 'Avila' report. And we've seen she probably doesn't know Harvey Delsanter, which would account for him not being mentioned. Remember he hasn't been at MRSU since she joined the department."

"I've never considered her to be very caring, though, and that's supposed to be an important part of the profile."

"It is, Theresa, and you're right if you compare her to someone like George Frazier who just oozes niceness. But Elsie Martin describes her as a wonderfully kind individual donating her time to women in distress, and Jim and Tom saw a softer side during their interview with her. I don't believe she fails that criterion."

It's my turn again. "Also, recall what she's capable of with a computer. The woman's a genius. Hell, I've told you she's helped everyone in the department at one time or another, including me. I was configuring a new computer the department issued me. I followed all prompts to the letter, and the damn thing didn't let me access the internet. So I did what we all do, turned to Susan. She came to my office, sat down at the console, and flew her fingers over the keyboard. Within minutes I was hooked up and I've had no troubles since. My point is, she *understood* all the behind-the-scene details associated with internet connections. And that's significant because they're not trivial. I'm sure she could figure out a way to alter the internal clock in Ken's computer."

"Oh, come now," says Theresa, "I agree your arguments are strong, but no more so than, say George Frazier's."

We knew this would be her reaction, but Donna's ready with a response. "You're right. But there's more. For example, don't you think it's odd that, spurned as a lover, she chose to remain as the man's secretary? I would think that would be an untenable position for most women."

"Yes, I can see that could be awkward. And you think that points to her guilt?"

"Certainly it does. Of course, what she claims is Ken treated her well as a secretary and the prospects of working with a man of his enormous technical talents and international prestige excited her."

"And you don't believe her?"

"Oh, I guess it could be true. It would take an extraordinary woman, which she is, but even so it's hard to accept. Other possibilities seem more likely, don't they, Tom?"

"Yes. It seemed to us she might want to be near Salter so she could more easily plan her revenge. She could have been waiting for the right opportunity. And finally it came along last Sunday. Recall she knew on Friday that Dr. Salter would be working in his office that day, and she easily could have slipped the extra evaluation into Salter's pack Friday afternoon. Her presence in the Dean's office would be the most natural thing in the world."

"All conjecture, though, isn't it?"

"Of course, although she begins to look like a more plausible candidate as these individual pieces of evidence mount."

"Is there more?"

"There certainly is," I announce proudly, for now it's time for my friend Elmo to shine. "You know Elmo has been saying there's something special about the last page of Ken's proof. Well, he's found a clue there that's pretty damning for Susan." At this point I hand out a reprint of the page to everyone. Of course, they've seen it before and should have it in their records. But you know how people are, never bringing what's needed. Here's a copy of what I distributed. I apologize anew for the imprint of the bloodstain.

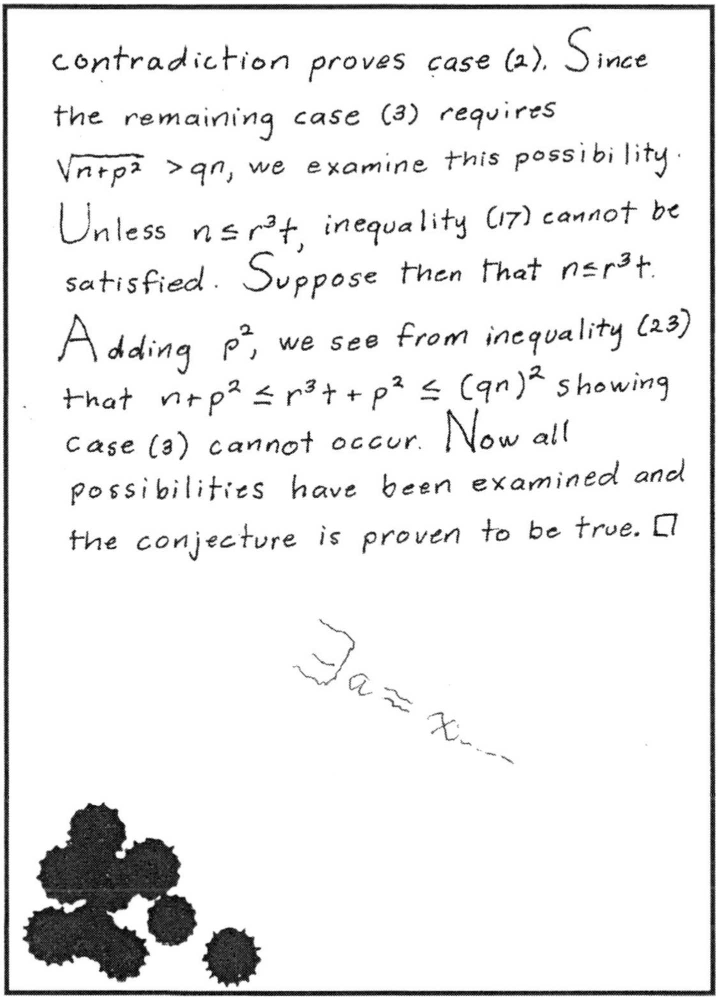

contradiction proves case (2). Since the remaining case (3) requires $\sqrt{n+p^2} > qn$, we examine this possibility. Unless $n \le r^3 t$, inequality (17) cannot be satisfied. Suppose then that $n \le r^3 t$. Adding p^2, we see from inequality (23) that $n+p^2 \le r^3 t + p^2 \le (qn)^2$ showing case (3) cannot occur. Now all possibilities have been examined and the conjecture is proven to be true. □

We take a moment to reexamine the sheet, with the silence finally broken by Theresa asking, "And what do you see here, Elmo?" There seems to be an element of respect in her tone that's been noticeably absent in the past.

"Well, um, look at all that pretty writing at the top of the page. Not the blood."

Theresa's acceptance is conditional. "Yes, Elmo, I think we could have figured out you didn't mean the blood."

"Well, of course, of course. Prissiest writing I've ever seen. But boy oh boy, what that writing told."

Gently I nudge Elmo along. "Get on with it."

"Oh, sorry. But every time I think of what that man has accomplished."

"Elmo!" Donna screams at him.

"Er, so look at that writing. Fairly shouts at you, doesn't it?"

Elmo settles back in his chair, quite certain, I'm sure, that he's adequately explained his finding to us. Of course, we all, except for Theresa, know from our earlier discussions what he's getting at, but I think our ex teacher's ready to brain him. And in truth he was much clearer when he explained it to us.

"That's the poorest excuse for an exposition I've ever seen. What the hell do you mean?"

Elmo's shocked there's still a question. "Oh. Thought it was obvious." Now there's a phrase that'll endear him to her. "Take a look at that writing. Mighty peculiar, isn't it? Those big capital letters at the beginning of each sentence followed by all those itty bitty letters. The whole damn paper's that way. Drove me crazy reading it. Guess that's how he always wrote?" I nod. "Well, I kept staring at this page, hours and hours. Nothing hit me. Then it suddenly became clear. Look at those great big capital letters. Them and nothing else. What do they spell?"

Theresa peruses the sheet one more time. "SUSAN!" she exclaims softly."

"Yep. Sure looked like Salter was finding some clever way to tell us Susan Barber killed him. Mebbe after she left the room. Probably wanted to find a way she wouldn't notice if she returned."

Theresa spends a moment digesting this, then responds slowly, "That's pretty convincing, all right. But how can he have known it was Susan? He was stabbed in the back."

Tom replies, "That's no problem. Remember Doc Pritchard said the victim could have taken up to two minutes to die. And the killer had to mess with the computer time, right in front of Dr. Salter."

"Yes, I can see that. So Susan Barber really did kill Ken?" And Theresa shakes her head slowly.

Donna, Tom, and Elmo look at me uncomfortably. I say, "Er, there does seem to be a hitch, though."

Theresa appears surprised. "Oh, what's that?"

I look at her, my stomach sending signals reminiscent of the many times I had to argue points in her class 20 years earlier. "If Susan killed Ken," I say, "why didn't she search for her love letters afterward, before she left his office on Sunday?"

> Ah, that *is* a difficulty, isn't it? Can you explain it? We're certainly going to have to if we're to make the charge against Susan stick. Can you figure out what we say next? Am I sounding superior? I apologize, but it's hard not to because I know the answer.

CHAPTER 43

Saturday Evening

Theresa seems unmoved, even annoyed, by my question. Disgust permeates her voice as she answers. "I should think that's fairly obvious, Jim, even to you." Ouch! "Murderers, at least ones who aren't professional hit men, often panic, usually even. And it's a damn good thing they do, because it's their mistakes that lead to their apprehension. In Susan's case it's clear she didn't even think about the letters until later. That's why she went in early the next morning. Probably never occurred to her you'd have the place watched." Theresa shakes her head at the naïveté of the amateur crook. Or maybe at that of her former student.

Donna, however, isn't buying this argument. "Normally I'd agree with you," she says, "but not with this killer. Remember, he or she was cool enough at the time of the murder to position the 'Avila' report so we'd be sure to find it. And even more so to create an alibi on the spot by those computer shenanigans. If Susan could have handled all that, she'd have had what it takes to remove the letters. You know they had to have been preying on her."

"Something even stranger knocks her out," mumbles Elmo.

"What a lovely turn of phrase. And just what do you think that is?" I fear Theresa's reevaluating her recent upgrade of his standing.

"All I said before's bunk—stupid nonsense."

"What the hell are you saying? You spent all that effort convincing me Susan's guilty, and now you tell me you didn't even believe it? I'm disappointed in all of you, wasting my time that way." Her eyes sweep over her former students, purposely avoiding Elmo.

Tom intervenes quickly. "We did no more for Ms. Barber than we did for any of the other suspects, Theresa. It's just that the case against her is stronger and it took more discussion to air it. I think it's important to finish the exercise. Go on, Elmo. Explain yourself."

"Geez, just think of what I've asked ya to believe. Impossible really."

"Oh, cut your rambling, Elmo, and get on with it." Theresa's really mad.

"Okay. Just imagine the situation. Here you've got a guy who knows he's just been stabbed in the back. He says, 'Ha, I'll give a clue that's so clever I'll fool my killer and so clear that any idiot, even that imbecile Sherwin, can understand it.' So all the time he's dripping blood, pretty sure he's going to die any second, he plans what to say. No sense of urgency in him. No siree. But then, he was a genius, huh? Then what? Well, he had a problem, you know."

"What was that?"

"He hadn't finished his proof! Got to do that. After all, it's the most important work of his life. So he says, 'Aha! I've got it. I'll simply complete the proof using sentences that point to Susan.' And he's probably grinning to himself as, weaker than ever, he meticulously writes his foppish script, undoubtedly thinking how it's gonna drive me crazy, and finishes it all with the mathematician's end of proof box. And in spite of any pain, and certainly the fear he must be feeling, he gets the damn proof right. No errors. No extraneous words. No sloppy writing. A concise, clear, technically correct masterpiece of mathematics. I'm tellin' ya, Theresa, it defies belief."

Theresa sees the logic of Elmo's argument just as we did earlier. "So you're saying his sentences beginning with the letters of Susan's name are a coincidence?"

"Yep. Amazing, ain't it? But they're perfectly natural sentences to write, given what he wanted to say mathematically."

Theresa thinks about that a moment. "What does this do to your and Tom's argument, Donna, about Susan staying on in her position in order to more easily plan revenge?"

"There are other explanations for it. We mentioned one earlier—she simply enjoyed the challenge of the job. I indicated then it was possible, and that may be a part of the reason. But I think there's more to it. I'm not sure, of course, but I suspect she felt, perhaps subconsciously, that staying in familiar surroundings might aid her healing, even though she would see Ken regularly. She never had a real home or family, you know. Maybe she thought that the university, and more specifically the math department, in some way provided a sense of security." You can count on Donna to put an unusual spin on a person's behavior.

Theresa appears confused. "Have I missed something here? Haven't we gone through all seven of our suspects and you're convinced each one is innocent? Are we back to square one? I thought you said you were done."

"We are," replies Tom. "Let's review for a minute the characteristics we've ascribed to our killer. He—or she—should be able to write well, know the format of MRSU reports, be familiar with the five individuals described in the 'Avila' report, care about people enough to do something to protect them, and have extensive computer knowledge."

"Yes, yes, we've been through that over and over. Don't waste time repeating yourself. There must be many fitting that profile."

"Perhaps, but as we've shown, only George Frazier and Susan Barber among our suspects come close, and they can be excluded for other reasons."

"So you're saying . . ."

"Remember Elmo commenting, when we were discussing who wrote the Avila report, that there were options other than the ones we were considering?"

"Vaguely."

"Well, I don't think he fully realized what he was implying, but the upshot is we've got to look elsewhere. None of our seven did it."

"Well, I'm not sure I agree with you. But I assume you have some ideas?"

I look at her directly, surprisingly feeling full of confidence. Could I be growing up? "Let's consider this computer business. We've stood on our heads trying to justify how someone could break through the protection system and alter the clock so as to provide an alibi. We realized he'd have to be a damn good hacker. We even went so far as to explore the possibility that the killer might find someone else to do the dirty work. But, as you recall, we decided that didn't make sense since changing the clock had to have been a spur-of-the-moment decision. So let's assume it was a dedicated computer nut. Even the best of them would require time, precious time it would have been dangerous to take in Ken's office, to figure out how to violate the system. Like Elmo says, 'It defies belief.'"

"I'm not sure what you're getting at."

"What if, instead, we ask who's likely to have what it takes. Such a person would, of course, have the expertise to understand and alter the clock. Also, and this is a key point, such a person would have *legitimate* access to that part of the system where such changes are possible."

"But there aren't very many people possessing that degree of access. We've talked about that. I'm not sure who's authorized in the computer services area. Oscar Shepinfield certainly, and I suppose others in his unit. But why on earth would any of them be involved in this killing? I'm sure you must be wrong, Jim."

"Recall, though, that Shepinfield indicated another group of authorized users."

"He did? I don't remember. What did he say?"

"He mentioned 'certain key administrators.'"

"Oh, probably that's the case. But I'm not sure which ones have the passwords, and it doesn't make much difference. They simply don't have the knowledge."

Damn. We finally get to this point and I don't want to go on, 'cause in a minute the shit's going to hit the fan. And I'm the one selected to initiate this somewhat less than salubrious event. "Would one of the authorized administrators be the Vice-President for Academic Affairs?"

Her steely eyes bore into me. You may think this is poetic license, but let me assure you I feel dual laser beams piercing my innards and pinning me to my seat. "James Albright," she says for the second time this week and for the second time it means trouble for me, "are you accusing me of Kenneth Salter's murder?"

I try to reply. I really do. But I guess I haven't matured all that much after all. My tongue moves and my lips part, but no sound emerges. Donna takes sympathy with my plight and says the words that were to be mine. "Yes, Theresa. We think, are sure really, that you're the killer."

Our mentor is furious. Her face is turning red. She stands. "How dare you! After all we've meant to each other, all I've done for you, and you turn on me like this. So you think, because I knew the people described in the report and wasn't aware of Delsanter's existence or Steve Farnsworth's ugly background, that I'm the author of that insidious paper. Or because at one point I knew a lot about computers. God, those arguments carry less strength than those you've given about other people. Really!"

I, stung by her view of our analysis of her computer expertise, seem to have found my voice. I have this eerie feeling that was her intention. "It's just not correct to say you *once* knew a lot about computers. You *still* do. Somehow or other, in a rapidly changing field and with all your other duties, you've remained the expert who can speak with authority. So much so that you've moved MRSU into the computer age with a vision that has placed and then kept us as a leading university in this field. You know these machines, all right."

"Even if that's the case, and I will admit I'm probably on the official access list, your so-called justification of my guilt is mighty weak."

Theresa has been pacing the floor during my response. Donna gets up and attempts to enfold her in a hug, but Theresa draws away. She does let Donna lead her back to her chair, though.

Then Donna says sorrowfully, "Oh, Theresa, there's so much more." She shakes her head sadly. "So very much more." And tears roll down Donna's face.

Theresa sees them and snaps, "Oh, stop your sniveling and tell me all that you think you have on me."

I jump to attention. I don't like anyone coming down on Donna like that. And the fact that it's Theresa makes it even worse. She *never* is angry with Donna. My wonderful wife, though, isn't offended in the slightest. I often seem to produce knee-jerk anger. Donna offers understanding. I wish I could be more like her. But not at this moment. Because it's her job to lay the foundation for our case, which will culminate in the devastating evidence uncovered by Elmo.

> Did you guess Theresa was the murderer? Oh, she is, all right. No more tricks in the offing. But she's correct, don't you think? The case is pretty weak, at least what we've outlined so far. But we're sure we've got the correct person, so you know there's more to the story. But how can we be so confident? The clues have been right in front of us, and I've set them down with meticulous accuracy. But I didn't recognize them myself, except for my own small contributions, until we'd shared our findings earlier this evening. I bet you can figure out our reasoning. If your mind's devious enough. If, however, you tend to more normal thought processes, read on.

CHAPTER 44

Saturday Evening

Theresa's looking a bit wild, not saying anything, just staring at Donna who has returned to her seat by my side. Unlike me, Donna doesn't shrink from the penetrating glare, nor the rancorous tone when Theresa says, "Well, aren't you going to start talking?"

"First, there's the evidence we've already discussed." Seeing Theresa's exasperated expression, Donna quickly proceeds. "Yes, I know it's no stronger against you than it is against some of the others. But it's important to recognize you do match rather well the characteristics we've ascribed to the murderer. What made me think you might be the killer went further, involving several more or less psychological factors."

"Psychological?"

"Yes. I'll never forget where I first heard of the psychological make-up of a killer. It was in your class. In this case we never formed anything as specific as a psychological profile, but perhaps we should have. It might have helped me understand concerns that nagged at me from the beginning."

"Are we ever going to get to them, Donna? Or are you going to babble all night?"

Damnation, this isn't the Theresa we know. She might speak sharply to Tom or me, but never to Donna. At least in the past. The target, though, takes it in stride and continues in an even voice. "We've spoken over and over about the killer being a caring individual, based on our interpretation of the 'Avila' report. And to some extent you are. You care about us, for example. But as I read the report, especially the excerpts we covered in our meeting Wednesday night, the writer seemed to be describing a strong need for justice, rather than a sense of caring."

Is it truly only three days ago Donna read us those words which we now know were penned by our teacher? It seems like an eternity. Tom takes up the recital. "No one, Theresa, has pressed the search for justice more than you. You've spent a lifetime pursuing it, mostly with the sheriff's office and at MRSU. You've inspired two generations of students."

Donna continues. "I think over the last couple of years you've observed first-hand how Ken treated Dick Brighthurst, Harriet Salter, Susan Barber, George Frazier, and, more recently, David Simmons. You became infuriated, thinking here was a man committing no crime, and hence untouchable through legal channels, but causing unimaginable harm to so many. This wasn't justice. *True justice* would alter the situation. You decided to administer *true justice.*"

I add, "I was reminded of the question you posed at dinner Sunday evening. You know, the one related to that TV show *Dexter.* Were you setting the stage for justifying what you had already done?"

Tom says, "When Jim told us about that, we wondered what you were thinking; could you be considering dealing with Dr. Salter in an *unofficial* manner, creating your own brand of justice? After all, you've never been one to shirk unorthodox behavior."

A wild look enters Theresa's eyes, and when she speaks her voice is pitched high. "He deserved to die. You're right, I'm glad he's dead. I bet there are any number of others he's hurt we don't even know about. And think of how many more there would have been if he'd remained alive."

There isn't much that angers Elmo, but this speech is one of them. "And think how much more brilliant mathematics he could have produced if he'd lived. Who knows the practical applications that might have been spawned by it, how much good they could have done mankind. I'm damned tired of self-appointed hypocrites taking it on their own to kill bright people, either by sending them off to war or," and he glares at Theresa, "by stabbing them in the back."

Theresa's somewhat less than cowed. "Say what you will, Elmo, but Kenneth Salter was a despicable man. And, remember, I said I was glad he's dead. I didn't say I killed him."

I'm glad to hear her voice returning to normal. I wonder how long it'll stay that way as Donna continues the indictment. "If you'll recall, I've also been convinced that the report's author has strong feminine and masculine sides to his personality. I'd say that applies to you. Certainly your regard for justice, your interest in the three of us, your concern for MRSU and all its students shows the feminine side. But you've also risen to the top in a man's world, both in the Sheriff's Department and at the university. That can't have been easy, especially at the time you did it.

It's likely you were treated unfairly at some point, as Tom's friend Barry Schwartz hinted the author would have been. You had to be as tough as the men, probably tougher. And you are, you know, a very tough woman. So tough that it's easy to envision you having the courage and creativity to carry out this crime. Remember the handwriting expert said the killer was innovative and willing to take risks like what was required to change the computer clock."

"Speaking of that," Tom continues, "you've had a great deal of experience in the presence of death. It's a lot easier imagining you calmly altering the clock to give yourself an alibi and positioning the 'Avila' report after killing Dr. Salter than it is to think of any of the amateurs doing it."

"There's one other thing I noticed," adds Donna.

"And what's that?"

"One of the chapters of the report is titled "Perpetrator."

"So?"

"It's not a word most people would employ. Perhaps 'villain' or 'scoundrel' or 'devil' or any of several others, but not 'perpetrator.' That's a common law enforcement term. It would be natural for you to use it."

Theresa looks scornful. "Oh, children," she says without a trace of endearment, "this is nothing but surmise and conjecture." She glares at Tom, "Maybe these others, who've never been involved in a homicide in their lives," she says, making it sound like a deprivation, "can believe this game you're all playing. But, Tom, I'd expect better of you. You know full well no jury would convict me on the basis of what you've said. Hell, any half-assed defense attorney could poke a million holes in your argument."

For the first time, Stuart Chen speaks. "That's what I thought too."

"Well, at last a sane voice. Perhaps you should be the sergeant."

Chen winces at the inappropriate statement. "*But,*" and he emphasizes the word, "it does represent powerful backup evidence if there's anything more conclusive."

Theresa appears surprised. "And you think there is?"

"Yes," nods Chen who continues softly, "I think there is."

She sighs. "All right, then, let's hear it all."

Tom takes up the argument. "Remember when I was a student you advised me to use my electives to take as broad a spectrum of courses as possible?"

"Not specifically, but it would've been consistent with what I believed then, and still do."

"Well, I recall it clearly. You said one never knew what might come in handy in a police investigation."

"What does this have to do with my situation?"

"One of the courses I took was the history of religion. The name 'Avila' seemed familiar to me, and I don't mean because of any modern surname. I checked it out online and that made me take a look at my old text."

Theresa seems pleased. "And what did you learn?"

"Ãvila is a town in Spain. Back in the 16th century there was a Spanish nun from there who founded the Reformed Order of Carmelites. Because of her good works, she was canonized in 1622."

"Well, this is an interesting history lesson, I'm sure, Tom, but what the hell are you getting at?"

"This nun's name was Theresa, Saint Theresa now. She's known as Theresa of Ãvila."

"That's it? You think this somewhat unremarkable coincidence means I murdered Kenneth Salter?"

"That taken with all the other evidence, yes."

"You still don't have a damn thing that's concrete. No case at all."

"There's more, Theresa."

"Well, you'd better have something other than the crap you've given me so far if you think you're going to make this ridiculous charge stick."

"Oh, it will, Theresa. It will."

Elmo's been waiting for this moment. Normally the most non-vindictive of men, he can't abide the thought of taking a human life. Any life. And especially that of a gifted mathematician. He doesn't share our concern about Theresa at all.

"Well, I know you've been sitting on something all evening. Here's your big chance."

Her tone is sarcastic and even a little threatening. Elmo seems not to notice, so intent is he on his carefully selected words. "You see, Kenneth Salter did tell us who the murderer was, just like I said before. Only he didn't name Susan. He named you."

Theresa seems confused by this. "Where? How?"

"Oh, on that last sheet of his proof." She still is puzzled. "First of all, you've got to understand that the proof was completed when that end of proof box was placed on the sheet. It needed nothing additional. Salter certainly would have left the rest of the page blank. He wouldn't have tarnished the work of his life—unless he was desperate." Elmo pauses a moment. "Hate to think how he'd feel about that bloodstain."

"Elmo," Donna says gently, "please get on with it."

"Er, yes, of course. You see, the only thing out of place, except the stain, of course, is that funny writing after the end of proof symbol."

Elmo now pulls from under his chair a manila envelope. I've been wondering what it was all about. He undoes the flap, pulls from it a letter size whiteboard and dry erase marker, holds it up for all to see, and makes a fairly accurate copy of the writing he had referred to. It looks like this:

$$\exists a = x \ldots$$

"Course it's not as shaky as the original."

Theresa stares at it in amazement! "You say those scribbles indicate I'm a murderer?"

"Yup. Without a doubt." Elmo shakes his head in awe. "I said before that Salter was damn clever to leave that clue about Susan Barber even while he was dying. And he sure would've been if that's what he did. Course he didn't. In fact, it was too much to believe. That's why we threw the idea out."

"Elmo!" says Donna sternly. It's an admonishment surprisingly not lost on my genius colleague.

"Right. Well, anyway, notice that the writing up to then was in that disgustingly cute script of his. And then the proof was done. So what was this scrawl underneath? Not prissy at all, but sort of wild. Nothing like his normal writing. So it doesn't take a great leap of faith to believe this was something he'd scribble while not his normal self—while dying maybe."

"And he wrote mathematics at that time?"

"Well, that's what I've been asking myself. Seems crazy doesn't it? It didn't make sense. But then I started wondering if he was planting a clue to his killer. Didn't seem likely. But then why the hell write it at all?"

"Why couldn't it have been something he'd written earlier, well before he was killed?"

"Thought I'd explained that. This was his most important work ever. He'd never have messed it up under normal circumstances, not a perfectionist like him. No, it took something mighty special to force that writing. And I'd say dying was special enough, wouldn't you?"

Theresa is scornful. "So how do those hieroglyphics indict me?"

"Once you accept they were written while he was on his last legs—well, on his last rump . . ."

"Elmo!" Donna screams.

"Quite right, terribly sorry. As I was saying, under that circumstance you have to look at 'em pretty damn close. And they don't make sense from a mathematical point of view. Of course, no one, not even me, I bet, would be writing mathematics at a time like that." Seeing Donna stirring restlessly, Elmo hurries on. "So what could they possibly mean? Take a look at that backward ***E***." He's talking about the $\exists$ that's on his board. "You know what that means to a mathematician, Theresa?"

She shakes her head. Tom says, "No reason you should. I just learned on Wednesday when I sat in on George Frazier's class. It's sort of a shorthand for 'There exists.'"

"Right!" says Elmo, as proud of Tom as he would be of any promising student. "So our little expression would read '***There exists a equal to x.***' Now that doesn't make much sense. But then, and clod that I am it took several days to realize it, you could interpret that backward ***E*** symbol as 'There are' or 'There is,' or any similar wording that makes sense from an English point of view."

Elmo continues, "Let's say it's 'There is.' Then our sentence is '***There is a equal to x.***' Not much help, is it? Suppose, though, we write 'There is' as 'There's' and drop the apostrophe."

Theresa's fascinated, and I think she has the answer. She starts to speak softly. "So then your phrase is '***Theres a = x!***'"

"Absolutely correct, and I can see you've got it. Yes, push the '***a***' with 'Theres' and it reads, '***Theresa = x***', or Theresa is equal to the universal symbol for the unknown, in this case the identity of the killer." Elmo stares at our teacher with a hatred I didn't know he could possess. "Theresa, you murdered Kenneth Salter and I'll gladly testify at your trial."

Theresa is as subdued as I've ever seen her. She's whispering, more to herself than anyone in the room. "God, what a clever cuss! I saw him scribbling, but when I looked it was the same crap all you mathematicians produce."

I'm hurt by this, but I guess nowhere near as much as I am by the fact that this woman I've so admired took another's life.

Donna rises, walks to Theresa and kneels in front of her. "Why, Theresa? Why?" Her voice pleads for understanding.

Theresa peers down on her, a more normal look than I've seen all week. "Because he was an evil man. You analyzed my motives pretty well before. I'd been planning it for some time, and had the report saved to a flash drive for weeks, waiting for the right time to print it. Then, last Thursday, Elsie, my secretary, told me she was going to play bridge Sunday evening with Susan Barber. Said she hoped Susan wouldn't have to work that day. She was worried because Susan had mentioned Ken would be in the office Sunday. I saw my chance. Later on Thursday I had to go to Steven Farnsworth's office and I saw Ken's student evaluations on the counter. There was a blank one lying there too, so I filled it in and inserted it with the rest. Never thought about removing another one so the count would stay the same." She looks at my colleague. "Elmo, you're a pain in the ass, but you're damned clever."

The despair in Donna's voice wrenches my heart. "You'd have let us find an innocent person guilty. And we might well have."

"No!" she says with force. "If you hadn't determined the truth by the end of this weekend, I'd have confessed."

Donna looks at her incredulously. "So you've been playing a game with us, seeing how we'd do at coming up with the answer?"

"Yes. I don't blame you for being angry. But I hope you'll forgive me. It's a foible of an old woman. I wanted to see the best team I've ever taught in action one more time." She turns to Elmo again. "I don't like you, Elmo. But I've got to admit you have a flare for the detection business. Unraveling that clue was masterful, the equal of the best detectives of fiction or life. I'm proud of you all."

Elmo, usually merely uncomfortable with praise, appears to hate accolades from this woman who deprived the world of a great mathematician. As far as I'm concerned, for the first time ever there is no joy in her approval.

Donna still fails to understand. "Theresa, you've spent a lifetime upholding the law. How could you . . . ."

"And I've spent a lifetime watching scum beat the system, or not even be threatened by the system," Theresa interrupts. Then, more gently, "I don't think I can make you understand, Donna, and I'm not going to try. But what I did was bring justice, just like you said. You had me pegged perfectly." Donna looks miserable and there's nothing I can do. Theresa reaches forward and places a hand on Donna's shoulder. "I'm dying, Donna. The doctors give me only a few weeks. I've a brain tumor, and sometimes it affects me in strange ways. But I'm not offering that as an excuse. I'm glad I killed Ken."

We're all immobilized by the news of her impending death. Eventually Tom recovers enough to approach her and state he's placing her under arrest. She interrupts him to say, "Just a minute, Tom." She looks at us each in turn, even Elmo, with a gaze filled with such love it makes me want to cry. Then she lifts and drains her previously untouched coffee cup. Soon her body shakes and she slumps in her rocker.

Donna and I gasp. Tom pulls her from her chair, places her on the floor, and begins chest compressions. Stuart Chen calls 911. But nothing can stop the effect of whatever she had in that cup. Within minutes our beloved mentor is dead.

EPILOGUE

Two Months Later

Donna and I are on our way to a local restaurant to have dinner with Tom. We haven't seen him since that awful Saturday night when Theresa died. The horror of it has pervaded almost every thought I've had since then. But it's starting to fade, and life is returning to normal. I'm beginning to be able to think of work without associating it with death.

Dick Brighthurst was promoted to permanent chairman. I'm glad of that, and he's doing a damn fine job. I found it impossible to accomplish any research for a while. I couldn't concentrate. My mind always returned to that tragic week, or sometimes to happier days with our favorite teacher. Elmo, whom I foolishly once considered the most imperceptive of creatures, understood. He must have picked up on my mood during his frequent phone calls, and my evasive responses to his inquiries about my work. So what did he do? He sent me a problem to attack, that's what. One he knew I'd be interested in and could handle. And it did get me off my duff. For the first time since Theresa's death, the joys of research are meaning something as I start to make headway. Hopefully Elmo and I will wind up coauthoring a paper on the subject.

Donna was upset too, but for different reasons. While I just couldn't accept the way Theresa had changed from the woman I had so long admired, Donna associated herself with the pain that had brought Theresa to her deadly end. We'd talk about it some, but not much. I guess we each had to work it through in our own way. By tacit agreement we've avoided all attempts to contact Tom. Until now. Suddenly, though, we both became ready and we pinned him down to dinner this evening.

So here we sit at a plastic-covered table in an unpretentious Spanish restaurant, working on our first carafe of sangria and waiting for Tom and the paella that we've ordered for the three of us. Hopefully Tom will appear first. And he does. I see him enter the door and scan the room. I wave vigorously, hardly necessary since there are only 12 tables.

He reaches us, kisses Donna on the cheek, and warmly shakes my hand. "It's good to see you."

"You too, Tom," I say. And I realize with surprise I mean it. For the last couple of months he's been too closely tied to unpleasant memories. But I've advanced along the recovery road enough to wonder if we three can recapture the deep friendship of college days. We chat for a while of inconsequential matters while we dive into the scrumptious rice dish loaded with mussels, shrimp, lobster, sausage, and chicken. I tell Tom of my work with Elmo, and Donna describes her newly redecorated office. He recounts a recent experience a friend of his on the city police force had. Seems a burglar attempted to rifle a local butcher's freezer. The guy was lifting a carcass off a hook when he lost his balance and fell, along with the hunk of meat. The future steaks tipped over a cart piled with boxes of frozen shrimp and the entire assemblage wound up on top of the would-be robber, pinning him to the floor. The early-arriving butcher found him almost, but not quite, frozen, and turned him over to the police who agreed to keep him on ice. Tom concludes his story by saying the crook is planning to sue the butcher for operating a dangerous establishment.

We smile and continue to talk around the subject foremost on our minds. But after the food is consumed and while we're sipping an exotic Spanish liqueur, it's inevitable that Tom says, "Whatever happened to those poor people we suspected of Dr. Salter's murder?"

I tell him about Dick Brighthurst, and Donna describes a supermarket encounter with Harriet Salter. "She looks great, is doing well, and has had a couple of promising interviews with accounting firms." I don't know if Donna's still seeing her professionally, and, of course, Donna would never say.

"Did Professor Frazier get his promotion and tenure?"

"The process isn't complete yet, but I think he's a shoo-in," I reply. "Dick gave him strong support and he whizzed through the department and college committees. The university committee has met and rumor is there was only one dissenting vote. So it's up to the Vice-President for Academic Affairs, and he'll undoubtedly approve. If so, the President's signature is assured."

"Vice-President for Academic Affairs? Wasn't that Theresa's position?"

"Yup!"

"They filled it already?"

"Acting—while a nationwide search is carried out." I grin. "Guess who's in the position."

"You mean I'd know?" Tom thinks for a moment. "No! You can't mean Dean Farnsworth?"

"Oh, but I do. I don't think President Mulholland is especially pleased with him, but I guess he figures he can stand it for a year."

"Are you going to say anything about the stolen research?"

"Nah. I guess I believe the story, but I don't think there's much proof. And, besides, it's not the sort of thing I want to do. The guy's a weak fish, but he's essentially harmless. And it was so long ago."

Tom smiles. "You'd never make a policeman, Jim."

"No surprise there. This murder convinced me all my future crime involvement will be confined to books."

"How about Harvey Delsanter?"

"Oh, I suppose he's doing all right. I don't have any contact with him. Elmo got Ken's proof published in record time and all the mathematical community's agog over it. When it came out, the journal asked Delsanter to comment. He said it was a wonderful piece of work by a master of mathematics, terrible shame he was lost to the world, blah, blah, blah. I could just see the guy planning how he could build on Ken's work, without the fear of his competition."

"You really don't like that man, do you?"

I shrug, and then say, "Susan Barber seems fine. She still rules our roost, but appears more human with Dick as her boss. I know she likes him." Seeing Tom's questioning glance, I say, "No. Get your mind out of the gutter. It's strictly professional." I pause for a moment, reflecting on what I've said. "But, then, that's what I thought when Ken was chair, wasn't it?"

"Let's see. That's everyone, isn't it?"

"You've forgotten David Simmons, Tom," says Donna. "Do you know anything about him?" and she looks at me.

"Yeah, as a matter of fact. He took me up on my invitation and stops by my office once a week. George seems to have pulled him out of his shell and he's acting much more self-assured. He's got a long way to go, but I think there's real hope for him."

We're silent for a moment, until finally I blurt, "Why did she do it? How could she kill someone, and then let us put others through hell while we investigated them? How is that any different from the way Ken was?"

Donna reaches across the table and takes my hand. "Who knows how her illness affected her. Are you upset because she killed someone, which is natural, or because it seems so out of character?"

"Well, both, I guess. Somehow I feel cheated. I guess that sounds crazy."

"No, it doesn't, darling. I think we have to accept that the woman who killed Kenneth Salter was not the woman we loved. I fear that tumor was wreaking havoc with her neural connections."

"And that's also why she allowed others to be suspected?" I say bitterly.

"Maybe. It's so hard to tell. But I've got a theory about that."

"What?"

"We know she was aware of her approaching death. We know she loved us and enjoyed our team efforts when we were in her class. On the rare occasions our paths crossed she never failed to mention them. We obviously were special to her in some way none of her other students were. And, as she said, she wanted to see us in action one last time. Remember how quickly she backed including Elmo in our group when it appeared you were ready to withdraw if we didn't? But I'm absolutely convinced she was telling the truth when she said she'd never have let anyone else be accused of the crime, that she'd have confessed at the end of the weekend if we hadn't figured it out."

"But what if she'd died or something? After all, she couldn't tell when the tumor would take her."

"She allowed for that possibility," says Tom. "We found an envelope stuck in a book in her office containing a full confession, dated the Sunday of the killing."

"But it might never have been found."

"Oh, she made sure it would be. She created an email message to her secretary telling her to show the envelope to the police. She placed it in a queue with a delayed transmission time so it would reach its destination on Monday, eight days after the murder. I suppose, if she'd lived, she'd have removed the message from the queue. As it was, she didn't have the opportunity, so we learned about the confession just as she'd planned."

"So," I say, "it *was* all just a game." God, this is hard to take.

"I'm sure of it," responds the wife of the luckiest man in the world. "Think again about the actions Theresa took that were just so unnecessary. In particular, I'm referring to the report with an author whose name we now know pointed to Theresa, and the extra student evaluation that gave us further insight into the characteristics of the killer. And she was the one who pointed you to Oscar Shepinfield who helped explain the time discrepancy. Now why would she do all that? None of it contributed to the creation of a perfect crime."

I'm slow, but finally I understand. "She was giving us clues, enjoying watching us unravel them."

"I believe so. It was her last hurrah, as both a law enforcement officer and a mentor. I hope it helps, Jim, to remember she never attempted to place the blame on any of the other suspects. Her sense of justice hadn't eroded so far as to allow that." It does help a little. Then Donna shakes her head sadly and lifts her glass. "I really don't think she fully comprehended the misery she was bringing to others. I believe we should let go of our resentment towards her. Let's just remember her for the good woman she was, and for all her many accomplishments which did so much for so many."

So it ends as it as it had begun for me; with good food, special companionship, and a fine liqueur. Tom and I join Donna in a silent toast to Theresa Wilson Bedlow: outstanding homicide detective, innovative teacher, productive administrator, dear friend—and loathsome murderess.

Lightning Source UK Ltd.
Milton Keynes UK
UKOW041836160613

212335UK00001B/65/P

9 781469 797281